I0817867

"Bowler...depicts his special needs kids not as victims, but as real heroes. Will both warm the heart and chill the spine."

— Kirkus Reviews

"*Spinner* incorporates elements of horror into a young adult read that is riveting and centered upon powerful protagonists that are well-drawn. The 'added value' in this story...lies in its...scenes that take the trappings of teen horror and turn them into something much more developed. Young adult to adult readers will find *Spinner* compelling and vivid."

— Midwest Book Review

"Michael manages to include many topics within the story, from bullying, to dealing with being in a special education class, to what it is like to be in love with someone who does not love you the same way, and much more."

— Readers' Favorite

"Bowler has created a tangible cast of characters who nearly leap off the page as they come to life in this highly suspenseful book...which is sure to keep readers enthralled clear through to its finale."

— Literary Classics

"Bowler offers some astute observations about teen life - capturing the doubt and insecurity of adolescence - and addresses important themes for maturing young adults, channeled through realistic character dynamics and camaraderie."

— Red City Review

"It's a very well-written story and very well thought of. I like how Alex is portrayed in the struggle he has using his wheelchair. I say this because I'm in a wheelchair, as well, and it's very nice to see a character who has similar struggles in their everyday life."

— Stephanie on Amazon

"The book is littered with those A-ha moments that will arouse powerful emotions in readers. I loved Bowlers remarkable cast of characters, solid, convincing, and compelling enough to attract the sympathy of readers. I loved the humor. I loved the colorful and vivid descriptions that make readers feel like they were part of the intense drama, and I love the breathtaking action, the frenzy, and the race against time."

— Romuald Dzemo on Amazon

"*Spinner* is a paranormal story told from a special ed kid's perspective, which does make it somewhat unique. I live the SpEd mom life, and I love seeing disabled children portrayed as heroes rather than useless. I also work in adoption, and enjoyed seeing that play a part in the story, as well."

— Ebienic on Amazon

"It's a story Stephen King would rightly be proud of."

— Lynne on Amazon

"OMG! It's Horror, Paranormal, Urban Fiction…and Scary Great! And I couldn't wait to finish this book… This is the first teen book I've chosen for a personal favorite! If you're willing to admit you read books for teens, then go for this one… Better yet, get it for a teen you know who loves horror at its finest, and a paranormal skill that I guarantee you will have never seen or read anywhere else."

— Glenda on Amazon

"There is danger, adventure and evil… real evil. The characters are fantastic, and the relationships intense. I couldn't put this book down."

— Author S.L. Dearing

"A book that will stand the test of time by approaching sensitive and delicate subject matters and mixing them with the supernatural."

— Author Wesley Thomas

"Terrific, upsetting, emotional, horrifying, and thought provoking."

— Melissa on Goodreads

SPINNER

MICHAEL J BOWLER

Spinner

Cover and interior design by Streetlight Graphics

ISBN-10: 1974520471
ISBN-13: 978-1-9745-2047-3
EAN-13 9781974520473
Hardcover ISBN: 978-1-7333290-7-1

Second Edition September 2017

First Edition Published by
YoungDudes Publishing
a subsidiary of
CoolDudes Publishing Pty (LTD)
2015.

DEDICATION

This book is dedicated to all the wonderfully diverse kids
I've taught throughout the years. You all rock.

AUTHOR'S NOTE

Whether labeled general education or special education, all children have unique gifts and talents and personalities and, despite so-called disabilities, can contribute positively to this world. I've lived with a disability my entire life – hearing impairment – and I met no one close to my age with hearing loss until after graduate school.

My disability was a drawback with teachers who talked a lot or didn't articulate clearly, but it didn't stop me from learning. It made me a visual and tactile learner. It allowed me to see more of the world around me because I couldn't "hear" the world with the same precision as my peers. It *did* make playing on sports teams a frustrating experience because of all the mistakes I made through mishearing the coach or other players on the field. It *did* make discerning song lyrics difficult, especially through radio speakers, and isolated me from most of my peers who could quote songs from memory.

But the "disability" never defined me.

Later, as a high school teacher who worked with kids like the characters in this book, I strove to emphasize their abilities, not their disabilities, and they accepted my own disability without question.

We spend way too much time in this country focusing on what we perceive to be the weaknesses of others. As the kids in *Spinner* clearly prove, our strengths always outweigh our weaknesses. If more adults would focus on the strengths of kids, especially kids with disabilities, instead of trying to "fix" the disabilities or make all kids conform to a normative standard of learning, then every child would have a real chance to soar.

No matter what we look like or how much money we have or how smart we are; no matter our race, gender, or orientation; no matter our abilities or disabilities – at the end of every day we're all the same. We're all human. We're human first, and everything else second.

For every "disability," there is an equal or more powerful "ability." Every kid I ever taught showed me this universal truth. I love you guys. You've made my life magical.

MJB 2017

DAY 1

CHAPTER ONE

WHAT ARE YOU?

Alex fidgeted as he lay in bed and listened to the wind outside. It had been an okay day at school – he'd only been called "Roller Boy" twice, which was almost a world record. After school, he'd kicked it at Roy's house and they cranked *Hawthorne Heights* tunes and chilled. Even Jane hadn't bitched at him.

So why can't I sleep?

He didn't know the answer. His eyes returned to the dancing shadows that flitted across his floor from the window. His drapes were closed, but the wind whistled through the trees, and the shadows mesmerized him. The patterns of light and dark pulled on his eyelids, dragging him sunder. A dream loomed at the edges of his consciousness. One of *those* dreams. Sleep overcame him, and it began....

Ms. Ashley trudged down a flight of stairs from her second floor apartment, carrying several overflowing bags of trash. The traffic sounds were omnipresent, but otherwise the night was calm and clear.

A slight breeze ruffled her long brown hair as she slunk to the rear of the complex. Rounding the building, she passed alongside a sloping hill of ivy-covered ground toward the row of trashcans in the far corner.

Looking chilled and unsettled, Ms. Ashley lifted one lid and struggled to get all her bags in without spilling anything.

A rustling noise startled her and she whipped her head around.

The ivy-covered hill ascended upward into darkness, but there was no movement. Only a creepy silence.

She tossed her bags into the can and dropped the lid back in place with a hollow *clang*.

A large cat dropped onto the top of the can from somewhere above. She uttered a startled cry and leaped back a few steps.

The cat meowed and she chuckled, extending one trembling hand.

The animal snuggled against it, wanting to be stroked. She ran her fingers through the fur around the cat's neck and under its chin.

More rustling leaves drew her attention to the ivy.

The darkness in this corner was deep and penetrating, with the vines and leaves snaking their way up the slope barely visible. Another cat materialized from beneath the thick cover of ivy.

Then another.

And another.

In seconds, the hillside seethed with cats of all shapes and sizes. Their glowing eyes shone like eerie beacons in the night. The cat beneath Ms. Ashley's fingers hissed and swiped its claws at her, raking the top of her hand and drawing copious amounts of blood.

Startled, she cried out and yanked her hand back, gazing in shock at the dark liquid spilling onto the concrete at her feet.

Her body trembled with fear as she backed away.

The cats crouched on the hillside, poised and threatening.

The one she'd been petting wailed into the night, and then they were on her, leaping and clawing at her face and hair. Hundreds of cats streamed down the hillside and flung themselves at her while the big one sat and watched like a general commanding his troops.

Ms. Ashley screamed, but loud traffic sounds drowned out her cries. Flailing, she turned and stumbled along the side of the building toward the street, crying out for help.

Claws dug into her back and raked across her neck.

Teeth sunk into her arm.

She shrieked in agony as they yanked out chunks of her hair and raked at her legs, shredding her sweat pants and digging into her soft flesh.

Blood spilled from everywhere on her body.

The street loomed just ahead. She tossed one cat off in a frantic attempt to save herself, only to have three more replace it. She didn't have much time before she'd topple beneath a tidal wave of claws and fur.

A large truck roared up Lincoln Boulevard as Ms. Ashley staggered toward the curb. The headlights were bright and blinding. The biggest cat flew from the retaining wall at her face and gouged a chunk of flesh out of her cheek, exposing the bone. She wailed in agony.

Her knees buckled, but Ms. Ashley managed to stay on her feet while stumbling headlong into the street at a frantic pace.

Suddenly aware that the truck was almost on her, she clutched at the nearest light post in desperation. One bloodied hand caught the post and slowed her momentum as the cats ceased their brutal attack. She gesticulated with her free hand, hoping to attract the attention of the driver. With her urgent gaze fixed on the truck, she didn't see the figure in black leap from behind the retaining wall right at her.

Strong hands pressed hard into her back and propelled her forward.

The truck mowed her down in a splatter of blood and gore, flinging her broken body to the pavement and then crushing it beneath massive tires.

As the truck screeched to an ear-piercing halt near the corner, the figure in black melted into the darkness. Several cats sniffed the dead woman's remains before they, too, disappeared into the shadows. The first cat was the last to depart, watching as the horrified driver jumped from the truck cab and pelted toward Ms. Ashley's broken body.

The cat seemed to grin before vanishing into the night....

Alex screamed and bolted upright in bed, hair plastered to his sweat-sheened forehead. Heart thumping with urgent terror, he scanned his darkened room. The door leading outside was closed, but the ominous shadows still crept through the window. His desk was messy as usual, and the door to his bathroom stood ajar, but he'd left it that way. Everything looked like it had before he fell asleep.

Dropping onto his pillow, Alex fought to control his breathing and calm his pounding heart. God, he hated those dreams! Poor Ms. Ashley. He lay there, sweat making his t-shirt cling to his chest as his heart rate drew down. Could this dream be like the one about his parents? It seemed so real!

He lay in bed worrying about the morning, and what he'd find when he got to school.

Gradually, tree branches tapping against the house lulled him to sleep. The last image to assail him before he went under was that ugly-ass cat grinning at him before running off into the dark.

***

The following morning, Alex regarded himself in the bathroom mirror as he brushed his teeth. He'd showered and blow-dried his shoulder-length, choppy white-blond hair and it looked clean. People liked his blue eyes, when he didn't hide them behind his flowing bangs.

Alex finished pushing the brush up and down his teeth, and spat out the mint-flavored water, staring a moment at his soft, hairless cheeks and milky white skin. Sure, he seemed so innocent, a "sweet-faced boy," as his social workers had always described him to prospective foster parents. That's what made the whole thing worse. He *did* look like a nice kid. But no matter how hard he tried, he always screwed everything up. He always started spinning people. He couldn't help it. And once they figured out he was doing something weird, they got scared and wanted nothing more to do with him.

He'd already been through ten foster homes, and the only reason Jane kept him at this one was because she'd figured out what he could do.

"What are you?" he asked his reflection.

As always, it didn't answer.

***

Jane Walters stood at the door with her ear pressed against it, while two boys sat at the kitchen table watching her.

Carlos, a burly high school junior, wolfed down his cereal, while freshman Juan glared with barely contained fury. Carlos grinned at the smaller boy. Juan flinched in fear and Carlos sniggered. Juan's cereal sat untouched in front of him as he reached with trembling fingers to touch his face, wincing at the pain. The left cheek and eye were black and blue and swelling rapidly.

A motorized sound came from behind the door, like a rising elevator. Jane stepped away and jerked her thumb at Carlos.

"You, out!"

Carlos's previous bravado with Juan dropped instantly. He swallowed his final mouthful and leapt from his chair. Snatching up a backpack from the floor, he bolted out the side door, never even glancing at Jane. She regarded the sullen Juan, folding her arms across her chest.

"You know what to do." Her tone left no room for argument.

"What if he don't wanna this time? He said he wouldn't no more."

"You know what'll happen to you if he won't," she snapped.

Juan nodded.

Jane observed her reflection in the large, ornately framed mirror, obviously looking pleased with what she saw.

She turned to him, practically pinning the petrified boy to his chair. "I'll be watching."

The motorized whirring s ground to a halt as Jane darted through the door into the hallway.

The door beside the rectangular dining table popped open and Alex rolled out in his wheelchair, wearing a *Hawthorne Heights* band t-shirt, black hoodie, skinny black jeans, his black and white high-top Converse shoes, and a backpack resting on his lap. He had Roy to thank for most of these clothes since Jane never spent a dime on him unless she had to.

He popped a small wheelie and shoved the door closed with a swipe of his hand, and then turned to Juan, whose head was bent toward his cereal bowl. Alex noted the behavior and frowned. It bothered him that he frightened Juan, but he didn't blame the kid. After all, he frightened almost everyone.

"Mornin', Juan," he offered in his most upbeat tone of voice as he dropped his backpack by the door. Was that upbeat? He so seldom felt that way he really didn't know what it sounded like.

"Hi, Alex."

Juan didn't look up. Alex noted the other bowl and half-filled glass of orange juice on the table, and frowned.

"Carlos must 'a heard me comin' and bailed, huh?"

Juan said nothing.

Attempting to seem nonthreatening to the younger boy, Alex added, "Left his dishes this time. Jane'll be pissed."

Juan looked up, revealing his bruised face. "You mean 'Mom', right, Alex?"

Alex ignored the correction, gazing in shock at the other boy's battered face. Furious, he wheeled over to Juan. "Did she make Carlos—?"

Juan cut him off. "I fell, uh, hit the bed table. That's all."

He indicated the mirror on the wall with a slight head nod. Alex caught the movement and looked at Juan, blinking twice in response, his anger roiling.

Juan pleaded, "Alex, could you, you know...?"

His voice trailed off and he looked down at his cereal again.

Alex scowled.

"I don't wanna go to school 'n look like this," Juan whispered, focusing his attention on the soggy corn flakes floating in his bowl like dead maggots.

Alex gazed long and hard at Juan. He was fourteen, but looked eleven or twelve, tiny and scrawny with brown skin, short hair, and big, fearful eyes. He wore baggy pants and baggy shirts, but they only highlighted how tiny he was. Had Alex ever seen the boy laugh or grin like a kid should? He didn't think so. But then, he didn't do those things either. How could they, living with a witch like Jane? He leaned in so Juan's head hid him from view of the mirror.

"You mean *she* don't want you to."

Juan's eyes looked round and filled with panic. "Please, Alex?"

"Aren't you afraid, like the other times?"

He reached out to touch Juan's bruised cheek, but Juan recoiled even before Alex's fingers reached him.

Alex felt that punch to the gut sensation each time someone flinched from him, which was almost everyone, except for Roy and the kids in his class. "You *are* afraid. Guess I don' blame you."

Juan flushed red with embarrassment, turning his bruises a brighter shade of purple. "Alex, please?"

Alex sighed with resignation. His frown melted into a look of deep compassion as he brushed his bangs away from his eyes so Juan wouldn't be scared. At least, he didn't think he looked scary. The blue always seemed to calm people.

"Okay," Alex said, steeling himself for the pain to come. "Tell me."

***

Jane stood in a small closet directly behind the two-way mirror in the kitchen, smirking at the two men beside her. All the kids knew it was there, but they never knew when she might actually be on the other side. Another technique she'd developed to keep them in line. The men wore business suits, and one held a GoPro camera pointing through the glass at the two boys.

"Now watch real close," Jane admonished, though both men were already riveted to the drama playing out in the kitchen.

The younger of the two, Phil, watched intently, as though not surprised by what he was witnessing. As silver-haired Bob lifted the GoPro, his mouth dropped open in stunned disbelief.

Jane grinned as she turned from the boys to eye the two men. Shocked by what he saw, Bob lowered the camera and watched with his own eyes.

"You idiot, keep filming!" Jane snapped, her voice like a firecracker.

Bob recovered from the initial surprise and whipped the camera up, continuing to record.

Phil's expression remained unreadable to Jane, but she didn't care. These men were flunkies. The moneyman was all that mattered.

"Wish we had audio," Phil muttered.

"You'll get it from the other camera," Jane said, directing his attention to the cupboard behind the boys. The door was ajar. From this angle, even through the two-way glass, she saw the blinking red light as it recorded.

Phil nodded while Jane watched, grinning at the stunned expressions of the two men beside her.

Through the mirror, she observed Alex spin his black magic, saw the pained expression on his face, and grinned when Juan, now uninjured, stared in wide-eyed fear at the freak beside him.

Yes, you're a freak, Alex, she thought, *but you're a freak who's going to make me rich.*

***

Alex's eyes remained closed, his features intent as his bruised face returned to normal. Several moments passed before his eyes fluttered open. "Man, Carlos—I mean that table—really hit you hard."

Juan had pulled away from Alex as far as his chair would allow. His eyes were wide and anxious, and his voice quavered. "Yeah. Well, I... uh, thanks."

He looked down at the table again, obviously afraid to meet Alex's gaze. Alex watched him sadly, and then glanced at the mirror. He scowled at his own reflection.

She was there, probably wearing that evil smile she had. Fighting down the temptation to flip his middle finger at her, Alex turned to Juan.

"C'mon," he said with a heavy sigh. "We gonna be late for school."

He smiled as best he could manage, and Juan nodded. He rose from his chair and snatched his ratty backpack from the floor at his feet. Alex grabbed his own pack and rolled to the door, pulling it open. Juan skirted past him, making Alex feel like he had a horrible disease or something. He'd just helped the boy—for the seventh time already—and Juan was still afraid of him. But Juan's reaction was typical. Unless he spun them afterwards, everyone who saw what he could do pretty much freaked. He rolled outside and yanked the door shut behind him.

***

Inside the closet, Jane turned to Bob, who continued to run the GoPro even though the kitchen was empty.

"You can stop recording now," she said, folding her arms across her chest.

Bob suddenly realized there was nothing left to film and shut off the camera, staring at Jane with amazement. His face was ashen, as though he'd seen a ghost. Phil's eyes glittered with excitement, which Jane interpreted as astonishment at what he'd just seen.

"A million, remember," she insisted. "You tell him. Not a penny less."

Bob wiped his sweaty palms against his gray dress pants. "Oh, we'll definitely tell him, Ms. Walters. You can count on that."

Jane grinned.

***

Alex followed Juan along the side of the house. On their left rose a high, wood-slat fence separating Jane's property from her neighbor. He allowed his chair to roll itself down the sloping driveway past the five-foot hedge that took over for the fence and ended at the sidewalk.

Just as the boys reached the sidewalk, a little old lady stepped from behind the hedge and Alex nearly cried out with fright. The dream images of the night before had not fully retreated, and he realized he was more unnerved than he'd thought. Juan jumped like a frightened cat, but Alex knew why *he* was jittery. The stooped, white-haired old lady offered a toothy grin and held out a small brown bag to each boy.

Alex found himself grinning in return, and his racing heart settled into its normal rhythm. "Morning, Mrs. Rhodes."

She kept herself on her side of the hedge. "Mornin' Alex, Juan. I made you tuna today, plus my chocolate chip cookies."

Even though this was a daily ritual, Alex couldn't help but feel extreme gratitude every time. "Thanks, Mrs. Rhodes. I din' even get breakfast this morning." As though on cue, his stomach rumbled.

She glared a moment at Jane's house. "Doesn't surprise me."

"*Gracias, señora,*" Juan offered shyly.

Mrs. Rhodes smiled and turned away, observing Jane's house as she hobbled to her front porch. Alex noted that she was using a cane today, not something she normally did. Must be that arth-something or other that always bothered her, he realized. He'd spin her again as soon as he got a chance. She was always nice to him, and since she never figured out what he was doing, making her feel better was pretty easy.

***

While Bob and Jane discussed particulars of the pending deal, Phil wandered to the living room window and pulled aside the drapes. He observed the old lady hand lunch bags to the boys, and watched as Alex wheeled away down the street, the other kid following. Phil slipped out his phone and typed the following message: 'You were right.'

***

Alex didn't attempt to make conversation with Juan as they made their way toward school. Roy would be along any minute, but Juan would beg off and choose to walk. That's what happened every time Alex spun him.

Roy's F-150 truck rolled into view, and Alex couldn't help but feel good at the sight. Roy's dad had helped him buy the used pickup, and Roy worked all summer buying parts from junkyards and after-market places to soup up the engine and transmission. As far as Alex was concerned, Roy was a genius when it came to anything mechanical.

Roy dramatically honked the horn, as though the two boys couldn't see him right in front of them. It was their usual morning game and Alex chuckled like he always did. Roy pulled the pickup to the curb and hopped out. Alex barely had time to note Roy's skinny jeans, *30 Seconds to Mars* shirt, and shock of brown hair spilling across his face like an old mop before his friend bounded over and grabbed the back of the wheelchair.

Alex's chair was his one prized possession. A few years ago, when he'd had a cool social worker, he'd managed to get a super-sturdy chair built like the one a famous guy named Aaron used for his incredible stunts. Alex had only been seven when he'd seen on the news how fourteen-year-old Aaron mastered the world's first backflip in a wheelchair. It had amazed and empowered Alex to see someone who couldn't walk accomplishing something so spectacular.

His caseworker at the time, a lady named Sandy Quigley, had convinced the county to pay for his special chair on the grounds that it would be nearly indestructible and would not need to be replaced or repaired often. Alex had been so ecstatic he didn't even feel guilty for spinning Sandy into thinking he needed something like that.

Roy pushed Alex's chair around the front of the truck to the passenger side and yanked open the door. Alex tossed his backpack onto the floor as Roy extended his arms and grinned. The double piercings at each side of his lower lip glinted in the morning sun. Alex smiled and slid forward, allowing Roy to sweep him up and toss him onto the passenger seat, grunting as he did.

"Getting too buff, Alex," Roy said. "You should be tossing me into the car."

"Yer just mad cuz I'm younger and can beat yer ass at arm wrestling," Alex retorted as Roy grinned and slammed the door.

Roy grabbed the chair, popped out the cushion, folded it into itself and slipped both chair and cushion up and into the bed of his pickup. He noticed Juan walking away in the direction of Mark Twain and called out. "Hey, Juan, doncha wanna ride?"

Juan turned and shook his head. "Not today, Roy. Thanks." He hurried away, as though trying to put as much distance between himself and Alex as possible.

Alex watched through the rearview as his housemate scurried away like a frightened rabbit.

Roy climbed into the cab and slammed his door, flipping his ragged bangs off his face and jerking a thumb behind him. "'Sup with him today?"

Alex shrugged. "Jane had Carlos beat him up so I hadda spin 'im. You know how he trips."

Roy cast a disgusted look Alex's way. "I hate that bitch. You need to spin her but good."

Alex tried for a smile, but those horrific dream images returned in force.

"Don't tempt me."

When Roy didn't start the engine right away, Alex looked at him through his surfer-white bangs. "We're gonna be late."

Roy shrugged. He wore the black Levi's jacket Alex loved, the one with the rips in it that looked so cool. If Roy wasn't Special Ed like him, he'd be one of the sickest kids on campus.

Roy reached down to the floor beneath his seat and pulled out a small package wrapped in black paper. "Happy birthday, fool." He tossed Alex the box.

Oh, crap! Alex thought as he fumbled to catch the box that fell into his lap. He'd completely forgotten! What with his latest nightmare and having to spin Juan, his fifteenth birthday never even crossed his mind.

Blushing and making his pale skin look like a tomato, Alex grinned. "Thanks, man. I forgot."

Roy shoved his bangs aside again. "I didn't. Open it."

Almost giddy at receiving a real present, Alex tore off the paper with gusto, and gaped at what he found underneath. A Nexus phone, still in the box. Brand new!

His chest tightened, like the wind had been knocked from his lungs. Other than his wheelchair, he'd never been given anything this nice since he was four. He looked at the grinning Roy with open-mouthed astonishment. "Oh, man, Roy, I dunno what to say."

Roy laughed, a rarity for him. "How 'bout, thanks, Roy, for being my awesomest friend."

"Thanks, Roy, for being my *most* awesomest friend. But, this is too much, man. And I got no money for a plan. You know how Jane–"

"Screw her!" Roy spat. "You know I make money fixing engines and stuff and my dad let me put you on our plan. He hates that bitch as much as I do."

Alex felt funny, like he was taking advantage of Roy. "I never had a phone before...."

"It's time you did," Roy said, grabbing the box and ripping off the plastic covering. As he opened the box and slid out the smartphone, he added, "Now you can call me any time. I know we can't text a lot, but I'll put apps on it so we can see each other when we talk."

Alex grinned. Jane never let the boys use her house phone, and she didn't allow them to have cell phones, either. The others were on probation and she'd convinced their probation officers that "Cell phones are an invitation to trouble."

"I gotta hide this from Jane," Alex said, his face clouding over. "She'll take it away."

"Over my dead body."

Alex loved how protective Roy was of him.

"Thanks, Roy," he said shyly, gazing in awe at the bright, crystal clear home screen. *His own phone! Wow!*

"We better get to school," Roy said, turning the ignition. "You know how Ms. Ashley gets when we're late."

The mention of Ms. Ashley pushed aside all the joy he felt at receiving Roy's gift, and flooded his mind with bloodied images of her demise in his dream. He shivered, seeing once more the face of that huge, grinning cat.

"Yeah, let's get going."

Suddenly, he wanted to get to school. But he feared it, too, because deep down he knew his teacher wouldn't be there today, or any of the days to come.

Roy made a U-turn and pulled out into the quiet residential street toward Mark Twain High.

CHAPTER TWO

SOMEBODY KILLED HER

Mark Twain High School sat on the corner of Birch Street and El Tercero Boulevard in the city of Hawthorne. It had been undergoing serious reconstruction for the past couple of years and part of the campus sported fancy new buildings. But for some reason Roy didn't understand, the construction had stopped and left most of the school looking ghetto.

Room 17-5 was as far from the main quad as possible, forcing Roy and Alex to push and shove their way through hundreds of oblivious students talking and texting their way to class. Roy heard a few shouts of, "Hey, look, there's Roller Boy!" which caused him to stop and glare out into the crowd. Alex nudged him and he reluctantly followed.

Pablo Medina and his girlfriend strolled past them arm in arm. Pablo played football and she cheered for the team, the typical couple Roy had seen on every teen show ever made. But Pablo was built and Jolene hot, and both showed off their bodies with tight clothes or, in Pablo's case, one of those skin-tight muscle shirts with no sleeves, revealing his big-ass arms to the world. She wore pants that couldn't have been any shorter if they'd been a hat, revealing her tan athletic legs. Roy followed the couple with his eyes as they passed, cursing himself for looking yet *again*.

A crunching noise distracted him and he turned to find Alex had stopped to stare at some kind of necklace on the ground. His wheelchair had run over it, smashing the clasp. But the main ornament was undamaged, and caught Roy's eye with its unusual design.

Alex reached down and scooped it up as Roy stepped to his side.

"What's that?" he asked, studying the intricate pattern.

"Dunno," Alex replied as he examined it.

Roy noted the design over Alex's shoulder. It resembled a complex spider web set within a triangle and encircled by silver.

"That's pretty wicked, Alex," Roy gushed. "And it would look badass on you. Another birthday present."

Alex shrugged. "Yeah, it's kinda cool. One of the Goth kids probably dropped it. Chain's broken though."

"We'll fix it later, man. We're late."

Alex stared at the unusual pattern, and gasped.

"You okay?" Roy asked, leaning in to look.

Alex swallowed hard. "I thought I saw a weird looking face in there."

"Yeah?" Roy felt a sudden chill that wasn't from the breeze.

"Just me being a dumb-ass, I guess," Alex said with a shrug and slight grin. "Let's go." He slipped the medal into his pants pocket and pushed hurriedly forward as the tardy bell blared like a super-loud doorbell. They were now officially late.

***

Yanking open the classroom door, Roy held it as Alex wheeled into the room. Roy followed, leaving the door ajar. Their four classmates were inside, but not Ms. Ashley. The other boys were engaged in loud arm wrestling matches.

Alex noted the absence of Ms. Ashley with concern, while Roy was relieved they wouldn't get detention for being late.

"Where's Ms. Ashley?" he asked.

Cuong, a thin, tiny Vietnamese boy was in the process of losing his arm-wrestling match to Jorge, who was big and soft-looking.

Cuong grunted, "L-l-l-late," as he struggled against the bigger Latino.

"She's never late," said Roy, turning to Alex. His friend looked paler than usual, and afraid.

"You okay, man?" Roy asked. Concerned, he squatted down to meet Alex's eyes.

Alex didn't respond.

Java, the only black kid in class, beefy and broad-shouldered, easily beat pretty-boy Israel at the same moment Cuong lost his match. Java raised his thick arms in triumph and crowed, grinning at Alex and Roy.

"Okay, Alex, I'm ready to try you again," he announced in a challenging tone, his voice deep with encroaching manhood. "I been doing tons more curls at home."

Lost in thought, Alex didn't even hear the challenge.

"Hey, Alex," Roy said, snapping his fingers in front of his friend. "You're zoning again."

Alex suddenly seemed to realize Roy had squatted in front of him, eyes wide with concern.

"Huh?" Then he glanced at Java. "Oh, not now, Java."

"C'mon, Alex," Java begged. "I feel strong today, man."

Israel chimed in with, "Go fer it, Alex. Don't be a pussy."

A young woman stepped through the door, silencing all the boys at once, except Cuong, who had pulled out a Gameboy and begun playing. Java stared with wide eyes, while Israel gaped, his tongue hanging out.

Alex looked at the newcomer with concern in his eyes.

"Hi," she said, her voice light and perky. "Is this room–" She glanced at a slip of blue paper in her hand. "–17-5?"

Java and Israel nodded.

"What happened to Miss Ashley?" Alex asked, his voice sounding small and breathless.

The lady smiled and shrugged. "I don't know. They just called me in to sub." She walked across to the teacher's desk up front. All eyes followed her movements, except for Cuong and Roy.

Roy watched Alex, and cast several glances toward Java and Israel, noting their tongues hanging out. This lady was hot. Of course, the short, tight dress didn't help matters. Roy clearly understood that she wanted to be noticed—strange for a woman working with teen boys at a high school. Her long blond hair fell about her shoulders in light waves, and her face displayed a remarkable lack of makeup. Roy was used to seeing the female teachers at Mark Twain trowel it on. But then, this lady was young and beautiful, and she knew it.

A pervasive, expectant silence hovered over the room like a raincloud, punctuated only by the sound effects from Cuong's Gameboy. The sub dropped her purse and satchel of materials onto the teacher's desk and turned to face them. They stared at her in silence.

She laughed. "This is a small class. Is everyone here?"

All but Alex and Roy nodded in unison.

Roy squinted. She was acting this way on purpose, almost flirting with them the way girls did for hot guys like Pablo Medina.

But we're the losers, he thought, *and no one flirts with us. 'Specially grown ladies like her.*

"My name is Ms. Garrett," she announced. "But you can call me Ms. G. if that's easier." Her voice sounded sultry to Roy, like some of those hot chicks in movies he used to watch with his dad before the drinking took over. His dad had taught him that word, had told him with a sly wink to beware of "sultry chicks."

She wrote her name on the whiteboard in flowing cursive, then turned to face them. Roy chewed his fingernails as he stared.

"You're all so quiet," she went on, like this was always the reaction she got from teen boys. "I shouldn't say this, I know, but I'm kind of new at this. I'd really like to know something about each of you before we start. Anyone?"

Roy didn't want to answer, but he didn't have to. As usual, Israel started his mile-a-minute-yammering. As soon as he began, Roy knew his classmate had not taken his meds. *Again.*

"I can tell ya everything," Israel began. "That guy's Roy. He can't read good–"

"None a us can, fool!" Roy shot back. "That's why we're special ed."

Israel went on as though Roy had said nothing. "But he's good at fixin' stuff an' he bites his fingernails."

Roy yanked his hand away from his mouth. "Do not."

Again, Israel ignored him. This time he pointed to Cuong. "That's Cuong. He's a nip."

"I-i-i'm V-v-v-i-i-etnamese," Cuong said.

Israel ignored the interruption. "Same thing. He just plays that stupid game all the time and he s-s-s-stutters."

Cuong glowered, and turned red with embarrassment. "D-d-d-do n-not." Seeing the new teacher watching him, Cuong stashed the game under his desk and tried to look innocent.

Then Israel went on, pointing to the boy who beat Cuong at arm-wrestling. "He's Jorge, but it's pronounced in English like 'George,' so just call him that. He's autistic and shit, but he remembers everything he hears, like a tape recorder, ya know? Show her, Jorge."

The other boy turned his soft round face toward the newcomer and said in a monotone voice, "I shouldn't say this, I know, but I'm kind of new at this. I'd really like to know something about each of you before we start."

Then he smiled so sweetly that Ms. Garrett laughed. "Wow, I better be careful what I say."

Israel swept his pointing finger at the black youth who'd beaten him at arm-wrestling. "An' that's Java. He thinks he's all bad."

Java glowered, his expression angry and proud. "At least I ain't no damned *ese* like you."

Israel ignored the dig. It was the standard play-by-play between them anyway and Roy knew they always had each other's backs if something went down.

The grinning Israel now pointed to the silent Alex. "An' this is Alex. He's a cripple, an' he don't read good, but he's the strongest guy in the class. And he can spin–"

Roy cut him off. "Izzy!"

As though suddenly realizing he'd gone too far, Israel looked at Roy, abashed. "Oh, yeah. Sorry."

The substitute stood regarding Israel with amusement. "And you are?"

Israel offered his loopy grin. "Huh? Oh, I'm Israel. Dumb name, I hate it. But I'm the hottest guy in here – everybody says so – and I have ADHD and I get kicked outta every class cuz the teachers say I cuss too much, but I don't think so. And these fools always think I need more meds, but I don't, and–"

"You do!" shouted Java, stormy brown eyes narrowed to slits. "Now shut up 'fore I hafta pound yer ass!"

Roy watched the sub's reaction to his classmates. Normally, substitutes looked shocked or offended when the guys cussed or called each other names, and tried to get them to be "polite." But it seemed this one had already known what to expect, which didn't sit right with Roy. The lady in the front office who scheduled subs never told them what this class was really like or else they wouldn't take the job. They'd never had the same sub twice. Of course, Ms. Ashley was almost never absent.

The lady smiled at them as though they had just acted like an honors class or something. She rubbed Roy the wrong way. Big time.

"Well, nice to meet you all. I don't know how long I'll be–"

A clearing throat startled them, and drew their attention to the open door. Mrs. Davis stood just inside, and the boys instantly sat to attention. For such a small lady, she didn't back down from any teacher or student, and ran her school like the Marines.

"Good morning," she said, shuffling uncomfortably.

Roy noted her unusual behavior, and saw Alex look at her with wide-eyed fear.

Israel blurted, "That's the principal."

Ms. Garrett ignored him and focused on the newcomer.

Mrs. Davis swept her piercing gaze over the boys in the room, but Roy noticed it wasn't with her usual disdain. She looked sympathetic. "I'm afraid I have some sad news for you boys."

"Miss Ashley's dead," Alex said, and Roy looked at him sharply

"The hell?" Israel blurted.

Mrs. Davis stared at Alex. "How did you know that?"

Alex stared at her without expression. "Dreamed it."

Mrs. Davis averted her eyes from Alex and took in the others' shocked expressions. "For now, Ms. Garrett will be your teacher until we find a replacement. Please don't drive her away."

With that, she turned and exited the room. Roy could make out the clicking of her heels against the concrete for several seconds until it faded into an awkward silence.

"Shit," Java whispered, his usual booming voice without timber or power.

Roy teared up, images of his mother filling his heart with sadness, especially since Ms. Ashley had been like a second mom to him.

He glanced around at his classmates through blurred vision. Even Cuong hadn't pulled out his game, and seemed to have a wide-eyed understanding of what Mrs. Davis had just told them.

The substitute cleared her throat. When he looked at her, he saw sadness on her face, and that disarmed him. Had he imagined her sultry behavior?

"I'm very sorry, boys," she said, looking uncomfortable and uncertain. "Do you want to talk about it?"

The boys remained silent for a moment.

Israel said, "Ms. Ashley was cool and I never once cussed her out."

Roy cast him a "look," but Israel kept going. "Well, only that first day, you know, cuz I didn't feel like doin' no work. But she just stood there and looked at me all calm and shit and waited till I finished talking, which took, like, you know, a few minutes, and then she went back to showin' me what she wanted me to do, and–"

"Izzy!" Java barked.

Israel looked at him, and Roy was shocked to see tears in his eyes. Israel never took anything seriously enough to cry.

"Sorry, man," Israel replied. "She was just so cool, that's all."

Roy watched him cry, his own emotions welling up from deep within him. Ms. Ashley *had* been cool, the coolest teacher he'd ever had. She'd loved them, and always celebrated everyone's birthday like it was a huge deal. She would've had a party today for Alex's fifteenth.

Now Jorge began to cry, and did something Roy had never seen before – he reached out and put an arm around Izzy to comfort him. Jorge hated being touched and *never* voluntarily touched anyone. Even Izzy looked shocked, but he wrapped his own arm around his classmate's shoulder and they cried together.

Roy locked eyes with Java. The black youth, who prided himself on being tough and manly, suddenly looked lost and fragile, like the little boy he once was, and Roy knew exactly how he felt.

But his main concern was Alex. He squatted again beside his best friend, vaguely aware that the substitute was saying something about making sympathy cards for Ms. Ashley's family, and did "anyone know if there were art supplies in the room?"

Wiping tears from his cheeks, Roy made eye contact with Alex. "What did you dream?" he asked quietly so the substitute wouldn't hear.

A tear rolled down Alex's soft white cheek and dropped into his lap. "Somebody killed her," he whispered.

Roy nearly gasped, his teary eyes wide and round. "For real?"

Alex nodded.

Roy felt the blood drain from his face. He was already pale, but now must've looked like a piece of printer paper. "Did you see who?"

Alex shook his head as more tears fell. He swiped at them in annoyance. Throwing caution to the wind, Roy leaned forward on his knees and enveloped Alex in a tight hug. He wasn't sure Alex would like that, but *he* needed it. To his immense relief, Alex returned the hug and they remained locked together in grief for a few moments.

The rest of the morning seemed to take forever. All of them kept quiet as they used their feeble artistic talents to make a card for Ms. Ashley's family. Since Cuong was the only one who could actually draw, they let him do most of the work, occasionally making a suggestion about adding this or that.

Israel wandered around looking at everything, hovering near Ms. Ashley's desk and playing with the plastic apple that held all her rubber stamps. He took a piece of paper and kept stamping it over and over again with every single one. Because none of them could read, and all had language processing problems, Ms. Ashley only used stamps with symbols they could understand: the Superman "S," a thumbs up image, the "Like" button from Facebook, smile faces, an angry face, and a host of others.

When one or more of them would be acting out or driving her crazy, she would simply walk down the aisle and stamp their papers with a sad face to indicate she was unhappy with them. No words were spoken or needed. They got the message and would usually settle down. Roy suspected Izzy felt guilty for all the times he hadn't settled down when she'd stamped his paper.

Roy remained by Alex's side the entire morning, especially when the substitute would sidle really close to the wheelchair like she owned Alex or something. That irked Roy, and he kept telling her they were fine and to help Jorge instead.

This class being the last stop, the six boys stayed there all day for every subject. While there were other Special Ed teachers and classrooms, none could handle them, and the other Special Ed kids always talked mess to them, which usually ended in a fight if the one being made fun of was Java. He was strong enough to kick ass on even the jocks, and didn't take crap from anyone.

No girls, not even the Special Ed girls, wanted anything to do with them. There had been one girl in their class for a while, but Israel and Java kept hitting on her every day, and then cussing her out each time she turned them down, that her parents moved her out.

Yup, Roy knew, this bunch had more than earned its school wide nickname: The Losers.

Finally, after what seemed an eternity, the lunch bell rang and the guys bolted from the room, leaving the substitute uselessly calling after them to clean up their stuff.

CHAPTER THREE

LOOKS LIKE WE FOUND THE REAL ONE

Once the others had gotten their food in the crowded cafeteria, they pressed their way through the milling students in the quad to join Alex at their usual table as far from the main traffic areas as possible.

The old picnic tables were made of metal, with peeling red paint and bench seats, and no one ever approached The Losers' table except to mock them or throw food. As the others scooted into the benches, Pablo and Jolene strolled past, and Alex saw Roy's eyes follow them.

Alex noted Roy's fixed gaze, as he had on several other occasions, and without even planning to, spun him. What he felt confused him, until something more distracting wandered past their table.

Israel called out, "Hey, Tami, wanna go out with me?"

The attractive sophomore stopped and looked over, obviously focusing her mind on what Israel had just said.

As always, when Alex looked at her, he blushed. She was the prettiest girl he knew, and one of the most popular at school. She was a cheerleader with a fit figure that she wasn't shy about showing off, and short wavy black hair. Her full lips were, at the moment, twisted into a scowl directed at Israel.

"I heard you broke up with Rick," Israel added, and Java elbowed him hard in the gut. Java always tried to look cool and buff around girls, hoping they would ignore the Special Ed part. He wore those tight, long sleeve shirts like the big-time NFL players because the shirts made him look more built. Jorge sat munching on his microwave burrito, and watched the exchange with a blank look, while Cuong ignored everything in favor of his Gameboy.

Tami's scowl turned fierce and stormy, and for a moment Alex thought she might grab Izzy's burrito and throw it in his face. Instead she stepped over to the table and thrust a thumb in Israel's direction.

"You better get Mr. ADHD back on his meds before he gets the shit beat out of him."

"Hey, bitch, I was just asking," Israel said. "Don't need to go all drama on me."

Java glowered at him as Tami's fists flew to her hips and she glared pure hate at Israel.

"I'm sorry to hear about Rick," Alex offered, even though he wasn't.

Alex's voice seemed to calm Tami, as it always did. "He was such a jerk, Alex. Snapchatting every girl on campus while telling me I'm the only one he cared about. I thought I could trust him, but guys are all alike. Well, I'm done with him and every other jock!"

As she spoke, Alex spun her. The others watched in silence. His face went from sad to angry within seconds, while Tami's relaxed into a look of resigned peacefulness.

"Don't worry about Rick," Alex said through gritted teeth. "He's not worth it."

And suddenly Tami agreed with him. "You're right, Alex. I don't know why I ever got mad. It's not like he's important."

Then she obviously noted the anger on Alex's face. "You okay, Alex?"

Roy said, "He's upset." She turned to him. "We, uh, we found out Ms. Ashley, well, died last night."

Tami's hand flew to her mouth. "Oh, my God, what happened?"

"She got attacked by cats and run over by a truck," Alex said.

Her mouth dropped open in stunned surprise, and Alex heard Java behind him mutter, "The hell?" Even Roy gulped in shock.

"That's horrible," Tami said, clearly shaken. "How did you find out?"

Alex realized he'd said too much. The story might have been on the news by now, but did they say anything about the cats? "Mrs. Davis told us," he said, knowing Tami would never ask the principal about anything.

Just then another girl trotted over. "Hey, Tami, I heard about Rick," she said, ignoring the boys. "Told ya he was an asshole."

Tami nodded, clearly upset by the news about Ms. Ashley.

The other girl, a cheerleader named Maribel, tossed the boys a look of contempt before addressing the silent Tami. "Why are you with these losers? C'mon, let's get out of here before anyone sees you with them."

Israel couldn't let that insult pass. "Bite me, bitch!"

Maribel looked at him like he was an old food wrapper. "In your dreams, loser."

Then she grabbed Tami by the arm and started dragging her away. Tami turned her head and offered a sympathetic smile. "See ya, Alex."

Alex's breath almost stopped. But only for a second. The truth practically slapped him. Her liking him even a little was only due to the spinning.

"Is that what really happened?" Java asked, planting his big arms on the table and leaning toward Alex so other students wouldn't overhear them.

Alex nodded and described his dream as best as he could remember. Israel said it sounded like a horror film, and even the tough and unflappable Java was shaken.

They resumed eating in silence. Israel drummed his hands against the table top, his eyes flitting to this girl or that one as they passed, his tongue hanging out like a dog's. Jorge doodled the letter "V" on his left arm with the Sharpie he held in his right hand. Cuong returned to his game. Java finished his burrito and asked Alex if he wanted the tuna sandwich in front of him. Alex shook his head, so Java shrugged, snatched it up and wolfed it down in three bites.

Alex observed Roy, but forced himself not to spin his friend any more than he already had. Roy seemed to be the one exception to his ability – even without words being spoken, Alex could pull feelings directly from him. It must be, he thought, because Roy was the only person to whom he felt close.

A shadow fell across their table. The bright October sun was behind the person, giving him a menacing silhouetted look. The figure studied Alex a moment before turning to Roy. The shift in position revealed his face, and Alex sighed. It was just Roy's older brother. Alex knew he was twenty-one and worked with the maintenance staff at Mark Twain and that he and Roy hadn't grown up together because they had different moms.

The man stood looking down at them, dressed in the standard blue shirt, with MTS above the pocket, and brown work pants.

Roy shifted with discomfort. Dane was six-foot-three and cast an intimidating shadow. "'Sup, Dane?"

Dane had longish brown hair, tied back off his thin face, and deep-set brown eyes that seldom, if ever, revealed what lived behind them. He looked to Alex like he wanted to be sympathetic, but didn't know how.

"Heard about your teacher," he said, with no inflection in his voice. "That sucks. You okay?"

Roy squinted against the sun, and nodded.

Dane returned the nod, as though that was all he wanted to know. Then he looked down at Alex again and fixed those unreadable eyes on him.

Alex squirmed with discomfort as he always did whenever Dane looked at him, which lately seemed to be pretty often. Alex knew Dane was embarrassed to be around his Special Ed brother because he'd been a loser at this school, too. Roy told Alex that only because Dane's mom knew people on the school board did Dane ever get his diploma, and a job on the maintenance staff. Dane couldn't read any better than Roy, and Alex had never seen him in any mood other than grumpy.

Abruptly, Dane turned and struck out toward the center of campus, working his way through the milling students toward the gym. The students cleared a path for him, and he didn't acknowledge any of them as he passed.

"Your brother's an asshole," Israel tossed out in between drumbeats.

Roy locked eyes with Alex, who shrugged and offered a smile. "Least he thought 'bout you."

The bell signaling the end of lunch ding-donged, and The Losers left their table to return to class.

***

After receiving the call from his agent in the field, Mark Davalos rubbed a hand though his silver-gray hair and sat a moment in contemplative thought. Finally, after thirteen years, a solid lead!

Since the enemy had never accomplished anything of note during that time, Davalos always suspected that the myth of "the other one" was just that – a myth. But the one they snatched all those years ago obviously proved to be a dud, which meant the existence of a second one made sense. Davalos now understood with crystal clarity that he had to move forward with care.

Snatching up his phone, he punched in a number and waited for someone to answer. When he heard the click, he said, "Davalos here. Looks like we found the real one. I'm sending over the info. Keep constant surveillance, but under no circumstances arouse suspicion. We can't let the enemy know we're on to them. Yes, report directly to me."

He hung up and swiveled around to scan the bulletin boards surrounding his desk. Newspaper and Internet stories were tacked up, some on top of each other, many brown with age.

Healings.

Miracle cures.

Supposed unexplained phenomena involving children.

All false leads, he now knew. The real deal, it seemed, had been under their nose all along, hiding in plain sight.

Kid's mom pulled a fast one, he thought, feeling deep admiration for the long dead woman.

"But not fast enough," he murmured to himself as he turned his chair around and stood to leave the office.

CHAPTER FOUR

STUFF MAKES ME WANNA KILL MYSELF

The substitute seemed more "normal" after lunch, and did her best to help them through the day, but Alex was still wary of her.

After school, they'd all piled into Roy's truck to kick it at his house. Roy's dad didn't get home till dinnertime most nights, and then he always went straight to the fridge for a six-pack and upstairs to his room.

The boys would often gather in Roy's downstairs room and argue about which music to listen to since Java and Israel disdained "that emo shit you guys listen to," referring to him and Roy.

"What is it with you white boys and emo?" Java once asked, messing with them. "Stuff makes me wanna kill myself."

Alex and Roy gave him a canned laugh, and Alex said, "Well, your rap music makes me wanna kill somebody *else*."

Java's mouth had dropped open in shock, and then he'd grinned and raised a meaty fist. Alex bumped it and they'd settled for ear buds, like always.

Today, Roy grabbed a six-pack of his dad's beer from the garage and they'd hung out in Roy's room drinking and trying not to talk about the teacher they'd loved, even though kids weren't supposed to like their teachers. Normally, Alex wasn't much for beer, but his sadness won out and he swigged the sour liquid with desperation, despite knowing the buzz wouldn't take away his pain.

Jorge had both arms covered with "Vs" and had even lifted his shirt to draw them on his soft belly. This was standard routine, so the others paid it no mind. Cuong had found some binder paper and drew a sketch of Ms. Ashley that the others agreed was a good likeness. Java and Israel mindlessly played Roy's PS4 while listening to music from their phones.

As it neared dinnertime, the others drifted away to their own homes in the neighborhood, leaving only Alex and Roy. The friends sat in silence, the beer having mellowed them, adding to their already dark, emotional natures.

They watched Roy's favorite video on YouTube. It was these three church boys singing a song called "Tears in Heaven" that Roy had found on the Internet right after his mother died. The blond singer named Patrick had a really high voice that Alex thought angels must sound like, and the song made him wonder if his parents and Roy's mom might know each other in heaven.

That video, while not an emo song, had cemented the friendship between Alex and Roy because both teared up every time they watched it. Roy always joked that Patrick looked like Alex, but Alex only wished he were that good looking.

They watched the video twice, thinking of their parents and Ms. Ashley. Father Pat always told Alex that he would see his parents again someday, but he wasn't sure he believed that. He even wondered if Patrick believed the words he sang so beautifully, or if they were just words to him. And he couldn't help noticing Roy stare fixedly at the younger boy on screen, as though remembering something else besides his mother. But he refused to spin Roy any more. It was wrong, and he had to control it.

The video ended and Roy pressed the pause button, glancing at Alex with a sad smile. Alex returned it. Yes, that song spoke to both of them in ways most other kids couldn't begin to understand.

Another few minutes of silence passed between them. Alex fiddled with the colorful friendship bracelet Roy made for him, and which he'd promised never to take off. Finally, he said it was time to head home before Jane "spazzed out." As always, Roy offered to walk with him.

When they arrived at Jane's house, Alex saw Mrs. Rhodes picking some flowers from her garden and waved. She returned the wave. It was nearly five o'clock, but since Daylight Savings hadn't ended yet there was still some sunlight.

"Thanks, Roy, for my birthday present," Alex said, patting his pants pocket.

With all that had happened, Roy had clearly forgotten. "No prob."

They looked at one another for a long moment. "Well, gotta go. See ya tomorrow."

"Yup," Roy said, and Alex turned and pushed his way down the side path to his room entrance. Jane's house had steps leading to the front door, so the only way Alex could enter was through his back door or the one into the kitchen. Roy watched his friend disappear, and then thrust both hands into his pockets and headed home.

CHAPTER FIVE

I HEARD YOU SCREAM

ALEX REPLAYED THE WHOLE DAY in his mind as he sat in his room listening to the wind howl outside. He'd said nothing at dinner, despite Carlos taunting him about school and whether he'd learned how to spell his own name. Obviously, Alex figured, the big gangster hadn't heard about Ms. Ashley, so the nightly ritual of mocking his learning disabilities was a relief by comparison.

Juan had sat shoveling in his macaroni and cheese, knowing better than to challenge the older boy and risk a beating from him or Jane for "starting trouble." That was Jane's favorite phrase. Whenever she was in the mood to punish any of them, she accused them of "starting trouble," whether they'd actually done anything wrong or not.

Jane, herself, never ate with them. She put out the food, gave them a thirty minute window to show up and eat it, or they went hungry that night. No exceptions.

Because he'd skipped lunch, Alex was hungry, gobbling his macaroni and cheese and a healthy serving of salad. The other boys ignored the salad, but Alex needed the roughage for his bowels, as well as lots of water throughout the day. He still didn't know why he couldn't walk or use his legs. He was told the doctors suspected an odd variation on spina bifida, but one that didn't come will all the usual problems. His lower body was weak and always had been. He had minimal feeling, but not strength enough to walk or even crawl as a baby.

After eating, he'd descended into the welcome solitude of his basement room to brood, and lament the loss of someone he cared about. He showered and took care of his bodily needs, which included feeling beneath his legs and buttocks for pressure sores. Thankfully, he found none.

Slipping workout shorts on over his boxers while lying on the floor, he'd pulled himself into his chair and sat shirtless, fumbling in his backpack for his iPod. He popped in the ear buds and cranked some

Hawthorne Heights tunes, hoping the music and lyrics would free his mind from the images assaulting him. But it didn't work. Ms. Ashley's broken body, and that gigantic cat grinning at her bloodied corpse, kept flashing through his brain like lightning.

For some reason, the image of that necklace he'd found at school intruded. He'd forgotten all about it. Wheeling to the corner where he'd tossed his jeans, he scooped them up and reached into the pocket, pulling out the necklace. He held out the medal and let it dangle before his eyes. He examined the design, marveling at the intricately woven strands that formed the web. He touched the webbing with his left forefinger, and shuddered. It felt weird, not like metal at all but more like... skin.

Human skin.

Still, it *was* pretty wicked looking, and would look kickass with his band shirts. Shoving aside junk in his desk drawer, he found a pair of needle-nose pliers and focused on repairing the clasp, bending it into place where his tire had damaged it.

The clasp was worn, and he proceeded with caution so he wouldn't break it. The entire chain, and the medal dangling from it, seemed really old. There was a word for really old stuff like this, but he couldn't think of it. That was part of his trouble. He'd be taught a new word and understand what it meant, but couldn't for the life of him remember that word the next time he saw it in print. So he couldn't read well because his screwed up brain wouldn't let him remember enough words. It frustrated him because, unlike walking, he felt it was something he *should* be able to do.

After several minutes of tinkering, Alex had the clasp in working order. Dropping the pliers onto his cluttered desk, he placed the medal and chain in his lap and wheeled to his closet. Pulling open the door, he studied himself in the full-length mirror attached to the inside. Whoever had lived here before must've liked seeing themselves every time they went to the closet for clothes. Alex didn't. He always tried looking away because whenever he looked at himself, all he saw was a freak.

He had a decent upper body because that's all he'd used his whole life, and his arm and shoulder muscles looked pretty yoked. He had a couple of dumbbells that had travelled with him from foster home to foster home, and had used these to do chest exercises he found on the Internet. He even had better abs than many of the guys he'd seen in P.E. last year.

But then his weak, useless legs filled his vision and choked off all possible thoughts. It wasn't that he felt sorry for himself; it was just that the chair, combined with his unnatural nature, convinced him he could never have a normal life, and that thought depressed him.

Brushing his hair away from his eyes, Alex yanked out the ear buds, snatched the necklace off his lap and wrapped the chain around his neck. The spider-web medal dangling between his pale pecs looked cool as he brought the two ends of the clasp together beneath his hair and joined them.

The door to the outside flew open and slammed hard against the wall.

Alex wheeled out of the closet and stared up at the open door. The lift was down, and wind howled through the room, encircling him, flinging his hair every which way and tossing leaves down onto his lap. He sat frozen in place, his eyes riveted to that open door, the cold wind raising goose pimples on his naked torso.

Something was out there.

The hackles on the back of his neck rose and tingled.

Something was coming.

Something bad.

And then the lights went out.

***

With the hood of his pickup raised, Roy had his head and arms buried deep within the engine, making some adjustments to the fuel injection. Outside, the wind howled and sounded louder than usual, especially with the garage door down. He had made some microwave dinners for himself and his dad, but when he'd taken one upstairs he found Nathan Phillips passed out on the bed, an entire six-pack reduced to empty cans in the waste basket. Dejection filling him again, Roy had decided to work on his truck. Other than being with Alex, there was nothing that made him feel better than tinkering.

Wind whipped up and swirled through the garage, tossing his mop of hair into his face and almost causing him to drop the wrench. He jerked his head and arms back just as the heavy hood slammed down with a loud *bang*! He stared aghast at the now closed hood of his truck. It could've killed him! And it hadn't dropped like normal - it crashed down, almost like someone… pushed it!

The wind continued, a cold, unnerving wind that set Roy's heart to thumping. He stepped around the truck and scanned the dimly lit garage. The wind blew around him. How? All the doors were closed. There was no way! Then, without warning, the tools hanging on the pegboard began rattling and shaking. Roy flung his hair from his eyes and just managed a dive to the floor as the tools flew off the rack right at him.

***

Java's bedroom looked more like a weight room than a place to sleep. His parents couldn't afford a membership for him at that gym next to school, so his dad had gone to the swap meet and bought a bench, some bars, plates, and quite a few dumbbells. Java knew he'd never be a reader and go into business like his dad, but he determined in middle school to be big and strong so no one could ever call him a dummy and get away with it. His parents didn't understand his "special ed-ness"—as Alex called it—and he overheard his dad on the phone telling grandma in Jamaica that he was "just stupid and lazy."

Well, Java would show them. He'd go into bodybuilding or powerlifting or boxing - something physical that didn't require reading. He was already one of the strongest kids at school, despite being only sixteen, and everyone was afraid to mess with him.

As usual, he worked out for at least two hours every night. Shirtless, sweat sheening his torso, Java used the curl bar to work his biceps. He tried to count reps, but always got confused and had to start again. So he used the stopwatch on his phone to keep track of the time and would curl fifty pounds for two minutes straight, rep after rep, nice and slow, until he couldn't feel his arms any more.

He was on his second minute when the window flew up in its frame with a crash, shattering the glass, and letting the howling wind pour into his room. The wind felt like a tornado, whipping around and around his head, drying the sweat on his chest, assaulting him with its intense coldness. Startled by the crash, he dropped the curl bar, staring in shock at the shattered glass near his bare feet, his heart racing along with the wind. When one of the forty-five pound plates rose into the air toward him, Java dove over his bed for cover.

***

Israel watched a movie on the small flat screen TV in his bedroom. The lights were off and the normally hyperactive teen sat riveted to the screen. Even though he'd seen almost every horror movie, his favorite was the old version of "The Omen," the first one, because of that creepy-ass little kid and the way it all seemed so real. His parents believed in the Devil, so he supposed he did, too, and a movie about the Devil's son seemed all too possible to him. Adorning his dresser on either side of the television were model kits he'd built as a boy. He had The Wolfman, Dracula, Michael Myers, Jason, Frankenstein's monster, and, of course, Freddy Krueger, his all-time favorite bad guy.

His parents loved those models, even though they hated horror films, because building them had actually kept Israel occupied for hours without needing his medication.

Israel felt a chill run down his spine, and figured it was due to the movie combined with the crazy wind howling outside his bedroom window. Suddenly, both his window and door burst open, and the wind whipped around him, causing him to practically leap off his bed in fright. Even as he swiped greasy hair from his eyes, the wind beat at him, and he noticed something odd about his models.

They were moving!

He blinked a few times, sure the dark and his own fear were responsible. Crawling off the bed, Israel stepped toward his dresser, the movie forgotten as his squinting eyes saw Michael Myers raise his knife and Jason swing his machete. The two looked ready to fight. A chuckling laugh almost made him scream as he whipped his gaze around to the Freddy model. It held out that claw glove and leered. It wasn't possible. None of this could be happening. Must be the beer he'd drunk at Roy's, 'cept he'd only had two.

I'm never drinking again, he swore to himself as he leaned closer to Freddy, his heart thumping like a bass drum. The other statues had stopped moving. He leaned in to Freddy and squinted in the darkness as the wind swirled around him.

Suddenly, the statue turned its head and grinned. "I'll kill ya slow," it said, and then slashed Israel's cheek with razor sharp claws. Israel shrieked.

***

Jorge had become obsessed with the letter V since watching the old sci-fi miniseries about alien invaders on cable, and now he drew or spray-painted red Vs everywhere he went. He'd drunk a beer at Roy's house, a first for him, and quoted from every Bud Light commercial he'd ever seen while doing so. Now, wearing only his boxers, spray can in hand, Jorge stood in his bedroom spray-painting the letter "V" in red all over his walls. Outside, the shrieking of the wind and the rattling of his windowpanes seemed to excite him, and his hand flew up and down with V after V.

The door flew open and his mother burst in, crying out, "*¡Dios, mío*!" She ran forward to try and take the can away, but he turned and grabbed her arm so hard she winced in pain. "Jorge!"

The wind smashed through his window and blew shards of glass everywhere. Jorge's mother screamed and covered her face, but Jorge merely stared at the fluttering drapes and bits of glass embedded in the carpet. The wind forced his screaming mother onto the bed as Jorge raised the spray can toward the now-shattered window. The can flew from his grasp as though snatched, ricocheted off the wall he'd been painting and struck him hard to the forehead. With a grunt he dropped to the floor as his mother screamed again.

***

Cuong sat in his room riveted to the TV, playing the Wii version of Super Smash Brothers against the computer. His family was embarrassed to have a Special Ed kid, so he never made any attempt to interact with them. He played Wii 24/7 and only came out of his room for dinner or to use the bathroom. On some occasions, he'd become so fixated on a game that he'd wet his pants and not even notice. That embarrassed his family even more. A fourteen-year-old wetting his pants!

Always oblivious to his surroundings when engrossed in a game, Cuong didn't even realize that a wind had kicked up and swirled about his head, even with his window closed and locked. The wind snatched the Wii remote from his hands and flung it at the television, cracking the screen from top to bottom. Cuong stared at the damaged television while his character of Link suddenly stopped fighting Donkey Kong and turned to lock eyes with him.

"You stupid little bitch!" the cartoon character spat, and then cackled with glee as he flung his sword right out of the TV at the wide-eyed boy.

***

Alex sat in the dark staring up at the open door. The swiftly falling temperature turned his exposed skin to ice. The wind made the room even colder and froze the blood in his veins.

When the lights went out, Alex had nearly screamed with fright. But the last thing he wanted was Jane down here. He rolled his chair closer and closer to the lift leading to the open door. Leaves littered the floor of the lift, but so far nothing but the wind, and those leaves, had entered.

His wheels creaked against the carpeted concrete floor, and he glanced around the shadowy confines of his room. In every corner lurked something hideous, something his imagination created to menace him.

He stopped at the lift and gazed upward. The wind banged the door against the wall every so often just to further unnerve him. Steeling himself, Alex pushed his chair onto the platform and pressed the up button. The door was only about eight feet above floor level, but it felt to Alex like an eternity as he watched the opening come more fully into view. The lift stopped at the top, and Alex nearly cried out in terror.

Sitting just outside his door, gazing in at him with shiny reddish-orange eyes, was the biggest cat Alex had ever seen, easily as large as the cocker spaniel one of his old neighbors had owned. But what froze Alex's blood and sent his heartbeat into overdrive wasn't the size of the cat, or even the way the longhaired animal seemed to tilt its head and regard him with thoughtful intelligence.

No, it was the fact that this was the same cat, the one from his dream, the one that led the attack against Ms. Ashley!

Alex stared, barely able to breathe. It couldn't be! How could it be here? Why was it here? The cat tilted its head from side to side, regarding the boy as though trying to decide whether to befriend him or claw him to death.

Trembling, Alex rolled himself onto the platform and reached with his right hand toward the door, intending to slam and lock it before the enormous animal could leap. The cat's creepy eyes followed Alex's hand, and then narrowed to angry slits. Alex stopped instantly, his outstretched arm shaking, his eyes never leaving the cat. It growled.

Alex gulped and pulled his arm in, resting it with great deliberation onto his lap. The cat's eyes were still narrowed, but they once again locked on his. Alex felt trapped, almost like the cat was spinning him the way he spun other people.

That's when the cat smiled. "Hello, Alex."

Alex freaked. He screamed at the top of his lungs. He didn't care if Jane heard him or not.

The cat's smile grew even bigger.

Roy's voice called from somewhere outside the house. "Alex, you okay?"

"Roy, in here!" Alex shouted, his mouth agape as the monstrous cat sat watching him.

Footsteps pounded on the gravel alongside the house. "I'm coming!"

The cat glanced once to its left, and then turned back to face Alex. It seemed to be mocking his quavering fear. With one final grin, the mountain of fur whipped its tail up, turned and fled into the night, taking the howling wind with it.

Roy bounded through the door, panting and heaving, gripping at a stitch in his side. "You okay, Alex?" Roy asked, his voice flush with fear.

The sudden absence of wind was more unnerving to Alex than the wind itself. He fought to control his shaking, but his shirtless state and that freaking cat sent wave after wave of icy cold fingers up and down his back. "Did you see it?" he gasped.

"See what?" Roy asked, suddenly aware that Alex was shirtless. "Shit, Alex, you look frozen!"

Alex's teeth were chattering and he could no longer speak. Roy closed and locked the door, and returned the lift to the floor. Alex stiffly slipped on the t-shirt Roy snatched from a dresser drawer, and then allowed his friend to pull a heavy black hoodie over his head and flip up the hood to warm his face.

The overhead lights burst to life, blinding both boys and almost causing them to cry out in surprise. Blinking back the painful shards piercing his eyeballs, Alex gasped. Roy's face was cut and bleeding. There was a bruise on his cheek and several more blackening bruises on his upper arms. Roy wore nothing but a t-shirt and jeans, and shivered as he checked Alex for injuries.

"Roy, what happened? You're bleeding!"

Roy told him what went down in his garage, clearly shaken by the experience. "I barely saved my ass by rolling under the truck till everything stopped flying around."

Alex wheeled himself into the bathroom and snatched up a hand towel. He turned on the faucet and wet the towel with warm water. He re-entered his room to find Roy sitting in his desk chair, head in his hands, shivering and almost hyperventilating with fear.

"Lift your head, Roy."

Roy complied, and Alex wiped the blood from his face. He handed Roy the towel to hold against the big cut on his forehead.

"When everything went down, Alex, all I could think about was you and was something like this happening to you cuz, you know, you can't spin yourself."

Alex nodded, feeling good that someone cared about him.

"What happened to you?" Roy went on, his voice tight with fear. "I heard you scream."

The image of that cat filled Alex's mind, the fluffy light brown fur, the big bushy tail, the sheer size of the animal, those weird eyes. And that grin. That voice… Had it been real or in his head? "In a minute. Let me spin you first."

Roy hesitated, and then nodded. He described where he had been hit, how the pain felt, exactly where it was, and Alex took it all.

Roy lowered the bloody towel to his lap and waited.

Alex felt Roy's pain pull at his every nerve like the plucking of guitar strings. It filled his brain with agony as he purged himself of the aftereffects.

"So," Roy said after a few moments, "what happened to *you*?"

Alex told him.

"Huh?" Roy said, shivering anew, his thin face scrunched with fear. "The cat said your name?"

Alex nodded, his mind replaying that scratchy, inhuman voice coming from the mouth of the cat. Or had he only heard it in his head? Now he wasn't so sure. "You think the other guys are all right?"

"How you mean?"

Alex wasn't sure why, but he sensed that all of his friends were in danger, too. "You an' me got attacked, so what about the others?"

"Oh, crap. I don't got their numbers, and Jorge and Cuong don't even got phones."

They sat a moment in a fearful silence. Wind buffeted the house.

"This is my fault, Roy," Alex whispered.

"How?"

"It was the same cat, the one that killed Ms. Ashley. Whatever tried to hurt you gots to do with me. I feel it."

Roy sat up straight and took on a look of fierce resolve. "Nobody's hurtin' you, Alex, not so long as I'm around," he declared. "I'm stayin' tonight. Keep you safe."

Alex reddened with embarrassment. "I'm not helpless, Roy, just cuz I'm in this chair."

"Never said you was. But two is better'n one, and I'm stayin'."

Alex nodded, feeling better than he should. "Thanks, man."

Roy shivered again from the cold. "You got some extra blankets so's I can crash on the floor?"

"Hell, no, the floor's cold as hell. I got a big bed, enough room for two."

Roy blushed and looked away.

Alex frowned, recalling his unplanned spinning of his friend, and refused to do it again.

"I don't know, Alex. Seems kind a kinda weird, ya know? 'Sides, I might, like, roll over in my sleep and hurt you."

Would people ever stop thinking because he used this wheelchair he could break like some glass statue? "Roy, I'm stronger than you, man. My legs just don't work. You can't hurt me 'less you push me off a cliff or somethin'."

That added a tiny smile to Roy's troubled expression, and he nodded. Alex pulled off the hoodie and tossed it onto the floor, wheeled himself to the big double bed in one corner of the room and slid himself out of his chair onto it.

He pulled his legs up and onto the bed and rolled himself over so he lay on the side next to the wall. He turned to face Roy and grinned. Looking more relaxed, Roy turned off the overhead lights and moved to sit on the other side of the bed. Slipping off his Converse, he pulled his legs up and slid them under the covers, pulling the blanket and coverlet to his chin as Alex did the same beside him. He finally turned his head to find Alex watching him in the shadowy darkness.

"Thanks, man," Roy said, his voice quiet and breathy.

"Thanks for coming to help me."

Alex turned away to face the wall and Roy settled into the mattress beside him. He felt Roy's back touch his own, and even through their shirts that touch felt warm and comforting. Images of the evil, grinning cat filled his mind as he drifted off to sleep.

The music box tinkled its soft, soothing melody, relaxing and distracting him like always. Her face loomed above, the image hazy and indistinct. A lovely, joyful face. She held the music box out to him, speaking comforting words he couldn't make out, in a voice tinged with love. There was someone beside him, someone he should know, but didn't. And he heard a name. Andy.

I'm Alex, he wanted to say. *Andy's my middle name*. But he couldn't talk. He wasn't even sure he knew how yet.

All the while the music box kept playing, repeating its lilting tune again and again. Suddenly, everything changed. Darkness surrounded him. A small pool of light was all he saw. There was a body lying in that pool. Alex felt himself moving toward it. The body was Roy. He'd been stabbed in the chest and blood was everywhere. Alex tried spinning him, but the spin wouldn't come because Roy couldn't talk. And the music confused him. He wanted to shut it off, but couldn't find the music box.

The pretty lady who had it was gone. There was laughter, and the cat. The nasty, evil, grinning-ass cat laughed as Roy's life bled out from his damaged body.

Alex tried to speak, but no words came. He was frozen, the music taking away his willpower. He could do nothing but watch as Roy groaned one last time, and died.

Alex screamed.

DAY 2

CHAPTER SIX

I'LL SPIN YOU GOOD

Alex opened his eyes to find Roy shaking him.

"Wake up, Alex, you're dreaming."

Heart thumping, Alex threw his arms around his friend. "I dreamed you died, man, an' I couldn't save you!"

Roy gasped, and held Alex close. "Tell me what happened."

Alex slipped his arms from around Roy and slid down onto his pillow. Roy noted the sweat plastering Alex's white hair to his forehead and the dampness of his t-shirt.

Alex described the dream, reminding Roy that the music box had been in every dream he could remember. But he was sure he'd never heard that song before.

Alex shivered. "When you died I–"

Roy put a hand over Alex's mouth gently. "I'm fine, Alex. I'm not gonna die."

He lowered his hand, and Alex stared at him with wide, frightened eyes. "But sometimes my dreams come true."

"Like Ms. Ashley?"

"Yeah."

Roy chewed on his lower lip. "Don't worry, Alex, nothin's gonna happen to me."

He lay down beside Alex and this time they faced each other. Alex found his friend's closeness comforting. They drifted off to sleep within minutes, and mercifully Alex had no more dreams.

***

When he heard his alarm chirping, Alex woke to find Roy sleeping peacefully. After all they'd been through the day before, he wished he could let Roy rest, but Jane wouldn't hear of him missing school; not because she cared if he learned anything, but because she didn't want him around.

He nudged Roy, and watched his eyes flutter open. "Time for school." He didn't want to go, but he *did* want to check on the others.

Roy nodded and climbed groggily out of the bed, watching as Alex deftly slid himself across and into his chair. "Uh, Alex," he began hesitantly as Alex adjusted his feet. "Think maybe I could shower here?"

"Sure. You can wear some of my clothes. We're about the same size, when you sit, anyway." Alex grinned.

"Thanks, man." Roy ducked into the bathroom and Alex set about finding clothes for the both of them.

***

So Jane wouldn't know Roy stayed overnight, Alex let him out the back door and told him to wait five minutes before knocking on the kitchen door. Jane would be watching from behind the two-way mirror and might not bother challenging the intrusion.

Alex threw on a *Fall Out Boy* tee and another pair of skinny jeans. Because the wind blew hard that morning, he snatched his black hoodie from the clothes pile and pulled it over his head before heading up to the kitchen.

When he arrived, only Juan was eating. Carlos must've taken off already. The bowls sat atop the counter next to the sink, while the cereal, milk, and juice were already on the table.

He grabbed a bowl and rolled to a stop beside Juan who gave him the silent chin raise greeting, and then poured his cereal. Roy knocked at the door a few minutes later, and Alex let him in. Knowing Jane was probably watching, Roy said, "Hey Alex, remember we gotta be at school early."

"Oh, yeah," Alex said, pretending to recall. "Grab a bowl and have some cereal."

"Thanks, man." Roy snatched a bowl from the counter, and turned around. He froze.

Jane stood in the doorway glaring at him. "Who invited you to eat my cereal?"

"I did," Alex said.

Jane pulled her vulture-like gaze from Roy and pinned it on Alex like she wanted to nail him to the wall. "I don't spend my money on food so you can have your degenerate friends eat it. Especially ones with metal through their lip."

Roy flinched.

"I'll give him some of my food," Alex announced, his voice taut with anger. He fought for control. "You get money for me every month that I never see, so don't worry about it."

Jane's face became explosive as she stepped further into the kitchen. "What did you say to me?"

Alex met her gaze straight on, and kept his voice calm. "I said don't worry about it. You don't need to be angry." He winced then as he felt the full force of her irrational rage fill him like a hot air balloon.

Her eyes grew feral, and, for a split second, she looked exactly like that cat. "Enough!" Jane cracked, her voice like a gunshot. "Stop spinning your black magic on me. I know your tricks."

Alex grinned, trying for an arrogance he didn't feel. "No, you don't, Jane. See, now I can spin people without 'em even talking." This wasn't true except for Roy, but she didn't know that.

She gasped, suddenly not as confident, or confrontational.

"So, you better watch it, Jane, or I'll spin you good." He tried for an evil laugh like he'd seen in the movies, but it came out flat. "I might even make you nice."

Jane blanched beneath her heavy coat of makeup, and Alex smiled. "C'mon, Roy, have a seat. We gotta get to school."

Giving Jane a wide berth, Roy sat down. Jane said nothing as Roy poured some cereal and milk into his bowl.

Jane glared at him "I've said it before, Alex. You're a freak. And like all males, you're evil." She turned on her heel and bolted from the kitchen.

Alex turned to Roy and shrugged. Roy opened his mouth to say something, but Alex indicated the mirror with a nod of his head, and Roy got the message. They ate their cereal in silence.

***

After breakfast, the boys hurried to Roy's house to get his backpack. Alex whistled with surprise at the dents and scrapes along the passenger side of the truck where flying tools had struck it. His alarm meter went into overdrive about what might have happened to their classmates, so they hurried to school as quickly as possible.

They arrived at seven-thirty and classes didn't begin until eight. Some students milled around, while others sat at outdoor tables chilling before their first class. Most ignored Alex and Roy as they made their usual way past the cafeteria, but Alex heard a shout from somewhere, "Hey, Roller Boy, what's your hurry?"

Roy turned in fury to find the shouter, but Alex pushed him forward and reminded him they had bigger problems.

No one loitered by their classroom, and the door was locked. Ms. Ashley had always been there early in case any of the kids needed something. The two boys anxiously waited, Roy chewing his fingernails down to the quick, and Alex popping wheelies in his chair.

Finally, the others arrived.

Alex instantly stopped his wheelchair stunts and turned to greet them. "You guys all right?" he blurted.

Java sported a large bandage on his forehead, while Band-Aids crisscrossed Israel's cheek. Cuong and Jorge looked unhurt.

"What happened guys?" Roy asked anxiously.

Israel and Java related their stories, but said they were too afraid to tell their parents what really happened because they knew they'd be called liars. They'd made something up about how they'd sustained their injuries and allowed their moms to bandage them up.

But Israel was clearly shaken, and didn't ramble on like usual. "Shit, man," he said to Alex, "I got so scared I took my meds!"

Alex and Roy exchanged a worried look, but said nothing of their own experiences until the others were finished. Then they recounted what each had gone through, leaving out the part where Roy had slept in Alex's bed. Roy didn't think that would go over well, especially with macho Java.

All the while, Jorge and Cuong stood watching.

"You guys okay?" Roy asked when everyone else had fallen silent. "Anything weird happen to you last night?"

Jorge smiled and said, "Anything weird happen to you last night?" He pushed the black hair off his forehead and Roy gasped. A lump the size of a walnut shell, fresh, black and purple, had risen above the boy's left eye.

"What happened?" Alex asked.

Jorge turned to Alex. Normally the boy refused to make eye contact with anyone. But now he looked straight into Alex's eyes. "For victory. Go tell your friends." He pantomimed spray painting, swung his hand holding the imaginary can at his forehead, and flung himself to the ground. He smiled at Alex and rose to his feet.

Alex nodded and turned to Cuong. The boy, as always, was dressed in a cartoon hoodie, wearing his Pokémon backpack, and clutching tightly to his Gameboy. "What about you, Cuong? Anything happen last night?"

Cuong merely stared, and then used his free hand to pull up his hoodie and t-shirt, exposing his scrawny torso and little-boy physique. Roy gasped and Israel cursed beside him. There was a small wound in Cuong's midsection where he had been stabbed.

His face riddled with guilt, Alex said, "I'm so sorry, Cuong."

"Why?" Java demanded. "You didn't do it."

"Alex thinks it's his fault we got attacked," Roy explained, "cuz of his spinning and all."

That silenced them until Alex spoke again. "I don't know why this all went down, but I can spin it. Hurry, 'fore the sub shows up."

Israel nodded and stepped forward, prepared to speak, but Java placed a meaty hand on his arm to stop him. "No can do. Our parents seen us already. We go home lookin' all fixed up and shit and how we gonna 'splain that?"

"Oh, shit, he's right," blurted Israel. "How come I din' think of that?"

"Cuz yer a dumbass, that's why," Java sneered.

"He's right, Alex," Roy said. "You can't."

Alex looked more guilt-ridden than before.

Just then the substitute arrived, dressed even hotter than the day before. Israel and Java gaped, but Roy just shook his head in disgust. His dad had warned him about chicks like this, and he guessed once a hoe always a hoe. She smiled at the two gawking boys and patted Alex on the shoulder before glancing in Roy's direction with a grin.

She doesn't like me, he realized. *Good, cuz I don't like her either.* He tried to catch Alex's eye, but found him staring at her, too, as she slipped the key into the doorknob and turned it. Java hurried to pull open the door.

"Why thank you, Java," she cooed. "Nice to see a gentleman in the group." She cast another unreadable look at Roy before entering the room and flipping on the lights. Israel leered, and high-fived Java before following her. The others entered, leaving Alex alone with Roy.

"I don't like her," Roy said.

"Me, either." He wheeled himself into the room.

His words gave Roy hope, and he followed.

Once they'd all retrieved their personal folders from the counter where Ms. Ashley had them organized, the boys sat down to work. Java and Israel kept calling Ms. G. for help they didn't need, Roy noted, just to watch her strut up and down the aisle, as well as bend over when helping them.

Roy noted her snug jeans and tight shirt that showed off the curves of her tits, leaving nothing to the imagination. Not to mention the way she swished as she moved. Slinky. That's how she looked today. Another word his dad had taught him. He and his dad had many talks about girls when Roy was in middle school. Dad would point out this girl or that one at school or on TV, explaining how some are better than others and how the right girl would make Roy's life magical, but the wrong one would ruin it.

Roy loved those talks, even though they'd always made him uncomfortable. But he loved his dad's stories about how he and his mom met in high school and had been crazy in love. Then, after high school they'd separated and his dad had hooked up with Dane's mother.

"Worst mistake I ever made, son," his father had told him. "Don't get me wrong, I loved Dane and still do. But that woman was trouble from the get-go. She was slinky *and* sultry and I fell for it." Roy knew all too well how much trouble Dane's mother could be. She'd talked enough mess to him through the years to make that clear. But then, after splitting from her, his parents got back together and lived happily ever after.

Until the cancer.

During second period, a student dropped off a hall pass for Alex. A summons, from the principal. Of course, Ms. G. had to read it to him because he couldn't, and of course Israel had to pipe up with, "What did you do now, Alex? Man, that bitch is gonna slap you down," and Roy glared at Israel.

"Israel, please, watch your language," Ms. G. said as she handed Alex the note.

Israel pulled a face and blurted, "Why? She *is* a bitch!"

His words almost distracted Roy from noting how the substitute returned the note to Alex. She brushed her hand against his, like in a sexy kind of way, before opening Alex's hand with her other and pressing the note into it. A chill ran up Roy's spine. The hell? Was she flirting with Alex?

Alex noticed, too, because he took the note and met her gaze with his own. Yes, Roy knew her type. Definitely the kind of girl his dad had warned him about. Except this was a grown-up coming on to a fifteen-year-old! Roy wanted to say something, but Alex shook his head slightly. Then he wheeled himself from the room, leaving the others in silence.

Ms. G. clapped. "Okay, boys, back to work. How are you ever going to read if you don't try?"

Roy pulled his gaze from the open door, wondering what the principal wanted with Alex. His work forgotten, he sat chewing what was left of his fingernails, and worried about his best friend.

CHAPTER SEVEN

HE LOOKS PROMISING

Alex pushed his way across campus toward the principal's office. It was located in a brand-new building at the front of the school, and Alex hadn't even been inside it yet. The building had only opened when school began in August. The nurse's office was there, as well as the counselors'. But his counselor never wanted to see him. The Losers hardly saw their counselors, he supposed, because they were pretty much a lost cause, and never got put with any other teachers anyway.

Compared to Building 17, the new one looked pretty amazing to Alex. Everything was fresh and clean. His classroom smelled of sweat and mold and dirt all the time because it was never cleaned well. But the new carpet in the front office felt soft beneath his wheels, and so smooth it almost looked brushed. Once he entered the building, the principal's office was on the left. Straight ahead, he spotted the entrance for parents and visitors, but he always came and went through the gate outside.

He entered the principal's outer office and held out his pass to the young secretary who took it and waved him on in.

The door was ajar and Alex saw a nameplate that probably said 'Principal' because it started with a "p." He knocked.

"Come in," came Mrs. Davis's throaty voice.

Alex pushed open the door and rolled in. Mrs. Davis sat at her desk. Two men occupied the chairs in front of her. The men stood when he entered, but Mrs. Davis remained seated. As usual, she was dressed in a bland-looking dress with her hair styled up around her head in a way that made it look like an animal was sleeping there.

"Come in, Alex, and close the door," she said, her face and voice giving nothing away. Alex had heard the word "cool" used for some people, not like kids used it, but to mean someone who was kind of cold and didn't show their feelings much. That was Mrs. Davis every time he'd seen her - cool.

Alex stopped before the two men, both of whom wore suits. They reached into their jacket pockets and pulled out badges. Police badges.

What did the cops want with him? He and Roy had gotten in trouble last summer when Roy was driving his truck and pulling Alex along by a rope behind him. It was the fastest Alex had ever gone in his chair, and the rush was more than worth the "warning" he'd gotten from the police.

"This is Detective Cole and Detective Gordon," Mrs. Davis announced. "They have some questions for you."

Alex immediately felt scared and small, and wished Roy was with him. "I'm not racing my chair in the street no more," he assured them.

The one named Cole smiled, while the other one mad-dogged him. "That's not why we're here, Alex. We're homicide."

"Homa-what?"

The younger one, Gordon, rolled his eyes and muttered, "Sheesh," but Cole, who looked older because he had some grey hair near the ears, glared at his partner and said, "Homicide. We investigate murders, Alex."

Alex's heart revved up. They were here about Ms. Ashley! But what did they want with him? "I don' know nuthin' 'bout no murders." His voice trembled, despite his best efforts to keep it steady.

Cole smiled. It was a warm, friendly smile, which made Alex distrust him even more than the guy mean-mugging him. At least that guy was being straight up. "That's what we're here to find out, Alex. It seems a student overheard you yesterday talking about the death of your teacher."

Alex was sure no one had overheard him. No one but Tami. She'd never call the cops on him.

"She was a good teacher," Alex offered, sadness at her death welling up again within him. "Aren't we allowed to talk about her?"

Cole nodded. "Of course, you are, Alex, and we don't want to upset you more. It's just that, well, you gave your friends information that wasn't on the news. About the cats?"

Mrs. Davis looked startled. "What cats? It was my understanding Ms. Ashley was struck and killed by a truck."

Gordon turned to her and shrugged. "That's the official story. But your kid here knows more than he should." He turned and squinted at Alex, as though trying to spin him.

Cole cast a warning look at his partner. "I got this, Joe." The other man shrugged and went back to glaring. Alex felt like a bug in a jar.

"Alex, you told your friends Ms. Ashley was attacked by cats and then *pushed* in front of the truck. Is that right?" Cole asked.

Mrs. Davis gasped and put a hand to her mouth in shock.

Knowing there was no way he could lie his way out of this, Alex nodded, but said nothing.

Cole appeared unruffled by the admission. "Can you tell us how you knew that?"

Alex shivered as the images flooded in on him yet again. "I dreamed it."

Gordon grunted. "Bullshit!"

Mrs. Davis normally hated swearing, but she looked ghostly white behind her desk, and Alex figured she was too upset to care.

Cole remained calm and steady. "And you actually *saw* someone push her in front of the truck?"

Alex nodded again.

Gordon opened his mouth, but Cole raised a hand to silence him. "What did this person look like?"

Alex shrugged. "All dressed in black, some kinda mask over the face, like for skiing or a ninja or something. That's all I could see."

Gordon expelled a heady breath of disgust. "Bill, you're not gonna–"

Cole again cut him off with a raised hand. To Alex's surprise, the other guy shut up. Cole must be the boss, he decided.

"Are you in the habit, Alex, of dreaming things before they happen?"

"Yes."

Now Cole looked surprised, though Alex couldn't tell if it was from what he'd said or the fact that he'd admitted it. Gordon looked even angrier, as though he thought Alex was making fun of him.

Cole cleared his throat. "That's very interesting, Alex. Can you give us an example of another dream you had?"

"I dreamed my parents died in a car crash."

"Alex, we checked on you before we came," Cole went on. "Your parents *did* die in a car crash. When you were four. It's natural you'd have nightmares about that."

"*Before* the crash?" Alex replied, brushing the hair away from his eyes so he could see those of the detective. "I dreamed it the night before. But my parents didn't believe me. I was only four and already a dummy so what did I know, right? They were dead before preschool was over." His heart pounded, the emotions of that long-ago moment rearing up and threatening to overwhelm him.

He met Cole's steady gaze and didn't flinch. He was tired of people calling him a liar. To his immense shock, Cole nodded.

"I believe you," the detective said, causing his partner to curse under his breath, and Mrs. Davis to look at Cole like he was Special Ed, too.

"Why?" Alex couldn't help but ask. No one but his classmates believed him about stuff like that.

Cole shrugged. "A gut feeling. I was a big fan of The X-Files." He tried for a smile, but when Alex frowned, it faltered.

"The X what?" Alex asked.

Cole suddenly looked uncomfortable and shifted in place. "Uh, before your time, I guess." He slipped a business card from his jacket pocket and held it out to Alex. "If you think of anything else, or if you have any more strange dreams, call me, okay?"

Alex reached out and took the card. For a split second he almost blurted out about the cat, but forced himself to remain quiet. Dreams were one thing, but a talking cat? The detective would never believe that.

"Thanks," he said, lowering his gaze and slipping the card into his jeans pocket. Then he looked at Mrs. Davis, who appeared ashen.

"Can I go now?"

Unusually for her, she nodded without saying anything, and he spun around quickly to exit the office.

Pushing himself out the double glass doors, Alex wheeled his chair around the building to where the gate entrance was closed and chained. His breathing became ragged, and his heart beat like crazy. Not because of the cops, but because of his parents, a memory he'd tried *so* hard to keep away. Now it all came flooding back, and his eyes burned with tears.

Two cops in uniform entering his preschool classroom. The teacher pointing at him and waving him over. The social worker. The first foster home he stayed at. The funeral. It was in a church, and he remembered seeing the coffins, but when his social worker asked if he wanted to see his parents one last time he'd turned and wheeled from the church to sob outside the front door.

As he sat behind the principal's office crying softly into the sleeve of his hoodie, Alex recalled faces and moments, pain and tears. Lots of tears. And then the string of foster homes. No one wanted to keep him. A few tried, but he couldn't control his power and spun them all the time, stealing their emotions and making them feel weird. He was a freak, like Jane said. Evil. He stole from people. Sure, he fixed them, too, but the stealing happened more often and he still couldn't fully control it.

He saw the two detectives stroll across the parking lot to their unmarked car. They didn't see him, for which he was grateful. He hated for anyone to see him crying, except Roy. Roy was cool about everything.

Wiping his face with one sleeve, he turned and wheeled across campus. The cool October breeze felt good against his cheeks and dried the remnants of his tears.

***

By the time Alex returned to class it was almost break time, so when Roy raised his eyebrows to ask what the principal wanted, Alex nodded toward Ms. G. bending over to help Jorge, and mouthed, "Nutrition." They'd have almost fifteen minutes to talk about his meeting with the cops.

When the bell chimed, the boys bolted from the classroom without a word and gathered around their usual table outside. No one headed to the cafeteria for food, and Cuong didn't even pull out his Gameboy. Obviously, they all wanted to know if Alex was in trouble.

He filled them in on his meeting with the policemen, eliciting scowls of distaste from Java and Israel. Both of them'd had several unpleasant encounters with the local police. When he finished, Roy looked worried, but Israel said, "Screw the cops, man!"

He and Java did the fist bump. "Crack Head is right, Alex," Java said in his usual serious tone of voice. "Don't matter how nice that cop was. He's a cop, and they lie to kids. Don't trust 'im."

Jorge watched the exchange, but said nothing. Cuong, Alex noted, seemed to be paying close attention, a rarity.

Alex sighed. "Don't worry, Java, I don't trust 'im. But I do wanna know who snitched on me."

Israel's handsome face lit up like fireworks. "It was Tami! I knew you couldn't trust that bitch! Shit, she won't even go out with me so she's gotta be a snitch."

Alex pulled a confused face, and Roy shook his head. "That didn't make no sense even for us dummies."

"'Sides," Alex said, "Tami wouldn't call the cops on me."

Java squinted. "You sure?"

Israel snorted. "Why, cuz you're all blond and cute? Hell, Alex, I'm better looking and she'd call the cops on me."

Alex and Roy exchanged a look of dismay.

"Uh, Izzy?" Roy said.

Israel raised his eyebrows. "Yeah?"

Roy glanced at Java and together they said, "Shut up!"

That made Jorge smile. "Shut up!" he repeated in his soft, quiet voice.

Even Cuong laughed.

Israel looked offended, and then sighed. "Okay, ADHD going crazy again." He paused a moment. "But she's still a bitch."

The bell chimed in their ears, signaling the end of Nutrition, and the beginning of third period.

"Listen guys," Roy said before they re-entered the classroom. "I think we need to stick close together after what's been goin' on, ya know?"

He stuck out his fist sideways, like he was gripping a bat. Java nodded and placed his fist atop Roy's, followed by Israel, Jorge, Cuong, and lastly Alex.

"For victory," Jorge said, and somehow that made Alex feel good inside. Jorge was just repeating a line from that TV show, but the words gave him hope.

They separated and scrambled from the table back to their classroom.

As though she'd just noticed the injuries, Ms. G. commented on their bandages, adding, "I hope nothing bad happened to you boys."

Java, who was the smoothest liar amongst them said, "Naw, Ms. G. Just us boys doing crazy stuff, you know, like guys do." He puffed out his chest as he said it, and she smiled at him in a way Alex didn't like. Again, it almost looked like she was flirting, the way he'd seen guys flirt with Tami.

"I worry about you, boys," Ms. G. went on, her voice taking on a purring tone. "Especially after everything that's happened. It's too bad you can't heal faster so those bandages don't cover your handsome faces for too long."

As she said that last part, she turned to focus on Alex. But her innocent smile never faltered, and Alex didn't know what to make of her comment.

She can't know about me, can she?

The same question was written all over Roy's face, but nothing more was said.

And then she was clapping—something she'd started doing that morning to get their attention—and when Alex looked at her again she appeared to be an ordinary substitute teacher. Weird. He bent his head over his work and struggled to write out some basic sentences without making a bunch of mistakes like always. He felt Roy's eyes on him, but he didn't want to attract any more attention from Ms. G., so he ignored his friend for now.

***

The building was large and corporate-looking, but nondescript, with only a sign affixed to the cyclone fence fronting the parking lot and the logo of the company in bold lettering above the front entrance. There were glass windows indicating offices on every floor, but even a window washer right outside would not be able to see in due to the extreme tinting on every one of them. The dark windows gave the entire building an uninviting air, something its owner cultivated.

Russell Shaw lounged in a plush leather chair behind an antique desk in his office that sported a bathroom and shower, a full wet bar, a large screen television, and famous works of art adorning the walls.

Handsome and well-tailored in an expensive suit, Shaw gazed at several TV monitors embedded in the wall behind his desk. A large bookcase had been slid to one side so the screens could be viewed. Two of these monitors displayed different angles of Alex spinning Juan the previous morning in Jane's kitchen. One had no sound other than the voices of Jane, Phil and Bob. The other played back Juan's tremulous voice as he described his injuries.

Phil and Bob, once more dressed in staid business suits and standing at attention, waited for Shaw's reaction to the video. As the tapes rolled to their conclusion, Shaw pressed the pause button on the remote, freezing both images on two different views of Alex's face. The phone rang and Shaw snatched up the receiver.

"I said I didn't want to be disturbed," he barked. He listened a moment. "All right, put him through." After a momentary pause, Shaw said in a cold voice, "Senator Harding, you have not lived up to our arrangement. You will vote my way on the technology bill or those photos of your liaisons with the Latino pool boy will find their way to the press. Good day."

He hung up, never taking his eyes from Alex's face. "He looks promising. What do the doctors think?"

Bob shrugged. "They really can't tell much from this video. It looks legit. I mean, I filmed the one angle myself, so there's no way the woman could've faked this."

Shaw nodded, staring at Alex's startling blue eyes partially hidden behind a straggly waterfall of white hair. "A million, you say?"

"Yes, sir," Phil answered.

"Hmm." Shaw pressed another button and the wall of books slid into place, concealing the monitors. He drummed his fingers against the burnished mahogany of his desk. Then he looked at his two underlings with a firm, but guarded expression.

"Keep him under surveillance. Let me know if you see him cure anyone else. We have very little time, so watch him closely. Find out everything about his background, and the woman's. That's all."

CHAPTER EIGHT

I FEEL LIKE DOING SOMETHING CRAZY

After lunch, Alex had to use the bathroom. Ordinarily, he tried not to use the nasty-ass school toilets, especially since he couldn't stand like the other boys, and there were never any seat covers when he went in. Because of his chair, he was always allowed to go out in the middle of class to avoid the crowds during passing periods.

As he wheeled himself out of the bathroom, a running Maribel collided with the footrest of his chair, and with a startled cry went sprawling to the ground. Alex gasped as she went down hard.

Gripping her ankle and keening with agony, she flashed her heavily made-up eyes his way and practically screamed, "Watch where you're going, you stupid cripple! You messed up my ankle! Now how am I supposed to cheer tomorrow night?"

Alex felt like he'd been kicked in the gut. *Stupid cripple? She'd run into him!* But, as always, seeing someone in pain, even someone like her, softened his heart.

"Where does it hurt?" he asked, knowing what he was doing to be highly dangerous. You never knew who might be looking out a window and watching. But even though it hadn't been his fault, and even though she didn't deserve it, Alex listened and focused while she railed on about the pain stabbing her ankle and foot and how it was probably sprained and she wouldn't be able to walk on it, let alone jump up and down at Friday night's football game.

Alex felt pain in his ankle, even though he wasn't supposed to. It dug at his nerves and radiated outward all up and down his leg. Of course, it wasn't his throbbing or damaged nerves causing him to wince and groan. No. It was the freak within him feeling *her* agony. He shut his eyes and concentrated while Maribel kept railing about how much suffering he'd caused her and why he was such a loser.

She suddenly stopped, and stared at her ankle. Slowly, she released her grip and stretched out the foot. She rotated her ankle, and her face relaxed into calmness. "That's weird. It hurt like hell. I don't –"

Alex felt her looking at him. He opened his eyes, and fought down the pain. That had been a bad sprain and would've kept her out of cheer for weeks. He could always sense the seriousness of an injury by how much effort he needed to rid himself of its effects. He noticed her open-mouthed expression and bewildered eyes.

"What the hell just happened?" she barked, sounding angrier than she'd been before.

Sheesh, Alex thought, *can't this girl ever be nice*?

He tried to look relaxed, hoping she didn't notice the beads of sweat brimming his forehead, and shrugged. "Must not have been as bad as you thought. Want me to help you up?" He reached out a hand, but she slapped it away.

"I think you done enough!"

Once again, the insult landed like a knife to the heart.

Maribel stood while Alex fought to avert his eyes from her tiny shorts that left little to the imagination. After the way she'd already treated him, if she caught him staring she'd tell everyone he was a pervert on top of being a cripple. She tested her weight on the injured ankle, but Alex knew it was fine. Good as new. Maybe better.

Once she realized her ankle was all right, Maribel flashed Alex an icy look of contempt. "Next time watch where you're going, crip!" Then with a flounce of curly brown hair, she turned and stormed off in the direction she'd been going in the first place.

Alex was stunned. He knew he was a loser. But did she *have* to call him a 'crip'? That wasn't his fault! Despite vowing never to let crap like that get to him, it still did. He brushed away a tear as he struggled to regain his composure. Whoever made up that stupid nursery rhyme about sticks and stones breaking bones had never been a freak cripple in a wheelchair! Broken bones healed! Hell, *he* could heal 'em. But who ever forgot hateful words hurled at them? He never had. He remembered every joke at his expense, every harsh word, everyone who'd ever made fun of him. He'd been called "crip" exactly three hundred thirty-six times in his life. *Bring on the sticks and stones!* Those wounds went away. "Crip" never did.

Wiping tears with the sleeve of his hoodie for the second time that day, Alex wheeled himself back to class, desperately wanting this day to be finished. He didn't think it could get any worse.

He was wrong.

***

The instant Alex rolled through the door, Roy understood that something had happened to him.

But Alex merely waved his silent questions aside until school ended and they were on the way home. Roy hated not knowing, but at least Alex looked physically unhurt and that was a relief. It baffled Roy how Alex could fix everyone but himself, even when he felt depressed. He'd spilled his guts a bunch of times about his mom and dad, and Alex had simply taken his pain away, made him feel better while making himself feel worse. Alex was like that. You never had to ask. He hated seeing people suffer, which was one of the things Roy loved most about him.

The last hour and a half dragged on for Roy because of Alex's silence. For her part, Ms. G. didn't flirt with them anymore and seemed less annoyed with Israel than any other sub they'd ever had. She also noted Alex's behavior and attempted to draw him out, but Alex just shrugged and said he was fine and returned to his work.

When the bell finally chimed at two-fifty-eight, Roy was desperate to get out of the classroom and talk with Alex. But as the others scrambled for the door, Ms. G. called out for Alex to remain. Roy glared at her a moment, but she flashed him an innocent smile and tossed her long blonde hair away from her face.

"Don't worry, Roy, I'm not going to steal him from you."

Roy blushed. Fortunately, the other guys were already outside and hadn't heard. He nodded at Alex. "Wait for you outside." Then he left the room.

Israel was shuffling from foot to foot and rapping as other departing students gave them a wide berth. Cuong had his Gameboy out and was lost within the video world. Roy moved to Java.

"What she be wantin' with Alex?" Java asked, clearly anxious to get going. Java hated staying on campus one minute longer than necessary.

The more time there, the greater the possibility of him getting into another fight with some prick.

Roy shrugged. "Dunno." He slipped his phone out of his pocket to check the time, and kept glancing at it every few seconds for the next five minutes. By the time Alex emerged, Cuong had stopped his game playing and joined Israel in the rap. As always when he rapped, he didn't stutter. It usually amazed Roy when Cuong did that, but today he barely noticed.

When Alex wheeled himself outside after that excruciating five minutes, Roy slipped his phone into his pocket.

"What'd she want, Alex?" he asked, his heart pounding with worry.

Alex merely shook his head in dismay. "She just said how I looked really down all afternoon and was there anything I wanted to talk about. I told her no, but she kept saying she was a really good listener." He used the air quotes with "good listener."

Roy shook his head. "What is it with grownups? They always think we wanna talk to 'em when we don't even know 'em."

Alex nodded. "C'mon, let's get outta here."

Roy really wanted to ask what had happened when Alex went to the bathroom, but Alex had already begun wheeling towards the main parking lot and he scrambled to keep up. The others followed.

***

Roy parked his truck not far from Cuong's house and the others clambered out of the bed to hear Alex's story. Roy's blood boiled as Alex told them what happened, especially when Maribel had called him a crip after the whole thing was her fault.

Israel snorted with disgust. "You shouldda left her there, Alex. She won't go out with me, so screw her."

Java sighed with annoyance. "Look, fool, no girl at MTS wants to go out with you so drop it, 'kay?"

Israel flashed his goofy, toothy grin and said, "They just don't like Mexicans." He ran his hand through his hair like it made him sexy.

Roy wanted to throw a shoe at him.

"I-i-izy," Cuong said with complete sincerity, "a-a-all t-t-the g-g-girls at M-M-MTS a-a-are M-M-Mexican."

"I-i-i k-k-know t-t-that, f-f-f-fool," Israel stuttered, sticking out his tongue and grinning.

Cuong smiled. "I-I-I'l k-k-kick y-y-your a-a-ass."

Israel smirked. "B-b-by t-t-t-the t-t-time y-y-y-you g-g-g-get a-a-around t-t-to s-s-saying i-i-it, I-i-i'l b-b-be g-g-gone."

Cuong laughed and they high-fived. Ordinarily, Roy enjoyed the banter. They could make fun of each other's disabilities, but no one else could. And even then, they all knew which words not to use, like crip or retard. Those were off-limits even for them.

Roy was worried that someone might have seen Alex spin Maribel, or that she'd blab about it, but Java was sure she wouldn't. "Hoe like her don' want nobody to know she even be talkin' to one 'a us. Trust me, she won't say shit."

"I still say we hire us some hit chicks to kick her ass, ya know?" Israel said while drumming his hands endlessly against the sides of Roy's truck. "Bitch like her talkin' shit to Spinner like that. T'ain't right!"

Jorge and Cuong's parents wanted them home right after school because Jorge, in particular, had a tendency to wander off and couldn't find his way back, so Roy pulled himself into the driver's seat and dropped those two off. Then he drove to his house so he and the others could kick it as usual before dinner.

This time they stuck to sodas and chips, and the others watched in amazement as Israel shoved food and soda into his mouth while rapping and dancing around Roy's room. Java played football on the PS4. Alex sulked and Roy sat in silence beside him.

After an hour, Java rose and dragged Izzy out the door. "Later, guys."

Roy heard the front door open and Java's exasperated voice, "Watch where you're going, fool!" before the door shut and silence returned.

Roy studied Alex a moment. "You wanna hang out after dinner?"

Alex nodded. "I feel like doing something crazy."

"Like what?"

Roy watched as Alex descended into thought.

"I haven't done any stunts in the dark before. Let's go to the skate park and I'll show you some kick-ass tricks."

Roy stiffened. Alex liked doing crazy stuff in his chair, stuff that scared the crap out of *him*. Alex was always so down on himself that he got reckless, and Roy panicked every time his friend fell into one of these moods.

He always wanted to tell Alex how amazing he was, but was afraid of how it might come out. So, he'd say nothing and just bite his nails every time Alex sank into one of his funks.

"Okay. I'll meet you out front at seven."

Alex grinned, which worried Roy even more. He'd have no fingernails left on either hand before seven o'clock even rolled around. Roy asked Alex if he wanted company on the way home, but Alex said no. He needed to think. Then he wheeled out the door and down the driveway, and Roy felt empty, as always. He sighed and closed the door.

Time for another microwave dinner. He'd already checked on dad when they arrived, and the man was passed out on the couch this time, beer in hand. It seemed to Roy that when his mom died, his dad died, too. He sighed, and headed for the kitchen. Yep, life sucked.

***

Alex ate his microwave dinner by himself. He absently chewed his chicken-fried steak with fake mashed potatoes and some rubbery vegetables, enjoying the silence of the kitchen and the sound of his own heart beating in his chest.

He kept hearing the word *crip* again and again, and hated himself for dwelling on it. He'd show her and everyone else how much of a crip he *wasn't*! He'd never attempted a real flip before, but tonight he would. He had a helmet, and if he broke his neck, so what? Roy would be sad, but no one else would really care. Yeah, he'd show Maribel and everyone else just what he could do!

After cleaning and putting everything away, Alex took the lift down to his room to change for his night at the skate park. He slipped out of his hoodie and t-shirt, replacing them with a long-sleeved compression shirt and a thick leather jacket he'd gotten at a thrift store. It was old, but kept him warm. And it offered pretty good protection on the rare occasions he'd fall from his chair doing stunts.

Lastly, he retrieved the necklace he'd found at school. He'd forgotten it in the bathroom that morning. Holding it in his hands, Alex stared into the intricate webbing, fascinated by the flesh-like feel as he touched it, and the pattern of the webbing seemed haunting. He couldn't pull his eyes from the twists and turns of the spun metal. The pattern filled his mind until he could no longer see himself in the bathroom mirror.

He gradually became aware of a hand on his shoulder. Shaking his head to clear it, Alex saw Roy crouched down before him.

"You were s'posed to meet me outside, Alex," Roy said. "You okay?"

Alex felt foggy, like he'd just awakened from a nap. "What time is it?"

Roy pulled out his phone. "Seven oh five."

"Oh." What had happened? Alex knew he sometimes zoned out, went to some emo place for a while, but that was usually when listening to his music. He shrugged. "Zoned, I guess." He slipped the necklace over his head. "I'm ready now."

Roy eyed the necklace shimmering beneath the fluorescent lighting above the sink. "That does look pretty sick on you."

Alex grinned. "You wanna see sick? Wait till we get to the park."

Roy stood up, frowning, but stepped aside so Alex could wheel himself from the bathroom. Without another word, the boys rode Alex's outside door lift to ground level and slunk along the side of the house to the street.

***

Eucalyptus Park was lit at night, but dimly, and the shadows seemed to grab at Roy from every direction. All the weird stuff happening to them the past couple of days made him jumpier than usual. It was stupid to be scared. Hell, he'd grown up in Hawthorne and had hung out at this park after dark many times, he thought, as he parked his truck on 123rd Street and they entered at the south side.

Tonight, however, seemed especially cold. The wind had kicked up again, and the chill sank through Roy's thick hoodie into his bones. Alex looked warm enough in his leather jacket and jet black helmet, but Roy felt strange. The empty play area and dried up wading pool loomed ahead between willowy trees, and both looked sad with no kids playing in them. The two shelters with their stonework columns and picnic tables seemed especially menacing, though Roy couldn't have said why. It just felt like someone was watching—hiding and watching—and a chill wrapped itself around him like a blanket of snow.

They moved past the public bathrooms. A *crack* startled Roy and he spun around toward the men's room entrance. The light above the doorway cast a yellow pool on the concrete in front, but no one emerged, and no one was anywhere around that he could see from this vantage point. He looked ahead at the empty basketball courts. Leaves spun in circles, and the wind sounded hollow as it forced its way through the tree branches overhead, like an old man groaning in pain. Roy felt certain someone was watching them, but his roving eyes revealed no one.

You're just spooked from last night, he told himself, as another shiver worked its way down his back.

Alex paid no attention to the wind or the dark or the huge shadows that seemed to come at them from every side. He simply rolled toward the skate park in silence.

Roy fought down his fear. He was more worried about what stunts Alex might try in the dark. His panic meter had gone into overdrive when he'd asked his friend, and Alex just grinned in a reckless, scary kind of way.

They passed through the basketball courts and stopped in front of the skate park, looking through the fence. There was a big, empty concrete pool with sides that weren't too steep, a cool-looking spine, some rails and ramps that Alex could easily jump without breaking a sweat.

The skate park didn't close until nine, and usually there were other kids skating, even on weeknights. Roy used to spend a lot of time here in middle school. But tonight, the place was cold and empty, and somehow threatening, even beneath the soft lighting. He hoped Alex just needed some exercise to shake off his sad mood. Roy usually did that by working on his truck or fixing some other mechanical device around the house. He'd completely revamped the heating system, but his dad never even noticed.

The wind suddenly blew leaves right into Roy's face. Startled, he jumped back with a cry of surprise.

"Nervous?"

"No," Roy lied, his breathing a bit ragged. "Just surprised me, that's all."

Alex nodded, gazing again through the fence at the empty skate park before him. The entrance was on the far side and they'd have to go around. Roy watched Alex and waited for his friend to move. But Alex merely stared at the shadowy slopes and curves of the park in silence.

"I'm gonna try, Roy," he finally said, his voice an excited whisper. The helmet covered most of his hair and with his face turned away, Roy almost missed what he'd said.

"Uh, try what?" Roy had a bad feeling.

Now Alex turned his head and looked at his friend, a fiery look in his blue eyes. "I'm gonna do a flip, like Aaron."

Roy sucked in a breath. He'd seen the videos of that Aaron kid doing flips, and crashing hard when he missed them. "No way, Alex! It's too dangerous, man."

"For who? If I kill myself, I'll just be a dead freak. But I won't kill myself."

Roy's heart thumped wildly. He could almost hear it against the weird quiet surrounding them. "Please, Alex, this is crazy! It's too dark. Please."

Alex didn't respond. He simply grabbed his wheel handles and started forward, around the perimeter of the park toward the entrance. Roy scrambled to stay by his side, not knowing what to say. When Alex made up his mind to do something, he did it.

The wind became stronger, whipping the hood off Roy's head and flinging his ragged bangs in front of his eyes. He had to push them aside and nearly collided with Alex, who'd stopped moving and stared straight ahead.

"What?"

Alex pointed toward the open gate into the skate park. Someone small stood there staring at them. Roy was as bad with numbers as with words and had no idea how far away the guy was, but it was close enough to look creepy. And he was blocking the entrance.

"Do you know him?" Roy asked, even as the wind penetrated his hoodie and sent shivers straight into his heart. Something about the figure, all dressed in black, some kind of ski mask covering his face, made him nervous. It wasn't *that* cold for the guy to have his face covered.

Alex shook his head, his eyes riveted to the unmoving figure.

Roy felt panic well up within him. This was bad. The wind increased. Leaves spun around him. Still Alex stared. Roy jostled his shoulder. "You okay?"

"Something about him…." Alex mumbled, clearly lost in thought. He rolled himself forward before Roy could grab for the chair. Roy started after him when an ear-piercing yowl shot through the night and he jumped back in fright.

Perched atop the skate park fence was the biggest frickin' cat he'd ever seen—like a dog almost—light brown and furry with shining eyes and gleaming teeth. "Holy crap!"

Alex stopped and spun around, following Roy's gaze towards the enormous animal.

"That's the cat, Roy, the one that…."

Roy swallowed hard. "Knew your name?"

Alex nodded, but neither boy could pull his gaze from the monstrous cat. Roy's breathing came in fits and starts and he had no problem admitting he was terrified.

That's when the music started. It seemed to be all around them, and in his head at the same time. A tinkling kind of music, like an old music box his grandmother once had. But he didn't recognize the tune. Then he remembered Alex's dream. "Alex, is that the music–"

He stopped short because Alex's gaze was frozen, staring up at the cat, but seeing nothing. Roy had seen his friend zone before, but nothing like this. He glanced at the entrance. The figure began walking – straight toward them. Roy dropped to a crouch in front of Alex. "Alex, what's wrong?"

Alex didn't respond. The wind grew stronger, and colder. Icy cold. Colder than Roy had ever felt. He glanced up at the cat and shivered. It looked like it was smiling. Then he turned to see that the approaching figure had cut half the distance and was coming on fast.

Roy snapped his fingers in front of Alex's face. "Alex, man, snap out of it! That guy's coming! We gotta jet!"

No response.

Roy grabbed Alex by the shoulders and shook him hard. "Wake up!" His wide eyes fixed on the approaching figure, and then turned to the size of dinner plates when the figure raised a knife. A big, shiny kitchen knife! "Holy shit!"

He grabbed Alex by the face. His skin was cold and clammy. "Alex, man, we gotta run!"

It was no good. Alex was unresponsive, and a sitting duck. Roy heard a growl and spun around to find the cat poised to leap on his back. That's when he grabbed the chair from behind and bolted, pushing Alex along the shadowy path in the direction of his truck. The park was at least a block long, and his truck was at the far end of it. Loud footfalls and mewling came from behind him.

They were coming.

Lights went out one by one, plunging the path into darkness. The streetlights outside the park dimmed to nothing. The wind rose to gale force levels. It forced Roy back and threatened to rip Alex from his grasp. But Roy gripped that chair harder than he'd ever gripped anything in his life and pressed his way forward.

His lungs burned. The cold air almost froze in his chest. His breath came out frosty and his hands were numb on the chair. He glanced back. The cat trotted after him, but not the guy with the knife.

What the hell? Where'd he go?

He panicked even more, slowing to a stop so he could check his surroundings. Nothing. Then, with a loud *crack,* a large branch dropped down from the tree overhead and struck him in the chest, knocking him backward onto the walkway where he cringed with pain. Gasping for air, he looked over his shoulder. The cat had stopped. It sat there staring at him.

The figure lunged from behind the tree right at him.

With a shriek of fear, Roy kicked out at Alex's chair.

It plowed into the figure and sent him sprawling. The knife clattered from his grasp to the walkway where it glinted in the moonlight.

Roy scrambled to his feet and grabbed for the chair. Alex stared sightlessly ahead. The figure rose, and Roy lurched forward, the muscles of his calves burning as he barreled down the winding path, pushing the wheelchair and dodging branches and trash cans flung in his path by the twisting wind. It was like everything around him–the park itself–was trying to prevent his escape. In his terrorized state of mind, Roy knew one thing for sure – if he got out of this alive he'd never come back to this park again!

Through his blind panic and hitching breath, Roy heard that music. It surrounded him, repeating itself, becoming louder and filling his head with its tinkling melody, driving him to distraction.

He stumbled over a branch and staggered, gripping the wheelchair for support, and nearly tumbled them both to the walkway. But he kept his footing and pressed on.

Roy ran hard, but the darkness and wind confused him. He veered off the path and slammed into the empty wading pool. As the chair plunged downward several inches, Alex toppled forward and Roy flung out his arms to snatch at his friend's jacket. One arm missed, but his right hand clamped onto the shoulder and he lurched forward, banging into the chair while pulling Alex back toward him. Then they were both upright and Roy drove the chair toward the other side of the dry pool.

He popped Alex into a wheelie and almost lost his balance from pulling back too hard. But the front wheels dropped onto the concrete, and Roy plowed his weight into the chair, knocking it up and onto the walkway.

He risked a quick look over his shoulder, his hair whipping into his eyes as he spun his head. The path behind was empty.

No cat.

No guy with kitchen knife.

Roy didn't wait to figure out where they went. He pushed the oblivious Alex into a powerful headwind that forced them back. Roy dug in his Converse and pressed forward. The wind felt like a whole football team pushing against him.

One of the picnic areas lay just ahead, and Roy almost screamed aloud as he spotted a heavy metal trashcan rolling across the grass directly toward him. He swung Alex a hard right, nearly plunging them both into the sand of the play area. At the last second, Roy swung Alex left and the clattering trashcan crashed into one of the slides with a loud *bang*!

They finally cleared the play area. The buffeting winds whipped

Roy's baggy sleeves so wildly they sounded like the flapping wings of a hawk, but he dug in and made steady progress.

Sweat dripped into his eyes despite the wind and cold, and his legs began to cramp. He squinted ahead in the windswept darkness.

There it was, the parking lot! And just beyond, his truck!

His breathing came in fits and starts, and his heart thundered like a bass drum. Roy couldn't focus on anything but the sight of that distant truck. Pelting forward, he drove Alex's chair like a sports car through the empty parking lot. His truck loomed ahead. They were almost home.

Roy ran fast and nearly pushed Alex right into the side of the truck. He just barely turned the chair sideways at the last second so his shoulder slammed into the passenger door instead of Alex. Pain swept through the whole right side of his body straight into his brain. He bent over, the stich in his side making it nearly impossible to breathe, the cold sapping what little strength he had left. He looked all around him. The street was deserted and dark. The streetlights were out, just like the ones in the park. He looked behind him, panting and mewling with terror.

Nothing! Had he lost them?

He didn't have time to think, and that damned music was driving him crazy, confusing him and almost making him forget about Alex. No way! He reached for the driver's side door handle.

The knife blade plunged downward and embedded itself in the door.

With a startled cry, Roy yanked his hand away and turned to face the black clad figure as it pried the knife free.

The guy looked small, Roy noted in that blind moment of sheer terror, but the huge knife more than made up for his size. The face was covered by a black mask and in the dark Roy couldn't even make out the eyes.

A meow startled him.

The cat sat on the roof of the truck licking its chops and grinning.

From the corner of his eye, Roy caught a glint of metal and lurched back as the blade slashed down and across, slicing open his hoodie at the chest and cutting into the skin.

Blood welled as Roy tripped over Alex's feet and sprawled to the sidewalk.

The masked figure stood over him, the blade raised for the kill.

Roy snapped his eyes shut, his last thought, *I'm sorry, Alex, I couldn't save you.*

"No!"

It was Alex's voice. But not his voice. It sounded far away, even though Alex sat right beside him. Roy opened his eyes and looked upward.

The knife had stopped in midair, the figure frozen with indecision, as though it had never expected Alex to speak.

The music increased in volume.

Alex looked at the rigid black form standing in front of him. "Harm him and I will destroy you."

The figure flinched, and Roy felt both fear and elation. Alex never talked like that! The figure seemed to forget Roy and stared at Alex without a sound. The music continued. Alex met the figure's gaze with his own, and Roy saw a look of such fierce determination on his friend's face that he suddenly didn't feel so afraid. Alex would fix this like he fixed everything, was his irrational, but very real thought.

Roy waited, afraid to even move.

The masked guy finally broke eye contact with Alex and looked at the cat.

The animal growled menacingly and swished its tail in anger.

Then it leaped from cab to the hood and down to the street where it melted into the darkness. The guy with the knife glanced once more at Alex. Then he followed the cat out of Roy's line of sight.

The music stopped.

The wind died.

The streetlights slowly rose to their full illumination.

Everything returned to normal, as though nothing had happened.

"Roy?"

Roy nearly screamed at the sound of Alex's voice. Sprawled where he'd fallen, he looked up as a confused Alex turned to him.

"What are you doing on the ground?" Then Alex took in his surroundings. "Wait a minute… I thought we were…."

Roy gasped for air, his entire body shaking, the tremors making it hard for him to even get his thoughts straight. His hand brushed against his exposed chest, and blood stuck to his fingers where the knife had slashed him.

"Roy, you're hurt!" Alex blurted. "Did that guy…?" Then he squinted at the park and the street in confusion. "Roy, I'm scared. What happened? Why can't I remember?" Those blue eyes, so wide and filled with fear, calmed Roy a little, and made him feel protective instead of weak.

Slowly, because his legs still shook, Roy rose to his feet, using Alex's chair for support. As he pulled open the passenger door to his truck, he haltingly explained about Alex zoning, and the guy who chased them.

"It don't make sense, Roy," Alex murmured, his voice shaky. "How could I zone out like that? I heard the music and then… nothing. It was the same music from my dreams!"

Roy placed a shaking hand on Alex's shoulder and squeezed. "What the hell is going on, Alex?"

Alex absently shook his head, obviously unable to come up with an answer.

The cold stung Roy's flesh where he'd been slashed. "I'm takin' you home now." He paused, and knew he looked as embarrassed as he felt. "Can I stay with you again tonight? I don't feel right leaving you alone and…." He trailed off. "I'm scared, Alex."

Alex nodded. Careful not to get blood on his clothes, Roy lifted Alex from his chair. Alex grabbed the interior handle and plopped into the seat, reaching down to pull his legs in after. Roy lifted the chair into the truck bed before taking his place behind the wheel. Just as he put the key in the ignition, a *Fall Out Boy* song blasted from his pants pocket.

Roy jumped and nearly hit the roof of the truck, while Alex blurted, "Oh, shit!" Then both grinned with relief as they realized it was only Roy's ring tone. Roy slipped the phone from his pocket, and frowned. "It's my Dad." He tapped the green button.

"Hey, Dad, what's up, everything okay?" he asked, the hand holding his phone trembling. His dad *never* called him. "Yeah, Dad, I'm fine. I'm with Alex. We… you what?" He listened a moment longer. "Uh, yeah, sure, Dad. I'll be right home. Soon as I drop off Alex." He ended the call.

"What's wrong?" Alex asked, his soft voice filled with anxiety.

Roy bit his lower lip. "My Dad just had a nightmare… that I got killed."

Alex gasped.

"What's happening, Alex?"

"I don' know. I just know it's my fault. You almost died, just like in *my* dream, all because–"

Roy's hand on his arm stopped Alex in mid-sentence. "It's not your fault, Alex, that you're the way you are. If somebody's after you they *better* kill me first cuz I ain't lettin' nobody hurt you!"

Roy felt strength and determination as he uttered those words. *Nobody* would hurt Alex if he had anything to say about it. "But I gotta go home. I hate leaving you alone–"

"Your dad needs you, man. I'll be fine."

Worry filled Roy's stomach. "Lock your doors and don't go out till I come in the morning, 'kay?"

Alex nodded. "Kay." They did the fist bump. Then Alex's eyes traveled to Roy's torn chest. "Let me spin you first."

Roy started the truck and pulled away from the curb. "It's just a scratch. Makes me look wicked, don't it?"

"It *is* pretty sick."

They rode the rest of the way to Alex's house in silence. Roy waited until Alex pushed his way down the path to the side door and entered. Hearing the lock click, he sighed with anxious relief and then sprinted back to his truck.

CHAPTER NINE

YOU'RE BLEEDING ALL OVER

When Roy pulled into his garage and killed the engine, his father was waiting. The man's eyes lit up as Roy opened his door and hopped out of the cab. Then his dad did something he hadn't done since Roy was twelve – pulled him into a tight hug, almost driving the air from his lungs.

Roy was so shocked he just stood there a moment before returning the hug.

"I'm okay, Dad," he said with assurance, even though it wasn't true. He was in trouble, because Alex was in trouble, but he didn't want his dad to worry.

"Oh, Roy, I'm so sorry, son. I've been a horrible dad."

Roy pulled away and saw dampness in his father's normally distant eyes. But now the eyes were alive with fire and love, the things Roy used to see in them back in the day.

"No, you been a good dad," Roy said. And he meant it, too. "You just miss mom. So do I."

Nathan Phillips looked long and hard at him, and Roy felt the man's calloused hands caressing his shoulders with a gentleness that surprised him. Roy couldn't remember his father's age, maybe somewhere in his forties, but the weight of years since his mom passed made the man look older, especially with the gray hair peppering his crew cut.

"You're right, Roy, I do miss her," Nathan said, taking a deep breath before continuing. "You look so much like her it scares me."

Roy knew he looked like his mother from pictures, and those delicate features had often gotten him called names at school. But he wouldn't trade his looks for anything in the world because he thought of her every time he looked in a mirror.

"But I'm the parent, Roy," Nathan went on, "and I forgot that." He stared at Roy, sizing him up, seeming to notice the snakebite piercings in the lower lip for the first time. "You grew up and I missed it. When

I woke from that dream… it was so real, son! Somebody stabbing you over and over again, and the blood…."

Roy gasped as his father trailed off, dropping his arms to his sides.

"Scared the shit outta me, Roy," Nathan went on, not noticing Roy's reaction. "Just the thought of losing you…." He shook his head. "I'm done being sorry for myself. You're my son and it's time I remembered that."

Happiness filled Roy. The prophetic nature of the man's dream having almost come true vanished in the desperate hug he threw around his dad's beefy frame. Nathan returned the hug, and the two stood in silence for a long moment.

Roy didn't care what Alex said. Here was another example of him making something good happen because of what he was, freak or no.

Once they entered the house, Nathan noticed Roy's torn clothes and the jagged cut across his torso. "What happened to you?"

Roy looked down, embarrassed about having to lie, while scrambling to invent one. "I, uh, I just scraped it on a tree branch while I was chasing Alex in the park. He's pretty fast in that chair, ya know?"

It sounded lame, but his brain never worked fast enough to lie convincingly. Nathan peeled away the remnants of his torn clothes to examine the wound.

Roy added, "Alex thinks it looks sick and I kinda like it, too. Be a wicked scar."

He must have sounded sincere because Nathan grinned. "I got my fair share of wicked scars, too. You go get cleaned up. I'm gonna make something you can take for lunch tomorrow so you don't hafta eat that garbage the school calls food."

Roy's mouth dropped open in shock, and Nathan chuckled, the crow's feet around his eyes crinkling in a funny way that Roy wasn't used to.

"Yeah, I remember how to cook something that doesn't need a microwave."

Roy smiled and held out a fist. Nathan eyed it curiously, as though trying to recall this gesture. Then he bumped it with his own.

Despite everything that had happened, and his continuing fear for

Alex's safety, Roy let the warm shower water rinse away a lot of despair, and hope filled his heart that things were going to get better.

***

Alex sat in his room staring off into space, thinking about what had happened. He struggled to pull up any memory of what went down after the music began playing, but there was nothing. His mind had simply gone blank, and that scared him almost more than the attack itself. Roy could've been killed right in front of him and he wouldn't have even known! And the dream he'd had the night before… he dreamed Roy had been stabbed to death! But it hadn't come true this time, not like his other dreams. Something changed it. What was going on?

The dreams he'd been having off and on his whole life had never been threatening, except that one about his parents when he was four. And there had never been a talking cat and guys in masks chasing him and his friends. *He* was the key. His spinning was the reason. Maybe it was like the magnets Ms. Ashley let them use in science class. Some, he recalled, pushed each other away, though he didn't understand why. But others pulled metal in from all directions. Was he like a magnet, pulling in evil things?

Jane always called him evil, and so had the old foster parent who'd first told him he was "spinning evil spells" when he was eight. She had prayed over him and tried to get him to read the Bible with her. When he kept insisting he couldn't read it because he was Special Ed, she accused him of being able to read when he wanted to and that his refusal to read aloud from the Bible was due to the evil inside him.

"You're the devil's child, Alex." She'd called his social worker the next day and had him removed.

Evil or not, something bad was happening all around him, and his friends were in danger. He had to figure out what it was so he could protect them. He removed his helmet and hoodie and gazed at himself in the closet door mirror, fiddling with the necklace around his neck. The round ornament still felt like human flesh as he caressed it, but that sensation no longer sent chills up his back. It almost felt comforting, as though he was touching another person.

***

Tami's house was smaller than Jane's because it was older, and only one story like most of the homes in Hawthorne. Painted a peeling green color by her dad several years ago, it sat on a corner not far from Eucalyptus Park and Mark Twain High. Tami was an only child and everyone told her she looked exactly like her mother. She didn't mind the comparison since her mother was beautiful.

She'd been hit on by lots of boys at Mark Twain because her light skin set her apart from the other girls. Her mother always said that was the Spanish blood in her. But her parents didn't want her dating seriously yet, so when she "went" with a boy like Rick, that pretty much meant at school or sporting events. Her mother always told her to pay close attention to how boys treated other people, because no matter what they said, that's eventually how they'd treat her, too. She hadn't done that with Rick, and she'd been burned.

She and Maribel had been practicing a few cheers for the next night's football game. Maribel was the polar opposite of Tami in temperament, not to mention a year older, but they got along mostly because of Cheer. On the subject of boys, however, Tami knew Maribel had no perspective. Just tonight, she'd gone on and on about how that "stupid crip" tripped her and almost messed up her ankle.

Tami had objected to the word "crip," but Maribel just kept on and on about how weird that kid was and how he'd done something to her, she just didn't know what, and how all Special Ed kids should be killed as babies because they were a burden to society. Tami tried to interject, but Maribel was so wound-up that Tami merely tuned out the diatribe until they could return to the work at hand.

Her mind drifted to her few encounters with Alex Maracle. Of course, they moved in different circles, but she liked him. Just being around him made her feel good. She hated to think it was because the wheelchair made her grateful for her legs, and considered this possibility. She loved Cheer, not to mention other sports, so not having the use of her legs would suck big time.

No. It wasn't the chair. There was something about Alex. Maribel was right about that. But Tami didn't think it was bad. He seemed like a nice, shy boy and made her feel good just by being those things. He was Special Ed, and her reputation would be ruined among the other kids, especially the athletes, if she hung out with him or even, God forbid, dated him. She blushed at the thought, but Maribel was too busy going on about the latest boy she planned to ensnare and didn't even notice.

Tami wondered, *could I date Alex Maracle*?

His stunning blue eyes and emo hairstyle practically took her breath away, and she loved his smile, even though he seldom used it. Alex and Roy were pretty much the only white boys on campus, so they kind of stood out. She thought Roy was cute, too, but liked Alex more. Must be the emo style, she decided.

She'd observed lots of boys at MTS and the more she observed Alex, the more she realized he was exactly what she was looking for in a boy – cute, good-natured, caring, a good listener, and not a poseur. Without having consciously made a decision, Tami decided to seek out Alex more often and chat with him.

By nine o'clock, Maribel announced she had to get home, and Tami was relieved. She escorted Maribel to her front door and pulled it open.

Dark, threatening rain clouds hung overhead, obscuring the moon and making her normally ordinary street look creepy and unsettling.

"Night, Tami," Maribel offered in her flighty style. "Sorry again about you and Rick."

Alex's face flashed before Tami's eyes and she shrugged. "No worries. He was a jerk."

"What about Jesse Herrera? He's hot."

Tami shrugged again. "Yeah, he's good-looking, but…."

She hadn't meant to lead Maribel on, but now the other girl hung in the doorway.

"You like somebody, I can tell," Maribel said, throwing her hands to her hips with annoyance. "Why didn't you say so? Now I *can't* leave till you tell me."

"I like the kid you were trashing, Maribel," Tami grudgingly admitted. "I think he's sweet."

"Roller Boy?"

"His name is Alex, not Roller Boy!"

"You're joking, right?"

Tami glared with defiance. "No. I think he's sweet, and he's a lot better looking than Rick or Jesse."

Maribel looked at her like she was crazy. "Girl, he's a crip who can't even get it up!"

Tami blushed, and burned with anger at the same time. "That's cruel and stupid. There's a lot more to relationships than sex."

"There is?"

Tami almost called her a hoe, but bit back her words at the last moment. "That's because you don't look," she snapped. "Anyway, it's none of your business who I like."

Maribel assumed that haughty stance she'd so perfected. "As co-Cheer-captain, anything that makes the team look bad *is* my business, and you being seen around campus with that loser will make us look super bad."

Tami trembled with anger and didn't trust herself to speak.

"You know I'm right," Maribel went on, her tone laced with smugness. "So, think before you do something really stupid."

With that, she turned and sashayed down the street.

Tami watched her go, furious and confused. She'd just gotten into a fight with her friend over a kid she barely knew. How the hell had that happened? But she didn't regret her words. Alex was a nice kid who got a raw deal at school, and Tami didn't care if it hurt her "status" – she determined to treat him like a human being. His friends, too. Even Israel. Feeling like she'd crossed some major threshold, Tami closed the door and returned to her room.

***

Alex heard the wind beat against the house, and realized the storm must be getting ready to break. He thought about Roy and wondered what his father wanted. Since Alex had known him, Roy's dad had hardly ever said much to either of them. He'd never been rude or anything. He just wouldn't talk a lot, and always disappeared somewhere in the house as soon as he got home from work. Roy had told Alex that these behaviors had been on and off since he was twelve.

But now the man was having dreams that showed the future. Alex knew it had to be his fault, but he didn't understand the connection.

He hoped everything was all right, and felt tempted several times to call Roy to find out. His new phone lay on the desk before him, sleek and beautiful and available. But each time he reached for it, he thought maybe he might be interrupting something, and knew Roy would call him when he could.

Without warning, the door leading outside burst open and slammed against the wall with a *crash*! Alex nearly jumped from his chair to the floor.

The wind poured in through the open door, bringing scores of leaves with it. Alex recalled the same thing happening last night, and gazed upward in fear. He'd locked that door. How had it opened on its own? When nothing else occurred, he relaxed. He had to close the door before the rain began or his room could easily get flooded, being underground and all. So, he pushed himself to the lift and pressed the up button.

The platform rose on creaky wheels. The wind howled about him. A cold wind. Colder than it had been when he and Roy left a couple of hours before. Almost like the North Pole had come to Hawthorne.

The lift lurched to a stop and Alex rolled forward onto the floor leading to the door. He stopped in the open doorway and peeked outside. To his left, Jane's backyard loomed in the darkness. Nothing moved except tornadoes of leaves spinning in circles.

Then Alex felt them.

Eyes.

Watching him.

His heart began pounding, and his breathing hitched as he turned his head to the right, knowing with a solid lump of fear in his throat exactly what he'd see.

The cat.

It sat there in the wind, its long fur blowing every which way, its shimmering reddish orange eyes fixed on him, its mouth grinning with pleasure.

Alex slowly backed into his room. But then the lights winked out. The music box began playing. And Alex knew no more.

***

Maribel strutted down the darkened street toward Eucalyptus Park, intending to take a shortcut to beat the impending downpour. She'd already felt a few sprinkles and knew she had to hurry or her brand-new hairdo would be ruined and she'd look crappy at tomorrow night's game.

The wind grew progressively stronger, forcing her to press down on the top of her hair to keep it from becoming disheveled. The deserted street creeped her out, even though she walked it every day. Eucalyptus Park loomed ahead, and she quickened her pace as larger drops began striking her in the face with increasing force. The unusual level of quiet sent her heartbeat to racing. Hawthorne was *never* this quiet at night. There weren't even any cars passing on Inglewood Avenue as she hurried along the sidewalk. Suddenly, she heard something, and whirled with a gasp.

Only shadows met her gaze, mocking her with their agitated movements. The wind whipped overhead tree branches into a frenzy. Pools of illumination from the streetlights revealed nothing.

"Is that you, Tami?" she called into the darkness with a timidity she never displayed at school. "C'mon, this isn't funny."

There was no answer. No sound but the howling wind. Thunder rumbled and she jumped in surprise.

"I'm sorry I made fun of the crip, okay? Come on out."

No one responded.

A streak of lightning ripped across the sky, revealing for a split second a small, black clad figure standing, or sitting on something, across the street. She couldn't tell which it was before the entire block went dark, plunging her into complete blackness. The sky broke open, and rain poured down in torrents. Thoughts of her hair long gone, Maribel shrieked with terror and ran headlong into the park.

***

Juan was scared. He knew he shouldn't be. There had been bad storms before, and power outages, too. But this felt different. This felt *bad*, like some*thing* bad had descended on this house. Jane's room was upstairs and she'd never come down to check on him. Neither would Carlos, who had the other second floor bedroom.

Juan stood at his window dressed in a t-shirt and sweat pants watching the hard rain sleet against the glass. The wind was so strong that the individual drops made a *pop pop pop* sound like bullets he'd sometimes hear in the neighborhood at night.

He shivered. The power had only been off for an hour, not long enough for his room to get *this* cold. Something bad. That's what it was. His *abuelita* would say the Devil was afoot, though she'd say his name in Spanish – *Diablo* – and that always made him sound more real. But she wasn't there, and *El Diablo* was.

He grabbed the thick hoodie draped over his desk chair and slipped it on, hoping the fleece would shield his skinny frame against the intense cold. He felt so chilled he didn't think he'd ever get warm again. Suddenly, he didn't want to be alone. He knew it was stupid. He was fourteen-years-old. He'd been arrested. He'd been in juvenile hall. But this was different. *This* was scary.

Using the tiny flashlight he kept in his drawer, Juan left his room and moved into the darkened hallway. Flashes of lightning outside the windows sent grotesquely shaped shadows dancing across the floor and walls. The house was locked up tight. Jane was paranoid about stuff like that. Still, he inched his way slowly along the carpeted floor, his rubber shower shoes squishing slightly with each step. Another flash from the open kitchen door blasted its way into the hall, and Juan gasped.

Fear gripped him like a vise. He inched his way to the door and peered cautiously around the jam into the dark, empty kitchen. The door leading outside was closed. Weird shadows danced outside the curtained windows, but nothing moved. And there were no sounds except the pounding of rain against the roof and the glass, and the rumbles of thunder rolling through the night every so often.

Juan stepped cautiously into the kitchen, waving his tiny beam of light around in every direction, knowing nobody was there, but *feeling* a presence nonetheless. The door leading down to Alex's room was closed. Alex wouldn't laugh at him, or tell him he was acting like a baby. Alex would protect him.

He reached out and gripped the knob, pulling the door open slowly. He looked into the small elevator shaft leading down to the basement. The lift was at the bottom, which meant Alex was, too. Just to one side of the shaft was a metal ladder attached to the wall so people could climb up and down. Jane told Alex the previous owners had a crippled kid like him and set the room up special. That's why social services placed Alex there, because the setup was ideal. The ladder existed in case of emergencies, and in Juan's mind, this was an emergency. Alex could climb it if he needed to, so he must be okay down there. And "okay" was what Juan needed to feel.

Another blast of thunder, and a streak of light illuminating the shaft spurred him forward. He turned and gripped the top rung of the ladder, swung his feet around, and descended to the floor. He alighted to the carpet and turned to scan the room with his beam. The cold was worse down there, almost like being inside a freezer. He shivered and pulled his hoodie more tightly around his torso, flipping up the hood to warm his frigid ears. There were leaves all over the floor and water dripped from above. He raised his beam, followed the dripping water upward, and gasped.

The outside door stood open, and the elevator platform on that side of the room was at the top. Alex was there, sitting on the platform staring out the open door. Rain blasted in from all directions because of the frenetic wind. It splattered Alex and dripped from the edges of the platform, coloring the white carpet a dark, ominous black. Yet Alex did nothing. He sat there like he couldn't move, and Juan's heart began pounding even more.

"Alex?" he said, his terrified voice barely a whisper against the thunder and pounding rain. "You okay?"

There was no response. Juan tiptoed across the room, the beam of light wavering because his hand shook. The outside lift had some kind of backup power in case Alex needed to escape a fire or something, so he went to the power switch and flipped it to "Down." The motor whirred to life, startling Juan with its invasion of the otherwise disturbing silence, and the platform descended.

He shuffled back and forth, his flashlight beam aimed at the descending platform, his breath visible on his lips. The whirring motor ceased its grinding as the platform came to a halt.

A flash of lightening revealed Alex's face.

He stared straight ahead like a zombie. Juan moved around to face him, lowering his beam to the floor as he did. With one trembling hand, Juan reached out to squeeze Alex's shoulder. He felt something sticky and yanked back his hand. Whipping up the flashlight, he shone the beam onto his hand and gasped. Blood smeared his fingers and palm – fresh blood! He raised the beam to Alex's face. Blood droplets were sprinkled on his soft, white cheeks. Heart thumping, Juan lowered the beam to Alex's shirtfront. He recoiled. The shirt was soaked with a mix of water and blood.

Alex blinked and groaned, and Juan stepped away even further. Alex blinked against the harsh light, his blue eyes iridescent like a cat's. He pushed back his chair in fright.

"Who are you?"

Juan shone the light on his own face, and Alex sagged with relief. Then he looked down at himself in confusion, noting his wet clothes and dripping wheelchair.

"Alex, what happened to you, man? You're bleeding all over!"

As though to prove his words true, Juan shone his light onto his own hand and then onto Alex's shirt, while a wide-eyed Alex followed the beam with his eyes. He gaped at his blood and water soaked pants, and the blood on his hands. He glanced down at his wheels and saw they were slick and shiny.

Juan watched as Alex assessed his situation, afraid the other boy might be seriously hurt, but more afraid of Alex's strange behavior. "What happened, Alex?"

"I don't know. Where was I?"

Juan waved the beam at the open door as more rain spilled in and dripped down the walls. "You was just sitting up there." He watched Alex digest that info, but Alex's eyes revealed he had no idea how he'd gotten there. "You hurt, Alex, want me to get Jane?" Juan didn't ever want Jane for anything, but she was a grown-up and whatever was happening wasn't something he could handle.

"No! I, uh, I don't know what happened." He looked across the darkness at Juan. "I'm, uh, gonna get in the shower and clean off, figure out where the blood's from."

"You need help?"

Alex shook his head. "No. I got it."

Juan nodded. "Okay. But I wait here." When Alex gave him a

questioning look, he added, "Alex, there be something here in the house. Something bad. It come in with the wind."

Alex shivered. "I know. I feel it, too."

He wheeled himself across the floor to the bathroom door, flung it open and entered without another word. Juan heard the lock click and, trembling, surveyed the room. There were bloodied tracks along the carpet leading into the bathroom, and the area beneath the outside door was getting more soaked by the second. He stepped onto the platform and pushed the up button. He wanted that door closed and locked, even though something worse than human had already gotten in.

***

Alex practically slammed the bathroom door and pushed in the lock button. He sat in the dark a moment, his whole body shaking with cold and fear and dread. What had he done? Despite the wet clothes sticking to his frozen skin, he knew he wasn't hurt. So, whose blood was it?

Suddenly the overhead lights burst to life and nearly blinded him. He squinted and blinked several times against the stinging pain until his eyes adjusted. He also realized that the wind had stopped pounding against the house.

Shaking and quivering, Alex slipped off his shirt. The necklace struck him in the chest, and felt heavier than it had before. He tossed the bloodied shirt into his hamper and slipped the chain over his head. The webbing looked clotted with blood. Sickened, he tossed the necklace into the sink and slid from his chair to the tiled floor. He couldn't stop shaking, making removal of his tight, wet jeans more difficult than usual. He sat up to yank off his Converse and then pushed his pants down around his ankles, lying back to pull his legs the rest of the way out. The pants and his drenched boxers went into the hamper and Alex sat on the floor, naked, exposed, and panicked.

What did you do?

Terrified of the answer, he pushed his way to the standup combination bathtub and shower. Easing himself over the lip, he used the pull bars to heft himself onto the seat. Closing the door and sealing it with the heavy silver handle, Alex spun the handles and sent hot water cascading from the showerhead into his hair. He tempered the hot with some cold, but not much. His entire body felt numb with fear and fatigue. He sat beneath the spray of hot water and closed his eyes when blood whooshed down the drain.

Whose blood is that?

Alex absently soaped himself, terrified because he couldn't remember a thing after the music started playing. No, wait. There was something! He'd dreamed that Maribel ran through the park, and it felt like... *he* chased her!

Why would I dream about her?

He looked down at the last remnants of reddish water swirling down the drain and almost cried out in horror.

Could this be her blood?

But how? He'd been in his doorway the whole time. Or had he? What time was it, anyway?

He stuck his head out of the shower far enough to see the luminescent numbers of the digital clock he'd installed on the wall. Ten fifteen. He was pretty sure it had been around nine when he'd spotted the cat outside his door. Was that enough time to get to the park and back? Enough time to.... *No!* He couldn't believe that! He looked down at his pale legs.

I couldn't have done it.

So, whose blood is this?

He stayed in the shower for a long time, the cold not wanting to leave his body. When he finally toweled off, he slid from the shower to his low chest of three drawers. Pulling out clean boxers, a plain tee, and his MTS P.E. shorts, he dressed as the storm outside abated. In fact, he realized, he hadn't heard any thunder since entering the bathroom.

After wiping all the bloody water from his tires, Alex placed a thick towel on his seat cushion, pulled himself into the chair, and rolled to the sink. He wanted to see that necklace. The memory of it thick with blood wouldn't go away. He reached into the sink and lifted it by the chain. Another shock roared through him. It was perfectly clean! Not a trace of blood or even dirty water. The webbing glittered and shown like it had been polished. Almost as if....

No, that couldn't be!

He'd seen the webbing filled with blood and now it looked almost like the web had.... eaten it. Eaten it and licked itself clean in the process.

Alex shook his head and dropped the necklace behind the faucet, not wanting to look at it anymore. Maybe he was going crazy. Whatever was happening, he didn't want to be alone. He wanted Roy. He needed Roy. Roy would help him understand, or at least make him feel safe.

But Roy was home with his dad, and Alex didn't want to mess with that, especially if he and his dad might finally be talking. But Juan was there, and Juan was scared too. They could keep each other company until daylight arrived.

The lights in his room were on and Juan sat at the desk, twirling the cord of his flashlight around his forefinger. He jumped in fright when Alex popped open the door and wheeled out. Standing and backing away from the desk, he stared at Alex with fear in his wide eyes.

Alex couldn't blame him. At this point, more than ever before, he frightened himself.

"You, uh, you okay?" Juan whispered, his body tense as though ready to flee.

Alex nodded, trying to spin some of the fear from the boy.

Juan relaxed somewhat. Then his face scrunched up with confusion. "So where was you bleeding from?"

Alex stopped his spinning suddenly, realizing he hadn't come up with a good answer. If he said nowhere, that would make Juan even more scared. His mind raced. Then he thought of Roy's scrape across the chest. He pointed to his chest. "I had a bad cut along my chest that was pretty deep, but I fixed it."

Juan's eyes squinted with uncertainty. Alex had told Juan he couldn't spin himself, only others, but he hoped the younger boy thought he meant the legs only.

"There was a lot of blood."

Alex tried for a smile he didn't feel. "Yeah. Sometimes I'm good to have around."

Juan glanced down at the carpet. "Too bad you can't fix the carpet."

Alex looked at the carpeting around his chair, especially beneath the outside door. It would definitely need a cleaning. "Jane never comes down here anyway," he told Juan with a shrug. "Roy and me'll clean it up."

Juan looked at him in an odd way. "Roy's awesome."

Alex caught something in Juan's voice that reminded him of what he'd seen when he spun Roy during lunch yesterday. But then Juan yawned, and Alex suddenly felt exhausted. The following day was Friday, a school day, and he needed sleep.

"I'm gonna knock out, Juan." The other boy glanced past him at the bed. "It's okay if you wanna stay. I got me a big bed. Lots of room." Juan's eyes widened and Alex noted the fear. "Up to you. There's blankets in the closet. You can wrap up and sleep on the floor near me where the carpet didn't get no water on it. Better wash that blood off your hand first."

Juan nodded, and hurried into the bathroom. Alex backed up his chair and turned it. Locking the brakes, he slid out and onto his bed in his usual fluid fashion. He pulled his legs up and under, tugged the covers to his chin, and lay shivering from the intense cold permeating the room. Juan came out of the bathroom.

"Uh, could you kill the lights?" Alex asked, trying to keep the nervous tremble from his voice.

Juan padded to the switch and flipped it. The room went dark and only shadowy moonlight peeked in through the window. Even the lightning had stopped, almost like it had never been there.

The tiny beam from Juan's light moved across the floor. The closet door creaked open. The light pointed into the closet for a moment, but nothing else moved. Then the door closed and the light beam skittered over to the bed and winked out. Juan slipped under the covers beside him and pulled them over his trembling body. Alex wanted to reassure him that everything would be all right. But he didn't believe everything would be all right. Ever again. Grateful for the other boy's presence—and body heat—Alex turned to face the wall, slipping into a deep slumber almost at once.

DAY 3

CHAPTER TEN

I KNOW YOU'RE HIDING SOMETHING

CARLOS WAS RINSING HIS CEREAL bowl as the door popped open and Alex rolled out of his elevator.

Upon seeing Carlos, he stopped short. He thought the bigger boy would be gone by now and whipped his head around toward the interior of the elevator with a warning look on his face.

Carlos sniggered. "Hello, Juan," he announced. "I know you stayed all night with Roller Boy."

Self-consciously, Juan stepped through the door and stood beside Alex.

"So, Juan," Carlos said with a grin, "could Alex get it up for you or not?"

Alex felt his body temperature soar with anger, but Juan shocked him by lunging at Carlos with a fist to his jaw, knocking the stunned bully to the floor. Alex had never seen Juan so furious before. The tiny boy had both fists raised, his face twisted with rage as Carlos recovered himself and jumped up to grab him.

Jane's voice cracked like a whip. "Freeze!"

The boys froze.

Jane stood in the hall doorway glowering at them. "You know the punishment for fighting in my house."

"But he said–" Juan began.

"Silence!" Her voice ripped through the quiet kitchen like a sonic boom.

The usually belligerent Carlos shrank back like a little boy.

Jane pulled open a broom closet beside the door and extracted a large cricket paddle. At least, that's what she'd told the boys it was used for. None of them had ever heard of that game before. She held it out.

"Who's on first?"

Carlos and Juan exchanged a fearful look.

"No," Alex said.

Jane flinched as though she'd been slapped. "What did you say?"

Alex rolled his chair past the others and stopped right before her. She could easily swing the paddle and do serious damage to his head, but he was done with her bullying.

"I said no. You ain't hittin' them no more. Take off guys."

They didn't need to be told twice and turned to the back door.

"Stop right there!" Jane barked, and lifted the paddle like a baseball batter preparing to swing.

The boys stopped and turned, unsure what to do.

"Forget it, Jane. I'm not gonna let you keep hurtin' them so's I gotta spin 'em. You're scared of me, I know. I told you before I don't even need you to talk no more. I can spin everything outta you till there's nothin' left. Then you'll be more special ed than I could ever be!"

Visibly shaking, Jane lowered the paddle, fighting to regain her take-charge demeanor. But Alex knew he'd gotten to her. He saw it in her eyes, and the fact that she wasn't speaking. When he'd first moved in, she'd talked all the time, criticizing the boys, yelling at them, berating them. But he started spinning her so she did those things less and less, until she figured out what he was doing. He'd never found out how she did that, but now she hardly talked much when he was around.

Alex smiled, and she recoiled. "I can do it any time, Jane, and you won't know till it's too late." Knowing he'd won this round, Alex spun his chair around. "C'mon guys, we're outta here."

The other boys were outside in an instant without saying a word. Alex grabbed his backpack from the floor by the elevator door and turned to face Jane. He was pleased to see her breathing was ragged, her beady eyes wide with fear. He grinned.

"You're evil, Alex," she said, her usually strong voice quiet and timid. "You're a freak and you're evil."

Alex flinched at her words. She'd said them enough times before that they should have no effect on him. But they did, because he believed her. He looked her in the eye.

"I was born this way, Jane," he said, his voice stronger than he felt. "What's yer excuse?"

He turned and wheeled out the door.

***

Juan and Carlos were long gone when Alex rolled down the driveway to the sidewalk, but Mrs. Rhodes was there, "Like clockwork," she always said, with his lunch. Shaken by his latest encounter with Jane, on top of the nightmarish events of the night before, Alex found himself grinning with relief at the normalcy of the moment. With gratitude, he reached for the bag and dropped it into his lap.

"I tried to catch Juan, but he was running with that hooligan and didn't stop," the old lady prattled on. "Jane up to her old tricks again?" Alex nodded, still smiling. He really liked this lady, not just for the lunches and the concern, but more because she felt like the grandma he never had.

"I figured," she said, her voice like sandpaper, swiping some strands of gray hair off her face. "They should take her license away, they should." Then she stopped because Alex had said nothing. "Look at me, making you late for school and all. Here comes your ride. Scoot now."

She waved a wrinkled, liver-spotted hand above his head, but Alex didn't need to turn to know Roy was approaching. He knew the sound of that truck like it was his own wheelchair.

"Can I hug you, Mrs. Rhodes?" he blurted, not even sure why he'd asked, but suddenly feeling the desperate need for a hug from "grandma."

Her toothy grin of joy was all the answer he needed. "Course you can, honey," she said, and wrapped her thin, frail arms around his shoulders. In turn, he wrapped his own around her waist, being careful not to squeeze too hard. She released her hold on him and he gazed at her sallow, happy face with joy in his heart. Just that simple moment buoyed his spirits and made him feel better.

"Thanks, Mrs. Rhodes," he said, blushing.

She tousled his mop of hair. "You're a good boy, Alex. Stay that way."

He nodded. Somehow, when she said it, he could almost believe it was true. Waving goodbye, he turned and rolled the rest of the way to the street, avoiding the massive puddle pooling at the foot of the driveway. Roy jumped down from the cab of his truck and waved at the retreating old lady. Alex glanced at the sky. Dark clouds hung above the city like a thick blanket threatening to suffocate them. Roy started around the front to the passenger side, but Alex intercepted him first.

Roy noted Alex's facial expression. "You okay?"

"Yeah. What's with your dad?"

Roy grinned. "Don't know why he dreamed about me getting killed," The grin made his snakebites glint in the hazy sunlight. "That part's weird. But he promised not to drink no more and wants to be a real dad again."

For the second time that morning, Alex smiled. Much more of that and his emo cred would be dashed for good. "That's sick. Think he means it?"

Roy's grin grew larger. "Yup."

He held up a fist and they bumped. Alex knew he had to tell Roy and the others about what happened to him, and Roy had to share the episode in the park with them, too, but he didn't want to relive the horror right now. Right now, he needed the wind in his hair. He needed the thrill of doing something extreme since he'd been denied the night before.

"C'mon," Roy said, popping open the door. "Let's get going. We gotta tell the others about the park stuff."

Alex nodded, but made no move to roll closer. "I want you to pull me, Roy, like we done before, remember?"

Roy laughed. "Yeah, I almost got a ticket, fool. Not good."

"C'mon, chicken, it's just a few blocks. And I got the need for speed."

"Okay, but not too much speed. I *am* going into school, ya know."

Alex pushed himself around the pooling water to the rear of Roy's truck, while Roy climbed into the cab and started the engine.

Alex found the handle at the passenger side of the tailgate and gripped it with his left hand. After the rope incident, he'd taken to using this handle because the cops never said he couldn't. He threw his right thumb high in the air so Roy could see it in the rearview, and the truck moved away from the curb. His hair blew in all directions as the truck picked up speed, and he whooped with childlike joy.

***

Roy cruised down Birch Street toward the narrow driveway into the school parking lot. Excited at the delight he saw on Alex's face through his side view mirror, Roy lost focus as he approached the entrance. Suddenly, the driveway was there, and he swerved to enter, flinging Alex loose.

"Oh, shit!" Roy blurted as his friend vanished behind the truck. Slamming on the brakes, he shoved the gearshift into park and jumped from the cab. He heard a crash of metal against the curb and ran around the truck in time to see Alex fly out of his chair and go sprawling onto the sidewalk. The chair upended on top of him.

Arriving students gawked, but no one made a move to help Alex, who groaned as he sat up. As Roy ran forward, Dane appeared through the crowd of looky-loo students. He squatted down beside the disoriented Alex as Roy joined them.

"You okay, Alex?" Dane asked, his voice gravelly.

"Alex, I'm sorry!" blurted Roy. "I wasn't thinkin', man."

Dane spun his head around to Roy. "You never are, fool! You couldda killed 'im!"

He grabbed the wheelchair and placed it upright. "I'm gonna put you back in the chair, okay?" Dane said, but Alex pulled away.

"'S'okay, Dane," he said. "I fall all the time at the skate park. I got this."

Dane stood as Roy stood up beside him. The two brothers refused to look at each other, but focused on Alex using the strength in his arms to pull himself up into the chair.

Dane turned to Roy. "You dumbass piece 'a shit, Roy! I told you before you drive like a fool!"

Roy looked abashed. "I can't help it, Dane. I guess I got distracted."

Dane's eyes blazed with fury. "You got distracted. You won't get distracted when I kick yer ass!"

He turned and stalked off toward the front entrance.

Embarrassed, Roy looked at Alex. Alex grinned self-consciously and shrugged.

Honking horns reminded Roy that he was blocking the entrance to the parking lot. He jumped back into his truck to find a parking place. Alex pushed himself along behind, ignoring the sniggers of his fellow students.

He was so absorbed in not responding to the students around him that he missed the white van parked across the street. Had he been less distracted, he might have noticed that the driver, obscured behind dark sunglasses, was clearly watching him.

***

Ms. G. pointed to something on the white board, but no one paid attention. Cuong played with his Gameboy while Israel sat behind him watching the images on the screen with a mesmerized expression. Roy bit his fingernails and looked lost in thought. Java doodled, while Jorge drew the letter "V" over and over in red ink on his vocabulary paper. Alex stared out the window.

Roy and Alex had told the others about the events at Eucalyptus Park, and Alex had shared his "dream" with them. And about the blood. As always, Israel freaked out, rambling on a mile a minute, lacing every sentence with cuss words as he tried to make sense of what was going on. Java threatened to punch him out if Israel didn't shut up, and the other boy wisely did so.

None of them had any idea what was happening, or why. Java agreed that these things seemed to focus on Alex, but that didn't help them understand it any better.

Ms. G. strode down the aisle to Cuong. "I'll take the game, thank you."

Israel scowled as Cuong handed it to her, but wisely kept his mouth closed.

"You can have it back after class."

Cuong looked down at the floor. "S-s-sorry."

She moved on to Jorge and his "V" covered paper.

"When will he stop obsessing over those Vs?"

Israel looked confused, and annoyed. "Ob-what?"

She placed a hand gently on Israel's shoulder, which caused him to drop his mouth open comically. "Sorry. When will he stop drawing those?"

Israel looked up at her with obvious desire in his eyes. From across the room, Alex saw it clearly. What was this woman doing?

"He'll start on somethin' else one of these days," Alex said, drawing her eyes away from Israel. "Last year it was all Star Trek stuff."

She pulled her hand away, and Israel lost the glazed look. He fell silent and looked down at the floor in embarrassment.

"Look, guys, I know you're upset about Miss Ashley–"

Alex broke eye contact and wheeled himself out the door. The last thing he wanted to hear her talk about was Ms. Ashley!

Ms. G. started after him. "Excuse me a moment."

Alex wheeled himself toward the rear fence. He felt her presence before she spoke.

"Are you okay, Alex?"

Alex remained silent. He had so many emotions running through him that he didn't know what to say even if he'd wanted to talk with this creepy stranger. She moved around and hunkered down before him.

"It's okay to feel bad. Miss Ashley's death was a terrible accident."

"It wasn't no accident."

"How do you mean?"

Alex shrugged, and didn't raise his eyes. He'd already said too much.

"Alex, if there's anything I can do for you, just ask, okay?"

"Uh, thanks."

"I really like you, Alex." Her voice sounded silky and tempting, and Alex shivered when he saw her hand land on his thigh.

Fixing his eyes on that hand resting *very* near his privates, he wondered again what she was up to. He was getting tired of people and their bullshit games, so he looked her right in the eye.

"Is it right for a lady your age to be puttin' her hand like that on a boy *my* age? Don't seem like it to me, but then I'm just special ed and you're the teacher."

She removed her hand, but not before Alex caught something in her eyes, something that reminded him of a lion he'd seen on TV getting ready to eat some helpless animal. She stood and silently entered the classroom.

***

The boys sat at their usual table during Nutrition and Java nudged Alex playfully. "She put her hand on you, fool. She got the hots for you."

Around mouthfuls of his breakfast burrito, Israel said, "I'm better lookin' than you, Alex. She must got a thing for cripples."

He cackled and dodged the cookie Alex threw at him.

Roy shook his head in disgust. "You guys are sick. I don't trust that chick, the way she rubs up against everyone, puttin' her hand on Alex like that. Something's wrong with her."

Alex looked at his friend, sitting and chewing his fingernails again. "You're right, Roy."

Just then, Tami approached and hovered near the table, as though trying to make an important decision. Alex noted how the morning sun shimmered against her dark hair and lit up her face so she looked like a movie star.

"Hi, guys," she finally said, her voice quiet, her gaze flitting to other students nearby, who'd stopped talking to observe the exchange.

The boys fell silent, even Israel, and waited for her to continue.

Before anyone could say anything else, the two senior bullies strolled past.

"Hey, Roller Boy," one of them yelled, the voice dripping with mockery.

Not allowing himself to appear pathetic, Alex met the laughing eyes of the bigger boy with his own.

"Why doncha ask her to the Homecoming dance?"

The second senior, Saul, grinned. "Yeah, man, we hear you can really rock and *roll.*"

The boys laughed and high-fived. Many of the observing students laughed as the seniors sauntered off to find another hapless victim.

Java stood as if to pursue them. "Assholes."

"Forget it, Java," Alex said.

"Why? You know I can beat the shit outta them!"

Alex nodded. "I know. But they ain't worth it."

Tami said, "Just ignore them, Java."

Reluctantly, the brawny boy resumed his seat, glowering out into the crowd of students, even though the two offenders were long gone.

Tami's next words nearly floored Alex. "Would you like to go to Homecoming with me, Alex?"

Alex met her gaze, and saw sincerity. But what could he do at a dance except look like a total loser?

"You don't have to be nice to me, Tami," he said, feeling embarrassed and terrified at the same time. Could she possibly like him for real, or was it just his spinning that had trapped her? Tami looked hurt by his words, and he wished he hadn't said them.

"I'm not just being nice, Alex," she insisted. "I really like you and I wanna spend some time with you. Homecoming would be fun."

"Those guys'll just make fun of us in front of everybody."

Now her soft brown eyes became stormy, like the ocean before a hurricane. "They won't make fun of *me*, Alex, and I won't let them make fun of you."

"I'll go with you, Tami," Israel blurted, his tongue hanging out at the prospect.

Tami flashed Israel an annoyed look. "We'd have fun, Alex. I know *I* would."

All of Alex's insecurities about his disability and his freaky nature welled up and nearly choked him. "Yeah, I can dance so good."

"I don't care about the dancing, Alex," Tami said, more insistently this time. "I just wanna spend time with you. Call me, please?" She handed him a slip of paper.

Alex took it and almost choked. It was her phone number. Before he could respond, Mrs. Davis was suddenly beside them. He'd been so engrossed in Tami he hadn't even noticed her approach.

"Excuse me, boys, but I need to speak with Tami."

Tami smiled at Alex and mouthed, "Call me," before following Mrs. Davis off to the side by the rear fence, away from the other students. Alex and the other boys watched the exchange closely. Suddenly Tami cried out and put both hands to her mouth in shock.

"Maribel *is* dead," Alex said. "She got killed, just like I saw."

Roy gasped, and Israel muttered, "Shit," but the others gave no reaction. Alex's gaze remained fixed on the now-crying Tami, who was led away through the curious crowd of students by Mrs. Davis.

Roy turned to Alex with concern. "Whadda we gonna do, Alex?"

Cuong held up his game. "P-p-play N-n-nintendo?"

Java rolled his eyes while Cuong returned to playing. Jorge handed Alex a big red "V" that he'd scrawled on his burrito wrapper.

"Thanks, Jorge."

"Hey, Alex," Israel said in his usual booming voice. "You think that blood on you was Maribel's?"

Several passing students eyed the table as Java turned to Israel with an upraised fist. "Why doncha say it louder, fool?"

Israel looked sheepish and shrugged, but Alex considered his words. After all, he'd wondered the same thing all night.

"Dunno" was all he could say.

***

After Nutrition, Alex took his midmorning bathroom break. Sitting on the toilet and concentrating on emptying his bladder, he heard two voices enter the bathroom. He recognized them at once – Saul and Tony, the seniors who always mocked him.

Anger assailed him. His mind replayed every insult thrown his way, from Roller Boy to crip to shorty, not to mention the word 'retard' flung at Jorge. And he still fumed over the time they stole Cuong's Gameboy and hid it in a pile of dog shit out by the railroad tracks. Alex hated even the idea of hating anyone. It was just who he was. But if anyone should be hated, it was these guys.

Tempted as he was to say something, he froze and remained silent. If they knew he was there in the stall, helpless and at their mercy, who knew what they'd do? So, he did what he was born to do – he spun them, and spun them hard.

Piss splattered against the porcelain of the urinals as they talked about sex. Each tried to outdo the other with their stories about girls they'd gotten drunk and taken advantage of.

Alex took it all. He felt stirrings in his body that weren't physical. He felt his body temperature rise. He felt their arrogance. He absorbed the sensations they described. He spun them harder than he'd ever spun anyone before. Every good feeling they expressed, he stole, pulled into himself, and relished until it faded from his mind and body.

The boys fell silent, and Alex listened for more.

"I feel like shit, Tony."

The voice was so empty and filled with despair that Alex stopped spinning and focused on what they were saying.

"Me, too, Saul," said the other one, his voice filled with sadness. "I feel like an asshole. A second ago I was great. What happened?"

"Dunno," answered Saul, his voice a dull monotone, like he'd lost all his energy. "But I gotta get outta here. Go home, go somewhere. My life is shit, Tony. *I'm* shit!"

Alex heard footsteps along the tile floor.

"Wait for me!"

Then silence as the two boys left the bathroom.

Alex allowed the last bits of pleasure to filter through him before they vanished into space, or wherever the stuff he spun ended up, and then he bowed his head in shame. Yes, those guys were assholes and deserved to get some of their own medicine. But what he'd done was wrong. He'd stripped them of every good feeling he could, feelings they will never get back. Maybe now they'd treat girls better, but did he have the right to make them feel like they were worthless?

Feeling alone and empty, Alex finished his business and returned to class, where he said nothing to anyone for the rest of the morning. Roy could tell something was wrong, but he wasn't sure he could even tell Roy what he'd done. He might lose his best friend, and he couldn't risk that. So, he said nothing and just gave Roy the head nod whenever he felt the other boy's gaze on him. He tossed off a couple of shy smiles to further calm Roy, and that seemed to work.

***

It was right before lunch that Alex was once again summoned to the principal's office. Roy looked at him with worry, but Alex gave him a head nod to chill. He already knew this had to do with Maribel. He didn't need his dream powers to tell him that.

With a pounding heart belying the calm he'd shown to Roy, Alex once again wheeled himself into the administration building and into the principal's outer office. The secretary gave him a sympathetic smile. "You're becoming a regular, Alex."

Alex mumbled, "Yeah." He looked down at his feet until Mrs. Davis appeared at her office door and ushered him in. Not surprisingly, he found those same two cops waiting. The nicer one gave him a curious look, while the other one glowered something fierce.

Mrs. Davis closed the door. "These detectives have some more questions for you, Alex," she said as she resumed her seat.

"Hello, Alex," said the light-haired cop, the one that had been nicer the last time. "Do you remember our names?"

"No."

The man nodded, as though expecting that answer. "I'm Detective Cole and this is Detective Gordon." The other guy said nothing.

"Did I do something wrong?"

Cole smiled, but it was one of those smiles that hid the truth behind it. "Not yet."

The other cop grunted, but a quick glare from Cole cut off whatever he planned on saying.

Shifting with discomfort, Mrs. Davis said, "Alex, some students overheard you talking about Maribel this morning."

Alex said nothing. *Izzy and his big mouth!*

"How did you know she was dead?" Gordon asked. "Did you kill her, kid?"

Mrs. Davis gasped, and Cole scowled at his partner.

Alex tried not to let the man's words affect him, but memories of his blood-soaked clothes swept over him and filled him with terror. Instead, he mumbled, "Dreamed it."

"Tell us about it," Cole prodded, and so Alex told what little he actually saw. He left out the cat and the fact that he'd zoned out, and of course, the part about the blood.

The two men exchanged a curious look, and Gordon whistled a tune Alex didn't recognize. Cole glared at him and turned to Alex. "Sorry. That's the X-Files theme. My partner thinks he's a comedian."

Alex didn't know that word and didn't respond. He waited for them to say something more.

"Did you get a look at the killer?" Cole asked, his voice serious and earnest.

Alex shook his head, thinking of the guy Roy said had chased them. Was it the same guy who chased Maribel? He never saw anything. In his dream, it felt like the person chasing Maribel was… him.

Cole hesitated and rubbed his fingers across his chin like he was thinking about something. "How much do you know about your birth, Alex?"

That caught him by surprise. His birth? "Uh, not much. I mean, my parents died when I's four."

"Your file with Children's Services is, of course, sealed," Cole went on. "Short of a court order, I can't see it. However, your social worker told me you're free to share any information that you know."

Alex didn't know where this was going. What did his birth have to do with these killings? "I told you, I don't know nothing."

Gordon cussed under his breath. "Look, kid, we know your mother left a package that you got when you turned fourteen last year. We wanna know what was in it."

"Joe," Cole said in a warning tone, but Alex didn't notice.

"What package?" he said, feeling stiff and fearful and chilled all at once.

Cole looked sympathetic. "Your social worker said there was a package held by some attorney until you turned fourteen. It was from your mother, delivered nine months ago to your houseparent." He flipped open a small notebook and checked something. "A Jane Walters?"

Alex felt like he'd been slapped. A package from his mother? And Jane kept it from him?

"She, uh, she never gave it to me," he answered, fury welling up within him.

How could she?

Gordon stepped forward and put his face down right in front of Alex's. "Don't lie to us, kid. I know you're hiding something."

"Back off, Joe," Cole barked, and Gordon, with obvious reluctance, stood and glared at Alex as he retreated.

"Detective Gordon!" Mrs. Davis said. "May I remind you that you are a guest in my office and Alex is one of my students? You will behave with respect."

Cole fought back a smile as Gordon looked suitably chastised by the principal, like he was a student about to get suspended.

Alex's heart pounded. *How could Jane do that to me?*

Cole hunkered down so they could be face to face. "So, this woman you live with never gave you a package from your mother?"

Alex shook his head.

From my mother...

Finally, he found his voice and stammered, "Do you, uh, like, know what was in it?"

"We were hoping you could tell us."

When Alex didn't respond, the man placed a hand on Alex's shoulder.

Why did adults always think troubled kids wanted to be touched? *Jeez!* He wanted to shrug the hand off, but he just looked at Cole without really seeing him.

My mother...

"Can I go now?" he asked, looking at Mrs. Davis.

She came around the desk. "Are you all right, Alex? You look so pale."

"I don't feel good," he whispered, looking at her with such desperation that her hard exterior began to crack. "You think maybe I could go home now?"

Mrs. Davis placed a hand on his shoulder, but he no longer cared. He was lost in thoughts of his mother, of what she might have sent, of how Jane had stolen his past from him.

"Of course, Alex," Mrs. Davis said. "I'll call your housemother."

"No!"

Mrs. Davis pulled her hand back and recoiled. Even Cole stepped back and studied him.

Alex realized he'd overreacted and looked at his principal. "Please, Mrs. Davis, after what she done to me I don't wanna see her. Can't Roy drive me home? He always does anyways."

She looked uncertain, and glanced at Cole as if to get his support.

"It's probably not standard procedure, Mrs. Davis," he offered. "But under the circumstances, I think it's warranted."

She paused a moment. "I'll have the attendance office mark you excused for your afternoon classes, Alex. Both of you."

Alex nodded, shaken and unsteady. "Thanks, Mrs. Davis. I'll go get Roy."

Before he could turn to exit, Cole's hand was outstretched, another business card between his thumb and forefinger. "In case you lost the other one."

Alex took it. The other one had been ruined when his pants got wet in the rain. He slipped the new one into his pocket, nodded at Cole and wheeled himself from the office.

He raced past the secretary and out into the hall, afraid he would cry or scream or something. He shoved open the heavy glass door so hard it struck the rubber stopper with a loud *thud*, and then he was speeding across campus.

How could she? The only thing I would have from my mother and she hid it from me!

So many emotions churned through Alex he didn't know which to feel first. But he did know Jane wouldn't get away with this. She'd already done too much to him. This was the last straw!

Pumping his chair as hard as he could, Alex was sweating and slightly out of breath by the time he returned to the classroom. Thankfully, the lunch bell rang as he neared the door and his classmates poured from the room.

Roy was out first, and he looked afraid when he saw Alex's condition. At first Alex couldn't talk, just waved off their questions until they got to their table. As always, Jorge and Cuong looked unconcerned, but even the usually taciturn Java noticed how upset Alex was and punched him on the arm in support.

Cuong handed Alex a drawing he'd made of all of them gathered around their table laughing. It was good, but Alex couldn't do much except say thanks and offer a small smile in return. Jorge handed him a pencil into which he'd carved numerous Vs, and Alex took that with gratitude. He really did have good friends, friends that nobody could ever take away from him.

Once he calmed down and stopped hyperventilating, Alex told the others what Cole had said. Of course, Israel started in on Jane with every cuss word in the book, and for once no one stopped him.

Alex told the others to make sure Ms. G. didn't know why he and Roy had left

"Why *are* you going, Alex?" Java asked, careful not to raise his voice like Israel and attract unwanted attention.

"I'm going to the house and get back what's mine."

"B-b-be c-c-c-areful, A-a-a-lex," Cuong said.

"I will. Roy's gonna help me."

He glanced at his friend.

Roy didn't even hesitate. "Yup."

"Why don't you want her to know?" Java asked, aiming a thumb toward their classroom.

Alex shrugged. "Don't trust her."

Java nodded. That was good enough for him.

"Just tell her I felt sick and Roy took me home."

Java grinned and held out his fist flatways. One by one each boy placed his fist atop each other's, and the pact was sealed.

"We'll call ya later, tell ya what happened," Roy said as Alex started across the campus. Then he hurried to catch up.

CHAPTER ELEVEN

WHAT AM I LOOKING FOR?

ALEX DIDN'T SAY A WORD once they left school behind.

"Um, Alex," Roy began, keeping his eyes on the road.

Alex turned and Roy glanced over. Alex's eyes looked lost and sad, and Roy's heart thumped with anger. Even for a bitch like Jane, what she did was beyond cruel.

"Um, how we gonna make sure she ain't home?"

"I'll ask Mrs. Rhodes to call her and have her come over, like she needs help with something."

Roy frowned. "Help with what? You think Jane'll even care?"

Alex shrugged. "Ms. Rhodes'll think of something. She's smarter than me."

Roy fell silent. They only lived a few blocks from the school so he drove slowly to let Alex have his thinking time. He pulled up to the curb around the corner from Jane's house and killed the engine. He turned to Alex, who finally realized they were no longer moving. Blinking, as though coming out of a trance, Alex looked around in confusion.

"Why'd we stop here?"

"Jane knows my truck. Can't let her see it."

Alex nodded, and offered a tiny smile. "Smart, man."

"I can't read good, but I'm no total dummy."

Alex's smile broadened. "Smartest guy I know."

Roy grinned with gratitude.

"C'mon," Alex said, flinging open his door. "We gotta sneak around into Mrs. Rhodes' back yard so Jane don't see us. Oh, and bring your little tools. Jane keeps her door locked. You gotta pick it."

Roy hadn't considered that part. Sure, he could pick locks. He'd taught himself as a child, using his dad's tools. He could pretty much open any lock, but it wasn't like he went around breaking and entering. Still, in this case, he realized, it wasn't stealing. It was getting back something someone *else* had stolen. He jumped from the cab to retrieve Alex's chair from the bed.

Rain clouds cast dark, menacing shadows over the boys as they crept along the alley behind Mrs. Rhodes' house. They stuck close to the fence in case Jane was looking out the upstairs window. A dog barked somewhere in the distance. Roy's insides twisted into knots. Always nervous anyway, he had never been good at sneaking around, and never smart enough to learn how to get away with underhanded stuff like other kids.

What if Jane catches us, he wondered? *Will she call the cops?*

She probably would, but he didn't give a rip. What she'd done to Alex was so wrong on so many levels he couldn't think about it without his blood pounding.

When they arrived at Mrs. Rhodes' gate, Roy reached over the top and flipped up the latch, pushing the gate inward. Alex wheeled inside and Roy followed, closing the gate and latching it. Her yard was larger than Jane's, but not by a lot. Just some shade trees, a small, well-trimmed lawn, some lounge chairs, and a round table set beneath a dirty awning that Roy figured used to be blue and red, but now looked washed out.

Roy knocked on her back door and they waited. After a few moments, the door opened and an ancient, wrinkled face peered out at them through the screen. The prune-like lips breached into a huge smile and the screen door popped open.

"Alex, my love," she said, her voice breathy. "What brings you here? Hello, Roy."

Roy smiled shyly from behind his bangs. "Hi."

"Can I talk to you a minute?" Alex asked.

The old lady's grin widened. "Any time, Alex. I always love talking to you." Her smile faltered. "Aren't you boys supposed to be in school?"

Alex frowned, and Roy said, "Something happened and they let him come home. I drove."

Now the wrinkled face turned sympathetic beneath the coiffed white hair. "Come in."

Her living room, Roy noted, looked like his grandmother's, and smelled the same: musty with old age. The sofas and chairs were covered by what looked to him like blankets, and old black and white pictures hung on the walls and rested atop the fireplace mantle. Mrs. Rhodes wore one of those long, billowy old lady dresses that he'd often seen on his grandma, and he felt oddly at home in her house. He also loved her little dog. She said his name was Raphael and he was a poodle. Roy loved how the tiny ball of gray fur curled up in her lap and acted like he was listening.

She gave them cookies and milk, which made Roy feel so much like a little boy again that he actually cradled the glass in one hand and a cookie in the other, thinking back to the days when his mother would have the same things ready for him after he got home from school, even if she wasn't there to greet him.

Alex nibbled absently on his cookie as he haltingly told her what he'd learned about Jane. He left out the part about Maribel being murdered and just told her that the officers wanted to know more about his parents.

Mrs. Rhodes clucked her tongue in disgust when Alex finished, and expressed her hatred for Jane and "Her cruel ways with you boys." She'd tried to get Jane's house shut down as a placement before Alex had even arrived, she told them, but when social services checked it they found everything in order. "Damn government, they wouldn't know a crook if they saw one, since most of them are crooks themselves."

But the old lady was more than happy to help Alex retrieve what was rightfully his. She placed a wrinkled hand on his arm and offered a toothy, sympathetic smile. "That's beyond the pale, Alex, to keep something from you that your late mother sent."

Roy didn't know what "beyond the pale" meant, and doubted Alex did, either, but Alex nodded with gratitude.

She pulled her hand back and fell silent a moment as her fingers idly caressed Raphael's fur. Her face suddenly brightened, giving her the sudden appearance of youth reborn. "I know what I'll do." She reached for the phone sitting atop an old table. Roy was shocked to see that the phone had a real dial on it; not even push buttons like his cordless at home.

Placing the bulky black phone in her lap next to a bored looking Raphael, the elderly woman picked up a sheet of paper with something written on it and squinted through her small, plastic-framed glasses.

Roy wiped his sweaty palms on his jeans. He tried for a smile, and his heart leapt when Alex returned it. They were so alike in temperament that it sometimes scared Roy how in sync they could be. He truly *felt* Alex's pain over what Jane had done.

The old lady dialed and a deep old school ring tone came from the receiver as she placed it to her ear.

Roy fidgeted as he waited.

"Hello, Jane, dear, how are you?" Mrs. Rhodes asked, her voice sugary and sweet, but masking evident distaste. "Now that's no way to respond to a neighbor who's trying to help you."

The boys looked at each other with the same knowing expression – Jane was being Jane, obviously.

"Well, I got a call from the police," Mrs. Rhodes went on, and that caught both boys' attention. "They asked me some questions about your boy, Carlos. I assume they talked to you, too." She paused a moment. "No? How odd. It seems they've been watching him. If you have a moment to come over, I'll fill you in. Wouldn't want you to be caught in some kind of scandal. Bad for the neighborhood and all. Fine. I'll see you in ten."

She hung up and grinned with delight at the two open-mouthed boys.

"What did Carlos do?" Alex asked.

"Nothing, dear," the old lady replied as she replaced the phone onto its ancient table.

"Well, uh, whadda ya gonna tell Jane when she gets here?" he added.

The old lady looked unconcerned and shrugged. "I'll think of something. I never told you this, Alex, but in my younger days I used to write mystery novels."

"Novels?" Alex asked, hating himself for not knowing yet another word.

"Books, dear," she replied. "I have a vivid imagination." She winked. "Now you boys better get out back and watch for Jane. I'll keep her as long as possible, but you know how she is so you'd best make it snappy in there."

"Thanks, Mrs. Rhodes," Alex gushed, glancing at Roy with expectation.

"Yeah, thanks," Roy said.

He rose and followed Alex through the kitchen and out the back door. Slipping through the rear gate into the alley, the boys slunk along the beat-up wooden fence and hid behind Jane's house. They waited in silence, only their breathing and expectant expressions indicating they were even alive. After a few minutes, they heard the telltale sound of the bell, and Roy leapt into action.

Jane had her gate latched from the inside in a way that it couldn't be opened by anyone just by reaching over. He didn't know the word for it, but Jane was one of those people who trusted no one. He jumped up and grabbed the top of the wooden slats, pulling himself up and over as he'd done on other occasions when he and Alex had hung out without Jane knowing. Once inside, he undid the chain that latched the gate and swung it open with deliberation. From past experience, he knew it would screech something fierce if opened too fast, something Roy suspected Jane had done on purpose to better control her boys.

Using his key, Alex opened the back door and rolled onto the elevator platform, Roy crowding in with him. They descended to his room and hurried across to the other elevator, rising up to the kitchen within seconds. Roy didn't know how much time they had, but knowing Jane and how she treated people, she'd probably blow the old lady off pretty fast.

He followed Alex through the empty, silent kitchen into the hall and then they stopped at the foot of the stairs leading to the second floor. Alex suddenly looked weak and embarrassed.

"You gotta go up on your own, Roy," he said, looking embarrassed. "I'm sorry I can't help. It'd take too long to get me up and back down."

Roy nodded, his heart pounding with fear. Hell, this really *was* like breaking and entering! "Which one is her room?"

"Carlos's is over the yard, so try the other doors. I'll keep watch down here." He held up his new phone in trembling fingers. "If I call, that means bail. Run to Carlos's room and climb out onto the roof. You can use that tree in back to climb down. I'll meet you in the alley."

Roy nodded, barely able to breathe. He could do this. Hell, after what happened the past few nights, facing an enraged Jane almost seemed a relief. "What am I looking for?"

Alex shrugged. "The cop said a package. Guess my name be on it?"

Roy looked uncertain.

"You know how to spell my name?" Alex asked.

Roy felt his ears burning. Even after all this time, he couldn't remember the spelling of Alex's last name. "Your first name." That part he'd managed to memorize.

"That'll work. You better go."

Roy nodded and turned to the stairs. He'd seen them before, but somehow in the gloomy sunlight filtering in through the living room drapes they looked ominous and threatening. Fortunately, they were carpeted so he went for it, pelting upward two steps at a time till he got to the second floor. He turned to glance down at Alex, sitting at the foot of the stairs, offered a tiny wave, and took stock of his surroundings.

A hall branched out in either direction. There was a door at both ends, and one in the middle, not far from where he stood. He guessed the door closest to him was the bathroom and the other two were the bedrooms. Knowing the yard was on his right, he hurried left and approached the closed, heavy wooden door. Squatting, Roy brushed the hair from his eyes and examined the lock.

Definitely required a key.

He gripped the knob and tried to turn.

Locked.

Must be the one, he thought, and fished the small tool set from his front jeans pocket.

It didn't take him long to find the tumblers inside and click them to the open position. The knob turned, and the door cracked open. Even as a child, Roy's mom had often asked him to pick a door or a lock she'd closed by accident. She joked that Roy would make a killer second story man. He never asked what that meant.

Pushing open the door cautiously, as though expecting that talking cat to leap out at him, Roy stood and peered into the room. It looked like a typical bedroom. A large canopied bed lay against one wall, two tables on either side with a fancy lamp on each one. The heavy dark drapes were pulled shut, forcing Roy to allow a moment for his eyes to adjust to the gloom.

He slipped out his phone and glanced at the time. It had been five minutes since they'd entered the yard. He had to move fast. Ducking into the room, he held the phone in one hand so he'd know if Alex called. Sometimes he didn't feel the vibration, even in his tight pants.

To one side of the bed he spotted a sliding closet door with a huge mirror on its front. Seeing himself with his band shirt, skinny jeans, scraggly brown hair and snakebite piercings, Roy sighed with disgust.

Why are you such a loser?

Pushing such thoughts aside, he hurried to the door and slid it open, wary in case Jane had it booby-trapped. But the open door merely revealed clothes and dresses hanging within. A shelf ran along the wall above the clothes, but a quick glance didn't reveal anything that looked like a box or package. Just blankets and pillows and sheets, folded and stacked.

Flicking on the flashlight app on his phone, Roy reached in with his free hand and pushed the nearest bunch of clothes to one side, moving them into the corner so he could see behind them. He nearly cried out and stumbled back in shock.

The rear wall was studded with knives – *sharp* knives jutting outward and gleaming in the narrow beam of his light.

Catching his breath, heart thumping, Roy leaned in for a closer examination. Each knife pinned a page from a newspaper to the wall, and there were four in total. He shined his light on the picture each knife stuck out of – one looked like a college boy and the others grown men. He couldn't read any of the words above or below the pictures. But for some reason they reminded him of those missing children pictures he'd see sometimes on the Internet. Had these guys all gone missing?

And why the knives?

As he crawled along, pushing her dangling clothes aside to get a better view of the next brown news clipping, his hand bumped something, startling him.

Looking down, he found a small brown box with post office labels on it. His heart flew into his throat. Could it be? He shone his light directly onto the label. He couldn't make out any of the words, like who it came from or even the street. But one word seared itself into his mind – 'Alex'.

He'd found it!

Forgetting the weird pictures for now, he snatched up the box and looked inside. There were some papers and a CD sleeved in a plastic shell case. The case had words written in marking pen that Roy didn't know, except one – Alex. Upon closer examination, he noted that it was a DVD, not a CD, one of those homemade kind you could get at Best Buy. He was about to scout further back into the closet when suddenly his phone vibrated in his hand.

Startled, he dropped the phone like it had stung him. It landed face up with that one name he'd always remember flashing at him in big letters – Alex.

Oh, shit, she's coming!

Snatching his phone with one hand and grabbing the papers and DVD with the other, Roy scuttled like a crab out of the closet and jumped to his feet, terror assaulting him. Okay, he'd lied to himself. Facing Jane *was* worse than the guy in the park, especially after those knives in the wall!

He shut the closet and tiptoed to the door. His heart thundered so hard, he was sure all the neighbors could hear. Slipping into the hall, he eased the door closed and turned the knob to make sure it was locked. Then he hurried to the stairs.

That's when he heard the key in the lock and the front door swung open with a loud creak. Dirty sunlight spilled up the stairs and nearly caught him as he ducked to the opposite side of the staircase and pinned himself to the wall. Sweat dripping into his eyes, he slipped the phone into one front pocket, but clutched the DVD and papers in the other. For once he regretted his emo style – the items were too big to fit into his small pockets.

The invasion of dirty sunlight closed along with the front door and Roy heard the lock click. He didn't know where Alex had gone and didn't have time to wait. Glancing to his right, he sprinted on tiptoe to Carlos's room. Flicking his hair from his eyes, he grabbed for the knob as he heard the stairs creak behind him. He gripped it and turned, and the door swung open with ease.

Almost frantic with momentary relief, he ducked inside and closed the door so silently it didn't even make a click. His breathing came in agitated bursts and he fought to control it. She'd hear him for sure!

With hungry eyes, Roy scanned the room and spotted the window

Alex had mentioned, the one with the tree outside. He pressed his ear against the door, and his breath froze. Even with the hall carpet, he made out the sound of footsteps coming his way, getting closer by the second. Roy darted across the room to the closet and slid open the door. He just barely got it closed and had ducked behind hanging shirts and pants before the bedroom door opened.

He kept one hand over his mouth, forcing himself to breathe through the nose. Otherwise, his panting would give him away. The wood beneath the carpet creaked as footsteps approached the closet. He pressed himself as far into the corner as he could without falling right through the wall. The door slid open. Scattered light fell on him, filtered through the hanging clothes. There was a pause, as though she knew he was there and wanted to taunt him. Her hand appeared and he nearly shrieked in terror. But it only held a jacket on a hangar. She hung it on the bar and the hand withdrew. The door closed and Roy sat in huddled fear, waiting and listening for her to leave.

Birds chirped outside and they sounded agitated, as though the weather annoyed them. That dog barked again. But there was no sound of her leaving. He crept from his corner, swept the perspiration from his forehead with one hand, and crawled to the inside of the closet door. Fearful of his heavy breathing, Roy pinned one ear against the cold wood of the door, and listened.

What the hell is she doing?

Drawers opened and closed. She was looking for something.

"You boys are all the same. Smut and more smut."

Was she talking to him?

"Think you can hide your filth from me?" Something ripped, like papers being torn to shreds, and her breathing became ragged. "If girls don't have bodies like these sluts you don't give them the time of day." More paper ripped, and suddenly all was quiet once again. "You think I don't hear you boys in the bathroom at night? You're all disgusting!" One last *rrrriipppp* filled the air and then it sounded like she threw whatever it was onto the floor in front of the closet door.

She laughed, a small, inside kind of laugh, like she thought something was really funny. "I'll teach you animals a lesson you'll never forget." Footsteps crossed the room. The door opened and slammed shut.

He exhaled. She was gone.

To be safe, he waited a couple of more minutes, watching the time tick off on his phone, before he eased open the closet door and stuck his head out. He gaped in surprise. Torn pages of girly magazines lay scattered all around the floor in front of the bed, on top of the bed, and right by the closet. So *that's* what Jane had been doing. It still didn't make any sense, but he was too terrified of being discovered to think about it now. Rising, Roy slid the door closed and sprinted across to the window.

He slid it up and groaned with relief that there was no screen. Sticking one leg outside, mindful of the DVD in his hand, Roy placed his sneakered foot onto the nearest branch and reached with his free hand to grab the next branch up. Pulling himself onto it, he hunkered down to make sure he couldn't be seen by any neighbors, and reached over to ease the window back into place.

He was down that tree faster than a monkey. Scuttling across the yard, he sprinted for the gate, undid the chain, and flew into the alley, where Alex awaited him.

Gasping for breath, Roy put a finger to his lips and handed Alex the DVD, along with the papers he'd found.

"Did she see you?"

Roy shook his head, too breathless to speak.

"Can we go to your house?" Alex held out the DVD.

Roy understood at once and nodded, gesturing for Alex to lead the way. As Alex rolled on ahead, Roy turned his head to glance at the upstairs window of Jane's house.

The curtain was moving.

CHAPTER TWELVE

I GOTTA KNOW WHAT I AM

Both boys remained silent as Roy helped Alex into the passenger seat and put his chair into the bed. Roy climbed into the cab and gripped the steering wheel hard, his knuckles white with the pressure. His breathing had begun to return to normal, but his heart kept pounding.

He felt a hand touch his arm and looked over to find Alex's soft face and intense blue eyes fixed on him with worry. "What happened in there?"

Roy shook his head, not because he didn't know, but because he didn't understand. "Some weird shit, Alex."

He started the truck and pulled away from the curb, relaying what he'd seen and heard as best as he could remember. Unfortunately, he had a poor memory for things he heard, so trying to recall Jane's words as she tore up the magazines didn't come easy to him. But he thought he'd done better than he usually did in school, probably because he'd been scared out of his mind.

By the time he finished, they had pulled into his own driveway and he'd turned off the ignition. Turning to the silent Alex, Roy asked, "What do you think it means?"

Alex considered a moment. "I know she hates boys cuz she tells us every day. Ya think maybe it's cuz she thinks we all like the hoes she seen in them mags?"

Roy found himself turning red and had to fight the urge to look away. "Maybe."

Alex nodded, looking thoughtful, and for a moment Roy panicked. But then Alex gasped. "Roy, those knives in the pictures…." He gulped. "You think maybe she killed them guys?"

Now Roy's heart started hammering anew. "Oh, shit!" He looked at Alex with wide eyes. "Ya think?"

"She's evil, I know that." His gaze lowered to the DVD in his hand. "This was all that was there?"

Roy nodded, thinking of the box he'd found. Something about it seemed off… He had it! "But the box was too big."

"Huh?"

Roy sat up straighter, sure he was right. "That box was too big for just the DVD and them papers. I think there was somethin' else in there."

Alex's face darkened with fury. "I'm gonna get it back, whatever she stole. C'mon, let's watch this."

Roy nodded, threw open his door, and jumped to the driveway to grab the wheelchair.

Roy's dad wasn't home from work yet so they had the house to themselves. His father had promised to be home early to prepare dinner, but they had plenty of time to watch whatever was on the DVD first.

As they passed through the kitchen, Roy stopped at the fridge and grabbed a six-pack of Coke. As he was closing the door, he spotted a six-pack of his dad's beer. Alex continued on through the kitchen into the hall, but Roy hung back a moment. When they'd talked the other night, Roy had confessed to drinking his father's beer from time to time, and he'd promised not to do it anymore. But he still trembled after his narrow escape from Jane and Alex's idea that she could be a killer. Shuddering, Roy grabbed the six-pack and followed his friend.

I'll just have one, he told himself.

But that was before he saw what was on the DVD.

By the time he got to his room at the rear of the house, Alex was already in front of the flat screen loading the disc. Roy shut the door and pulled a chair over beside him. He held out a beer in one hand and a Coke in the other. Alex shook his head. Roy shrugged, put down the Coke and popped open the beer. He needed to calm his nerves.

Alex rolled back from the TV and held out the remote, but didn't press play.

"What's wrong?" Roy asked.

"I'm scared."

"Why?"

Alex shrugged, and pressed the play button.

A room appeared on screen that Roy didn't recognize. Alex didn't appear to, either. It looked like a bedroom because there was a chest of drawers in the background.

A lady moved around in front of the camera and sat down so her face filled the screen. She had long blonde hair and soft features and striking blue eyes.

"That's her, Roy," Alex whispered. "The lady from my dreams."

Roy opened his mouth to say something, but the lady started speaking and he quickly closed it.

"My dearest Alex," the lady said with a sad smile. "If you're watching this video, that means your dad and I are dead. I had a feeling we wouldn't live to see you grow up, but I know Ben and Joyce did a fantastic job raising you. You probably know some of this story by now because I told them to tell you when you were old enough, and all the information you need is in a sealed packet they can help you retrieve."

Alex's fingers gripped the wheel handles of his chair, and his lower lip quivered.

"Briefly, Alex," the woman went on, "when I was pregnant with you I had a lot of dreams that led me to certain books and documents and images. You probably know from Ben that he and I are half Iroquois Indian and grew up on the Onondaga reservation in New York. Your grandfather taught us that our people have always seen the future in dreams. It was a gift of the Great Spirit."

She smiled, but to Roy it looked really sad and thoughtful. "Anyway, the dreams led me to uncover evidence about you, though I didn't know for sure it was you they were talking about until you were born."

Roy saw by his rigid posture how freaked out Alex was becoming. He wanted to reach out and touch him, but wasn't sure of the reaction. So, he gulped his beer and focused on the video.

The lady suddenly looked puzzled. "But here's the part that seemed to throw everything off. None of the information I found mentioned twins, so I didn't know what part Andy would play in all of this."

Alex gagged.

Roy reached for the remote, wanting to give his friend a break, but Alex snatched it back and dropped it into his lap, never taking his wide eyes off the woman on screen.

"Your father and I could only guess that God threw a monkey

wrench into the deal to confuse your enemies." She frowned again. "Yes, my son, you have enemies. We knew we were being followed for months prior to your birth, but we could never find out who. We hired private detectives, but none were able to get any leads. These people were like shadows."

She sighed, her bright blue eyes brimming with sadness. "The bottom line, Alex, is that you're very special. And important. Your dad worked at the hospital where you were born, and because we feared someone would try to kidnap you, he created a birth certificate for you with my brother's last name. We made it appear that you were Ben and Joyce's son and we only had Andy. It was tricky to pull off, but we did it."

She smiled again, but it looked sadder than before. Roy's heart lurched at the sight of Alex's stricken face watching this woman he was supposed to know, but didn't.

"You babies were identical, Alex, except for the unusual form of spina bifida in you," she went on thoughtfully. Roy wondered how old Alex was when she'd recorded this. "I'd visit my sister-in-law and her 'new baby' often just so I could see you both together. Even then, Alex, you did things to people. You made them feel good or bad. If they complained about aches or pains, suddenly those disappeared. I noticed this seemed more intense when both you boys were together. That's why I enclosed this music box."

She held up a round, fancy-looking object with a lid on it. Alex reacted in such a way that Roy knew he recognized it. She raised the lid, and Roy gasped. The music tinkling forth was the same as he'd heard last night in the park!

"Alex, that's–" Roy said, but suddenly noticed that Alex had gone even stiffer, and his eyes had taken on a distant, faraway look. He was gone again. Roy snapped his fingers in front of Alex's eyes, but nothing happened. "Alex, man, you're zoning again. C'mon, wake up!"

He was frantic by the time Alex's mother closed the music box, and silence filled the room. Alex came back. That's the only way Roy could describe it. Just like in the park. The music stopped, and Alex returned.

Roy grabbed the remote and froze the image. "You okay? You tripped again."

Alex nodded, his face whiter than normal. "That music…" was all he said, glancing at Roy with wide, frightened eyes. His gaze lowered to the remote.

Roy unpaused the image.

"For some reason, this music box always soothed you boys, even when you were crying. And it seemed to almost mute whatever it was you could do to people. So, I played it a lot whenever you babies were together so no one would figure out you were different."

She set the music box down and gazed into the camera. "Here's the rub, Alex. We're dead. I don't know how, but they probably made it look like an accident. And they probably made it look like Andy died, too. But they wanted *you*, Alex, and I'm sure they took him by mistake because they didn't know there were two of you. Find him. Find your brother. And get the evidence I left for you. Ben and Joyce can help you make sense of it and maybe even find some kind of expert to advise you. Your father and I wish more than anything to still be with you, but, obviously, that can't be."

She looked even more grim, and it appeared whatever she wanted to say next was distasteful. "Since we knew we were targeted for death, your dad and I made our funeral arrangements ahead of time, hoping they wouldn't be needed. To keep all the information I uncovered out of the hands of our enemies, I hid it in the lining of my casket, Alex. It's buried with me. I hate to put you through this, but you and Ben will have to dig up the coffin and get it back."

Alex gagged again, and Roy went rigid with fear. Did he understand that part right?

Alex's mother offered a look of encouragement. "Don't be afraid of some old bones, Alex. That's not me in there. I've moved on, but my love for you hasn't. It's still here on earth, surrounding you each and every day as best as I can send it." She sighed again. "Some say you will be the great peacemaker, and others the great destroyer. But you're my son, and Ben's adopted son, and I know you will choose love over hate. We love you, Alex. Never forget that."

She smiled one last time. She stood and the front of her shirt filled the camera before everything went black.

Alex sat and stared like something was still happening.

Roy clicked off the TV and set the remote aside, watching Alex in helpless silence. He wanted to say something, anything, to help him, but what could he say after all that? He didn't even understand most of it, but he did get that everything Alex thought he knew about his life was a lie.

A fake.

Roy gulped the remainder of his beer and snatched another can from the pack. Not knowing what else to do, he held it out to the silent, staring Alex. Without even a sideways glance, Alex's trembling hand reached out to grasp it. Within seconds, he'd pulled the tab and begun gulping the beer like he hadn't had anything to drink in days. The sour smelling brew dribbled down his chin as Alex upended the can and consumed the entire contents in one long gulp. With an angry squeeze, the can was crushed between Alex's strong fingers and tossed to the floor by his front wheels. His arm stretched out again, and Roy slipped a fresh can into the open hand.

He'd never seen Alex like this, so lost and despondent. And he'd never felt so low in his life except when his mother passed away. He grabbed a second can of his own and gulped it down. The liquor soothed and relaxed him, and helped with his frayed nerves.

Alex still hadn't said a word. He just gulped down the second beer and tossed the crushed can to the floor by its fellow. This time Roy was ready before the hand came his way, and a third can passed to the boy whose entire life had been turned upside down in the space of five minutes.

By the time Roy swallowed the contents of his third can, the combination of alcohol, an empty stomach, and his sorrow for Alex took its toll, and tears burned his eyes. His inhibitions lowered, he reached out hesitantly with one arm and wrapped it slowly around Alex, scooting himself closer so he could pull the other boy into him. He feared Alex would push him away, but instead Alex turned to him with such a look of utter loss and despair that Roy choked on whatever words he'd planned on saying. Those brilliant blue eyes looked devoid of hope, and the soft, delicate features quivered with unchecked emotion.

"Who am I, Roy?" Alex finally said, his voice quiet and guttural and desperate with need.

Roy said the first thing that came to mind. “You’re my best friend.”

Alex’s blue eyes grew huge and magnified as they filled with water, and then he broke, throwing his arms around Roy and crying helplessly into his shoulder. Roy wrapped both arms around this boy who meant more to him than anyone, and held him, assuring him with his closeness that he wasn’t, and never would be, alone.

They sat together in pain and despair for several minutes, and the closeness to Alex combined with the alcohol weakened Roy. He gently pushed Alex away so their eyes met. Alex’s were huge with hopeless loss, and filled with fear of the unknown, and that desperate need only made Roy’s heart pull more tightly in his chest. With trembling fingers, he cupped Alex’s soft, damp cheeks, gazed into those eyes he loved, and leaned in suddenly to press their lips together. When Alex didn’t resist, Roy pressed harder.

His blood pounded and for a brief moment of ecstasy Roy felt like he’d tasted a bit of heaven. He suddenly realized what he’d done, and pulled away with a horrified expression on his face.

“Oh, shit, Alex, oh shit, I’m sorry, man, I’m so sorry!” He lurched to his feet and turned his back in shame, hands clutching his head in mortification. “Oh, shit, oh shit, oh shit!”

A moment of silence passed. He felt fingers touch his forearm, and turned, his eyes brimming anew, his face plastered with shame and humiliation. “I’m *so* sorry, Alex, it’s the beer. I never would’ve....” He trailed off, his heart hammering in his chest.

Alex looked at him with wonder. “But you been thinking about it?”

Roy nodded, not trusting his voice to work properly.

“It’s okay, Roy. I already, well, kinda figured out about you.”

Roy’s eyes widened. “You did?”

Alex turned red with shame. “I seen you a few times, you know, checking out Pablo Medina during lunch and the other day I, well, I kinda spinned you.”

Roy’s eyes grew even wider, and Alex looked more ashamed.

“I’m sorry, man, I can’t help it sometimes. It just happens, ’specially with you, and then it’s like, well, I feel what you feel.” Alex lowered his gaze to the carpet. “I’m sorry.”

Roy sat beside him and touched his cheek. Alex looked up and their eyes locked.

"I'm sorry, Alex. I just couldn't help myself. Oh, shit, you're probably never gonna talk to me again, but Alex, man, I'm so in love with you it hurts my gut to be this close and not hold you."

Alex looked sucker punched. "How can you be in love with me, Roy? Look at me. I'm a freak and a cripple who can't even stand or dance or…." He trailed off, and Roy's face fell into shock.

"How can you say that, Alex? You're, like, so sick and wicked and hot and I…." He paused a moment, his eyes wide and wet. "When I first found that vid of Patrick singing Tears in Heaven, I was so sad about my mom, and he was so beautiful, and I crushed on him big time. I think that's when I knew for sure I was gay."

Alex listened, eyes wide with understanding.

"I even asked my dad if I could go to school where he did, and my dad just gave me this weird-ass look and said he didn't have money to send me to school in England." Roy laughed. "I was so dumb I didn't even know how far away Patrick lived."

He paused and lowered his gaze, fearful of seeing Alex's face. "Patrick was the most beautiful boy I ever saw… until you." He turned red, and peeked at those amazing blue eyes that almost took his breath away. "I been wishing so bad you might be, you know… like me."

Another tear slid from Alex's eye as he shook his head. "I'm sorry, Roy. I mean, I love you, man, you're my best friend. Just not like that."

Roy nodded. Deep inside, he'd already known. "I was pretty sure, especially cuz you like Tami and all. I guess I just… hoped."

He looked away in embarrassment before Alex's words caused him to turn back.

"I wish I *was* like you, Roy," he whispered, his voice tinged with sadness and regret. "I wish I could make you happy. I wish I could be normal like you and love someone and not spin people and…." He trailed off.

"Alex, everybody hates queers. You wouldn't wanna be like this."

"At least there'd be other guys like me. You'll have a boyfriend someday, and I'll still be a… freak. There's no one like me, Roy. I'm alone."

He started to cry again. Roy reached out and pulled him into a hug. "You'll never be alone, Alex, not when you got me. I'll never leave you. I swear it. And there *is* someone like you. You heard your mom. You got a brother."

Alex nodded and struggled against the tears. "My mother," he whispered, as though confirming the truth of it. "And my brother."

"A twin brother," Roy added, as that detail finally solidified in his brain.

Alex met Roy's gaze with his own. Roy felt the urge to hold him again, but didn't trust himself not to try for another kiss. So, he asked Alex the question he'd wanted to ask ever since he'd found out what Alex could do.

"Alex, you think maybe you could, you know, spin me?"

Alex wiped tears from his cheek. "Whadda ya mean?"

Roy bit his bottom lip. "So I won't be gay no more?"

Alex's eyes widened in surprise. "I don't know. It's not like you're sick or nothing."

"Everybody says I am, right? Gay guys are sick and broken, like us bein' special ed and all."

Roy watched Alex consider his request. He recalled when Alex had tried to fix his classmates' special ed-ness, but it hadn't worked because there was nothing they could talk about that was wrong. No illness of any kind. They were all 'normal' for them and so there was nothing to fix.

"I can try. Tell me what it feels like to be gay."

Roy paused for a moment, sat up straighter, wiped tears from around his eyes, and sank deep into himself. How did being gay feel? He thought back on his whole life since he'd first felt different, but hadn't known why.

"I feel alone, and lonely. I see girls and I don't feel nuthing, 'cept I know I should, so I feel, like, broken and wrong. Then a hot dude like Pablo walks by at school and I…." He blushed. "I wonder if he thinks I'm cute. I wonder what it'd be like to kiss those guys, to hold hands and go to the movies and just hang out." He exhaled and turned to Alex, who watched him in silence. "Mostly I see them guys and wonder if any of 'em could be like… you."

He stopped, head bowed in shame. When Alex didn't say anything, he raised his eyes once more to find Alex looking at him with tearful compassion and love. "Nothing?"

Alex shook his head. "There's nothin' wrong with you, Roy, that I can spin. You're normal."

Roy gulped, stunned to hear that he wasn't a sick pervert like he'd always heard about guys like him.

Alex bowed his head in shame. "You're crazy, though, cuz you love *me*."

Roy gasped and cupped Alex's bowed head in his hands, raising it gently. "You're amazing, Alex. That's why Tami likes you, too."

Alex's face filled with sadness, and Roy knew Alex didn't believe him.

"I'm sorry I kissed you," he said quietly.

Alex offered a shy little smile. "I'm not. It was nice."

Roy smiled now. "Yeah?"

"Yeah. My first kiss." He laughed, and Roy joined in.

"And you don't get how I could fall for you?" Roy said with a shake of his head. "What straight guy would say that?"

"A straight guy with the best friend in the world," Alex answered, his voice choked with emotion. "I don't know what I'd do without you, Roy. I mean that, man."

"Thanks. Don't know what I'd do without you, either."

Roy wrapped an arm around the boy he loved and pulled him in close. They sat together in silence for several minutes. Then Roy rose unsteadily to ditch the beer cans before walking Alex home. He figured they both needed the cold October air to sober them up before his dad, or more importantly, Jane, discovered they'd been drinking.

As they moved slowly along the sidewalk, Roy asked hesitantly, "Alex, did you understand any of what your–" He stopped, afraid he'd upset Alex again.

But Alex merely looked at him. "My real mom?" He shook his head. "I'm too dumb to understand those words, Roy, but I guess she didn't know that." He paused a moment, stopping his chair and looking lost in thought.

Roy waited, the cold air against his cheeks beginning to revive him.

The light hoodie he'd thrown on wasn't keeping his upper body very warm, but at least the cold helped overcome the alcohol in his system.

Alex looked at Roy with a mix of sadness and determination. "Roy, I gotta find out what happened to them. I gotta know if my… if Andy is alive. That means we gotta…."

Roy's eyes widened with comprehension. "Dig her up like she said?"

"I gotta know who I am, Roy," Alex said, his voice almost a whisper. "I gotta know *what* I am."

Roy forced a nod. The idea of creeping around some graveyard and digging up bodies freaked him out. That was like whacked-out Goth stuff. But if Alex needed him, he'd be there. Always, like he promised.

"We'll get the guys to help," he said, though he wasn't too sure that was a good idea.

Alex must've read his mind because he said, "Only Java and Izzy. The others are too loopy sometimes."

Roy agreed, though he predicted Izzy would probably talk so much the dead bodies would tell him to shut up. That drew a tiny smile from Alex, and then they continued on to Jane's house.

Just looking at the second-floor window made Roy's heart thump anew. In his mind's eye, the curtain fluttered. It must've been her. And that meant she knew he'd been in her room. Feeling protective, he said, "I'm going in with you."

Alex nodded with gratitude, and wheeled around the side of the house. He let himself in through the kitchen door. Roy followed, and then froze in place.

Jane stood beside the table like a statue, red hair almost aflame, staring at them with piercing intensity. "Come on in, boys, and sit a spell." She smirked at Alex. "Oh, yes, you're *always* sitting, aren't you?"

Alex glared, but fury rose within Roy and he stepped around the wheelchair to confront her. But Alex shot out a hand and grabbed his, squeezing gently. Roy stopped and looked down at Alex, who shook his head and looked calmer than Roy felt. But he backed down and Alex released his hand.

Jane's penetrating brown eyes took note of the brief handholding, and the smirk grew larger. "Well, aren't you two just the cutest couple."

Roy opened his mouth in anger, but again Alex stayed his response with a simple hand to his forearm. Roy closed his mouth and seethed in silence.

"Whadda ya want, Jane?" Alex asked, his tone icy cold.

Her smirk changed to an evil smile that reminded Roy of the Grinch in that old cartoon. "It's 'mom' or 'mother' to you."

Alex glared. "You'll never be my mother. Now whadda you want?"

She chuckled. "I want to see the look on your face when the police arrest your boyfriend there for breaking and entering."

Roy gasped. He'd been right. She knew!

Alex, however, remained impassive, as though he'd expected this. Roy realized later that he knew this woman all too well.

"Go ahead and call 'em, Jane," Alex replied, sending new fear piercing through Roy like a knife. "All he was doing was getting something *you* stole from me."

She laughed. "Like the police will believe a punk kid with pins stuck in his mouth over me?"

Alex smiled and reached into one of his pants pockets. Roy watched him slip out some kind of card. Clutching it between thumb and forefinger so she couldn't snatch it away, he held the card out to her. "This cop will."

Losing her smile, Jane looked surprised as she stepped forward to study the card. "Who's Detective Cole?"

Roy was pleased that her voice sounded uncertain.

Alex grinned and pulled the card back, sending it disappearing into his pocket. "He's the cop who told me you stole that package from me. He asked me if he should come see you, but I told him no. Not yet, anyway."

Jane lost all her arrogance, and turned pale.

Alex pointed to the phone on the counter. "Why don't we call him now?"

Jane's eyes narrowed to slits. "You're the most evil child I've ever known."

Alex gasped with shock. "*I'm* evil? I finally get something from my real mother and you hide it from me? *That's* evil, Jane!"

Alex shook with fury, and Roy placed a hand on his shoulder.

Jane backed closer to the door into the hallway.

"That's how you knew about me, isn't it, about my spinning?" Alex went on, pushing himself forward so fast that Jane yelped as she jumped back. "I wanna know what happened to my music box!"

For a split second, Jane looked confused at the change of topic. Then she must've remembered because she said, with far less confidence than before, "I, uh, I sold it."

"You what! That was mine!"

Jane stepped back even more until she was pressed against the spy mirror next to the door. "Some lady showed up last week and offered me a thousand for it. Think I'm going to turn down a thousand dollars for some old music box?"

Alex rolled closer. "What lady?"

"Receipt was in the box. *He* took it." She pointed to Roy like everything was his fault.

Alex continued to fix his eyes on her frightened face. Roy saw beads of sweat creating runs in her makeup.

"You had no right!" Alex shouted. Then he stiffened. "Last week? What'd she look like?"

Jane's expression turned to disgust. "Young, blonde, curvaceous, slutty. The kind you boys like." She tried for a sneer at Roy, but didn't quite make it. "Most boys, anyway."

Alex stiffened even more, and Roy felt his breath catch in his throat. Alex turned to look at him, and Roy met his eyes. It was obvious they both had the same thought.

Ms. G.

Alex turned to Jane, and in a voice colder and less human than Roy had ever heard from him said, "Don't ever talk to me again, Jane. And I'm done helping you be the evil bitch you are. You hurt one 'a them other guys and my cop friend is coming to visit. I'm sure he wants to know about those pictures you got in your closet, them boys you killed."

Jane gasped, and Roy decided maybe she really *had* killed those guys.

Alex wasn't finished. "Course, I'm not sure how you'll be when the cop gets here, cuz I *will* spin you so hard you won't know yer name no more!"

Her mouth dropped open, and her eyes widened with terror, and then she was gone, around and through the door out of sight. Alex glared after her, his breathing heavy, his body tensed and coiled.

Roy approached and touched Alex's shoulder. "You okay?"

"Ms. G. has my music box, Roy."

Roy's throat constricted a moment, and he said, "Sounds like."

"I need to get it back."

Roy nodded. "Yup. And I'm gonna help you."

"Sorry for what she said about you."

Roy tossed off a shy smile, peeking out from beneath his bangs. "I don't mind being called your boyfriend. And she got it wrong, anyways." He pointed to his lip piercings. "They're snakebites."

He grinned, and Alex returned it.

CHAPTER THIRTEEN

SOMEBODY'S WATCHING US, AREN'T THEY?

ROY RETURNED HOME AND TOOK a shower. His mind kept drifting back to that kiss with Alex, despite his best efforts not to go there. Would he ever find anyone like Alex? No. That was a hard reality he'd just have to accept.

The cold water helped clear his head somewhat, but the alcohol in his system gave him that buzzed, unsteady feeling.

He dressed in clean clothes and went to see if his dad had gotten home. Peeking out the side-paneled glass of the front door, he spotted his dad's truck in the driveway next to his, and wandered into the TV room to see if he was there.

He froze. His dad lounged on the couch, head lolling to one side, a beer can in one hand.

"Oh, Dad," he whispered, his body sagging. "You promised."

Nathan's eyelids fluttered open and he peered a moment in sleepy surprise at his son standing before him. Shaking off the sleep, he sat a bit higher. "Hey, Roy. Must've dosed off."

Roy found himself glaring as he pointed to the can. "I wonder why."

Nathan sat up in surprise, glanced down at the can, and then held it out to Roy. "I had a hard day at work, son. This is *your* can. I found it in the trash."

Roy's anger vanished, and he lowered his head in shame. "I'm sorry, Dad. It's just...."

Nathan waited, and when Roy didn't go on he asked, "Just what? I thought we said we'd talk about everything, Roy, be a real father and son like the old days."

Roy knew he must look ashen, because he felt sick. Should he tell his dad about Alex? Would that be disloyal? He decided Alex wouldn't mind because Alex trusted him. So, Roy sat on the couch and explained about Alex finding out his parents had really been his aunt and uncle, and that his real mom and dad had been killed. He left out everything about the spinning. He had to ask Alex first before saying anything about that.

Nathan listened and didn't interrupt. Roy apologized for breaking his word about drinking, but they'd both been so upset and miserable that… He didn't need to finish the thought because his father nodded, and Roy knew he understood the power of sadness.

Nathan searched his eyes and his face, as if expecting him to say something more. "You really like Alex, don't you? Kinda the way you liked that choirboy kid when you was in middle school?"

Roy stiffened. Something about the way his father said those words…. Suddenly, though he'd never given the idea any thought at all, and had always planned to keep it a secret, he said, "I'm gay, Dad."

He expected shock, maybe an outburst, maybe even the silent treatment and a return to the beer. What he hadn't ever imagined were his father's next words: "I know, son."

Roy's heart pulled into his throat and his breathing stopped. In a quiet, breathy voice he asked, "How'd you know?"

"I figured it out when you was twelve, thirteen, and we had those talks about girls." He chuckled. "You never asked me a question. Not one. Then there was that choirboy. Why else would you wanna go to school with him?" He smiled, not in any nasty way, but more like he thought it was funny. "I think your mom had an idea before she passed."

That surprised, and frightened Roy. "I don't act like a girl or nothing, do I?"

Nathan held Roy's gaze with his own. "No, but even if you did, you're still my son and I'd love you anyway." He looked embarrassed, which surprised Roy since he felt like a disappointment right then. "You probably thought I didn't cuz of all the drinking I done, but trust me, Roy, there's nobody more important than you."

Roy's eyes widened. "Not even Dane?"

"Not even Dane. I love him, he's my first born. But his mother turned him against me. We never had a chance."

Roy nodded, digesting this new image of his father. "So, you're okay with me being gay?"

"You don't got a choice, Roy," his father said with understanding, "any more than you an' me had a choice about being special ed in school.

I know now that's all about genetics, but I sure as hell don't understand that science stuff."

He laughed, and Roy joined him, not quite believing this moment was actually occurring.

"So," Nathan went on, "are you and Alex, you know, like, I don't know, boyfriends or whatever the word is?" He sounded uncomfortable, but Roy realized it was only because he wasn't sure what word to use.

Roy lowered his head and shook it. "I wish. But he's straight." He lifted his desolate eyes to his father's face. "I love him, Dad, so much I get stomach aches some times. Do you know that feeling?"

Nathan nodded. "Had it with your mother 24/7, 'specially if I thought she might leave me cuz I did somethin' stupid."

Roy smiled. "I kissed him tonight when we got drunk."

Nathan's eyebrows shot up. "And?"

"He said it was nice. Can you believe that? He's the best friend I ever had."

"Lovers come and go, Roy, but best friends are forever."

Roy nearly cried, but fought back the tears so he wouldn't look weak. "Mom used to say that, didn't she?"

Nathan nodded, and Roy's vision blurred as emotion overcame him. He threw both arms around his dad and squeezed. "I love you, Dad!"

"Love you more."

They stayed together a few moments, and Roy hadn't felt this safe since he was a little boy. For a split second, he considered spilling his guts about everything that had been happening to him and his friends this week, but forced himself not to. He had to talk with Alex first, but he did know for sure they needed a grown-up. It had gotten too big for them to handle.

When they separated, his dad stood and Roy stood beside him. "You'll make some boy very happy one day, Roy, and he'll be damned lucky to have you."

Roy reddened and lowered his gaze to his Converse. "Thanks, Dad."

"What say we make dinner, huh?"

Roy grinned. "That'd be sick."

Nathan gave him a funny look, and Roy laughed with delight. "That means yes."

As they walked side by side from the TV room into the front entry hall, Nathan said, "Give Alex a call and invite him to dinner. God knows that bitch doesn't feed him for shit."

Roy laughed. "I'll call him right now."

***

When Alex got the call from Roy, he was sitting downstairs moping and brooding about what he'd seen on that DVD. The alcohol in his system didn't help. The parents he'd known were really his aunt and uncle, and his birth parents were killed by people who wanted to get him because he was a freak who could wreck the whole world.

Now he understood why people were after him and Roy at the park. Or did he? And why kill Ms. Ashley? *Oh,* he realized, *so Ms. G. could take her place.* But why? To spy on him? If they wanted to kidnap him like his mother said on the DVD, why didn't they? Why try to kill Roy?

Just thinking of Roy made him blush as he felt that tender kiss on his lips, the kiss of someone who'd *actually* fallen in love with him. He couldn't believe it. He remembered something he heard once about how loving someone meant you took the bad with the good, and Roy had sure done that with him.

But I'm not gay, Alex thought, touching his fingertips to his lips and seeing the love in Roy's soft brown eyes. *I'm not anything.* He sank into an alcohol-laced funk.

That was when the phone vibrated in his pocket. He slipped it out and smiled when Roy's sloppy grin and choppy hair looked back at him. He punched the talk button and put the handset to his ear. "Long time no talk." He found himself laughing, despite the pain he was feeling minutes ago. Maybe Roy was the real healer, not him. "Dinner? You know it, fool. I'll be right over."

He pressed end, slid the phone into his pocket, grabbed his hoodie, and pushed himself to the lift.

***

Alex hadn't felt so relaxed in months, despite everything that had been happening. Once they sat down to heaping portions of spaghetti with meat sauce and cans of Coke, Roy shared with Alex about coming out to his dad. Alex felt intense happiness that Roy's dad was okay with it, since lots of parents weren't. He'd heard enough stories.

Roy's dad even joked about what kind of boyfriend Roy might find one day and how he'd better not be "better looking than the old man," causing Roy to blush and playfully shove his dad around. Alex could barely recall such family moments of his own, and it made him feel like he was part of this family, too.

He dug into his spaghetti so they wouldn't see his eyes misting with sadness.

How the hell can I be so happy one minute and sad the next?

He felt eyes on him and peeked out from beneath his hair to find both Roy and his dad no longer clowning, but watching him.

"You okay, Alex?" Roy asked, his voice filled with concern.

Alex pulled a smile for their benefit. "Just being emo."

Roy nodded with understanding, and Alex took a drink of his Coke.

Nathan put down his fork. "Alex, you want for me to adopt you?"

Alex spat out the Coke all over his spaghetti, gagging and choking as the cold liquid went up through his nose and down his windpipe.

Roy exclaimed, "Dad!"

"Sorry, Alex," Nathan said. "I'm special ed, too, so, you know, we kind of just say what's in our head, right?"

Roy leaned in to him. "Did you mean that, Dad? You'd adopt Alex?"

Alex watched the middle-aged man grin like he'd just discovered a thousand dollars hidden under his mattress. "Why not? You don't mind, do you?"

Roy's face exploded with pure delight, something Alex had never seen there before. "Oh, hell, no!" He turned to Alex, shining his excitement right across the table.

Alex's eyes burned with impending tears. He must've looked like he was in pain because Roy's amazing smile faltered and began to crumble. That's when the tears came.

"Oh, shit, I hate crying!" Alex blurted, and pushed himself back from the table and out into the hallway. Nathan said, "What did I say?" and Roy called out, "Alex!" but he needed to be alone, like he'd been his whole life. He rolled himself across the hall into the TV room, and then the dam burst and he cried for the second time that night.

He'd learned through the years not to cry because it didn't do any good and always made the house parents mad, especially when they figured out he was "different."

"Do your black magic on yourself and stop acting like a baby," they'd say, but always from a distance because he made them nervous. No love meant no feelings, and he'd never truly felt any love since he was four. Until Roy. And now Roy's dad. So, he cried.

And that's how Roy found him, crying like a little kid who'd lost his mommy at the mall. But Roy didn't say anything. He just wrapped long arms around his quaking shoulders and held him from behind, hands clasped together with Alex's in his lap, and waited.

Finally, the battling emotions came together within his heart and soul, and Alex's hitching breath slowed to a steady, even rhythm. Roy released him and came around the front of his chair, hunkering down to look into his red, blotchy eyes.

"You okay, Alex?"

Alex nodded, unable to speak.

Roy looked down, refused to meet his eyes. "It's me, isn't it? It's cuz of what I did, how I feel? That's why you don't wanna live with us. It's okay, Alex, I get that. I just–"

He never finished because Alex grabbed him and pulled him into a crushing hug, nearly toppling Roy off-balance onto the hardwood floor. "It's none 'a that, Roy. I love you. It's cuz 'a me, cuz 'a what I am, cuz of what I might do to your dad or you–"

Roy's hand snaked up and covered his mouth, stopping him in mid-sentence. He pulled back so Alex could see his eyes. "You'll never do nothing but make us happy. You know I love you, and I know we can't be together like that, but my mom always said lovers come and go, but best friends are forever. We're forever, Alex, you and me. And my dad wouldn't have said what he said if he didn't mean it. Please, Alex, please be part of our family. I need you. *We* need you."

Alex fought back a resurgence of tears. "I need *you* more. I been on my own for so long...."

Roy's eyes went wide with hope. "Does that mean yes?"

Alex felt a smile slip onto his face before he could stop it. “Yeah.”

“Yes!” Roy shouted so loudly Alex laughed, and Roy was up and shouting, “Dad, he said yes!”

Alex couldn’t help but feel excited to see Roy so childlike in his enthusiasm.

Nathan called from the kitchen, “That’s cool.” There was a pause. “You kids still say cool?”

Roy laughed and rolled his eyes at Alex. “Yeah, Dad, ’cept this is *wicked* cool.”

Another brief pause and then, “Okay, wicked cool it is. But your food is getting wicked cold.”

That made both of them laugh and do the fist bump. Then something occurred to Alex, and he lost his happy grin. “You think maybe your dad can help us find out where Ms. G. lives?”

That sobered up Roy, and he leaned in so they wouldn’t be heard in the quiet of the house. “Maybe. He don’t read great, either. You wanna tell him everything that’s been going down?”

Alex considered a moment. “Maybe. But not tonight. I’m gonna see Father Pat at church in the morning and I’m gonna see if he might help us.”

Roy nodded.

Alex considered for a moment this priest he’d made friends with at St. Joseph’s Church in Hawthorne. Alex wasn’t Catholic, or any other religion, but had wandered into the church a few times to think, and maybe try to figure out the whole God thing and where he, with his freakish abilities, might fit in. This guy, Father Pat, had invited him to help out as an altar boy early on Saturdays or Sundays or both. Alex had made it a regular routine during the past few months because he found the man, and the church, comforting. He and Father Pat had talked about many things, including heaven, but never about his “differentness” and never about stuff like what had been happening to him this week.

“I’m just gonna talk about whatever, and, like, see if he might understand, you know?”

Roy nodded again.

“But I don’t wanna ask him about Ms. G’s address cuz he might wonder and look her up and call her or something," Alex went on soberly. "Think your dad could help?"

Roy shrugged. "I'm sure he will. But what about the, you know," he gulped, his excitement of a moment before replaced by fear. "The graveyard?"

"I looked at them papers you took, and I'm pretty sure one of 'em had my parents' names and the graveyard where they…." Alex trailed off, emotions welling up in him again that he didn't want to deal with. "We can Google it."

"Hey, guys," they heard wafting in from the kitchen. "Your food's gonna be cold as that wind outside if you don't get in here and finish it."

Roy grinned, and Alex returned it. "I'll let my brother go first," Roy said, extending a hand so Alex could lead the way. Alex's grin widened and his heart felt full, for once, instead of empty, as he turned and wheeled across the hall. Roy stayed by his side.

For the remainder of dinner, with Nathan making plans to contact Alex's social worker and clean the house for an inspection, and Roy gushing about how much fun they'd have together, Alex basked beneath a glow of happiness such as he hadn't felt since early childhood. All the danger, all the drama, all the evil and crazy things that had happened this week sunk into the back of his conscious mind because he wanted to cherish this singular moment of pure, childlike delight.

After dinner, Nathan helped them navigate the white pages on the Internet to try and locate Ms. Garrett's address. When he'd asked why the boys wanted to know and who this person was, Alex had partially given the truth: she was someone to whom Jane had sold something left for him by his mother, and he wanted it back.

Alex saw Roy nodding with approval, but Nathan looked concerned, and insisted that whenever they went to see this lady he would go with them. They assured him that would be great, and he retreated to the kitchen to clean up.

Alex hated lying to the man who'd just offered to adopt him, but he couldn't tell the full truth about Ms. G. without going into everything else, and he wasn't ready to do that just yet.

He and Roy agreed to meet in Roy's room with Java and Israel at lunchtime the following day, since it was Saturday. Had all of this stuff happened in just a few days? Yeah, his entire life had changed in seconds, like watching magicians on TV make elephants disappear.

Roy offered to contact the other guys since Alex couldn't use his phone at Jane's house, and Alex promised to give everyone a report on his talk with Father Pat.

As they made their way down the block, shivering against the cold, Alex felt eyes watching him. He glanced around and didn't see any movement. There was a white van parked just up the street on the opposite side that he didn't recognize, but the windows were tinted and he couldn't tell if anyone was in it.

They halted near Jane's house. "Do you feel it, Roy?" he whispered, the cold making his breath vaporous and ghostly.

"Yeah. Somebody's watching us, aren't they?"

Alex nodded, his eyes traveling from the van to the other parked cars to the surrounding homes with their brightly lit windows. Nothing moved.

Weird, especially for a Friday night in Hawthorne. True, it was coldern' hell and that probably kept people inside. But it felt more like everybody knew there was evil out here and were too afraid to meet up with it.

The wind gusted and swirled dead leaves around the wheels of his chair. Roy gasped beside him, clutching his arm in fear. Alex looked up and Roy pointed to the large shade tree bordering Jane's property with Ms. Rhodes'.

The cat sat on one of the lower branches staring down at them.

Alex locked his eyes on those of the animal. It didn't look away. In fact, Alex felt its eyes piercing his soul.

"Whadda we do?" Roy hissed.

Alex paused a moment, studying the animal, searching for clues, trying to spin it, if such a thing were possible. But he could spin nothing. All he felt were darkness and evil.

"You're gonna come in with me and stay the night, if your dad says it's cool," Alex answered, his eyes fixed on the cat. "No way I'm letting you walk home alone."

Roy looked relieved and nodded.

"C'mon," Alex said, and pushed himself into Jane's driveway. Roy followed close behind. Both gave the tree a wide berth in case the cat decided to jump them as they passed.

But it didn't move a muscle. Alex turned when they arrived at his outside bedroom door. The cat hadn't budged, but its eyes were still aimed squarely at him. Shivering, he slipped his key into the lock and pushed open the door. He ushered Roy inside and, with one final look at the cat, he followed.

Roy managed to convince his dad that both of them were too excited to sleep because they were so happy about Alex joining the family, and his dad agreed to let Roy sleep over.

"See ya in the morning," Alex heard from Roy's speakerphone.

"See ya, Dad," Roy answered.

"I love you, son."

Alex grinned, feeling happy for Roy, and for himself. If it weren't for that damned cat, everything would be perfect!

"Love you too, Dad," Roy replied before ending the call.

He sat with Alex and they talked about the cat and the murders and what they had to do the following night. Alex could tell Roy was scared as hell, but then, so was he. But he *had* to find out who he was and why all of this was happening. To do that, he had to get the music box. And he had to dig up his mother's grave.

When both began yawning so much they could no longer stay awake, Roy watched as Alex slid from his chair into bed, pulling his legs smoothly up under the covers.

Alex saw his best friend hesitating, and knew why. He patted the bed beside him.

Roy stood, slipped out of his hoodie and jeans, and stood in his band shirt and boxers. "You sure, Alex, now that you know 'bout me?"

"Wickedly sure. Get in here, fool, I'm freezing my ass off. And I can barely feel my ass."

That made Roy laugh. Shivering against the frigid cold of the room, he flicked off the lights and scurried to the bed, slipping beneath the covers. He looked at Alex a long moment, his expression uncertain. Then he said, "Night," and turned away.

Alex felt Roy's deep discomfort, and spun it from him as they lay side by side. Within minutes, both were sound asleep.

DAY 4

CHAPTER FOURTEEN

SO WE BREAK IN AND STEAL IT

When his alarm beeped at six o'clock, Alex killed it. But he needn't have worried. Roy was fast asleep.

Alex scooted down to the end of the bed, rolled his legs off the edge, and then lowered himself to the carpeted floor. He dragged himself to his chair and pulled himself up and in. Roy stirred, but didn't wake. Alex smiled, recalling dinner the night before, and retreated into his bathroom to get ready for mass.

When he rolled out of the bathroom shirtless, wearing just his boxers, he found Roy sitting up in bed gazing at him with wide-eyed wonder. Roy averted his eyes, but Alex didn't feel any such shame, and didn't want Roy to, either.

"Morning," he offered, wheeling himself to his large chest of drawers to pull out a clean shirt. He felt Roy's eyes on him as he slipped the shirt over his head, covering his chest. He understood Roy's discomfort, though it still amazed him that anyone could find him hot.

Tossing Roy a smile as he rolled to the closet, he said, "I'm gonna head over to the church." He grabbed a pair of jeans from the clothes pile on his closet floor and pushed out to an open area where he had room to change. Reaching down with the pants, he used one hand to load each foot through the leg holes. Then he grasped the pants with both hands near to the rear and pulled them higher.

Roy clambered out of bed. "You need help?"

"Nope." With a wink, Alex yanked hard on the pants and they came up under his buttocks with the ease of daily practice. "See, wicked skills." He grinned, and was happy to see Roy crack a smile. "Uh, bathroom's yours."

Roy nodded with gratitude and made his way to the door.

***

St. Joseph's Catholic Church looked huge to Alex every time he approached. It had tall double doors, a large colorful window that looked like an arch right above them, and a gigantic tower next to the main building. Both the tower and the building had big crosses on top, and the sight calmed him every time he approached. He forgot what those colorful windows were called, but he loved the images they showed, people with bright lights over their heads. He also loved the cool, shadowy interior with paintings and statues and lighted candles all around.

He'd been helping Father Pat long enough to understand about Jesus being the son of God and all, and how we were supposed to treat others the way we wanted to be treated. He wished everyone would do that, but his mind always filled itself with images of being called "crip" or Roy called "retard."

The whole God thing confused him, especially when Father Pat talked about free something or other. He couldn't remember, but it had to do with people making bad choices, like to hurt or kill others. Why would God give that to people and let them do those horrible things if God was supposed to be good?

He couldn't enter the church in front because there were steps and no wheelchair ramp, so he rolled around to where the priests and altar boys went in. Since mass was to begin at seven, and it was already close to that, Alex found Father Pat pulling that white thing that looked like a baggy dress over his head.

The priest broke into a big smile as Alex wheeled himself into the changing room.

"Morning, Alex," he gushed in that deep voice he had. "Wasn't sure I'd see you today."

Despite his anxiety and fears about what was happening, Alex returned the smile. He really liked this man. "I'm always here," he offered with a slight laugh, rolling to the cabinet where his own white dress-thing hung. As he pulled it out, he turned to find the man looking at him, as though seeing something new.

"And so you are," Father Pat replied, grabbing for the long cloth that looked like a scarf and draping it over his shoulders so it spilled down his front on either side.

Alex knew Father Pat wasn't that old, maybe forty or something like that, and he didn't have any gray in his hair. The front was neatly combed and gelled, but the back hung down and covered his neck. He had a smile that put people at ease, and he always acted like Alex being there beside him was the best thing in the world. Alex knew that had to be him unconsciously spinning the man when they talked, especially if the priest seemed down about some bad thing he'd had to deal with. Alex would take the pain away without even intending to, adding it to his own vast pool until he could get rid of it later.

As he slipped on his "dress" and pulled it underneath his buttocks so it covered most of his legs, he watched Father Pat adjusting that little white collar in the small mirror hanging on the wall.

"Father Pat, do you believe in evil?" Alex hadn't meant to blurt it out like that, but he did, and the man paused in mid-motion to look at him.

"What?"

Now Alex suddenly felt foolish, but he needed answers to these questions. "Do you, uh, you know, believe in evil?"

Father Pat turned fully around and leaned against his desk, gazing at the boy with curiosity in his deep-set brown eyes. "You mean like the Devil and demons and all that stuff?"

Alex shrugged. Was that what he meant? Yeah, he'd seen lots of those scary movies where something takes over somebody and makes them do bad things. Could that be happening now? "I guess so."

Father Pat placed both hands behind him on the desk and sat on it, bringing him closer to Alex's eye level. "No, I don't. I haven't bought into that since I was a kid. I know I'm supposed to, but the idea that outside forces influence us to spread evil doesn't make much sense to me."

Alex frowned, now feeling confused since he'd heard Father Pat talk about evil during their church services together. "Then how come there's so much of it?"

"Oh, it does spread, but people are the ones who do that, Alex. Evil is like a living organism, a germ that people pass along to each other, sort of like a cold." Father Pat glanced at his watch. "Almost time."

"Am I evil?" Alex's voice was so low he wasn't even sure the priest could hear him.

Father Pat looked at him with open-mouthed surprise. “You? Why would you think that?”

Alex hadn’t prepared an answer to that question. He didn’t want to tell the priest everything he’d done or could do, so he just mumbled, “Cuz Jane said–”

Father Pat cut him off. “I told you before not to listen to that woman! If anyone’s evil, it’s her. But you, never. You know why you’re my favorite altar boy, Alex?”

Alex shook his head. “No.”

The man paused, as though thinking how to say what he wanted. “It’s because I always feel good after I’ve said mass with you at my side. I confess I get very down, Alex, dealing with so many problems every day, so much cruelty and heartlessness. But you…you make me feel like there’s always hope. You’re a gift from God.”

Alex said nothing, knowing why the man always felt so good around him, and not wanting to give himself away.

“I was very sorry to hear what happened to your teacher. If you want to talk after mass, I’m willing.”

“Thanks.”

Throughout the mass, as Alex looked at the big cross with Jesus on it and heard the prayers, and handed Father Pat the water and wine, his mind kept returning to what had been happening, and how they really needed a grown-up to help figure it all out. On the DVD, his mother had said his aunt and uncle could do that. But they were dead now. He became convinced that Father Pat was the person they needed.

As usual, for a Saturday morning at seven, few people were in the church, mostly older ladies wearing shawls and baggy dresses. But Father Pat acted like the church was full and looked at each of those ladies as he spoke to them in English and Spanish. Alex never had picked up much Spanish, figuring his Special Ed-ness made it harder to learn, but the looks of peace on the faces of those elderly ladies assured him the priest was touching their souls with his words.

After mass ended, when they had returned to the changing room and Father Pat helped pull the “dress” off him, Alex made his decision.

“Um, Father, there’s something I wanna tell you. ‘Bout me.”

Father Pat was hanging up the "dress" alongside his own in the cabinet. "What is it?"

Alex felt his stomach churn with fear. "You said before I'm not evil or nuthin', but there's stuff you don' know."

"Like what?"

"Like…" Alex began, and then fear grabbed him, and he trailed off.

Father Pat must have misinterpreted his reluctance because he said, "You have bad thoughts, or thoughts you think are bad? That what this is about?"

Now Alex felt flustered, his fears jumbling his thoughts and confusing him. "Kinda, I guess…."

"You think about stuff like sex?"

Alex dropped his gaze, recalling how he sometimes thought about Tami.

"I thought so," the priest went on in that way adults always did when they were sure they'd figured a kid out.

But that's not what I wanted to talk about, Alex thought, his tongue failing him when he needed it most.

Father Pat squatted down so he and Alex could be at eye level. "Alex, everyone thinks about sex. Including me."

Alex looked up, surprised.

"Shocks you, huh?"

Alex nodded, though he wasn't sure why. He didn't know much about religion, but he supposed he thought priests gave up even thinking about sex when they became priests.

"Alex, it's human. Thoughts don't make us good or evil. Actions do. Your actions are good, and your heart is good. I've been around you enough to know that."

Father Pat placed a comforting hand on Alex's shoulder, and Alex nodded. But his tongue froze in place and he chickened out. He liked this man and couldn't bear it if he lost that relationship because of what he was – he couldn't handle any more rejection. So, he just offered a weak smile as Father Pat stood and pulled his hand back.

"You coming tomorrow?" the man asked, and Alex clearly detected the hope in his voice.

He smiled from beneath his sheltering bangs. "Where else would I be on a Sunday morning?"

That drew a laugh from Father Pat and Alex took off for home.

***

It hadn't rained the night before, but the sky looked dangerous anyway, and the home screen of his phone showed angry looking clouds and big raindrops, which didn't thrill Alex given what he had planned for that night. He just hoped the others wouldn't chicken out. Roy never would, but Izzy and Java were not as predictable.

As Alex wheeled along the sidewalk toward Jane's house, hungry and eager for even that small bowl of cereal, he spotted Ms. Rhodes sitting slumped on her front porch in a big, old-fashioned rocking chair, head bent in sorrow and crying softly into her gnarled hands. He paused a moment, wondering if he should intrude, and then remembered that he never thanked her for distracting Jane yesterday. He pushed himself up the walkway that split her well-kept lawn in two, and stopped at the foot of the porch, unable to go further.

"You, uh, you okay, Mrs. Rhodes?"

She raised her head. Her pale, leathery skin looked drawn with sadness, and the red puffy eyes glistening with tears struck Alex straight to the heart. It took her a moment to realize he was present.

"Oh, Alex, sweetheart." That was all she said, her tired old eyes almost looking inward at herself.

"What's wrong?" Alex asked. His stomach clenched just being in the presence of suffering. He didn't know why he couldn't handle people in pain, but he couldn't.

"Oh, Alex, my poor brother passed on during the night." She cried again, and Alex wanted to reach up and place a hand on her shoulder, the way Father Pat or Roy would do for him if he was hurting. But the porch wouldn't let him, so he said in a gentle voice, "Jeez, I'm real sorry, Mrs. Rhodes. You wanna talk about it?"

She looked at him with wide-eyed gratitude and proceeded to do just that. As she described the two of them growing up together and how her brother had always protected her and looked out for her and how she loved him even more than she had her late husband, Alex felt his belly fill with her pain and sorrow and loss. It always started in the belly, then spread upward to the chest where it would clamp onto his pounding heart like it never wanted to let go. But it always did let go, and today would be no exception.

Gradually, her sorrow decreased while his increased, and he felt full to bursting. He had to get away from her before she noticed something was wrong with him.

Finally, she sighed, and used a lace handkerchief to dab the leftover tears from her eyes. "I always feel so much better when I talk with you, Alex."

Alex knew his face must look angry, but it was all he could do to hold the pain within him and not start bawling himself.

"You're a good boy," the old lady went on, standing with great effort from the rocking chair and lurching down the steps to him. She placed a hand on *his* shoulder.

"I, uh, I better get home now," he croaked, struggling to keep his voice steady. She'd had a lot of pain in her, and now it was his.

He spun his chair to leave.

"Alex?"

He turned to face her, barely able to keep it together.

Mrs. Rhodes studied him with confusion, but no sadness. Her aged face looked peaceful and calm. "I don't know what it is about you," she murmured, as though talking to herself. "But… thanks."

He nodded, spun and fled her front yard, whipping around the hedge and up Jane's driveway, along the side of the house to his bedroom door. He finally broke, his body wracked with sobs, all of her pain draining out of him like floodwaters.

Juan poked his head out the kitchen door and spotted Alex. He ran over, worry etching his smooth young features.

"Alex, what happened?"

Alex held up his hand as the pain and heartache ran their course through his system. Gradually, the sorrow receded from his heart, released the tightness in his chest, and allowed his stomach to settle back to normal. He stopped crying and regained control.

Juan observed him with a mix of fear and empathy. "You spin somebody, huh?"

Alex offered a small smile to assure the other boy he was all right.

Juan glanced furtively about them, including up at the second floor. Alex followed his gaze and noted that the drapes were closed in all the upper windows. Then Juan leaned down close to Alex's face.

"The other day, when you spin me?"

Alex nodded, his stomach clenching again. *What now?*

Juan looked stricken, like a frightened little boy. "Jane, she have a video camera in the shelf with the cereal, filming you."

That surprised Alex. "Why?"

Juan glanced around and behind him again, but they were alone. "*No sé*. She tole me not to tell. She say she get me sent back to juvy." He bowed his head in shame. "I'm sorry."

This time Alex placed the comforting hand on a trembling shoulder.

"It's cool," Alex assured him. "But what's she gonna do with that video?"

Juan shrugged.

As though I don't got enough problems, Alex thought with anger as he followed the other boy into the house for breakfast. He couldn't move in with Roy soon enough!

***

The Hawthorne Police Department was a modern, plain two story building on Hawthorne Boulevard near the corner of Broadway. Cole sat at his desk within the Homicide Division squad room gulping coffee and gazing at some photos.

He examined Maribel Lopez's body as it had been found – dumped beside a tree in Eucalyptus Park with multiple stab wounds to the chest and abdomen. He flipped through the pile for the third time, studying the symbol carved into her forehead with some kind of sharp knife. Trails of dried blood wended their way down her face and onto her sweatshirt, but the symbol was clear enough to make out, and the lab had enlarged those shots so he could have a better view.

Gordon approached with a fresh mug of coffee and some donuts. He offered the box to Cole, but the other man waved it off. Gordon sat beside Cole to study the photos as he chewed off a huge bite of donut and washed it down with coffee.

"This is one sick puppy, partner. Serial, you think?" He took another bite.

"Not yet."

"Any leads come in?"

"Only this." Cole pointed to the enlargement of that symbol carved into her head. "Gotta be there for a reason."

"You ever see anything like that before?"

Cole looked up so quickly that Gordon stopped chewing.

"What?"

Cole shook his head. "Nothing. This case has me rattled. I'm sure this killing is connected to the teacher's death."

"And to your little bitch boy in the wheelchair," Gordon spat derisively. "Prophetic dreams, my ass. That kid knows something about these murders. I'll bet my bottom dollar on that."

"He does know more than he thinks he knows, that's obvious, but we're not going to learn what it is by treating the kid like shit or scaring him. In the meantime, this symbol is the key."

Cole tapped one index finger on the enlarged image of the symbol. It showed a circular web-like pattern set within a triangle. "We find this symbol, we find our killer."

***

Alex's fingers fiddled with the necklace while watching, for the second time, the video of a mother he didn't remember, except in dreams, reveal his life story.

Roy sat beside him, his arm resting on the wheel of his chair, while Israel lounged in the beat-up beanbag chair and Java sat cross-legged on Roy's unmade bed. Alex's fingers absently rubbed the fleshy web-like pattern as he fought hard against the tears burning his eyes.

When the moment arrived for his on-screen mother to play the music box, Alex stuffed in his ear buds and cranked "City of Angels" on his iPod to drown it out. He didn't want to zone again, especially since he had no idea what he did while zoning. The image of himself covered in blood the night Maribel was killed sent quaking shivers throughout his body.

Java's serious features remained impassive as he leaned forward with veiny, muscular forearms across his knees, while Israel fidgeted, munched on Hot Cheetos, and listened to the sounds of Roy's dad tromping around upstairs.

When the video came to an end, Roy turned off the television.

His mouth full of Hot Cheetos, Israel mumbled, "What the hell was that?"

"That was Alex's real mom, Izzy," Roy said, unable to hide his annoyance. "Didn't you get that?"

Israel's eyes flew open and his Cheetos-stuffed mouth ceased chewing. "No shit?" The words came out "O it."

Roy attempted to explain the video in a way Israel could understand. Java sat and listened, which irked Roy because he wasn't sure the other boy understood it either.

"So, Alex is some weird-ass freak who's gonna, like, turn the world into the walking dead or something?" Israel had swallowed his Cheetos and set the bag in his lap. He stuck his orange fingers into his mouth to lick off the residue.

"No, fool," Java said, finally coming to Roy's rescue. "He just got that spinning thing and people killed his folks over it. Right, Roy?"

Roy nodded.

Java turned to Alex. "What you need me for, Alex? I got your back."

Alex had watched the exchange with swirling emotions. Here they were, a bunch of dummies who couldn't read or write, who could barely make sense of his mother's words, and it was up to them to save the world? If he hadn't felt so stressed out, he'd have laughed.

He met Java's gaze straight on, and swept the careless bangs off his face so his blue eyes were visible. "You're not gonna like it."

"Try me."

"Jane sold that music box to somebody and I aim to get it back."

"So, we break in and steal it."

Alex nodded, exchanging a quick look with Roy, who also brushed away his sheltering hair.

"We know who gots it," Roy said.

Java's eyebrows shot up as Israel stuffed more Cheetos between his orange lips.

"Who?" Java asked.

"Ms. G.," Alex answered, and Israel spat out his Cheetos in surprise, spraying bits of reddish-orange all over Roy.

"The sub? We're gonna break into her place? Shit, man, she prob'ly gots, like, panties lying around everywhere and shit!"

"Izzy, what are you talking about?" Alex asked, beginning to feel it was a mistake to involve the other boy.

Israel swept a hand across his orange lips and said in his rapid-fire way, "That's what hoes do, right, like, take off their panties and bras and shit and leave 'em lying around everywhere?"

"Focus, Crack Head," Java said, repeating the word so often used by Ms. Ashley. "We ain't goin' there to steal her panties, fool, we're goin' to get Alex's shit back!"

"Well, how we know she not gonna be there screwing some crippled guy?" Israel went on without pause, Java's words barely seeming to register.

Alex's eyes flew open in shock, and he was about to respond when Roy said, "The hell, Izzy?"

Israel plowed on, clutching his Cheetos bag like it would save his life. "She's a hoe, right, we seen that at school with them tight-ass dresses and shit, and she got a thing for cripples, right, cuz she put her hand on Alex, so she might have some crippled guy in there and we'd, like, walk in and–"

Roy snatched up a roll of duct tape and threw it at him. Israel dropped his bag to fumble for it. The Cheetos spilled out onto Roy's dirty carpet, but the sudden need to catch the tape stopped Israel's mouth. Ms. Ashley used to do that as a reminder that he needed to pretend his mouth was taped shut.

Israel regarded the tape a moment before opening his mouth again. This time Java's upraised fist closed it.

"I'm gonna ADHD yer face, fool, if you don't shut the hell up!" he said, and that did the trick.

Israel recoiled and deflated. "Okay, I can do that."

Alex made to speak again when Israel mumbled, "I think."

Up came Java's fist again and this time Israel ripped off a piece of the tape and stuck it over his mouth. Satisfied, Java lowered his fist and turned to Alex.

Alex explained how Roy's dad helped them find out Ms. G's address and that they'd have to go there, break in, and get the music box.

With Israel threatening to remove the tape, and only Java's upraised fist stopping him, the others made plans about who would break in and who would stand guard. They'd found her phone number online and would call from outside the building before entering to make sure she wasn't home.

Java nodded, accepting that his role was the muscle guy, like always. He'd do any heavy lifting necessary, and he was a good fighter if anyone tried to stop them.

"How you gonna find her place when you can't read them street signs?" Java asked.

Roy slipped his phone from his pocket and held it out. "Google voice, fool," he announced like he invented it. "It tells me everyplace to turn and when to stop. It's pretty wicked."

Java's eyes widened in admiration. Since Roy was the only one with a driver's license, Alex figured the others had never thought of that option.

There followed a moment of silence while everyone waited for Alex to continue.

"We gotta do something else, guys, after we get the music box."

"Yeah?" Java asked.

"You heard my mother. She hid the truth about me. And I need to get it."

Java looked confused a moment. "But isn't she, like, in the ground?"

Alex nodded.

Java got it then, and his eyes widened with horror. Israel looked clueless. His head was tilted to the side as though replaying the punch line of a joke through his brain to see if he got it or not.

"We gotta go to that graveyard and dig up the coffin to get it out," Alex said, his stomach churning in knots at the thought.

Now Israel's eyes became the size of boiled eggs and he yanked off the tape so fast it made a loud *rrriiipppp* sound. "The hell? You want us to dig up a dead body? You crazy, fool? What if she's a zombie or shit or her ghost comes after us or–"

Roy held up a fist this time. "Dumb ass, that's Alex's mom we be talkin' 'bout, so shut yer mouth!"

"It's okay, Roy," Alex murmured. "Chill."

Roy fixed his angry eyes on Alex and the ire dimmed. He lowered his fist and glowered at Israel, who for once had the good sense to stay quiet.

"It's the only way, Izzy," Alex said. "I gotta find out who I am, what I am. You guys are the only friends I have, and I need your help. But I get it if you don't wanna. No hard feelings."

Israel listened, his terrified expression softening as Alex's words hit home. He looked down in shame. "Just scares the shit outta me, s'all."

Alex rolled over and placed a hand on Israel's shoulder. He found it trembling with fear. "Me too."

Java stuck out his fist flatways into the center of their grouping. "Well, I'm in."

Roy placed his fist atop Java's and awaited the others. Alex removed his hand from Israel's shoulder and placed it atop Roy's. Now all of them fixed their eyes on Israel, who sat a moment in uncertain silence. With a heavy sigh that spoke more than all the words he usually babbled, he stood and opened his hand, placing it atop Alex's.

They were ready.

CHAPTER FIFTEEN

YOU MEAN SHE KNOWS WE'RE HERE?

Ms. G. lived in a two-story apartment complex on Doty Avenue, not far from El Tercero Boulevard, and a short drive from Mark Twain High. The front entrance was on Doty, but there was an alley behind the building wide enough for trash trucks to drive through on pickup day.

After Roy's dad helped them locate the address, Alex and Roy had tinkered with the different Google map views to try and locate where in the complex her apartment was situated. In a stroke of good luck, her apartment was in the rear and there was even a little balcony jutting out over the alley. Roy had commented that "Only in Hawthorne would they put one of those things over a dirty-ass alley," and Alex had chuckled.

None of them chuckled now. It was after ten. Roy and Alex had swung by and picked up Java and Israel after they snuck out their windows and crept to the corner.

All of the boys wore dark pants and sported black or navy blue hoodies with the hood up in case someone should spot them breaking in.

Roy eased his truck into the alley and stopped beside a large dumpster with the lid standing open. The dumpster overflowed with plastic trash bags and other garbage.

By the time Roy got around to the bed, the others had jumped out and Java was already wheeling Alex's chair toward the passenger door.

Once Alex was in his chair, the boys looked around. The sky appeared angry again, with rain clouds threatening to attack them at any moment. Traffic sounds were constant from El Tercero Boulevard, but Doty was quiet.

Roy scanned the upper floors. Some of the windows were lit, some dark. He counted balconies from the corner until he came to her apartment. The window was dark. There were no people sounds, not even the loud music that usually accompanied Saturday nights in Hawthorne.

He looked to Alex for confirmation, and Alex nodded. He turned to the other two and pointed at the dark windows on the second floor. Israel looked ready to say something, but Java clamped a hand onto his mouth before he could. Roy watched as the trembling Israel calmed enough for Java to remove his hand.

Roy snatched his small pick set from the truck and slipped it into his pocket. Alex dialed the number they'd found for Ms. G. They didn't know if it was a home or cell number, but all had agreed that to hang up if she answered.

The phone rang in Alex's ear while the others shifted their weight from side to side and glanced around. Roy studied Alex's face as he listened. Alex hadn't said it, even to him, but Roy knew how hard all of this was on him, finding out about an entire past he'd never known, having to break into this woman's apartment, not knowing if she was part of the group that wanted to kidnap him, and lastly having to dig up his mother's grave. Roy felt sick about doing that. It just seemed so wrong....

Alex lowered the phone and pressed the end button. "Voicemail," he said, his voice a harsh whisper cutting into the darkness.

Roy's gaze drifted to Israel. The other boy was practically dancing with nervousness.

Oh, crap, he didn't take his meds like he promised!

As though on cue, Israel said, "Probably out looking for some cripple to screw."

Java's upraised fist silenced him, but Roy knew that wouldn't be the last outburst. This night just got a whole lot crazier.

They sent Israel around to the front. His job was to hide across the street and call Roy's number if Ms. G. showed up. That would give them time, Roy hoped, to get away before she got upstairs.

Roy had spent the afternoon creating a makeshift grappling hook like he'd seen in the movies. It wasn't fancy—just some old railroad spikes he'd found near the tracks that ran though Mark Twain. He'd tied them tightly together with strong wire, angling them out so they would be able to hook around the balcony railing, and then he used his dad's welding machine to lock the wiring in place and secure his "grapple."

He reached into the bed of his truck and pulled it out, along with the coil of rope he'd attached to it. As Java was stronger and used to play football, he'd been selected to toss the grapple up to the balcony in the hope that it would catch on the first try and minimize the noise. Roy handed over his creation.

Java gave him the chin nod and craned his neck upward, gauging the right angle. He took a moment while Roy and Alex watched in anxious silence. Then he stepped back, held the coil of rope in his left hand and let the grapple dangle from his right. He twirled it around and around. Up went his right arm and the grapple sailed into the darkness above.

The meager lighting of the alley made Roy squint as he watched the grapple fly up and over the second-floor balcony, where it came to rest on the floor with a solid *thud* sound.

Java tugged gently on the dangling rope. Roy's breath ceased as he watched the grapple drag along the floor of the balcony before rising upward along the metal bars of the barrier. It caught in the top railing, the spikes locking between the upright bars and the crossbeam. Java tugged, and it held. He turned to Roy with a grin.

"Sweet."

Roy exhaled and grinned nervously. He hated to have any of his inventions, no matter how simple, fail. And this one was crucial.

Now for the tricky part.

He looked down at Alex, whose upraised face bore no expression. "You ready?"

Alex nodded and Roy turned to Java. Java got the message and grabbed the dangling rope with both meaty hands. Using just his upper body strength, he pulled himself up and was over the balcony railing in seconds. He looked down and even though Roy couldn't see his face, he knew the other boy was grinning.

Roy glanced down at Alex. "Your turn."

Alex wheeled to the rope. He grabbed it with both hands, tugged to make sure it was secure, and began his hand over hand ride to the top. As always, Roy marveled at his strength. In less time than it had taken Java, Alex was up to the railing and pulling himself over. Java reached out to lift him up and set him down onto the balcony floor.

Never athletic, Roy had once in a while lifted weights with Java, and did use his own dumbbells with some regularity, but his tall, skinny frame and lack of muscularity were always an area of worry for him. He grabbed the rope, pulled himself up, wrapped his feet around it, and began the laborious, terrifying climb upward.

The rope swung and dangled like a twisting snake in his hands, and he was sure he'd fall several times. It took him much longer than the other two, but when he finally reached the railing Java lifted him over and Roy gasped at how hard Java's arm muscles were as the bigger boy set him down.

They had decided to leave Alex's chair in the alley in case of a quick getaway, and because they didn't want to take the time to haul it up to the second floor.

Roy doubled over, panting from the exertion, while the other two waited. He finally looked at Alex, sitting on the balcony floor, and offered a hangdog grin.

"Gotta get in shape like you guys," he whispered, and Alex grinned.

Roy stood to his full height. Java nodded his head toward the sliding glass door in front of them and Roy stepped forward. He slid the tools from his pants pocket, examined the door lock a moment before selecting one and getting to work. He felt Alex's eyes on him as he squatted down and poked his tiny tool into the locking mechanism. A few twists and turns and then the silence was broken by an almost inaudible click. They were in.

He stood and stepped back. Java would remain on the balcony to watch the truck and Alex's chair. If anyone showed and tried to mess with either, Java was the man to scare them off.

Roy cracked open the glass door and eased the hanging drapes aside. The lights were off and the place looked empty. He breathed a sigh of relief and slid the door all the way open. He turned to Alex. Alex nodded. Roy squatted down so Alex could wrap his arms around his neck. Then he wobbled to his feet, forcing himself not to grunt as he reached behind to grab Alex's dangling legs. Either he'd gotten weaker, or Alex was bigger because this was a lot harder than the last time he'd carried him. With his friend wrapped securely around his back, Roy stepped past the curtains.

***

Davalos was about to leave his office when a call came through on the secure line. He snatched it up.

"Davalos." He listened a moment. "We need that information." He paused. "It's imperative he trust you or we could blow the whole operation." Another pause. "Very well, keep on it. Don't screw this up. You know our timeframe. No margin for error. Call when you have something solid."

He slammed down the phone.

***

Alex let go of Roy's neck with one hand to slip the tiny LED flashlight from his front pocket and flick it on. He panned the room with the small beam. It looked like an ordinary living room: sofa, some chairs, lamps, and tables. Nothing fancy.

Roy lumbered through the dark, glancing down periodically to make sure he wouldn't trip over anything.

He stopped at an entertainment center, listening for any movement within the apartment. Nothing but silence. He lowered himself to his knees so Alex could reach out and pull open the double doors of the entertainment center. There were some CDs in there, but little else except a weird smell, like some kind of herb or spice, though nothing Roy could recall his mother ever using. Alex closed the doors and Roy muscled his way to a standing position.

"You can put me down, Roy," Alex whispered in his ear. "I can crawl."

Roy shook his head. "No. I got you." Even though he barely did, he hated seeing Alex on the floor, crawling like a helpless baby. Alex was strong and full of power, and that's how Roy needed to see him.

"Bedroom," he whispered hoarsely, and started down the small hallway. There was an open bathroom door on the left and a closed door at the end. If she had hidden the music box anywhere, it would most likely be in her bedroom. What if she was hiding there with a knife? Or what if… Izzy's talk of panties lying everywhere nearly made him laugh and he had to force it down.

Inching cautiously forward, he glanced into the bathroom before sticking his head all the way in. Empty. Phew! Pulling back, he looked sideways at Alex, who had twisted his neck to make eye contact. Alex's fearful expression mirrored his own. Not only could they be arrested for this, but if their teacher *was* part of the group that killed Alex's parents, they were in real danger.

He offered a smile he wasn't sure Alex could even see in the dark, and continued down the hall. His back and shoulders ached, and his biceps screamed with burning fatigue, but no way would he make Alex crawl. No way in hell!

Step-by-cautious-step, Roy moved down the dark hall to the closed door at the end. He stopped, his ragged breathing the only sound assaulting his ears. Alex's hand reached out and clutched the knob. He turned it, and the door pushed inward.

The room was dark, like the rest of the apartment. Alex swept the beam of light around the interior. There was a big bed, neatly made, nightstands on either side, a chest of drawers, some paintings on the walls. Looked ordinary to Roy, who sighed quietly, and then thought of the panties again. He stifled a chuckle.

"What?" Alex whispered into his ear.

"No panties," Roy whispered with a nervous laugh.

Alex sniggered.

As Roy stepped into the room, flickering light from behind the door caught their attention. Alex swung the beam to his right, and stiffened.

Roy's breath froze as he followed the beam of light. Off to one side, against the same wall as the door, stood a kind of altar, with flickering black candles casting a creepy glow on the contents of the table. Glancing around, Roy hefted the slipping Alex a bit higher and inched toward this strange looking table with its weird items.

He leaned closer to get a better view. There were two carved statues about as big as his hand, a male and female, but distorted and creepy, with jeweled eyes that glittered in the candle light and seemed to follow him as he moved. What looked like a goat skull sat in the middle with big curved horns. The white of the bleached bone sent chills down Roy's spine. Several stone bowls filled with different colored powders were set on either side of the two statues. The candles were numerous, arranged in a triangle. Set within the triangle of candles was some kind of webbing, almost like spider silk, but thicker. And under the webbing, like food awaiting the spider, was Alex's music box.

"There it is!" Roy blurted, cursing himself for the outburst.

"Yeah," Alex agreed with a nervous sigh. "And look what's covering it."

Roy studied the webbing again, and something clicked in his memory.

"It's like the necklace, Roy, the one I found."

Roy stiffened. That was it! It *was* the same.

"Put me on the bed," Alex whispered.

Grateful for even a brief respite, Roy backed a few steps to the edge of the bed and sat carefully so as to not crush Alex with his weight. He released Alex's legs and Alex let go, and then Roy was free. He scooted over next to his friend, feeling the warmth of Alex's hand brush his as he did, and shuddered at the weird stuff laid out before him.

Alex offered a grin. "Don't tell Izzy we was on her bed. He'll freak."

Roy almost laughed, and that felt good. His stomach was knotted up and his back ached from carrying Alex. That second of relief meant a lot.

Alex slipped the medal out from under his shirt, and shone his flashlight beam on it. It was identical to the web protecting the music box.

And then it began to glow.

"Oh, shit!" Roy blurted, clamping a hand over his mouth as he recoiled.

But Alex didn't say anything. He just stared at the glowing medal in his hand and then looked at the larger version covering his property.

It began to glow, too.

"What do you think it means?" Roy whispered.

"An alarm maybe?"

Roy's eyes grew so wide the whites flashed. "You mean she knows we're here?"

"Somebody does. You feel it? We're bein' watched again."

Roy leaped up and snatched the flashlight from Alex, waving its beam back and forth around the room. There was no one there. "Are you sure?"

Alex nodded. He glanced at the table, and his music box. "Think you can get that out from under?"

Roy swung the flashlight toward Alex so fast that his friend blinked furiously. Roy lowered the beam. "Sorry," he said, his voice barely functioning as he gulped with terror. "You, uh, you want me to, like, reach in there?"

Alex looked at Roy with obvious embarrassment. "I'm sorry, Roy. I would, but I can't." He indicated his position on the bed and the table several feet away.

Roy gulped again, and nodded. He inched forward, half expecting something to come flying at him like the other night in his garage. But nothing moved except the candle flames. He stopped just before the table. The colored powders looked scary in the guttering candlelight, and he kept his eyes off the goat skull altogether. He examined the glowing web, and the fancy-looking music box beneath it.

"Think there's electricity if I touch it?"

Alex shrugged, glancing around the shadowy room.

Turning to the web, Roy exhaled, fought his thrumming nerves, and reached out to touch the tip of his index finger to one of the strands. Revulsion filled him, and he yanked it back, his entire body trembling.

"What?"

He turned, his heart pounding, his eyes wide with disgust. "It felt like…." He couldn't say it.

"Like skin?"

Roy nodded with surprise. "Yeah. How'd you…."

Alex held out the medal dangling from his neck. "This feels the same."

Heart thudding, Roy returned his gaze to the webbing, and the music box. He leaned down to get a side view, gauging how much space there was between the webbing and the table. The music box was at least as tall as his middle finger and the webbing didn't quite touch the top of it. Yes, he could slide his hand under. But what would happen when he touched it? Would the webbing suddenly grab his hand and not let go?

Alex's eyes were fixed on the open door to the hall. Roy followed his gaze, but saw nothing. It was now or never. Sucking in another breath and releasing it, Roy squatted on his haunches, and with extreme care not to touch the webbing or the tabletop, slid his hand between the two and inched it closer and closer to the music box.

Silence surrounded him. There was Alex's breathing, and his own raspy, anxious breaths, but nothing else. He touched the plastic of the music box. Nothing happened. He exhaled and relaxed slightly. Wrapping his long, slender fingers around it, he slid the music box toward him.

With a hideous screech, the cat landed on the table behind the webbing and swiped at his face with a massive forepaw.

Roy yelped in surprise, yanked out his hand and tumbled back, landing on his butt and scuttling up against the bed. Alex's leg brushed his shoulder, but he kept his eyes riveted to the massive, crouching animal before him. It opened its mouth. Sharp, jagged teeth gleamed in the candlelight, and it let loose with a fierce growl that sounded more like a tiger than a housecat.

Roy jumped when Alex's hand landed on his shoulder. "You okay?"

Roy nodded.

"Did it scratch you?"

Roy shook his head. He wanted to look at Alex because that would make him feel strong. But no way would he turn away from that cat.

Please don't talk, he thought, his mind numb with fear

And that's when his phone vibrated insistently in his pocket.

Oh, shit! He yanked it out and opened the call. Izzy's frantic voice poured forth, "She's coming, she's coming! Get the hell outta there!"

The voice was so loud even the cat looked startled.

Alex reached for the phone and said, "Izzy, stay calm, man. Stop yelling or she's gonna hear you. Where is she?"

"Just went in the front gate," came the frantic, but quieter response. "Hurry!"

"Got it." Alex ended the call and handed the phone to an anxious Roy. "We gotta jet now." He glared at the cat. "I'm gonna get my music box back. You'll see."

Roy turned to look at the cat. It titled its head. It was listening, and it understood.

Please don't talk!

"C'mon, Roy," Alex said, nudging him with one hand. Roy didn't need to be told twice. Keeping an eye on the cat, he scrambled to his feet, squatted so Alex could wrap both arms around his neck, and lifted his friend off the bed. Clutching Alex's legs against his trembling body,

Roy pelted for the bedroom door. He was so terrified he ignored Alex's warning to shut the door behind them.

But Roy had had enough. He wanted out of there. He needed to get away from that creepy altar and that evil cat. He lumbered down the hall and through the living room to the sliding glass door. "Java!" he hissed.

Java shoved aside the drapes and stood in the apartment before them.

"She's coming!" Roy said, breathless and frantic.

Java didn't panic, but merely stepped to one side and pulled back the drapes for the others to pass through. Then his face twisted with shock. "Oh, shit!"

Roy whirled and nearly tripped over his own feet as the cat loped into the living room after them. Roy cussed silently and turned to Java. Just as he was about to stumble through the opening onto the balcony, the heavy glass door slammed shut, and the lock clicked into place.

Roy pulled up short to keep from colliding with the glass, and a startled Java turned to grab for the handle. The door wouldn't budge. He grasped the lock switch in his thick fingers and struggled to release the latch, but gave up with a grunt.

"It's stuck!" he hissed, turning to face Roy with hints of panic on his normally stoic face.

"It's not stuck," Alex said. "That bitch locked it."

Roy glanced back and saw Alex's eyes fixed on the cat, which now sat looking at them as though it had no worries in the world. But Roy could tell where its gaze rested – on Alex.

Alex stared at the cat with dangerous fury. "You listen good, bitch. I don't know what you are, but if you don't let my friends go, I'll spin your ass so hard there won't be nothing left to send back to Hell or wherever you came from!"

The cat flinched and moved back a few paces, which stunned Roy. He even heard a muted, "The hell?" from Java behind him. But he kept his eyes on the cat. It almost seemed to be thinking, but that didn't make sense, did it? Roy heard a click, and the door was flung open by Java.

"C'mon, guys, let's go!"

Alex stiffened on Roy's back. "She's coming."

Shit! Roy spun and followed Java out onto the balcony. Java slammed the door shut and turned to face them, panting from fear. "You go first, Roy, you're the slowest."

"I'll go last," Alex said. As Roy turned his head to protest, he added, "I'm the only one that can control that thing. Now put me on the railing and go!"

Not liking this plan, Roy backed up so that Alex's butt rested atop the railing. Java supported Alex until he had both hands firmly grasping the cold metal so he wouldn't fall over the side. Roy turned with wide, beseeching eyes.

"You gotta get down there first and start the truck, Roy," Alex whispered, offering a tiny smile. "You know I never fall."

His stomach in knots, Roy nodded and slid over the railing. With Java holding onto the top of the rope to support the grapple, he wrapped his legs around the twisting coil and began his descent. He had to hurry, but dangling like this in mid-air scared the crap out of him. Images of Alex's face, strong and confident, gave him courage and he quickened his hand under hand pace. A few feet from the ground his forearm cramped and he yelped with pain, releasing the rope and slamming hard into the asphalt of the alley. He landed on his butt and fell backwards, twisting just in time to avoid hitting his head.

He looked up and saw Alex craning his neck around. Java practically leapt over the rail to grab the rope, and began his descent. Roy stumbled to his feet as Java athletically navigated the whipping rope, barely requiring the use of his legs. Just as he neared street level, there was a groan and snap of metal, and Roy looked up to see his homemade grapple break apart. The pieces flew downward straight at him.

He leapt to one side. Java crumpled to the ground, and covered his head as the railroad spikes slammed into his shoulders and back. He grunted in pain and rolled over, the wind knocked out of him. But Roy was already looking upward.

The rope was gone.

Alex had no way down.

"Alex!" Roy called out, louder than he'd intended, fear controlling his common sense.

Java rolled over and clambered to his feet, clutching his left shoulder in pain. But his gaze was also on Alex stranded two stories above. "What we gonna do, Fix-It-Man?"

Roy looked around. His gaze fell on his ruined grapple. The welds had snapped and it was now a useless collection of railroad spikes. He stumbled to the wall below the balcony, his right ankle shooting pain into his brain. He ignored it and focused on a runoff-pipe snaking up the wall past the balcony all the way to the roof. He gripped it and pulled. Seemed solid enough. He stepped away and looked up at Alex. Trying to keep his voice steady, he called up, "Can you get to this drain pipe over here? You could use it to climb down."

Alex nodded, but didn't answer. Roy became frantic, wondering how close she was now. She could find Alex any minute, and he was helpless without his chair.

Java rushed over. "The hell, Roy? He's gonna climb down that pipe?"

"You know he can." Roy's eyes remained fixed on his best friend as Alex used his arms to push himself to the corner of the railing, and make the turn toward where it attached to the wall.

Alex had the ability to climb just about anything with his arms alone, but watching his best friend reaching out over empty space two stories up for a pipe that might or might not support his weight filled Roy with terror. He held his breath as Alex's left hand closed around the pipe. He nearly cried aloud when Alex tumbled off the railing, grabbing for the pipe with his right hand.

Roy's breathing stopped for those few seconds as Alex seemed to float in midair. Then Alex's other hand encircled the pipe and his chest slammed hard into the wall. He grunted in pain, but held his grip. And then, like apes Roy had seen at the L.A. Zoo with his mother when he was seven, Alex shimmied down that pipe like it was the easiest thing in the world.

Until his extra weight snapped the brackets holding the pipe to the wall and it tipped backwards.

Roy cried out. Java cussed as the pipe swung out from the wall at an angle with Alex dangling.

"Hang on, Alex!" Roy cried.

"Whadda we do?" Java hissed, his body crouched like a cougar ready to spring.

The rainwater spout above Alex's head snapped and came straight down with alarming speed, bringing Alex along with it. Roy and Java dove forward to break Alex's fall, and he slammed into both of them, letting go of the spout as he did and sending them all sprawling to the ground in a jumble of arms and legs, the spout landing atop Alex with a hard smack to his shoulder.

Momentarily stunned, Roy looked up from beneath Alex and Java at the balcony above. The cat had its huge head between the bars staring down at them. Then a muffled female voice called out from somewhere above, "Mr. P, where are you?"

"Guys, she's there!" Roy hissed. "We gotta hide!"

He and Java disentangled themselves, wincing with pain, and stumbled to their feet. Alex looked stunned, but unhurt.

"Roy, get yer truck outta here," Java hissed. "I'll hide Alex under the balcony."

"But–" Roy began, but Java pushed him toward the truck.

"Now!"

Roy lurched to the driver's door. Pain shot up his ankle and poured through his back and shoulders.

Don't matter, he told himself. *For Alex.*

He clambered up, inserted the key and snapped the ignition forward. The engine gunned to life and he floored the accelerator. He stopped the truck at the end of the alley where it couldn't be seen from her balcony, killed the engine, and limped along the building to where he'd left the others.

He found Java and Alex huddled against the wall beneath her balcony, the wheelchair beside them. Roy mouthed, "Are you alright?" Alex nodded and flung a finger to his lips, pointing upward. Then Roy heard it: her voice wafting out through the night like a nasty fog.

"I can't believe I left this door open," she said, obviously talking to the cat. "Did you have a party with your friends while I was gone? I heard a car racing through the ally just now. Or was it a pickup truck?" Roy heard a loud meow and a laugh from her. There was a pause. "Oh, my, that water spout is broken. How strange. Almost like somebody tried to climb it. Well, we'll just have to report that to the manager, won't we, Mr. P?" She laughed, and Roy's blood ran cold. Her laugh sounded nothing like her laugh at school. This one sounded cold and evil and… dead.

They waited a few more minutes until the door above slid shut. Java grabbed Alex and hefted him into his chair, and then they were rushing down the alley to his truck. They picked up Israel around the block, and he wouldn't stop yammering from the moment he jumped into the truck bed with Java.

Roy drove off into the night, his thumping heart winding down. He glanced at his friend, who sat observing him in the darkness. "You really okay?"

"I'm crippled, Roy, not made outta glass."

Roy's anger flared. "You're not a cripple!" He returned his gaze to the road, his cheeks burning with embarrassment. "Sorry. It's just, you know… I hate hearing you talk shit about yourself."

A hand landed on his forearm and he glanced over.

"I get it, Roy. But I'm okay."

Roy faced forward, cursing under his breath. The disgust he felt for himself, and his feelings for Alex, overwhelmed him. He wanted to cry. "I'm such a loser."

The hand squeezed his forearm with intensity, causing Roy to glance over once more.

Alex's face looked angry. "You'll *never* be a loser!"

Roy felt warmth overtake him. It swirled around his heart and filled his insides with safety and security. He offered a shy smile across the darkness of the cab. "Thanks, man."

Alex pulled his hand back and they drove a few more minutes in silence.

"Let me spin your ankle," Alex said. "I know you jacked it up."

Roy was going to protest, but the pain in his swollen ankle was severe, and he might need to run some more tonight. So, he described the pain, Alex took it, and his ankle felt good as new. "Thanks."

Alex nodded in the dark, obviously feeling aftereffects of the spin.

They drove for a few more minutes, Roy focusing on following the Google voice directions pouring forth from his phone that he'd stuck to the dash. He'd just made a turn onto Florence Avenue when Alex cleared his throat.

"You gonna be, you know, okay, with what we gotta do? I mean, with your mom dying and all…?"

Roy hesitated. It was true, he'd been dreading this part ever since Alex mentioned it, but he hadn't said anything. Leave it to Alex to figure it out.

"I, uh, I can help, you know with the digging and stuff." His mind retrieved memories he'd rather forget. "But I can't open the…." He trailed off, his heart filled with guilt and sadness. "I saw my mom in her coffin and…."

The hand was there again, gentle and warm, even through the sleeve of his hoodie. He looked sideways at Alex, fearing he might be letting his friend down. But the look of understanding on Alex's face calmed him. "It's okay, Roy. Java's got that."

Roy focused on the rain-slicked road, but there was a pause that made him glance back.

"I just need you with me, to keep me strong. 'Kay?"

"I can do that," Roy whispered. "I can always do that."

He resumed driving. Except for the Google voice telling him where to turn and where to stop, no other sounds were heard for the rest of the drive.

CHAPTER SIXTEEN

WHAT IF IT'S EMPTY?

Inglewood Cemetery wasn't far from Hawthorne – the two cities were neighbors – and it didn't take Roy long to reach it. Located off Florence Avenue, it was easily accessible. But Florence was too busy a street for them to try and sneak in unseen, so Roy drifted around the block to the rear of the graveyard where there wasn't even an entry gate. They'd already known they would have to jump a fence. They'd found the place on Google and looked at some pictures. The fence looked high and made of metal, but fortunately had a flat rail along the top instead of spikes like some other graveyard fences.

Roy pulled the truck beneath a thick shade tree that would hopefully shield it from prying eyes. This street was quiet and looked largely untraveled except by residents entering the neighborhood. He killed the engine, and silence surrounded them with such intensity that he shivered. He looked at Alex and found his friend staring at him. He nodded in answer to the silent question. Yes, he could do this. They would do it together.

Cracking open the driver's side door to keep noise to a minimum, Roy slid from the seat out onto the pavement and eased the door closed. He scanned the area. No one was around. Lights blazed in some homes, but otherwise nothing.

By the time he got around back, Java had hefted the chair from the bed and placed it on the ground. Israel stared at the dimly lit cemetery on the other side of the tall metal fence. Roy wheeled the chair to the passenger side, where Alex had the door already open. Java reached into the truck bed for the four shovels they'd brought.

Roy lifted Alex out and placed him in the chair.

"Thanks for doing this," Alex whispered.

Roy was too tense to respond, so he just nodded and turned to Java, who held the shovels. Roy admired his friend. Even after what they'd just been through, Java was cool and calm and ready to do what needed to be done. Roy wished he had that personality type, but he was still rattled by the episode at Ms. G's, and this graveyard gig tore at him for so many reasons. Especially because his mother was buried here, something he *hadn't* told Alex because that would make him feel worse. Roy forced himself to block out those thoughts. His mother was long dead, but Alex needed him. End of story.

He glanced at Israel, shifting from foot to foot as he gazed through the fence at the graves within. Might have been a mistake to bring him, Roy knew, but they needed as many people as possible to dig. Hopefully, the digging would help calm Izzy.

He surveyed the fence. Always bad with numbers, Roy used increments of his hand or height to gauge distance or how high something was. This fence was easily two heads taller than him, and he was five eleven. Getting Alex's chair over wouldn't be easy. They'd have to stand atop the cab of his truck on this side, but there wasn't anything on the other but grass. And his grapple had broken in that alley. He turned to Alex.

"You can climb over that, right?"

"I can climb anything. Let's do this."

Roy turned to Java, who handed him the shovels and scrambled up atop the cab. He reached out, took the shovels from Roy and tossed them one at a time over the fence. They each landed with a soft thud on the grass, the muted sounds disrupting the quiet of the night.

Roy glanced around, but nothing moved and no one was in sight. A quick look at the dark rainclouds overhead reminded him that they needed to hurry.

"Izzy!" he hissed, trying to get his attention. He finally had to go and tap the boy's shoulder, which made Israel jump and cry out in fear.

"Quiet, fool!" Java hissed from behind him.

"C'mon, Java'll help you over the fence," Roy whispered at the terrified Israel.

Israel clambered into the bed and up onto the cab next to Java. Without hesitation, Java cupped his hands together and squatted down so Israel could use the cupped hands as a step over to the fence. Even from below, with darkness surrounding them, Roy saw Israel quaking with fear. It surprised him when Java said in a gentle voice, “It’s okay, Izzy. I got your back.”

Israel nodded and stepped into Java’s cupped hands. With a quick upward thrust, Java powered Israel up onto the top rail of the fence. The other boy grabbed on and swung over, lowering himself and dropping to the soft grass with the ease of a boy who regularly hopped fences.

Now it was Alex’s turn. He gripped the bars of the fence and flew from his chair hand over hand up to the top with his usual monkey-like ease. Then the boy who called himself crippled flung himself up and over and shimmied his way hand under hand back down until Israel eased him onto the lawn beside him.

Now it was Roy’s turn. But first the chair. For being almost indestructible, it was small and lightweight, being built for speed, and Roy always felt strong each time he lifted it above his head. Java took it from him and set it onto the roof of the cab while Roy clambered up to join him. He grabbed the top of the fence while Java gave him a boost, and straddled the metal, wrapping his feet through the bars for support. Maintaining his balance, he reached out as Java handed him the chair. Holding it carefully so he wouldn’t fall, Roy lifted it over the fence and then, holding on to the top rail with his right hand he lowered the chair to Israel with his left. The other boy grabbed it and planted it beside Alex, who slithered in with ease. Then Roy was beside him and Java dropped down right after.

They were in.

Now to find the grave.

They had a map, of sorts. With the graveyard paperwork Alex’s mother had sent was a map that had numbers on it. Roy knew from his own mother’s funeral that those numbers meant where graves were located. One area was circled on the map, and Roy had told them that must be where Alex’s folks were buried. All they had to do was follow the map.

Yeah, he thought, as they stood in a darkened graveyard looking at a paper map with a tiny flashlight beam, trying to figure out just where in the hell on that map they were, *it sounded easy at the time*.

Since he was the only one who drove, the others let him plot their way. But he hadn't been here since last year on his mom's anniversary to put flowers and, well, that had been during the day!

Israel stood keening with fear, his eyes darting everywhere at once, while Java and Alex waited for Roy to figure things out. Their best landmark was a lake near to where Alex's parents were buried. They'd have to wander around till they found it.

"They're near some lake, and there's a fountain, I think, so we should, like hear water splashing, right?"

Java shrugged, but Alex nodded. "Yeah, we will. Let's look around till we hear it."

They moved out into the tree scattered, grave-filled cemetery with nervous anticipation. Java carried the shovels because he didn't trust Israel not to drop them if a gopher ran past in the dark.

The grass slowed Alex's wheels so he let Roy push the chair from behind to conserve his arm strength.

Most of the graves were the small ones like his mom had, just a flat metal plate with names and dates on them. The wind gusted and blew leaves from the fading trees onto the grass, swirling them around their feet as they walked. No one spoke. The silence crushed them. Dark, ominous clouds only added to the horror-film atmosphere, and Roy wished he hadn't watched so many of those movies at Izzy's house.

The grass rose up into hills and mounds, all scattered with graves that they passed between. Roy felt weird, walking on top of dead people like this, and he could hear Israel panting with fear. He was about to approach and calm the boy when Java stepped up and flanked Izzy, offering his own muscular body as protection. The gesture surprised Roy, just like the one atop his truck, given Java's daily frustration with Izzy's ADHD. But the move helped Izzy, who looked at Java and smiled with gratitude.

The flat graves gave way to the kind with tall headstones by the time the splashing of water came from somewhere ahead in the darkness. Roy increased his speed. The tall headstones looked really old, and for some reason they creeped him out more than the newer ones, like somehow older dead bodies would be more likely to haunt them.

The splashing grew louder, and the wind stronger. It also got colder. Roy shivered. Must be the lake water making him cold, he told himself, hoping that was the only reason. The image of that huge, evil cat crept into his mind as he pushed Alex toward his parents' graves. To find out what? That Alex was a bigger freak than he thought? That he might destroy the world some day? Roy knew these things could never happen, not from Alex. But Alex feared himself even more than he feared the cat. And that broke Roy's heart every time he thought about it.

The lake loomed ahead, not too big, but bigger than Roy could calculate using his body-height method. A jet of water shot into the air at its center and fell back, hitting the surface with the kind of splashing sounds he used to make in the bathtub as a child.

Java and Israel stopped by the shore of the lake and turned to face him. Roy let go of Alex's chair and slipped out the map. He squatted down so Alex could see and turned on the penlight. Together, they squinted at the circled spot and tried to figure out which direction it was from the fountain of water.

After a few moments of bobbing his head up and down from the map to their surroundings, Roy thought he'd figured it out. He pointed to their right, to an older part of the graveyard that was a mix of flat plates and stone markers. "Over there."

The others nodded and they set off. They passed through the rows of graves. Even though Alex hadn't said anything, Roy felt eyes on them.

Lots of eyes.

But every time he looked around there was nothing but the wind and rustling leaves and their own cushioned footfalls against the grass.

I'm crazy, he thought, *imagining dead people watching*.

Or maybe it was those creepy-ass stone angels bending toward a grave, hands clasped before them in prayer. Maybe they were watching. Whatever it was, Roy's skin crawled.

This was the section. He stopped pushing Alex, and the others stopped, too. Now was the part they all hated – reading. They had to look at each grave and try to figure out which one belonged to Alex's parents. Alex looked at him and Roy whispered, "The last name starts with 'O,' right?"

Alex nodded. Roy squinted at the paper and found the name. He could tell because there were two names in front of it and that meant the

"O" word was the last name. He pointed to it for Java and Israel. "That's the name we gotta find."

"Are dead people, like, you know, laid out by ABCs?" Israel asked.

Java looked at him in annoyance. "Fool, do you even know your ABCs?"

Israel shrugged. "Some of 'em. I always get stuck around, like, 'G' or 'P' or something like that. I never could–"

Roy whispered, "Just look for a last name starting with 'O.' Then we'll check it with the paper."

Java nodded, but Israel's mouth fell open. "You mean we gotta split up?"

"Just around here, fool," Java snapped, keeping his deep voice low and controlled.

"But there's dead people here!" Israel hissed, his eyes wide with fear.

"That's why it be called a graveyard," Java spat, his temper rising.

"Look guys," Alex said, "you two stick together and me and Roy'll stick together. 'Kay?"

Java grunted, but Israel nodded. "Yeah, that's better."

The two groups wandered off in opposite directions, each with a penlight.

Roy aimed his light while Alex wheeled himself between the graves. The beam struck each headstone or metal plaque long enough for both of them to squint at the last name, and then Roy moved it along to the next. He still felt that sensation of being watched, and it sent chills up and down his spine. The cold, biting wind didn't help, and he kept his hood up and over his head to keep his hair from blowing into his eyes.

He spotted the other flashlight beam a short distance away, but there seemed to be no one else anywhere around. So, who was watching them? Finally, he stepped closer to Alex and leaned down to his face. "Someone's watching us."

Alex peered out from his hood and brushed hair from in front of his eyes. "Not someone. Some *thing*."

Roy froze. "What thing?"

Alex shrugged, which didn't do anything to allay Roy's anxiety. "Dunno. Let's find my...."

He didn't finish, but he didn't have to. Roy nodded and stood, aiming the beam at the next grave over. Graves, actually, he noted, as there were three closer together than usual. He waved the beam so Alex would notice and they headed in that direction.

The three graves had those metal plaques on them so Roy knew they couldn't be super old. Alex wheeled up to them across the well-trimmed grass. There were no flowers on these graves, and like so many they'd already seen, fallen leaves obscured the plaques. Roy stepped past Alex and bent to brush away the leaves with his hand. He stepped back and aimed the light.

Ellie Maracle O'Sullivan

Walter O'Sullivan

Andrew Alexander O'Sullivan

Alex gasped, and Roy examined the names more closely. The last names all started with 'O'. Holding the light in one hand, he fished the paper from his pocket. His numbed fingers nearly made him drop the light. Gripping the paper in one trembling hand, he leaned down to Alex and held it out, shining the beam directly onto the names. It took both of them a moment to process all the letters, and Roy's heart rate quickened.

The names matched!

Alex looked at him with a mix of elation and sadness that touched Roy's heart.

"You okay?"

Alex nodded, but Roy could see, even in the dark, that his best friend was far from okay.

"Get the others," Alex whispered, his gaze once more on the three graves.

Roy scanned the surrounding area. Some distance ahead he spotted the bobbing beam of light and whistled as loudly as he dared. The light ceased moving and Roy waved his hand above his head, shining his light on the moving hand to draw their attention. The other beam changed course and moved in their direction.

Roy stood beside Alex, shivering in the cold, expecting the rain to pour down any moment, watching his best friend sit atop the bodies of the family he never knew. He tried to imagine how that would feel, and couldn't. Sure, he'd been denied the company of his older brother most of his life, and his own mother was buried somewhere in this place, but at least he'd had them and known them and shared memories with them. Alex had nothing but dreams, shadows of who he was and where he'd come from.

His gaze roamed to the grave of Alex's twin. It was smaller than the other two, about the size of a small child or even a baby. His heart sank even further at the thought that this baby might never have gotten to grow up and have a life like his brother.

The others arrived and Roy focused on them. Java was ready to get to work, but Israel looked like he might bolt any second. His eyes roved, his body reacted to every creaking tree branch and rustle of leaves at his feet.

Alex pointed to the first grave, the one whose name started with 'Ellie'. "That's my mother." His voice came out as a whisper against the increasingly loud wind.

"How you know?" Israel whispered.

"Looks like a female name."

Java nodded and thrust a shovel into Roy's hand and another at Israel. Israel jumped in fear, as though the shovel was out to hurt him.

"You can do this, Izzy," Roy offered, keeping his voice steady. "It's for Alex, remember."

Israel moved his fearful gaze from Roy to Alex and must have seen something on Alex's face because he expelled a breath and grabbed the shovel from Java, gripping it like a weapon.

Java turned to the grave. The grass was neat and trimmed, the exact dimensions of the grave unclear. As always with anything involving building or un-building, he turned to Roy, eyes wide with expectation.

Roy studied the ground around the grave and thought of his own mother's coffin, shuddering at the memory. He stepped up near the headstone and used his feet to measure out and then down about as long as he thought a coffin would be. He pointed out where to start digging.

Java went to the front and Israel to the back, while Roy and Alex took the sides. Alex set the brakes on his chair, hefted his shovel and made the first cut into the ground. The others followed suit.

Digging up a grave, especially one that's been in the ground a long time, was not as easy as the movies made it seem, Roy soon discovered.

The hard ground did not want to give way and he had to plunge the shovel downward at times like he was planting a pole into the ground. Java fared better due to the strong muscles in his arms and back, and even Alex managed to break up the hard earth with greater ease than Roy. But poor Israel had the most trouble. His un-athletic and underdeveloped muscles must have felt every strain and every pull as he fought to puncture the ground with his shovel. Roy, who'd done lots of work with his dad installing fences, showed the other boy the proper technique for using a shovel to get the most out of each thrust. While it helped, Israel cursed and swore under his panting breath as he struggled to heft the large clumps of hard earth up and back onto the growing pile behind him. But to his credit, he didn't quit.

Roy had no idea how much time passed as they dug. His hands were too numb to fumble with his phone, and it didn't matter anyway. They had to get this done no matter how long it took. The wind grew icier. It gusted and died, blasting them with leaves and then subsiding, as though trying to warn them off.

Roy locked eyes with Alex numerous times while they dug, and every time he saw the same truth – yes, they were still being watched. And that made him thrust, pull and toss with greater abandon.

Finally, after what seemed like forever, Java's shovel hit something hard. Something wooden. He looked up at Alex.

As the hole had deepened, Alex had been forced to stop digging because he couldn't reach far enough. Now he sat at the top of the deep opening looking down at his friends. He locked eyes with Java and nodded. Java dug around the front of the now exposed coffin, and Roy joined him. Roy remembered how these things could open from the front or the rear, so they likely wouldn't have to completely uncover the whole coffin.

Israel stood back, gaze flitting from side to side, while the other two flung the last clumps of earth up and over their heads. After another few minutes, the front part of the coffin was completely exposed, enough for it to be opened. That's when Roy stopped and looked up at Alex, feeling weak and guilty, but also vulnerable. Alex nodded.

Roy turned to Java and Israel. "I, uh, I already told Alex that I, you know, can't... open it." He looked down at his dirt-covered Converse in shame. "I seen my mom in her coffin and...."

He felt a huge hand grip his shoulder and squeeze. He turned to find Java gazing at him, not with his usual macho expression, but with compassion. "It's chill, man." He jerked his head upward, giving Roy permission to climb out.

Roy practically melted with gratitude. Man, Java just kept surprising him. His mother's words returned to him then: "You find out who your real friends are in times of trouble." He gripped the lip of the hole, threw one leg up and pulled himself out to lie on the grass beside Alex, who extended a hand to help him stand.

Java turned to Israel, who backed away. "Hell no, man, I ain't opening no coffin," Israel blurted, his voice breathless with exertion. "What if she's a zombie?"

Java shook his head in disgust. "Fool. You be watchin' too much shit on TV. I'll do it."

Israel nodded and clawed his way up out of the hole, leaving his shovel behind. Java handed all the shovels up to Roy, who grabbed them and set them aside.

Java stepped forward and placed both feet in the dirt at either side of the coffin. He bent down and searched around with his hands along the side of the box for the latch to open it.

Roy couldn't look. Instead he focused on the face of this boy he loved, whose entire life as he'd known it was about to change. Alex's face looked tight with anticipation, and fear. Roy heard creaking and groaning from below, and instinctively turned. Java had the front lid open, and Roy stifled a gasp at the sight of decaying bones, pieces of a skull and some long straw-like hair that filled him with revulsion. Did his own mother look like this?

Israel keened with fear and murmured under his breath, "Oh, shit!" Try as he might to avert his eyes, Roy found he couldn't. A cold hand grabbed his and he nearly cried aloud. Glancing down he found Alex's pale fingers squeezing his hand with desperate need. He squeezed back.

Java straddled the open coffin, the corpse visible beneath him as he looked up at Alex and awaited permission.

"Go ahead," Alex said.

Java slipped a pocketknife from his jeans and bent to the white cloth lining the inside of the coffin. He slit along the top on the corpse's left side and peeled it away. Roy shone his flashlight beam downward so Java could see better. There was nothing there – just unpainted wood beneath. Java leaned over to the right side and did the same. This time he grunted with satisfaction as he stuck a hand in between the lining and the wood to pull out one of those large brown envelopes people used for mailing. Java stood, looking big and menacing as he raised his arm and held up the envelope.

Alex let go of Roy's hand and tossed him a silent look. Roy stepped to the edge of the hole and took the envelope. Java proceeded to close the coffin lid as Roy handed Alex the thick, heavy envelope. It was sealed inside a large plastic freezer bag. To keep water out, Roy figured.

Alex regarded the stuffed envelope, turning it over and over in his hands as if it contained his entire life. Roy placed his numb hand on Alex's shoulder and squeezed. Alex offered a tiny smile of gratitude, but then his face darkened and his eyes teared up.

By this time, Java was out of the hole and dusting himself off, while Israel crouched nearby. Alex swept their expectant faces with his gaze. "Thank you," he whispered, his voice choked with emotion.

They all nodded, like digging up dead bodies for your friend was something they did every day.

Alex's face took on a pained expression that worried Roy. "I hate to ask after all you guys done…" he began, clearly not wanting to say what was in his mind.

"What?" Roy asked, his teeth chattering from the biting wind.

Alex pointed across the big graves to the tiny one. "I have to know if…. my mother said Andy might be alive." He met their expectant looks head on. "I gotta know if he's in there."

"The hell?" Israel shouted. "You want us to dig up *another* body? Shit, man, that's crazy. Let's get the hell outta here, I'm scared!"

Even Java looked dubious at this new request. "Alex, there be a grave here, so he gotta be in it, right?"

Alex met his gaze. "What if it's empty, Java? What if somebody took him and he's alive?"

Java paused a moment, and shrugged. "You the smart one here." He bent to grab the shovels, thrusting one at Roy and the other at Israel. Roy grabbed his, but Israel scoffed and backed away in terror.

"No, Java, I wanna go home." Despite the manly cadence to his voice, Israel sounded like a lost little boy. He stood wide-eyed and frigid with fear.

Before any of them could respond, Alex said, "Izzy, you're like my brother, man. I wouldn't ask 'cept it's super important. Please?"

Israel's eyes widened with surprise, as though he'd never known Alex thought of him like that. Roy understood. They all used to run their own program before Alex joined the class. But somehow, just by being Alex, he'd turned them into a weird kind of Special Ed family.

Israel stepped forward and snatched the shovel from Java's outstretched hand. "Okay, but let's get this shit over fast!"

He turned and stalked past the piles of dirt they'd already unearthed and stood atop the smaller grave. Roy and Java followed. Alex stuffed the envelope behind his back and pushed himself after them.

Getting to the smaller coffin didn't take as much time or digging, and the pile of earth on either side of the hole was smaller. Alex could only dig for a short time because Israel's frantic jabbing and tossing of dirt kept getting in his way. Even Java had renewed energy, and Roy understood. Those eyes were still on them, watching and waiting, and he figured the others felt it too. But waiting for what? To open *this* grave? Why?

Java's shovel striking wood caught his attention, and he looked down to see the lid of a small coffin, almost like a box for mailing one of those Chucky dolls. Once again Roy's heart pounded with dread at the thought of opening it and seeing the bones of a child, so he scrambled up top with Alex. Israel climbed up beside him, leaving Java alone in the hole.

Java gazed at them from beneath his hood. "Okay, I got this."

He tossed up his shovel, stuck his small flashlight between his teeth, and stooped to examine the burnished brown wood of the coffin lid. He felt around the edges, finally stopping along the right side. Roy held his breath as a loud *click* broke the suffocating silence. This time he couldn't look away as Java's dark hand reached out and gripped the side of the lid, lifting it slowly until it rested in the open position. The light beam wobbled as Java switched it from his mouth to his hand, and Roy watched as the light revealed the interior of the coffin. He inhaled sharply, and heard Israel yelp with fear.

"The hell?" Java muttered in bewilderment.

A doll lay within.

A boy doll.

Not Chucky - something even creepier. It had plastic hair, glassy eyes that stared up at them, and an open, grinning mouth with plastic teeth dirtied and brown with age. The expression looked both vacant and knowing, even within the small beam of light fixed on it, and Roy shivered.

Alex stared at the doll in silence, and Roy knew what he was thinking: if the coffin had a doll in it, where was Andy?

"Can you hand it up to me, Java?" Alex asked, his voice trembling.

Java grasped the doll by one arm and handed it to Roy.

Roy wasn't sure why he didn't want to touch it, but he gulped and took the toy from Java before passing it to Alex. Alex sat the doll on his lap and looked long and hard at it, as though it would give him the answers he sought.

The doll blinked and said, "Hello, Alex."

Israel shrieked.

CHAPTER SEVENTEEN

WHAT ARE THEY?

ALEX YELPED AND FLUNG THE doll to the ground in front of him while Roy lurched back.

Java jumped up and crawled out of the hole, staring at the doll in open-mouthed horror.

"Oh shit, Alex, it talked to you!" Israel cried out, no longer even trying to be quiet. "Oh shit, oh shit, oh shit!"

Java stepped toward him, but Israel scrambled away. "No, stay back!"

Roy's heart thundered with terror and he could scarcely breathe.

Alex had ceased his panting after that initial shocked reaction, and stared down at the doll with anger.

"Who are you?" he demanded, his voice rising against the increasing wind.

"We are you," the doll said, its voice raspy like sandpaper, the plastic mouth and teeth moving as it spoke.

Alex flinched, but didn't move his chair.

Israel went crazy. "Shit, Alex, it knows you!"

Java raised a trembling fist. "Shut up, Izzy, or I'll ADHD yer face!"

Israel threw his hands atop his head and started pacing frantically, ready to explode. Roy knew they didn't have much time before Izzy was uncontrollable.

Alex trembled with rage. "Whadda you want with me? And where's my brother?"

The doll smiled, and Roy would never forget that moment for the rest of his life. It actually smiled! And a more evil smile he never wanted to see.

"With us. You'll be with us soon," the doll replied around that smile, the voice sounding like what Roy imagined ripping skin would be like.

Alex recoiled, and Roy tried to focus. What did that mean, *you'll be with us soon?*

Java backed further away.

Israel spun around and danced on his heels and clamped a hand over his mouth.

Alex gripped the shovel lying across his lap and raised it above his head, the curved blade aimed down at the grinning doll lying in the grass at his feet.

"Like hell!" he spat and thrust down with the shovel, driving the blade into the doll and severing its head from its body. The plastic head rolled a few inches and landed face up, still displaying that hideous grin.

Rustling leaves sounded in the dark, and Roy whirled with his flashlight to look behind him. He gasped, and everyone turned. The cat sat on its haunches staring at them, those reddish-orange eyes gleaming in the light of Roy's beam.

"How the hell it get here?" Java hissed.

Israel whimpered and quaked.

"We're outta here, guys," Alex said. "I can handle this bitch."

"What about the others?" It was that raspy, ripping sound that pretended to be a human voice.

Roy twisted around to see the doll's smile had grown even larger.

And then he heard it.

Crackling movements among the fallen leaves.

Scuttling sounds in the trees around them.

Roy spun. They all did, shovels raised for protection. Eyes glowed at them from the darkness. Many eyes. Hundreds. Roy twisted his head around and saw more coming at them from the sides. Eyes and more eyes, closing in on them.

"Holy shit!" he muttered, unable to keep the shake from his voice.

"What are they?" Java whispered beside him.

"Cats," Alex said, his voice strained and afraid. "A shitload of cats."

"Like the ones that killed Ms. Ashley?" Roy whispered without taking his eyes off the sea of eyes closing in.

"Yep," Alex replied.

Israel started up again. "Oh, shit, we're gonna die. Oh shit, oh shit, oh shit!"

Java whirled angrily, but Alex's hand to his arm stopped the outburst. "Let's go. Slowly. Back to the truck. Maybe if we don't make 'em mad they'll leave us alone."

The doll head began laughing maniacally, and the clouds opened up to assault them. Rain poured from the sky like God was dumping buckets of water on them. Israel broke and ran. He turned and half-sprinted, half-stumbled away into the darkness.

"Izzy!" Alex cried out, but Israel kept going, completely out of control. Alex turned to Roy. "Push me!"

Roy didn't have to be told twice. He threw down his shovel, grabbed Alex's chair from behind and pushed as fast as the terrain allowed. Java brought up the rear, his shovel up and ready. The rain slammed into them, and they were drenched within seconds.

The cats made their move. A massive wave descended from the hills and rose from the valleys of the graveyard in pursuit, flowing across the grass like lava, oblivious to the driving rain and wind.

The boys plowed forward. The rain in his eyes made it hard for Roy to see ahead. He could barely make out Izzy's erratic movements and called out for the other boy to wait. But his words were ripped from his mouth and carried off by the wind even as he uttered them.

Alex's chair slowed his progress. It bounced and careened over the uneven grass and Roy's feet had little traction beneath the water sluicing down the hill and filling his shoes. He slogged and slopped along, his hood falling from his head, wet hair covering his eyes and blinding him.

Israel cried out, "Oh, shit! Help!"

Roy barely made out the writhing mass of darkness closing in on Izzy and toppling him. Izzy went down and didn't get up. His shrieks and agonized curses pierced the pounding rain like bullets.

"Izzy!" Java shouted and bounded past Roy and Alex to close the gap in seconds.

Roy pressed forward, the muscles in his arms and shoulders straining to keep Alex upright.

Java raised the shovel and swung wildly back and forth. Cats shrieked as they were struck, flying this way and that as Java plowed through them.

By the time Roy arrived with Alex, Java had cleared a path and was dragging a crying, groaning Israel to his feet. He had blood running off his arms and legs and back where his clothes had been shredded.

The cats massed on either side of them, and Roy made out a number of unmoving forms among them.

Java shoved Israel forward, glancing back for a split second to make sure the others were there. He swung his shovel up for them to follow and Roy pushed forward. The cats paused a moment, as though afraid of Java's wrath. But that break lasted mere seconds.

The boys had only gotten a small head start before the ocean of cats swarmed, moving like a tidal wave across the grass in pursuit. Roy kept looking over his shoulder, expecting any moment to be overrun. They were closing the gap and he surged on even faster. His arms and legs and lungs screamed with fire. Up ahead, Java pushed and dragged the injured Izzy while still gripping the shovel in one hand.

Roy had no idea how far they'd come or even if they were headed in the right direction. The dark and drenching rain confused his normally strong sense of direction. Suddenly, the cats were there, sprinting alongside him and Alex. But to Roy's shock and surprise, they didn't move in to attack. No, they stayed away from them and headed straight for Java and Israel.

"Java, look out!" he shrieked against the howling wind.

Java turned once and poured on even more speed. But as athletic as he was, there was no way he could outrun so many animals while dragging the stumbling Izzy.

Roy had mere seconds to wonder why the cats were ignoring him and Alex before the mass of vicious felines surrounded Java. He released Izzy, who staggered, and swung his shovel like a golf club. The sound of metal striking soft flesh, and the screeching cries of wounded cats pierced the wind and rain.

Roy dug in and ran all the harder, determined to help his friends. But then Alex's chair caught in a rain-filled rut and toppled forward before Roy could react. Pulled with it, Roy stumbled over the tipping chair and sprawled onto the wet grass entangled with Alex, the chair lying on its side next to them. The wind knocked out of him, Roy could only grab for Alex, struggling to see his face. Alex looked up from beneath him, rain running in rivulets off his cheeks, and blinked against the water.

"I'm okay," he grunted.

Roy was about to respond when from out of the dark a tall figure loomed and reached for him. A hand gripped him by his hoodie and hauled him to his feet. Roy raised a fist to swing on his attacker until a face pressed forward in the darkness.

"Dane!"

The taller man had already stooped to right the chair, and ignored him. Before Roy could respond, Dane snapped, "Can you carry Alex?"

Momentarily flustered, Roy couldn't answer. Dane shook him by the shoulders.

"Focus, little brother! Can you carry Alex or not?" Dane's face was right in front of his, dangerous and intense.

Roy nodded.

"Then grab him and run! I got the chair." When Roy hesitated, Dane shoved him toward Alex. "Now, 'fore your friends are dead!"

That snapped Roy out of his stupor. He bent and fumbled around for Alex, finding his legs with one arm and his upper body with the other. Alex scrabbled around in the dark for something and Roy realized that he was grabbing the envelope they'd dug up. Roy's legs screamed with pain as he lurched to his feet, cradling Alex in his arms.

By then Dane had the chair in one hand and a handgun in the other. "Run!"

Roy ran, gripping Alex hard. Dane ran beside him. He twisted and turned in every direction, firing the gun. Shots pierced the night like explosions of death. Small bodies twisted and flew to this side or that as the bullets struck them.

Dane got to Java and Israel first. Java held off the attackers with his shovel, but some had circled around and jumped Israel. Israel screamed and writhed, fighting to yank them off his head and back. Dane pelted alongside and, even with the gun in hand, snatched a big animal by the tail from Israel's head, tossing it into the dark. He grabbed for another and then another.

Gunshots sounded. Flashes lit the night, and cats screeched in agony.

Roy passed Dane. He ran and stumbled though the dark and rain up a sloping hill. The others fell in behind.

More gunshots and smacks of the shovel came from behind. Roy spotted a familiar tree.

"Almost there, guys!" he shouted, hoping to inspire the flagging Izzy to speed up.

Alex's weight in his arms ripped through his biceps and shoulders and he wasn't sure he could make it without falling. But Alex turned to look into his eyes and that renewed his waning strength. He pounded all the harder through the soggy grass, not even thinking about the possibility of slipping. Wouldn't matter anyway. If they didn't get over that fence in the next few seconds, they'd all be dead. He heard a clicking sound behind him. Dane's gun was empty.

He didn't dare look back, but the smacking of the shovel continued unabated. And then suddenly the metal fence was there, looming before him, both a blessing and a curse. It meant freedom.

If they could get over in time.

His breath came in short gasps and the stitch in his side nearly toppled him, but he reached the fence huffing and puffing, and shoved Alex at it. Alex didn't hesitate. The metal bars must've been slippery in the pounding rain, but he tossed the envelope through the bars and was up to the top and over in seconds. Izzy staggered forward, bleeding and whimpering and barely able to stand.

Roy instinctively stooped and cupped his hands together. Izzy stepped into the bridge and Roy lifted him with strength he didn't know was there. Then Izzy was up on the rail and swinging himself over to the other side, dropping into a crumpled heap beside Alex.

Dane and Java arrived, panting and wheezing from their exertions. Dane didn't hesitate. He dropped the chair and gripped Java by the waist, shoving the boy up to get a grip. Java threw the shovel down and grabbed for the bars, hauling himself up. Dane turned to Roy. "Go, I'll hand you the chair."

"But–" Roy began as the mass of cats closed the gap.

Dane didn't wait for an answer. He squatted down and grabbed Roy's legs, hefting him up so Roy had no choice but the grab the top rail. He straddled the fence and twisted around just as Alex's chair was thrust toward him. He grabbed it in both hands, heedless of falling. Java reached out from the cab of his truck and took the chair.

Roy slipped over just as the cats reached Dane. They flew at his back and legs as he jumped upward to grasp the bars of the fence. He grunted in pain, but the leather jacket he wore prevented them from digging into his back. Five cats clung to his legs, shredding his pants with their sharp claws.

Roy climbed onto the cab of his truck beside Java and together they reached out toward Dane.

Dane scrabbled for the top of the fence. A cat landed in his hair and raked at his forehead with its sharp claws. Dane let go of the fence with one hand to grab for it, and nearly toppled off. But Roy was there first. He punched out at the cat and knocked it loose. Dane flailed with his free hand and Roy grabbed it, anchoring his brother and pulling with everything he had left. Dane practically toppled forward and over the fence. He flailed out with his other hand and grabbed for the bars again, slamming into the metal fence with a thud. Then he slipped from Roy's slick grasp to crumple hard to the ground.

"Dane!" Roy cried out. He jumped from the cab to the hood and onto the ground to kneel beside his brother.

Dane groaned as Roy rolled him over. Blood streaked his face, but he was alive.

Roy looked through the fence. The cats had stopped. They just sat and stared, a whole sea of them. Roy had never seen so many animals together at one time. The massive leader, the big cat with the orange-red eyes, sauntered through the rest and sat at the front of them. But it didn't look at him. It focused on Alex.

Alex sat on the rain-soaked ground beside Israel, water running through his hair and down his face, his gaze riveted to that of the cat.

It's like they're talking to each other, Roy thought.

Suddenly, as though they'd never been there, the cats turned and melted into the darkness. And the rain stopped. Just like that. Only the big cat remained, and Roy saw it do something that freaked him out. It seemed to smile before turning to follow its fellows into the night.

Alex looked at Izzy, bloody and panting beside him, and then met Roy's wide-eyed gaze. Even in the darkness Roy saw the guilt on Alex's face.

Dane's strained voice interrupted his thoughts. "You okay, little brother?"

Roy nodded, studying Dane's shredded pants. Bloodied scratches were visible beneath the pale streetlight, and the scalp where hair had been clawed out in clumps bled profusely. He looked at Java and Izzy. Both of them were bleeding from numerous scratch wounds, Izzy most of all because he'd fallen under the attacking cats. Izzy lay in shock, staring at the blood running down his face and arms in disbelief.

And then it hit him. Neither he nor Alex had been attacked. Not even a scratch. Dane noticed it too.

"You didn't get touched," his brother said as he struggled to a sitting position, and Roy turned to meet his squinting eyes. "Why not?"

Roy shrugged. He didn't know.

"Let me spin you guys," Alex insisted. His voice sounded urgent, desperate and guilt-ridden, and Roy wanted to hold him and tell him it wasn't his fault. Except it was. All of this *was* happening because of Alex. But they were all too stupid to figure out why.

Alex faced Israel. "C'mon, Izzy, I know it hurts bad. Tell me. Please."

Israel looked up and into Alex's face. But he said nothing. For the first time since they'd known each other – and Roy had grown up with Izzy – the boy couldn't talk. That realization was almost scarier than anything else.

Alex looked at Java, standing and panting from his exertions. "Java? Tell me. This is all my fault and–"

Then a flashlight beam struck Alex in the face and stopped his words cold.

A voice said, "Now what have we here?"

Roy looked up in shock to see a man standing beside a car, aiming a large flashlight beam directly at Alex. He hadn't even heard the car approach. Had it been there before they came back over the fence? Darkness obscured the man's face behind the beam.

Alex blinked and the beam dropped to his torso. The figure stepped forward.

"Mr., uh, cop!" Alex exclaimed, clearly not remembering the man's name.

Roy had never seen this man before. He was dressed in plain clothes, a coat and tie, and didn't look like a cop.

Dane muttered beside him, "Oh shit, a pig."

The light moved to Dane's bloody, angry face. Roy placed a hand on his brother's arm to calm him.

"What's up, mister?" Alex asked, distracting the man and causing the flashlight beam to settle once more on him.

The man stepped closer. He observed Alex seated on the ground, legs pulled under him, the bleeding, panting Israel beside him. He looked at the truck and clearly saw the wheelchair in the bed. Squinting, he turned to Alex.

"It's Detective Cole, Alex, and I was about to ask you the same question."

Alex just looked at him, clutching the large envelope in his lap, unable to come up with an answer. Cole regarded him soberly, and then swept his eyes over the others. "There were reports of gunshots. I heard it on the radio as I was heading home. Cops are coming. I'm trying to help here."

Roy waited for Alex to say something. He didn't even know this man.

Alex held out the envelope, but clutched it tightly in case the man tried to grab for it. "From my mom," he explained, his voice trembling. "I had to get it."

Cole said nothing for a moment. "How'd *they* get hurt?" He waved his beam at the others.

"Cats," Alex said. "We was attacked by cats."

The man's eyebrows shot up and Roy was sure he didn't believe it. But he nodded again, like he'd expected an answer like that. "Okay. Which of you are hurt?"

Alex pointed to Israel, Java, and Dane, but none of them said anything. Cole looked them over, glancing at the two trucks parked next to them. "Who's driving these?"

Roy spoke now. "Uh, one's mine and one's my brother's." He indicated Dane, who glowered, but said nothing.

"You take Alex home," Cole said to Roy. Then he fixed his gaze on Dane. "And you, take these others to Centinela E.R. and get them stitched up."

"Screw you, pig!" Dane spat. "Don't give me orders!"

Cole flinched, but unlike most cops Roy had ever encountered, he didn't fly off the handle. "Look, kid, I'm doing you a favor. You wait for those beat cops and use that mouth of yours, you'll know why they're called 'beat' cops."

None of them reacted, and Cole shook his head. "Cop humor is wasted on you kids. Look, get out of here now before your asses are under arrest!"

"You're just letting us go?" Dane asked. "Why would a cop do that for us?"

"I'm doing it for Alex. Now move!"

His words acted like a gunshot, and set the boys to scrambling. Java yanked Israel to his feet and sprinted for Dane's truck bed as sirens could be heard in the distance. Roy lurched himself to a standing position, pulling Dane up along with him. Dane glared at Cole before turning to his brother. "You got Alex?"

Roy nodded, and Dane grunted, strutting past Cole and mad-dogging the man as he did. Then he was into the driver's seat of his truck with the engine cranked.

Roy stumbled to Alex.

"You need help with him, kid?" Cole asked.

"No, sir. I got him."

Cole stood aside as Roy stooped to scoop Alex into his arms, pressing him against his wildly beating heart. He turned to his truck and found Cole already there with the passenger door open. He stepped forward and slid Alex inside. With a nod at the man, he moved around to the driver's side.

Alex looked at Cole as the detective closed the door, and their eyes locked through the window.

"Thank you," Alex said as Roy started the engine. Cole stepped away, his expression unreadable in the gloom. The sirens grew louder. Cole slapped the side of the truck and waved them off. Roy gunned the engine, backed up, and sped off down the street.

***

They rode in silence as Roy navigated his way along the rain-slick pavement of Florence Avenue, heading toward Hawthorne. His clothes were soaked, his body numb, and he couldn't stop trembling. He glanced over several times to see Alex gazing out the window, his sad, almost angry face reflected in the glass.

Because he needed to hear a voice, Roy murmured, "I was scared shitless, Alex."

"Shit!"

He tried to keep his focus on the road, but looked sideways at Alex. "What?"

Alex turned his head and Roy saw such pain on that face his heart lurched. "You couldda died cuz a me, Roy," he whispered, like he was afraid to say it too loudly or it might come true. "I'm fifteen years old, practically a man," he went on angrily. "But you near died cuz you hadda carry me like I'm a baby!" His mouth twisted with self-disgust. "I hate being so damned helpless!"

Roy blurted out the first thing that came to mind. "I like carrying you." When Alex's eyes widened, Roy flung his gaze back to the road in front of him in time to slow for a red light. "I shouldn't have said that." He couldn't look, certain he'd see anger or even disgust in those amazing eyes.

Alex's next words froze his breath, and sent his blood surging. "I just wish I could carry you sometimes, you know? That's what friends are for."

Roy raised his head and suddenly didn't feel cold anymore. "You do carry me, Alex. Every day. Here." And he placed a hand over his thumping heart.

Alex smiled, and Roy felt renewed, as though this night hadn't even happened.

Alex whispered, "I'd kill myself if anything happened to you, Roy. I mean that."

Roy's mouth dropped open in shock. "Don't ever say that."

Alex held his gaze with his own. "It's true."

The light turned green and Roy had to focus on the road ahead.

"Can I stay with you tonight?" Alex asked hesitantly, as though Roy might say no.

"Like you gotta ask?" He glanced over and saw relief on Alex's face. "What about Jane?"

"Screw her."

The warmth returned, but still Roy looked at him with embarrassment. "Um, my bed's smaller than yours."

"Don't matter to me."

"Me, either."

They drove the rest of the way to Roy's house in the comforting silence of best friends who had no need of words to communicate how they felt. They already knew.

CHAPTER EIGHTEEN

PLEASE DON'T CALL ME A FREAK

By the time they returned to the house, Alex had calmed down from the ordeal, despite being soaked and cold. He understood now that whoever was after him wanted him alive.

You'll be with us soon.

The words of that hideous doll haunted him. They had Andy. His brother lived! Alex's heart beat with wild excitement at the thought. But where *was* he?

He also understood that his friends were in real danger. They might be killed to weaken him, to make him give up.

Because they know I love my friends.

He watched Roy use his key to open the back door. Roy hadn't been hurt. At all. Alex's mind whirled with questions. In Eucalyptus Park, he'd told the guy with the knife not to touch Roy or else. Could that be it? Were they afraid of him, like Jane was, and wouldn't hurt Roy because of what he might do to them?

Am I that scary?

Roy eased open the door and pulled Alex up the steps, making sure to lock the door behind them. Flinching at every creak of floorboards, the boys made their way down the hall to Roy's bedroom and slipped inside, closing that door ever so softly. Roy turned on the lights and the warmth of the room filled Alex with momentary peace.

Roy hurried to the bed and slid all the clothes, magazines, and game controllers onto the floor. Alex chuckled and Roy turned, looking embarrassed. "Kinda stupid, huh?"

"Yup."

Roy grinned and offered Alex access to the bathroom first. They pulled out some dry clothes that would fit, and then Alex rolled out into the hall and down to the bathroom. He could've used Roy's help with his pants because the water had made them even tighter on him than usual, and his fingers were numb. But he refused to embarrass Roy anymore, so he struggled and pulled for ten minutes before finally using one hand to draw each leg out, while the other tugged on the pants. Stripping off his sopping shirt, he dried his whole shivering body with a thick bath towel and slipped into the boxers and sweat pants Roy had given him. The *Hawthorne Heights* t-shirt felt soft against his frigid skin.

He would have loved a hot shower, but Roy only had the stand-up kind, the kind for people who *could* stand. He piled his wet clothes in the sink for now. He spread a dry towel atop his seat cushion before clambering into the chair, and then rolled his way quietly to Roy's room.

When he opened the door, he caught Roy standing shirtless and pulling on his own pair of sweats. Roy froze in mid-motion upon seeing Alex, and to defuse the awkwardness, Alex joked, "Stop trying to look buffer than me. Won't work."

That did the trick. Roy laughed and pulled his pants the rest of the way on. He grabbed his own tee and pulled it over his head. "I won't ever get buffer than you, Alex."

Alex tried for a smile, but his thoughts were on his friends. "You think the others are okay?" He picked up the plastic-covered envelope from Roy's messy desk and turned it over in his hands.

Roy held his wet clothes, his brows furrowed with worry. "I hope so. Izzy looked pretty scratched up, but he seemed okay, didn't he?"

Alex nodded, his eyes lowering to the thick envelope. "We need to get them over tomorrow to look at this stuff."

He had to know if any water had leaked in through the plastic, so he unzipped the surrounding bag and tore off a strip along the top of the envelope. Roy stepped up to him, soggy clothes in hand. Alex held his breath as he reached within. He felt plastic. Gripping it with his fingers, he slid out a large sealed plastic bag filled with papers. Double plastic. His mom had been really slick, he realized. Sadness filled him that he'd never gotten to know her.

Roy noted the double plastic, too. "Your mom was super smart."

Alex suddenly recalled what he'd forgotten to ask. "Why do you think Dane was there?"

That froze Roy in the act of opening his already overflowing hamper. He turned, clothes under one arm and looked at Alex, puzzled. "I don't know."

He dumped the clothes on top of the pile and tried in vain to close the hamper lid, but it barely went halfway.

Alex considered Dane showing up like he had. It was weird. How would he have even known where they were? But if he *hadn't* shown up, the others would for sure be dead. Alex knew that much. He thought back to when he'd noticed Dane at MTS the past couple of weeks. He'd feel eyes on him as he passed through the quad area, and when he'd look around it would be Dane staring at him. And last week he'd showed up at their table, supposedly to talk with Roy.

But he was looking at me. Why?

He wondered for a split second if maybe Dane could be gay like Roy. Could that be like Special Ed-ness and run in families? He'd always thought his reading disability came from the parents he'd known, but now he had no idea. He watched as Roy pulled extra blankets from a pile on his closet floor, and decided Dane's "looks" at him weren't the same as when Roy looked at him "that way." So, what was up with Dane?

"Can you ask him?" he finally said as Roy tossed the blankets onto the bed.

Roy turned. "Ask him what?"

"Why he was there."

"Yeah. I wanna know, too."

Alex set the plastic bag atop the desk and turned to see Roy turn red and look down.

"What?" Alex asked, though he thought he knew the answer.

"Um," Roy said to his bare feet, "which side of the bed do you want?"

Alex had been right. He hated making Roy uncomfortable, but there was no way he'd leave his friend alone until they knew what was going on.

He wheeled himself over and looked at the bed. It lay against one wall, like his own, but it was smaller and they'd basically be right up against each other, but Alex didn't mind. He needed Roy's body heat to remind him that there was still good in this world.

"I'll take shotgun," he said, pointing at the side near the wall.

Roy grinned.

Alex slipped out of his chair and onto the bed, pulling in his legs with his hands and pushing them under the covers. He scooted against the wall to make as much room for Roy as possible. There was only one pillow, and he wanted Roy to have it.

Roy padded to the wall switch and turned off the lights. Darkness engulfed Alex and he felt a momentary panic, a flashback to their earlier ordeal. But then he felt his friend slide under the covers beside him and lay there stiffly, obviously uncomfortable. But rather than push away more, Alex scooted closer. His body felt numb with cold, as though the evil in those cats had invaded him somehow. He needed warmth.

He could almost hear Roy's heart thumping, and determined to quell his anxiety. "Best friends are forever, right?" he whispered.

Roy's breath caught a moment in the dark. "Best friends are forever."

Roy rolled onto his back, and exhaustion pulled him down to sleep.

Alex listened to Roy's gentle breathing, the sound filling him with joy, before he, too, went under.

He awoke late and didn't need to look at a clock to know he'd missed seven o'clock mass with Father Pat. It struck him that he'd never missed before.

Roy still slumbered, and Alex felt bad about waking him. But he was anxious to check on Java and Izzy, and to crack open that stuff his mother had left for him.

He nudged Roy's chest with his hand, and watched his friend return to wakefulness. At first, Roy's eyes widened in surprise, as though he'd forgotten Alex was there. Then he grinned, which made Alex feel good to see.

"Morning," Alex said.

"Morning," Roy replied, pushing himself up onto one elbow and getting his bearings. He winced with pain. "Ooh, man, I'm sore today."

"Sorry. It's my fault."

Roy gave him a steady look. "Don't even go there."

"You think the other guys are okay? We need to call."

Roy slipped his feet up and under the covers to the floor. He sat up and said, "Gotta piss. Be right back." He was up and out the door before Alex could say anything more.

Alex pulled himself to the open side of the bed, slipped his feet out and onto the floor, and slid into his chair. The cushion had mostly dried, but he felt dampness from the rain so kept the towel in place. Ignoring the coldness, he wheeled to the desk to check Roy's phone for the time. Ten o'clock. Was that too early to call the guys? He wished he could write good enough to text, but the others wouldn't be able to read it if he did. Besides, they always had their phones on vibrate in case they called each other.

He scrolled through the contact pictures and found Java. He paused a moment to look at the unsmiling face, something he really hadn't taken the time to do. Java could be pretty good-looking, he realized, if he didn't try so hard to be badass all the time. He pressed the number and put the phone on speaker.

Roy stepped inside the room, shivering, just as the phone began ringing.

"'Sup, Roy?" came loud and clear over the speaker.

"It's Alex. I'm with Roy," Alex answered as Roy leaned in closer. "You and Izzy okay? What happened at the hospital?"

A grunt of disgust came from the other end. "We waited like, forever," Java's voice said with annoyance. "I only needed a few stiches. Got me some badass scars, man. Like you emo boys say, wicked looking."

"What about Izzy?" Alex asked anxiously.

Another grunt. "Man, he was spooked something crazy. He kept crying and be like, making weird sounds and shit all the way over. I guess he was hurtin', though, cuz he had some nasty-ass cuts and needed a crapload of stiches."

"And Dane?" Roy asked, trying to keep his voice steady.

Java's laugh wafted out of the phone. "That fool's crazy, Roy. I thought he'd beat the shit out of Izzy cuz of the crying. Anyway, he stuck around with us till our folks come and then he split. Needed some stitches in his head, but that was all."

"Were your folks pissed?" Alex asked.

"I'm, like, grounded for the next ten years, my dad said, but I think my ma was just glad I weren't killed. Izzy's, too."

"Um, what'd you tell 'em?" Roy asked.

Java laughed. "Dane told 'em some crazy ass story about how we was all fixing to go to a party and while we was cutting through the park a shitload of cats jumped us and he come to the rescue."

"And they believed that?"

"Why not? Doc said we was attacked by cats, looked like."

"Dane was always good at lies," Roy remarked and Java chuckled.

"You able to come over and look at the stuff we found?" Alex asked.

"No can do, bro," Java said with annoyance. "Grounded. Can you bring it tomorrow? We can check it out at lunch."

"Yeah, that'll work. We're gonna look now and I wanna show Roy's dad, too. That okay with you?"

"It's your stuff, man," Java replied. "Oh, gotta go. Ma calling." The phone went dead.

Alex gazed at the large, sealed plastic bag on Roy's desk – the bag holding… *everything.*

"Do you wanna get my dad?" Roy asked.

Alex shook his head. "Let's you and me look first."

Roy reached out to grab the bag, handing it almost reverently to Alex. Alex laid it on his lap and tore open the seal. Fingers trembling, he slid the sheaf of papers out and set them atop the desk. Roy shoved stuff onto the floor to make room. Together, they spread out all the papers and photos into a scattered pile so they could get a sense of what was in there.

There were *lots* of papers with writing on them that looked photocopied from books. There were lines and passages highlighted in faded yellow, none of which Alex could read. He glanced at Roy, who shook his head.

"Think yer dad could read any of this?"

Roy shrugged. "He's better'n me, but this stuff looks hard."

Alex pushed all the "reading stuff" aside. He grabbed the photos and laid them out on top. They looked like color copies from books - pictures or drawings - with writing underneath. He examined them, and felt Roy's warm breath on his cheek as he leaned in closer.

The first picture shocked them. It was of a necklace – the same necklace Alex wore, the same design they'd seen at Ms. G.'s apartment.

Roy blurted, "How'd yer mom know you'd find that thing?"

Alex shook his head, but his heart was already pounding. He flipped through the photos.

Some showed drawings on stone walls, and others displayed images painted onto big pieces of some kind of material Alex didn't recognize, but that almost looked like animal skins. The ones on the animal skins showed Indians. He was sure of that based on the feathers and other "Indian" stuff he'd seen in movies. Hadn't his mom said something about being part Indian? The other paintings had people dressed in sheets or just small towels around the private parts for the men and long bathrobes for the women. Alex didn't know what to call any of these things, but that's what they looked like.

Roy gasped, and pointed to a figure in each of the pictures. The same figure, but dressed differently in each picture. It was a boy. A light-skinned, white-haired boy. Everyone else had brownish skin. In some of the pictures, the boy stood, in others he kneeled. A couple showed a large male angel with big wings standing right behind him as the boy had his hands raised toward a group of people. One of the Indian drawings had the boy shirtless, the white hair going all the way down his back, on his knees with his legs kind of rolled up, almost curved under him. But every image of the white skinned boy showed him with really blue eyes.

"Holy crap, Alex!" Roy blurted in shock. "It's you!"

Alex nodded, lowering his eyes to some of the dates below the pictures. He read the letters "B.C." He remembered that. "Roy, member how Ms. Ashley taught us about B.C.?"

Roy nodded. "Before Christ." He blew out a frightened breath. "But that was, like… more than a hundred years ago!"

Alex's heart thudded. "We need to show this to your dad," he said finally, pulling his gaze from the old pictures and fixing it on the fearful face of his best friend.

Roy nodded and scooped up all the papers and photos, slipping them into the plastic bag.

They found Nathan in the kitchen preparing breakfast. He had a frying pan on the stove filled with scrambled eggs mixed with bacon and veggies. He looked up when the boys entered, clearly surprised to see Alex, but didn't ask any questions. Roy told him they needed to talk about something important, and he agreed immediately.

The smell of eggs, however, set Alex's stomach to rumbling. So, they all sat down to eat while Alex considered the best way to explain things to Roy's dad. After all the food had vanished – quickly between the two boys – Alex indicated the plastic-covered papers on the table beside him. He decided as they ate that he wanted to share the whole story. This man had offered to adopt him, after all, and he deserved the truth.

Alex, with Roy filling in some gaps, told everything that had happened over the past week, and shared his secret with the man who wanted to be his father.

Nathan listened to every word, occasionally asking questions along the way. But Alex could tell he was both worried and embarrassed. Alex saw it in his eyes – he didn't understand what this meant any more than they did, and felt guilty for that. Alex guessed grown-ups always liked to have the answers when kids needed them. But maybe, sometimes, there were no answers. Only questions.

When the boys finished, Nathan sat and stared at Alex intently, like maybe he expected to see a miracle or something.

Please don't change your mind, Alex thought.

Nathan took the plastic bag in his large hands and slid out the contents. Alex and Roy exchanged furtive glances while calloused fingers flipped through the documents, and squinting eyes studied them, especially the photographs. After about ten minutes, Nathan sighed.

"This is…." He trailed off. "I mean, Alex, you're…."

Alex blurted, "Please don't call me a freak, Mr. Phillips."

Roy gasped, and Nathan frowned.

"I would never say that to you." He sighed again, sounding old and tired. "It's just, well, this is way over my head, boys. I can't read most of this stuff, either. And these pictures… it looks like you're really important, Alex."

Alex blushed and glanced down.

"I'm only a construction guy," Nathan went on. "I can't help you with this, Alex, but I'll help keep you safe. Got me a hunting rifle upstairs."

Alex nodded, but he'd already expected this. "Thanks anyway, Mr. Phillips."

"Since I'm gonna adopt you, shouldn't you be calling me Nathan, or just Nate?"

Alex raised his head to find the man smiling. "You still wanna adopt me?" he asked, shocked. "After all this?" He pointed at the photos.

Roy's dad indicated the papers with a wave of his hand. "Don't mean nothing. You do."

Warmth filled Alex, and a tiny smile slipped onto his face. "I got a friend at St. Joseph's," he said. "A priest. He's been to college and everything. I'm gonna show this stuff to him."

"Great idea. I'll drive you," Nathan said.

That's when Alex felt it. He glanced toward the kitchen window, and gasped. Outside, perched on the fence like it owned the place, was the cat. Alex turned to Roy, and saw his friend's gaze shift from the cat to him.

Suddenly, the ground rumbled and shook. The house vibrated and rattled around them. The cat forgotten, both boys ducked their heads under the table, like they'd done for earthquake drills in school. As he slid back his chair to join them, a ceiling light crashed down on Nathan's head, sending him sprawling onto the tile floor.

DAY 5

CHAPTER NINETEEN

I'M NOT LEAVING MY FRIENDS

Roy and Alex sat in a sterile-looking room at Robert F. Kennedy Memorial Hospital and watched Nathan sleep. Machines beeped and whooshed and made blipping sounds, but Roy had no idea what any of them did. Once the shaking stopped, he'd crawled to his fallen father and felt terror engulf him at the blood pouring from the top of the man's head. He panicked, but fortunately Alex stayed calm enough to dial 911, and help came quickly.

The paramedics seemed confused when the boys said an earthquake had knocked the light fixture down, insisting there hadn't been any earthquake that morning. Roy didn't try to argue because he was too upset. Alex kept one arm over his shoulders while his father was placed on a gurney, given oxygen, and then wheeled outside to the ambulance. The boys hurried after. The paramedics told Roy where they were headed and sped off down the street, siren wailing. Roy put Alex into his truck and they zoomed off in pursuit as curious neighbors watched from their front porches.

Roy sat in a chair, elbows on his knees. He watched the rise and fall of his father's chest, noted the large bandage covering his head, and wondered if the man would ever wake up again. The doctor had talked to him and Alex, but neither boy understood much of it. Head injury was all they could get. He gave the nurses Dane's cell number because the doctor wanted a legal adult available in case any decisions had to be made. He doubted Dane would even come.

What decisions might have to be made?

His dad would be fine. He'd been hurt on the job tons of times and always joked to Roy, "Just a scratch," even though his whole hand would be bandaged.

Alex had one arm resting across Roy's shoulders for comfort. No words were spoken. None were needed. They sat and waited. It was late afternoon and they'd been there for hours. Sure, his dad had a large head wound that had been stitched up, but Roy didn't understand why Nathan wasn't awake yet.

The meds they gave him should've worn off by now.

As though reading his mind, like he always did, Alex said, "He'll be okay, Roy."

Roy looked at him, more afraid than he'd been in that graveyard. "How do you know? We didn't understand what them doctors said."

"It don't matter what they said. Soon as he wakes up, I'll spin him."

Roy nodded, feeling a little better. Alex could fix things better than doctors, long as the other person could talk, anyways.

Come on, Dad, wake up!

That's when Dane stepped into the room.

Roy was so shocked, he blurted, "Dane!"

Alex pulled his arm from Roy's shoulders and looked down at his feet.

Dane squinted at the two of them a moment before moving to the bed to check on his father. Roy noted he was dressed grunge, like usual, in ripped workpants, a long-sleeved flannel, and Army boots. He also wore an old black hoodie to complete the look. His mop of brown hair was messy, but his face looked worried, rather than its usual angry.

He regarded Nathan a few moments, and then turned to his brother. Closing the gap, he asked, "What'd the doctors say?"

Roy stood to look at his taller brother with embarrassment. He felt useless, like always. "I don't know, Dane. The guy used so many big words, I couldn't understand him."

"Dammit, Roy, why didn't you ask him to tell it different, with smaller words?"

Roy fought to meet his brother's intense gaze. "Doncha get tired, Dane, of always telling people to talk like you're a baby? I hate being a useless dummy!"

He looked down and met Alex's upturned eyes. Even in the dimly lit room, the blue of those eyes calmed him.

A hand on his shoulder startled him, and he looked up to find Dane gazing at him, not with anger, but with understanding. "I'll talk to 'em. You done good, Roy, gettin' him here. The old man'll be proud."

He strode from the room, leaving Roy feeling stunned. Dane was almost never nice to him, or complimented him. He sat again and this time he threw his arm over Alex's shoulders, relishing the comfort it brought him. They sat like that for several more minutes.

Finally, Alex said, "When Dane comes back, I'm gonna bail."

Panic overwhelmed Roy. "You are?"

Alex offered that smile again. "I think you guys need time with your dad, you know? Just yourselves."

Roy already felt lost without him. And the thought of being alone with Dane made him nervous. "You going back to Jane's?"

Alex nodded. "But first to your place, if that's okay. I wanna get all my papers and stuff we left on the table. Need 'em for Father Pat tomorrow."

Roy didn't hesitate. He pulled out his keys and slipped off the one for the house, handing it to Alex. "It's your place, too, man. You're gonna be living there soon, right?" Despite his dad's condition, the thought brought a smile to his lips.

Alex pocketed the key. "Soon as they let me."

They did the fist bump, and that's when Dane re-entered the room. Roy leaped to his feet. "Well?"

Dane stared at them a moment, and Roy noticed his eyes lingering longer on Alex. "Doc told me he got a concussion."

That was the word Roy hadn't understood!

"But–"

"Let me finish, little brother," Dane went on quickly. "It means he got hit hard on the head and they don't know if anything bad might happen to him later on. They took pictures of his brain and said they looked okay. They wanna keep 'im overnight to watch 'im. That's about it."

Roy nodded.

"Well, I gotta go," Alex announced, like he had a date. "See ya in school tomorrow?"

Roy raised his eyebrows at Dane.

"If the old man's good, he'll be there," Dane said.

"Remember to call me when he wakes up," Alex added.

As he turned to leave, Roy said, "Uh, how you gettin' home?"

Alex gripped the sides of his chair. "Got my own wheels, remember?"

With a whoosh, he was out the door and into the hallway, and Roy lost sight of him. He instantly felt alone, and resumed his seat, trying not to meet the piercing gaze of his brother.

But Dane wouldn't be ignored. Roy finally looked up. His brother stood in the same spot, studying him. "What?"

Dane's eyes narrowed. "Why's he wanna know when the old man wakes up?"

Roy heard suspicion in Dane's voice, and knew he had to come up with a reason. Then he thought of a good one – the truth. "Alex cares about Dad. Dad's gonna adopt him."

Dane stiffened, but kept his cool, as always. Roy had never seen his brother lose that cool, even when they'd been kids. If Dane got angry, and he often did, he always retained control – even if he was beating the living crap out of someone.

Dane chuckled. "So, the old man's finally replacing me, huh?"

"It's not like that. Alex got no one, and he's my best friend."

Dane stared at him, shifting his body weight from side to side without breaking eye contact. "Sure that's all he is?"

Roy's chest tightened, and his breath almost stopped. *He knows!*

When he didn't respond, Dane crossed the room. He slid the other chair over beside Roy and sat, dropping his arms to his knees and fixing those hard eyes of his on Roy's ashen face.

"I know, Roy. 'Bout you."

Roy couldn't speak. He was too afraid. Dane wasn't like dad. Dane wouldn't understand. "Yes, that's all he is."

"But you want more, don't you?"

Roy felt himself turn red. "How'd you find out?"

"I watch you at school. I seen how you look at guys. 'Specially Alex."

"He's just my friend," Roy whispered, not sure what to say. He twisted his hands together. Then it occurred to him what Dane had said. "You watch me?"

Dane nodded. "Hell, yeah. Nobody's gonna give *my* little brother shit."

He looked down and fell silent, and Roy understood the conversation was finished for now. Astonished by his brother's words, Roy could only wallow in confusion. He sat back in the chair, flipped up his hood and rested his head against the wall, listening to the sounds of the machines and Dane's even breathing beside him.

***

The sun was already setting when Alex set out from the hospital for home, and an ominous darkness had engulfed him by the time he rolled up in front of Roy's house. The street was empty of people, and the brooding rainclouds looked ready to reach down from the sky and grab him.

A chill wrapped itself around his heart as he stared at the empty house. Something felt different since they'd left, something just... wrong. Alex glanced up and down the street. He felt eyes watching him, but couldn't tell from which direction. Suddenly anxious to be in his own room with the doors locked, he wheeled around the side of the house to the back gate. Roy had months ago put in a long drawstring so Alex could unlatch it. He rolled into the empty yard and closed the gate. That feeling of being watched was gone, but the tightness in his stomach remained.

Forcing the fear to one side, Alex wheeled himself to the rear door and up the plywood ramp Roy had built for him. Fumbling for the key, he opened the door and entered the kitchen. The broken light fixture lay shattered on the floor, and the tiles beside the table were streaked with blood.

He glanced at the hole in the ceiling where the light had come loose. Alex looked around the kitchen. Nothing had changed. Not even the dishes on the counter had slipped to the floor. Of *course,* it hadn't been a real earthquake. He'd seen the cat. The cat didn't want Roy's dad helping them, so it took him out.

His mother's stuff was there, piled on the table just as they'd left it in their mad rush to the hospital. He felt cold, but not from the chill filling the house. Something was there with him. Something bad. He pushed himself to the table and scooped up the papers and photos. He slipped them into the plastic bag and shoved the bag behind his back for protection.

He looked around. He was being watched again. He turned to the window and looked out at the darkness beyond, but saw nothing except lights from the neighbor's house next door.

Taking a deep breath and expelling it, Alex wheeled himself to the door and outside, locking it behind him. He rolled down the ramp and out the gate onto the shadowy driveway. He heard something moving. Turning his chair, Alex watched the house. He looked at the upstairs windows, and then at the front door. Satisfied there was nothing moving, he wheeled around, and cried out in startled fright.

A figure stood in the dark staring at him, a figure silhouetted by the streetlight on the corner. He backed away until a familiar voice said, "It's okay, Alex. It's Ms. G." She stepped forward and to the side, so half her face fell under the light.

Ms. G. smiled in a way Alex knew was supposed to relax him, but it didn't.

What the hell is she doing here?

"Sorry I startled you, Alex," Ms. G. said as she stepped closer. Alex had to resist the urge to pull away. He noted she was dressed in pants and wearing a heavy coat, not the short skirts she usually wore to school. He said nothing; just watched her with suspicion.

She stopped right in front of him, close enough to touch his face, and stood gazing down at him.

She knows! She knows we were in her place!

But he forced himself to stay calm, hoping she couldn't hear his heart thundering in his chest.

Hands tucked into her coat pockets, she. said, "I heard about Roy's dad and wanted to see if he needed anything."

Alex's mind raced. Would something like Roy's dad being hit on the head make the news?

"I have one of those police band radios," his teacher went on, as though reading his thoughts. "I heard the 911 call you made."

Alex nodded, but offered nothing. She had his music box. She had that… that evil cat in her apartment! She was his enemy.

She pushed her long blonde hair away from her face as the breeze sent a chill through Alex. "Is he all right?"

Her question pulled him out of his thoughts and he gave her a steady look. "Yeah. Roy's with him."

She offered a smile of encouragement. "Good. I hope everything will be fine. I'd hate to see any one of you boys, or your families, get hurt."

Her face might have been smiling, but her voice wasn't. Alex wasn't so stupid he didn't know a threat when he heard it.

"You came to tell me that?" he said, letting her know he got the message.

She smiled again. "And I wanted to talk with your housemother about you."

Alex flinched. "What about? I do something wrong?"

She laughed, but Alex could tell it was fake. "You kids always think you did something wrong. How funny."

Alex didn't think it was funny. The only time his teachers ever talked to his house parents was because he was in trouble. He waited, hoping to spin something from her.

"I merely told Ms. Wilson that I thought you were misplaced in my room and should be in more challenging classes."

That hit Alex like a slap, and stopped his spinning. She grinned, and he understood that was what she'd wanted. "Whadda you mean?"

"Only that I think the others are holding you back. You're smarter than them, Alex, and I–"

"No," Alex said, his voice quiet, but forceful. "I'm not leaving my friends."

She smiled again, and the shadows made it seem crooked, like something you might put on a pumpkin for Halloween. "Of course, I'm just a long-term sub and can only make recommendations. Your counselor and Ms. Wilson have the final say."

He scowled at her, knowing she was messing with him, knowing deep down she wanted to separate him from the others. "I'm not leaving my friends. Ever."

That crooked smile appeared once more, and the tilt of her head with the light from above gave Alex the shivers. "We'll see."

He said nothing more, wanting to get as far from her as possible. Steeling himself, he said, "Well, night, Ms. G.," and wheeled around her before she could make a grab for him.

He made it to the sidewalk and started toward his own house when she said, "We don't want anything to happen to your friends, do we?"

Alex stopped and whirled around. She stood where he'd left her, the streetlight making her look like a monster from the movies. Her face was hidden in darkness, but Alex knew for sure she was grinning. He turned and pushed his way as fast as he could toward the safety of his own room.

***

Roy peeked out from beneath his hood at Dane. His brother sat in a chair across from him, sometimes looking at their dad lying motionless in the bed, but mostly fixing his hard, squinting eyes on him. Roy felt his brother's gaze drill into him with its intensity, as though Dane were spinning him like Alex could do.

He wanted to focus on his dad, but his mind kept returning to Alex, that evil cat, the earthquake that hadn't been an earthquake, and the real possibility that someone was going to die. He couldn't shake the feeling, and shivered in the cool room each time that notion entered his frazzled brain. Thoughts of Alex brought back memories of the graveyard, and the question he'd forgotten to ask.

Clearing his throat, Roy saw Dane turn his head and pin him to the wall with those eyes. "Um, Dane, how come you was at the graveyard last night?"

Dane's eyes narrowed, and his whole body stiffened, causing Roy to think his brother was about to go off on him. But Dane slumped in his chair like a deflating balloon.

"Dunno, little brother. I was sittin' on my piece a shit couch knocking down a few like I do every night of my sorry-ass life and…." He trailed off, his face scrunched as he sought to recall something. "Guess I knocked out, cuz I had a dream."

Roy sat up straight. "A dream?"

Dane nodded, his eyes staring off into space. "Yeah. You and Alex was in trouble, 'cept I couldn't figure out where. But somethin' bad was gonna happen to you. Then I woke up." He considered a moment, and Roy waited. "Dunno why, but I got in my truck and drove. Ended up at the graveyard."

Roy blew out a little breath. "I'm glad you did. We were goners."

Dane looked long and hard at his brother. "That wasn't the first dream I had about Alex."

Roy gasped.

"What's up with him, Roy? I know you know."

Roy squirmed beneath the intense look, and considered whether or not he should tell his brother the truth. Then he replayed Dane's earlier words in his mind: "Nobody's gonna give my little brother shit," and knew he needed Dane. Especially with his dad hurt and unable to help. So, Roy told his brother about Alex, and described everything that had happened over the past week.

Dane sat and listened, not interrupting once. Unlike him, Dane was good at listening and learned better that way. When Roy finished his story, Dane sat like a stone statue, and Roy was sure his brother hadn't believed him.

Dane stunned him by saying, "I seen those walls and shit with Alex's face, the ones you found in that grave."

Roy leaned forward. "How? We just dug that stuff up last night."

"I seen 'em in my dreams."

Roy knew he should've been surprised at that, but he wasn't. Alex had dreams, his dad, and now Dane. He somehow knew if he wasn't a dummy he could put everything together like a car engine and figure it out. 'Cept this wasn't a car engine.

"Roy?"

Roy jerked his head around at the sound of his father's voice, his heart leaping into overdrive.

"Dad!" He jumped to his feet and moved to the head of the bed.

Nathan seemed groggy, and the white head bandage made him look like someone from a war movie, but he was awake and alive. Roy grinned.

"How'd I get here?" Nathan asked, disoriented and confused as he took in the unfamiliar surroundings.

Dane stepped forward. "Roy got you here. He had it under control."

"Dane?"

Roy noted Nathan's obvious confusion at seeing his first-born. Roy understood. Dane hadn't seen dad for more than a year.

Dane shifted, shoving his hands into his hoodie pockets. "Yeah. Just came to make sure Roy was okay."

Roy saw the hurt drift across his father's face and said, "Dane talked to the doctors, Dad, and you're gonna be fine. Just got conked on the head."

Nathan looked from his first son to his second, and smiled gratefully. "Thanks, guys." He squinted at Dane. "What happened to your head?"

Roy suddenly noticed the stitching around the upper part of Dane's forehead, just below the hairline.

Dane shrugged. "Just a scratch."

That line seemed to run in the family, Roy thought, as Nathan accepted the obvious lie. "Is Alex okay?"

Roy nodded, but Dane scowled.

"Yeah, my replacement went home," Dane said, and Roy's mouth dropped open in shock.

"Dane!" he admonished, glancing at his father with embarrassment.

Nathan turned his head to focus on Dane, and Roy saw his brother squirm with anger.

"Dane, no one will ever replace you," Nathan assured him. "You'll always be my son. You're the one who didn't wanna be."

Dane's eyes widened. "That's cuz you made me a dummy like you! Mom said so."

For the first time in his life, Roy wanted to punch his brother.

Dad is hurt and Dane starts talking shit?

Nathan seemed to deflate beneath the blankets, his face looking old and guilt-ridden. "You're right, Dane. You and Roy came out like me. We can't read or write good. But I tried to raise Roy the right way, to stick by his friends, to treat people good. Is that worse than how your mother raised *you*?"

Dane's hands curled into fists within the pockets, and his whole body stiffened.

"I might be a dummy, like you said, and just a working man who didn't go to no college, but I tried to be a good man and a good father. You never gave me a chance."

Dane stared at Nathan in a brooding silence, but said nothing more.

Roy saw that his dad had fallen asleep, and turned to Dane. For once Roy felt he understood his brother because he'd experienced the pain of being different. Dane must've gone through the same crap his whole life. Only *his* mother blamed dad for it, and didn't do anything to help him.

"Want something to eat? They got a cafeteria in this place somewhere."

Roy nodded. "Sure."

Dane stared at him a moment longer.

"Thanks for coming, Dane," Roy offered. He tried for a smile, but felt so nervous it probably didn't look like one.

Dane squinted, his expression unreadable. "We're family." He turned and left the room without another word.

Roy watched his dad sleep for a few moments before returning to his chair to wait. He slipped out his phone to check the time, wondering if he should check on Alex.

I'll wait a little, he thought, *give him time to settle in.*

***

By the time Alex arrived home, it was past dinnertime and Jane had the food all put away. But he didn't care. He kept lots of snacks in his room for emergencies, and he just wanted to lock himself in his basement and try to feel secure, if that feeling was even possible anymore.

He slipped the packet from behind his back and tossed it onto his cluttered desk like it had bitten him. He'd always known he was a freak. But the stuff in that plastic bag, the stuff he couldn't understand, what did *that* make him? Evil? Good? Or both? Someone was after him, big time, and wanted to separate him from his friends. Ms. G. had just said so, without saying so. Should he bail, leave and go somewhere so his friends would be safe? Where could he go? Would they be in more danger if he wasn't around to protect them? That cat seemed scared of him. Sometimes.

Father Pat. He was a priest. He'd understand the stuff in that bag.

He'll explain everything and tell me what to do, Alex thought hopefully. *But what if I don't like what he tells me?*

He slipped the dangling medal from around his neck and studied the spider-web pattern. This necklace was a big part of what was happening, especially after seeing that picture of it with his mom's stuff, but he didn't know how. Still, he felt he should keep it with him in case someone was after it, too.

He suddenly heard raindrops pound against the house. Another storm. He shivered, but not from the cold. A storm meant something bad was going to happen.

He glanced around his room, his body tensing. The lights were all on and no shadows lurked anywhere that could lash out at him. The feeling crept over him that he wasn't alone.

The outside door flew open and slammed into the wall.

Startled, Alex dropped the necklace and gazed wide-eyed at the open door. The wind howled, the rain attacked, but no one appeared.

He knew what was about to happen.

Fumbling in his pocket, he yanked out his iPod, scrabbling through the other pocket for his ear buds.

Shit, where are they?

He spun around, setting the iPod onto his lap while shoving stuff off his desk. He spotted something at the corner of his eye and turned toward the bed. There they were, dangling off the rumpled sheets, out of his reach. He gripped his wheels and started in that direction.

But then he heard it.

The music box.

And blackness took him.

CHAPTER TWENTY

LET'S GET OUTTA HERE

Mrs. Rhodes stood at the kitchen sink washing the last of her dinner dishes. The sudden onslaught of more rain startled her at first, but then she relaxed. The rain chilled her to the bone, but California needed it, so she didn't really mind. All the more reason to build a nice cozy fire.

Finishing the dishes, she dried her wrinkled hands on the towel suspended above the sink, and puttered out of the kitchen, flicking off the lights as she did. Making her way into the living room, she spotted Raphael lounging on the couch. She reached down and scooped him into her arms. The miniature poodle seemed miffed by the interruption and squirmed in her grasp.

"Time for bed, Raphael. Yes, I know. I miss Joe, too. It's strange, but I don't feel so sad after talking to Alex. He's–"

Suddenly, the dog growled and leapt from her arms, darting from the room.

"Raphael? What is it, sweetie?"

The lights went out, plunging her into darkness. She cried out in startled fright. The absence of light through her closed drapes meant the street lights had gone out, as well. Wind pounded against the house. She mumbled to herself as she carefully made her way into the hallway toward the kitchen.

"You're too old to be scared of the dark, Liz," she said, but it wasn't the dark that put the edge in her voice. It was Raphael's aberrant behavior. And the weird feeling of something bad in the house. Something evil.

"Now where is that flashlight?" she asked aloud because she needed to hear a human voice.

She entered the kitchen, her heart thumping with a dread she couldn't overcome, and fumbled her way to the row of drawers by the sink. She rummaged around, and pulled out a small flashlight.

A gleaming knife whizzed past her field of vision. She stumbled back as the blade swung down and plunged itself into the drawer, right where her hand had been.

She screamed, and dropped the flashlight.

***

Roy had been trying to call Alex for the past two hours, but the phone just went to voice mail.

He'd left numerous messages, but none had been returned. The doctor had been in to check on Nathan, and said it was a good sign the man had awakened and spoke with the boys. Once he awoke for a longer period of time, he'd be given more tests to make sure there was no internal damage.

Roy had listened while Dane talked with the doctor, and he was impressed with his brother not letting the man throw big-ass words around. Dane didn't let anyone make him feel stupid.

Roy and Dane had eaten greasy grilled cheese sandwiches and drank soda and talked more than they ever had in their lives. Roy learned that Dane even liked some of the same bands as him, and had dressed grunge in high school. But mostly it was Alex on his mind, which was why his phone popped into his hand as if by magic every twenty minutes so he could leave a message.

He and Dane had been sitting in silence for a while now, digesting what each had discovered about the other. Roy tried Alex once more while Dane stood to stretch.

"I'll go see what's up with him."

Roy's eyebrows rose. "Yeah?"

"Yeah. Kid's special, that much I know," Dane said as he fished his truck keys from his pants. "And not just to you." He gave Roy a knowing look, and Roy felt his ears burn. "Let me know any change with the old man."

As Dane turned to pull open the door, Roy blurted, "I wish I grew up with you, Dane."

Dane turned and gave him one of those intense looks. "Yeah, well, I'm here now."

Then he was through the door and Roy was alone. Only the sounds of the heart monitor kept him company. As strange and dangerous as the past week had been, it had brought him closer to his Dad, to Alex, and to Dane. Didn't make sense at all, almost like life itself was Special Ed. For all Roy knew, it was.

***

Dane drove from the hospital in the rain, navigating the waterlogged streets with caution, thinking about his life. It was true, his mother had always talked shit about his dad, and about Roy, and from an early age had taught Dane to hate them. But now he realized who the real loser was – him. He'd missed out on a father and a pretty kick-ass little brother because his mom pumped his brain full of shit about how he was better than them and how he was gonna be a doctor someday so she could brag to her friends. Shit, he could hardly *understand* a doctor, let alone become one. But his mom kept pushing college on him, even forced him into El Camino so he could transfer to UCLA.

Dane's blood boiled as he thought of what a fool he'd been to listen to her. He was a dummy, just like the old man. But at least he'd finally wised up and wasn't full of shit like his mom. He hadn't even talked to her in the last eight months, and was better for it.

As his truck rolled toward Alex's house, Dane squinted through the windshield. The rain had let up, but was still a steady drizzle, and his windshield wipers were crap, so he had to peer through streaks on the glass to see out.

The hell?

Alex sat in his driveway staring at the house next door. Even through the streaking windshield glass, Dane saw the kid was soaked, like he'd been out there for a while. He eased the truck to a stop at the curb, killed the engine, and hopped down to the asphalt. Whipping up his hood, Dane sprinted around the front of the truck and stopped in front of Alex.

Alex didn't even blink.

Dane waved a hand in front of his face. "Yo, Alex, you okay?"

Alex's eyes remained riveted straight ahead, like he was seeing right through Dane. Dane turned to eye the house next door. It was dark. In fact, he realized, the whole street was dark. Power outage. Turning to Alex, he placed one hand on his wet shoulder. And that's when he noticed the blood. Watered down blood was all over Alex's pants and the sleeves of his hoodie. Rivulets of red rolled off the chair and formed tiny rivers on the cement, rolling down to vanish within the water gushing along the gutter.

Dane stiffened with dread. What the hell…? "Alex? Snap out of it, man." He shook Alex by the shoulders, harder than he'd intended, but he was spooked.

Alex's eyes lost that faraway look, and the wide pools of blue finally realized Dane was present. He squinted in the darkness at Dane's face. "Roy?"

His voice sounded confused, like he was drugged. "No, man, it's Dane."

Alex shook his head, the drizzling rain misting off his face, and he pushed back his sopping hair to give his eyes a better view. "Dane? What's wrong?"

"I came to check on you. What you doing out here in the rain, man? You got blood all over you. You hurt?"

Alex reacted with horror as he scanned his soaked, bloodstained pants and saw red water trapped in the grooves of his tires. He looked past the confused Dane at Mrs. Rhodes' dark house.

"Somethin' happened over there. Somethin' bad." His voice sounded garbled, like he'd just awakened from a long nap.

Dane followed Alex's gaze. The house looked quiet to him, nothing out of the ordinary. "How you know?"

"Just do." His tone of voice sounded so sure, and so afraid.

Dane offered a steady look and tried to keep his voice from shaking. "Let's check it out."

He went behind Alex's chair and started pushing, sensing the kid was dazed and confused. They made their way around the hedge and up the walkway. Rainwater sluiced off the old roof and down through the exit spout near the corner, rolling like a river past his feet as Dane pushed Alex to the porch.

Alex just stared at the closed front door, so Dane stepped around him and ascended the steps. Using the flap of his hoodie, he tried turning the doorknob. It didn't budge.

He turned to Alex and shook his head. Stepping down off the porch,

Dane started along the front garden to a side path leading into the back yard. Alex trailed behind.

Dane didn't believe in God or ghosts or any of that shit. But there was something here. Or had been. Something bad, like Alex said. It crept under his skin and chilled his soul.

Alex rolled past the kitchen window. Dane stopped and craned his neck to see inside for any sign of movement. But the interior was dark and silent. No power meant no appliances working, either, and that absence of sound unnerved him even more. When he pulled his head back, he found Alex awaiting him at the rear door. The door stood ajar. Suddenly, Dane wished he hadn't volunteered to come.

"You sure you wanna go in, Alex? Looks like everybody's sleepin'. Probably just left the door unlocked and the wind blew it open."

"She's not sleeping." Alex's voice cracked, and he looked away.

Dane stepped around Alex, careful to wipe his muddy shoes on the doormat as he used one elbow to push open the door. It creaked inward.

He stepped inside the kitchen, glancing right and left for the light switch. Spotting it on the right, he used the hem of his hoodie to flip it up and down. Nothing. Just as he'd suspected. Everything was out. He turned and pulled Alex's chair up the couple of steps and into the dark kitchen.

No moonlight filtered in through the window, and Dane could make out nothing at first. He waited for his eyes to adjust to the dark interior. Alex rolled forward slowly, and his wheels hit something, sending it rolling across the floor to bang into the refrigerator.

"What was that?" he hissed, his head tilted down at the shadowy floor.

Dane stepped past him and bent down by the fridge, grabbing the object and holding it out so they could both see. A flashlight.

Alex released the breath he'd been holding and turned toward the door to the hallway. He'd just started forward when Dane activated the flashlight, and then he shrieked in horror. Dane flung out a hand and clamped it over Alex's mouth as both stared in revulsion at what hung from the doorjamb – a dog.

Throat slashed, the dead poodle dangled from the telephone cord running along the top of the door, his eyes glassy and wide open, his mouth skewed crookedly to reveal teeth frozen in a growl of agony.

Blood dripped from the slashed and mutilated throat, pooling on the floor of the kitchen like some nasty soda pop.

Dane felt his heart pound with dread, and Alex trembled beneath his hand. Slowly, he lowered it and squatted down in front of him. Alex looked guiltier and more unhinged than he had outside.

"Let's get outta here, Alex. This is some crazy shit!" He hoped his voice didn't betray his unease.

Alex shook his head, and started forward, wheeling around Dane toward the pool of blood and the dangling dog.

Dane watched him roll through the puddle and duck his head to avoid drops of the animal's blood hitting him. However, several red spots appeared in Alex's wet hair, making him look like he was in a horror movie.

Body coiled for flight, Dane followed, turning sideways to slide past the dog, avoiding those huge glassy eyes that practically accused him of having done the deed.

Alex wheeled forward into the carpeted hallway, his chair leaving twin trails of dog blood embedded in the fibers. Dane stepped around in front with the flashlight, shifting its beam about the entry hall. The front door was closed, and locked. The beam halted on the stairs, and Alex gasped. The lower stairs glistened red, and a trail of blood led through the entry hall into the living room.

Dane aimed the flashlight at the carpet in front of Alex. The beam followed parallel tracks that crossed the entry hall and disappeared into the living room. Parallel *wheelchair* tracks. Except Alex hadn't been in the living room yet.

Other than last night in that graveyard, Dane could recall few times in his life he was really scared, and this was one of them. Could he have been wrong about Alex? Could Roy have been wrong? He waved the flashlight beam toward the living room. "Go on. I'll follow."

Alex looked at him a long moment, and Dane saw uncertainty flash across his face. Then he placed both hands on his wheel handles and pushed across the entry hall. Dane trailed behind, aiming the beam of light above Alex's head into the room.

Alex wheeled himself into the living room. Blood was everywhere. It looked like someone had dragged a dead animal across the carpet in a curving arc toward the sofa. Dane swung the flashlight beam along the floor, following the blood until it stopped in a large pool beside the sofa.

An old lady lay bloodied and crumpled on the floor. A weird design had been carved into her forehead – a kind of triangular spider web. Oddly, Dane didn't feel much of anything. He didn't know her, and had expected something like this anyway.

Alex whimpered and began to cry.

Dane placed a hand on his shoulder. "How'd you know?" he whispered, knowing that they needed to get out of this house before they got caught.

Alex looked at him, his face awash in tears. "Dreamed it, I think." His eyes widened as he stared at the woman's bloody face. "Oh, God…."

"What?" Dane swung the beam back onto the dead woman.

"That…." Alex began, his voice hitching with fear. "What they did to her head, it's…."

Dane lowered the light and leaned into Alex, squeezing his shoulder. "It's what?"

But Alex looked down and away, obviously unable to face the corpse any longer. He gasped, and Dane swung the light around to the floor where Alex's gaze was fixed. More wheelchair tracks. In a place Alex hadn't even been. Right near the woman's body.

"Oh, my God!" Alex said in a hushed whisper. "I was here, Dane. Before. I must a been here. And in the hall. But I don' remember. Dane, maybe I…."

He trailed off, but Dane already knew the punch line.

He glanced around with heightened anxiety. That bad feeling was everywhere now, and he itched to get out. "Look, man, we gotta bail. Just roll yer chair over them tracks, here and in the hall. Do it the same."

Alex's breathing had become ragged, and he clearly didn't understand. "Huh?"

"Snap out of it, kid!" Dane hissed. He planted his face right in front of Alex's. "Roll yer chair over them tracks."

Stunned and in shock, Alex nodded and pushed himself closer to the dead body on the floor. The smell of blood was overpowering, and Dane began feeling sick to his stomach. Alex attempted to roll his chair over the already existing tracks, but his hands shook and he wasn't precise. Dane worried that Alex wasn't matching them perfectly.

To fill the void, he said, "We tell the cops you went over there now. They'll never know you was here before."

A woman's voice said, "But we'll know, won't we, Alex?"

Alex stopped dead and whipped his head around. Startled, Dane spun and aimed the beam at the voice. A woman stood at the entrance to the living room, a woman with flame red hair, someone he didn't know, but clearly Alex did.

Alex's eyes bulged with terror.

The woman stood with her arms folded, as though she'd expected to find a house full of blood and an old lady carved up.

"Now what have you boys been up to?"

CHAPTER TWENTY-ONE

I AM A FREAK

Roy paced the hospital room, gripping his silent phone in his left fist and balling and unballing his right. Dane should've called by now. Or Alex. Something was wrong. He sensed it. He promised to protect Alex. What if something happened to him? Roy stopped his frantic pacing to look down at his father, asleep in a hospital bed, injured because of him. He hadn't wanted to put his dad in danger by telling him, but Dad *had* been hurt, and now Alex was in trouble.

Roy wanted to scream and shout, but there were no words for the kind of pain and guilt he felt. He couldn't leave his dad, could he?

What if Dad wakes up and I'm not here? He'd feel like I just left him or something.

No, he had to stay, but why the hell didn't Dane call? If he didn't hear something soon, he'd have to drive there himself.

Shit, he thought with despair, *I can't even leave Dad a freaking note!*

God, he hated being a dummy. His mind raced for some way to let his dad know he hadn't just walked out on him. He resumed pacing. Then he had it! He'd tell the nurse, that's what he'd do! Yeah, if he didn't hear something soon, he would go check on Alex for himself.

***

A lady was dead. A lady he liked, a lady who'd always been good to him. And it looked like he killed her.

Despair almost swamped Alex, dejection like he'd never felt even in the darkest moments of his sorry life. He had no idea how he could've killed her, or Maribel, since he couldn't even stand up. But the tracks were there. Wheelchair tracks. Why else would they have been there if he hadn't gone into the house and killed her? And what about the blood all over him?

Jane had followed them out of the house, and took them back to hers. She'd seen the blood on Alex's wet clothes and told him to change. "We wouldn't want you getting sick, now, would we?"

Her smile was so nasty Alex shivered. He wanted Dane to help him, but she insisted he stay with her in the kitchen. She did urge Alex to hurry, however. "I already called the police."

Dane had opened his mouth to say something, but Alex shook his head. To his surprise, Dane backed down. Alex didn't know him at all, but had always had the idea that Dane didn't back down from anything.

He knows he's in trouble, Alex thought, as he wheeled to his bedroom door and took the lift down to his room.

He pulled himself out of his wet clothes as quickly as his numb hands would allow. Thinking the cops might want to search his room, he pulled himself to his bed and shoved the wet pants and hoodie under his mattress so they'd have to pull apart the bed to find them.

By the time his lift returned him to the kitchen, he'd already heard the sirens. Red flickered outside Jane's kitchen window like those flashy lights people put out on Halloween. Dane sat at the table, staring at the floor, and Cole stood beside him. Jane was nowhere to be found.

"Hello, Alex," Cole said, the look on his face dark and almost scary.

He knows! Alex thought, his heart soaring into overdrive. *He knows I did it!*

"You don't gotta tell this pig anything, Alex," Dane said, lifting his head and glaring at the officer.

"Where's Jane?" Alex asked, more terrified of her than the cops.

"Outside, talking with my partner," Cole answered, his voice even and calm. "I wanted to interview you two separately."

"We don' know nuthin, pig!" Dane spat, his expression livid.

Alex noted the look and wondered why Dane hated cops so much, but then Cole spoke to him.

"Look, Alex, I did you a big favor last night," the man said, his eyes fixed with such intensity on Alex that he squirmed. "There's a shitstorm about those desecrated graves, and now I find you in the middle of *another* murder? Care to tell me what happened tonight?"

Dane opened his mouth to say something, but Alex gave him that headshake and Dane remained silent.

Cole looked from Dane to Alex. "All I managed to learn from your *friend* here was that he came to check on you because his brother was worried. How did you happen to go over to your neighbor's house so late at night?"

Alex felt another stab of panic to his gut. He hadn't even thought to make up an excuse, since he had no idea why he'd even been out in the rain. Except that he killed her.

"Uh, well… I, uh, when the lights, you know, went out, I thought I heard her scream. I thought maybe she fell or something an' got hurt."

Cole gave him a penetrating look.

He doesn't believe me!

"You see anyone suspicious around here, anybody who didn't belong?" Cole asked, glancing at Dane, who sat and watched Alex.

"No, sir."

"What time did you hear the scream?"

Alex fidgeted. "I don't know. I, uh, I don't tell watch time good 'less it's a digital." He didn't want to mention his phone in case Jane was just outside and might overhear.

"When's the last time you spoke with the lady?" Cole had his notepad out and was writing down Alex's responses.

For some reason, that notepad made him even more nervous. "Yesterday, I think, or maybe the day before."

Cole lowered the pad and paper with obvious annoyance. "Are you doing this on purpose, Alex?"

Dane stood and faced down the man. Cole took a step back and reached under the flap of his jacket for his gun. Alex could make out the gray handle poking out of a small holster.

Dane stopped moving. "Leave the kid alone. He gets enough of that shit at school."

Cole took a long look at Dane, and Alex was afraid he'd arrest him right on the spot. Instead, he said, "Sit down, young man. We're not finished yet."

Dane flipped his chair around and plopped hard into it, resting his thick forearms across the back.

Cole watched him a moment longer before removing his hand from the gun. "Tell me how you got into the house, Alex, and everything you did."

Alex attempted, as best he could, to relate the story, leaving out the part about how his wheelchair tracks were already in the house before he was.

Cole didn't interrupt any more, and took lots of notes. Not once did he ask Dane anything. Finally, he flipped closed the notebook and slipped it into his jacket pocket, along with the pen.

"Okay, Alex, that's all the questions I have for now. But I'll be back for more. You and I just can't stop meeting, can we?"

He walked out the back door without another word.

Alex turned to Dane. "He's not gonna arrest us?"

Dane shrugged as he stood and stepped to the window. The flashing red lights gave his face a creepy, cartoony quality. Alex wheeled himself closer to the door and craned his neck to see what was happening. Jane stood in the driveway talking to someone.

Probably the cop's partner, he thought.

He almost jumped when Dane leaned in over his head to look.

"Whadda ya think she's tellin' 'em?" Dane asked.

"Dunno. She must not 'a told 'em she thought we killed her or Mr. Cole wouldda arrested us, right?"

"Maybe." Dane's voice sounded suspicious, and Alex was about to ask him what he meant when Jane turned and looked his way. Even from such a distance, Alex felt her hatred of him. Then she smiled.

"We're dead," Alex whispered, and Dane nodded in agreement.

***

Two ambulance attendants wheeled a stretcher through the front door as Cole and Gordon watched it pass. A blood-soaked sheet covered the body.

The two men entered the house as technicians bustled around dusting for prints and taking blood samples from the hall carpet.

"Time of death is estimated at around nine o'clock, thirty minutes before those guys claim they found her," Cole said as they stepped past the forensics team in the entry hall and entered the living room. "You get anything out of the woman?"

"Says she didn't see or hear anything."

"Alex said he heard a scream."

"Not corroborated, by her or the neighbors."

Cole nodded, but Gordon wasn't finished yet. "I asked her if she'd ever seen the kid walk before."

That caught Cole's attention. "Why?"

Gordon smirked, obviously enjoying the moment. "The kid lied to you. He was in this house *before* he said he was."

Cole frowned. "How do you know?"

Gordon motioned him over to the bloody wheelchair tracks near the wall. Careful where they stepped, the two men squatted down.

"Look at these tracks - see how some are double, almost parallel? Like somebody tried to retrace the same path. Touch both sets."

Cole reached out a hand and touched the double tracks with different fingers. When he pulled his hand back, one finger displayed more blood.

"One's wetter than the other," Gordon said. "Because one had more time to dry. Same thing in the entry hall."

"Shit, Joe, how could a kid in a wheelchair do something like this?"

Gordon shrugged. "Hell, he's *your* X-file. You figure it out."

He stood and walked out of the room.

***

Jane relaxed at the kitchen table, puffing away at a long, thin, dark cigarette. Alex sat near the door to his lift, staring at her in silence.

Dane had split right after they'd seen that hideous smile come their way, promising Alex that he wouldn't let anything happen to him, but that he needed to get back to Roy.

As though knowing it would unnerve him, Jane had slid into the kitchen from the hallway instead of through the back door, puffing on that nasty-smelling cig and chuckling with amusement.

Her calm, controlled glee scared Alex more than anything else.

"Your accomplice finally go home?" she said between puffs.

As always, Alex felt stupid, just as she knew he would. "A kom what?"

Jane smiled, an even worse one than she'd tossed his way from the sidewalk.

"The guy who helped you kill that meddling old busybody."

Alex stiffened. "He didn't help me, cuz I didn't kill her." *Did I?* He paused when she didn't answer, and couldn't help himself. "That what you told the cops?"

Jane blew a smoke ring toward Alex. It wafted in front of his face and made his eyes water. "Maybe. Or maybe I just told them I saw you going over to the house earlier tonight."

"Did you?"

Another drag, another smoke ring, another wicked smile. "That's for me to know and you to worry about."

Alex gulped, his throat going dry, his heart thumping so loudly he felt sure the other boys in the house could hear it. Jane had confined them to their rooms once the cops arrived. "I mean… did you… really see me go over there?"

For the first time, Jane lost her smug expression and looked confused. "What do you mean did I really…?" She fixed her beady eyes on his. "You don't know?"

Alex didn't answer, but his fearful, puzzled facial expression told the story.

Jane laughed with delight. "Mr. Freak doing drugs now or what?"

Alex shook his head. His whole body felt numb with fear. "I just… I just can't remember. But I know I didn't do it." *Did I?* His voice came out weak and unsure, because that's how he felt.

Jane sneered. "Because you're Mr. Goody-Two-Shoes, always helping everyone?"

"No. I just… I couldn't do somethin' like that."

Could I? Did I? Why was I in that house if I didn't?

Jane's expression turned even colder, and her tone became how ice might sound like if it could talk. "Yes, you could. And you want to know why? Because you're a freak, Alex. Say it. I want to hear you say it."

Alex felt himself collapse inside at the realization that she might have been right about him all along. "Jane, please don't make me say that. Please?"

Her face looked like a stone statue. "Say it, or I call those cops right back here. I am a freak."

Alex bowed his head in shame. "I… I am… a freak."

"I am evil." Her voice became even colder.

Alex's breath almost stopped, and he could barely speak. "I… am… evil." His vision doubled and the tears forced their way out.

"Now both together."

Alex looked at her, tears of shame and defeat rolling down his cheeks to drop onto the hands in his lap.

"Now!" Her voice cut the air like lightning.

Alex fought to control himself. But his voice came out a guttural whisper. "I am a freak. I am evil." He lowered his head. He was beaten.

"Don't you ever forget it," Jane went on in a steady voice. "And don't ever forget who's in charge here. Do we understand one another?"

Alex nodded, his chest hitching with the desire to sob out his pain and sense of failure. But he wouldn't give her that satisfaction. He'd shown too much weakness already.

She sniggered. "Now who's afraid of who?"

Alex glanced up to see her gloating expression and those pursed lips taking another drag on the cig, and lowered his eyes once more. He shuddered to think what she might use him for now. He was lost.

***

Alex tossed and turned in his sleep. After Jane had "dismissed" him, he'd returned to his room and struggled with wakefulness for hours, his mind playing and replaying the night's events.

He'd found that Roy had blown up his phone trying to reach him, but he also knew Dane would've told his brother everything by now and Alex didn't want to worry Roy even more. If he told Roy about Jane, his friend would come right over to be with him. But Nathan needed Roy, and Alex refused to be that selfish, refused to be evil the way Jane said he was.

So, he'd lain in bed for hours and wondered if he was a murderer, if he could kill one of his friends without knowing it, even if Roy might be in danger hanging out with him. All of these fears twisted his stomach into knots and kept sleep at bay. Finally, exhaustion overcame him and he drifted into a fitful slumber.

But then the dreams began. Images of blood and knives and that horrible spider web carved into Mrs. Rhodes' forehead, and the bloody wheelchair tracks that could only have been made by him.

Suddenly, he was somewhere else. Kids his age dressed in fancy clothes danced. Flashing lights abounded and loud hip-hop music blasted from somewhere. Alex saw himself sitting in his chair, wearing a jacket and tie, watching the dancers spin and gyrate in front of him.

This must be the Homecoming dance, he thought as he watched the girls with their frilly dresses and the boys with their coats and ties bop and bounce around. *How'd I get here?*

And then Tami stood before him, and he gaped at her in open-mouthed shock. She looked dazzling, her hair done up in a kind of funnel with little bits dangling here and there. She wore a bright red dress that exposed her bare shoulders and Alex thought she'd never looked more beautiful. She smiled, and Alex put his breath on hold. She just laughed and reached out to him. He let her take his hand, and then saw himself do something he hadn't even dreamed of since he was small – stand up out of the chair and face her eye to eye. In fact, he was taller. She looked stunned, but this time Alex laughed as he put his arms around her and they danced their way into the crowd.

"You never knew I could walk, did you?" the dream Alex said.

She shook her head.

"The others didn't, either." He grinned at her mystified look, and then lifted his right hand into view, revealing a large, gleaming knife.

He laughed at her sudden expression of horror and plunged the knife toward her. As she cut loose with a blood-curdling scream, Alex shot bolt upright in bed, his face and torso sheened with sweat, his heart pounding.

He scrambled from the bed into his chair and wheeled to the cluttered desk where he rummaged through the rubble. He shoved papers and books onto the floor until he found it - the scrap of paper with Tami's phone number. He snatched his phone from the floor where it lay charging and punched in the number, tapping a pencil against the desktop as he listened to the rings in his ear. He glanced at his digital desk clock. Three-thirty a.m.

A voice came over the phone, a voice loopy with sleep.

"Tami? It's me, Alex."

Tami's voice sounded confused, and groggy. "Alex, why are you calling me?"

Alex dropped the pencil to wipe perspiration from his brow. "I can't go to homecoming with you." He fought to keep his voice flat and calm, but his racing heart made that impossible.

"You called to tell me that?" Now she sounded mad as hell.

Alex didn't care. He had to keep her safe. Better she be mad than dead. "No. Yes. I mean, I don't want you to come around me no more. I want you to stay away."

Now her voice changed. "Alex, what's wrong?"

"Nothing. I just don't wanna hurt you, 'kay? So, stay away. Please, please!" He ended the call.

The dream images assaulted him. The knife. Tami's scream of agony. The blood spurting and staining her fancy dress. No. He had to do something, maybe go away. Would that save her? What about Roy? What about the guy who chased them in the park?

Even if I did kill Maribel and Mrs. Rhodes, there's still another killer out there. I can't leave my friends. I can't!

He spotted the weird necklace that had been the beginning of all this. It lay on the floor where he must've dropped it. When had that happened? He bent and picked up the chain between thumb and forefinger. He no longer wanted to touch the fleshy skin of the web, and wished he'd never found the damned thing!

Father Pat. He was their only hope. If the priest couldn't figure out what was going on, Alex would go away with Roy. They'd have each other's backs and the rest of his friends would be safe. Tami, too.

He rolled to the chair where he had his clothes ready for school and tossed the necklace onto them. He'd bring it tomorrow with all the other stuff and show it to Father Pat. It wasn't much, but it was a plan.

He retreated to his bed, but sleep eluded him for most of that night.

DAY 6

CHAPTER TWENTY-TWO

TAKE HIM

WHEN ALEX EMERGED FROM HIS lift the following morning, the kitchen was empty. Cereal bowls lay in the drainage basket by the sink and he figured the others had already eaten and bailed for school. He wasn't hungry, but out of habit rolled to the table where Jane had laid out the milk, bowls, and utensils. He poured himself some cereal, doused it with milk, and shoveled it into his mouth.

He'd almost finished when the door to the hallway opened and Jane strutted in, looking pleased with herself. She was dressed better than usual, Alex noted, like maybe she was going out somewhere. And her hair looked even redder, almost like it was on fire.

She grinned, and Alex felt his blood turn to ice. "Good morning, son," she cooed, her eyes wide with amusement.

Alex glanced down at his cereal to avoid those empty eyes. "Morning."

"Morning, what?" The coo was gone, the threat obvious.

He scowled as he lifted the spoon to his mouth. "Morning…" He paused, and then spit out, "Mom," before shoving the Wheaties into his mouth and swallowing his pride along with the cereal.

"Much better."

He looked at her, grimacing at the expression of triumph on her face. "Whadda ya gonna make me do, J-mom, keep spinning them others after you beat on 'em?"

She made no move to approach.

I still scare her, Alex realized, his mind racing to figure out a way to use that against her.

"Of course, if the brats need discipline, I admit that having my own private freak boy is helpful." She chuckled. "But I have bigger plans in mind."

Alex stiffened. Plans? That sounded bad. His mind replayed what Juan told him about the video camera. "What plans?"

She grinned, spreading her gruesome red lipstick across her wrinkled face like a diseased Jack-O-Lantern. "You're going to make me very wealthy, Alex."

Alex wasn't exactly sure what "wealthy" meant, but just the tone of her voice told him it wouldn't be good for him. He said nothing and tried to spin something without her knowing.

Her smile dropped and she took a step back. "Don't."

Alex stopped spinning at once.

Her smile returned, even nastier than before. "It's time I got out of this rat hole and got on with my life. You're my ticket out of here, freak boy."

Movement behind Jane caught Alex's eye, and she must've seen his gaze shift because she spun around.

Carlos and Juan stood in the open doorway to the hall, Carlos aiming a cell phone at Jane.

"How dare you?" she barked, her voice shrill and strident, like it always got when she was flustered. "Where did you get that phone? You know my orders."

Carlos's voice came out hard and unwavering. "Yeah, cuz you didn't want us filming you like we just done."

Jane flinched and spun her head around to Alex, her face livid. "You put them up to this, didn't you?"

Alex shook his head. He had no idea what was going on.

"Alex didn't know nothing," Carlos said, causing Jane to turn around again. She backed toward the sink so she could watch both Alex and the other boys at the same time.

"We been recording you the past few nights, Jane, outside your door."

She flinched again and took another step back as Carlos and Juan pressed forward.

"You been talkin' some crazy shit, Jane," Carlos went on, his voice cold and commanding. "'Bout some *vatos* who treated you like the shitbag you are and it sure sounded like you off'd them guys." He turned to Juan. "That what it sounded like to you?"

The small boy nodded, but kept his wide eyes on Jane.

Alex watched the confrontation with uncertainty. This woman was dangerous. And there were kitchen knives right behind her.

Carlos smiled, and Alex imagined that was the kind of cruel smile he showed on the streets when he went gangbanging. "Now we got a vid of you saying how youse gonna beat us up and have Alex spin us. That ain't *firmé, mom.*" He said the last word with a sneer.

Jane said nothing. She looked like a cat cornered by a big dog, but Alex knew too well that cornered cats could be deadly.

"You call my P.O.," Carlos went on, "or his P.O., and these vids go to the cops."

Jane's lower lip quivered, not in fear, but in barely contained rage. "You do that and the whole world will know about freak boy here."

Alex stiffened as Carlos looked at him with raised eyebrows.

"It don't matter to me, Jane," Alex said. "Tell the world. Long as we put your ass in jail, I don't care." Alex hoped his voice sounded strong, because he *did* care if everyone found out. He cared a lot. But he would show no more fear in front of this woman.

Carlos grinned. "See? The homie be with us." He waved the phone around before slipping it into his pocket. "C'mon, guys, we're outta here."

The two boys started toward Jane, causing her to press back against the counter, her eyes wild and fearful.

Good, Alex thought, as he wheeled himself out the door behind the others. *Fear is a good thing for her to feel.*

Once outside and down the driveway, Carlos and Juan turned to face Alex.

"Uh, thanks, guys," Alex said, feeling stunned at what just happened.

"It was you, Alex," Juan said.

"Me?"

Carlos nodded. "Yeah, man. If you hadn't talked shit to that bitch last week we never wouldda had the balls to. You're *firmé,* homie." He raised a fist and Alex bumped it with one of his. "For a special ed kid."

Alex grinned. "And you guys are okay, you know, for criminals."

"You got that right. Wanna walk to school with us? We could use yer chair to do a drive by." Carlos pointed his finger like a gun at Jane's house. "Pow!"

He chuckled and Alex laughed. It seemed like he hadn't laughed for the longest, and to suddenly be tight with these guys against Jane was almost epic.

He was about to say yes when Roy's truck turned the corner and headed their way. Alex lost the smile, suddenly feeling guilty for not even calling Roy since he woke up. "Next time, guys. Roy's dad got hurt and I wanna find out what's up."

"Tell Roy I said hi," Juan said, turning red around the ears.

Alex nodded, noting the small boy's look and tone, but not really focused on it. The three bumped fists before Carlos and Juan sauntered off down the street in the direction of Mark Twain.

Roy's truck slid to the curb and he jumped down to the asphalt. Alex wheeled over to him. "How's your dad?"

Roy's face looked ashen, and he had dark circles under his eyes. "He's okay. I'll take him home after school." His face darkened as he scrutinized Alex. "Dane told me what happened. Shit, Alex, you didn't kill her."

Alex lowered his gaze to the sidewalk. "I might've."

"Never!" Roy's voice sounded like the crack of a whip, and Alex looked up, startled.

"But I don't remember nothing, Roy," Alex stammered. "And there was tracks–"

"You didn't kill her!" Roy snapped. "I know you."

Alex felt warm inside. Roy was such an amazing friend, so loyal.

Roy tilted his head toward the retreating boys. "Those guys giving you crap?"

Alex smiled. "No. We're buds now."

"Yeah?"

"I'll tell ya on the way."

Roy agreed and put Alex into his truck. By the time Roy pulled into the student parking lot, he'd heard everything that had transpired with Jane, and seethed with anger at the way she had treated Alex.

"She's the freak, Alex, not you," he spat as he scanned the busy lot for an open space. "I hate that bitch!"

Alex reached out and placed a hand on Roy's forearm as his friend slid into an empty space at the rear of the lot. "It's chill, Roy."

Roy put the gearshift in park and switched off the engine, turning to face Alex with a stormy look.

Alex offered a reassuring smile. "Long as I got the other guys with me, Jane can't do shit. We got her cornered."

Roy nodded, but looked worried. "If she really killed them guys from her closet, what's to stop her from killing you?"

Alex frowned. That hadn't occurred to him. "Well, I guess your dad better adopt me quick, huh?"

He raised a fist, and Roy bumped it.

***

When they arrived at the classroom, Alex and Roy found the others hovering outside the door. Israel looked scratched up, his face crisscrossed with stiches, but he offered that loopy grin and said the stitches made him look "Badass as hell."

Java had only a few stitches to his face. But when he rolled up the sleeves to his hoodie, Alex gasped at the raggedly stitched tears running this way and that, looking like blood-red rivers intersecting one another.

They waved away Alex's apology, admitting they had been "scared shitless," but afterward thought the whole thing "awesome."

Israel said, "That freaking doll knew your name, Alex! It's like Chucky and shit!" He lost the look of terror and added, "Did you guys see her panties and bras?" His tongue hung from his mouth, and Java shoved him playfully. Alex had to chuckle at that, and shook his head. Israel looked disappointed. "I wonder if she screwed some crippled guy 'fore she got home."

"Izzy!" Roy and Java said at the same time, making Cuong and Jorge both laugh.

"Izzy!" Jorge repeated, and even Israel laughed that time.

With only fifteen minutes until the sub arrived, the boys huddled together to plot their next move. Alex told them about Mrs. Rhodes, which caused Israel to recoil.

"The hell, Izzy!" snapped Roy. "He didn't kill her."

Israel nodded, but Alex noted that he kept his distance.

I don't blame you.

They all agreed that Ms. G. was the enemy, and made a pact not to do or say anything when she was around. They'd do their class work, but that was all. They sealed the pact with their fist ritual, and then the substitute arrived.

Despite it being a cool, breezy day, she sauntered up in one of those short skirts that, Alex noted, usually drew Izzy's eyes right to her. Which, he supposed, was her plan – to distract them, maybe catch them off-guard. But it didn't work this time. Izzy didn't even give her a look.

You're not gonna win, bitch, Alex thought as she offered him a sly smile before slipping her key into the lock and pulling open the door.

***

Phil and Bob stood to one side of the desk. Shaw sat back in his swivel chair, his eyes fixed on the two doctors before him, attired in their white lab coats.

"You've studied the tape. You've read Bob's observation reports from the past few days. Your impressions?"

The woman looked at him with conviction. "I don't think it's a trick. He did what we saw. What isn't evident is *how* he did it."

The middle-aged, balding doctor beside her nodded his head. "I agree with Dr. Stiles. The boy did something to heal the other one, but we cannot discern from this bit of tape the true extent of his abilities. It also appears from Bob's report that he made the old lady feel better, somehow took her pain away. There may be no limit to what he can do, Mr. Shaw."

Shaw considered a moment. "Thank you, Dr. Gluck. You may both return to the lab."

The two doctors departed the office as Phil and Bob stepped around to face their employer.

"You gonna meet that woman's price?" Bob asked casually.

Shaw snorted with disgust, glancing at the message Phil had handed him just before the doctors entered the office. It was an email sent to Phil from that housemother, Jane Walters: 'To Whom It May Concern: I've changed my mind. If you want Alex, it'll cost you five million. In cash. I have other buyers, so act fast.'

"Buy a child?" Shaw said after a moment, his voice tinged with distaste. "I may be many things, Bob, but I wouldn't go that far." He paused, considering his options. "Take him. Unharmed. Do it invisibly. Any mistakes will cost you."

"Understood, sir."

***

Ms. G. swished her way between the rows observing each boy's work. Cuong sat at his desk copying words from a picture dictionary, his printing uneven and illegible. Israel filled in some blanks with words to make sentences comprehensible, but he was skittish with her so close and became more unfocused than usual. She made sure to brush against him as she passed, and he recoiled every time.

She stopped by Jorge's desk and looked over his shoulder, leaning in so her arm touched his as she did. He looked at her warily. "Remember, Jorge, to put the 'de la' into your name."

She wrote it on his paper – Jorge de la Cruz – in between rows of "V's" scribbled everywhere.

Jorge continued to watch her, but did not otherwise respond. She stood and looked at him with a knowing expression.

Alex watched all of this from the corner of his eye as he pretended to read a short passage and answer the questions. He knew she understood that everyone had been told what went down on Saturday night and were now hip to her games.

As though reading his mind, the woman turned her head and fixed those amused blue eyes right on him, forcing Alex to look up and meet them. He squirmed, but was determined not to look scared in front of her. She sauntered in his direction.

She stopped by Roy's desk and leaned in to him like she was sharing a big secret. Alex couldn't hear what she whispered, but Roy's eyes bugged out with a mix of anger and fear. He twisted his head around to lock eyes with him even as the smirking teacher rose to her full height and approached.

Alex couldn't fully read Roy's expression, but his best friend looked really pissed. Ms. G. stopped before Alex her lips twisted into a lopsided grin. She bent and pressed her face so close to his he could have kissed her.

"Curiosity killed the cat, Alex," she whispered. "It can kill cripples, too."

He looked at her blankly. He knew what cripple meant, of course, and thought he recognized the other word, but was she talking about the big, evil cat? Why would she want it dead?

He must've looked confused because she chuckled with disgust. "Idioms are wasted on you dummies," she muttered before moving closer to his ear and brushing her lips against the blond hair covering it.

"We can and we will make you kill every one of these dummies you call friends, just like we made you kill the others." Alex gasped, and his heart pounded. "And we'll start with the queer boy you love so much. *We* may not be able to kill him, but *you* can."

She stood and looked at his horrified expression with amused detachment. "Really, Alex, your work isn't that bad. You just need to try a little harder."

She moved toward Cuong, who pressed back in his seat, as though afraid she might slap him.

Alex met Roy's gaze, and nodded to reassure his friend that everything would be all right. But, how could it? If he *was* the one doing the killing, what would stop Ms. G. from making him kill his friends?

I could even kill Roy, he thought, his heart thumping.

Feeling cold eyes on him, Alex looked away from Roy to find Ms. G. across the room near Java's desk, staring at him with intensity. She smiled.

Suddenly images flashed through his mind like a movie. It was the dream he'd had last week, the one about Ms. Ashley. It replayed itself in his head with more clarity than before. Suddenly the classroom was gone, his friends gone. It was like he was sitting on the sidewalk watching his favorite teacher staggering out toward the street beneath the weight of all those cats. He wanted to rush over and save her, but he couldn't move. He could only watch helplessly as the dark figure shoved Ms. Ashley in front of the oncoming truck.

Alex gasped, because this time the face of the killer became clear beneath the glow of the streetlight – it was Ms. G!

Then Roy was there, his face in front of Alex's, his words cutting through the movie images playing out before him.

"Hey, Alex, you okay, man?"

Ms. Ashley's scream of terror almost drowned out Roy's words, and Alex gasped again, causing Roy to grab his hand and squeeze.

Roy froze. The image of Ms. G. standing beneath the light as the truck plowed into Ms. Ashley filled his head and almost caused him to cry out.

He whirled around to face Ms. G. along with Alex. Together, they stared at her, causing the woman to frown. Her smugness of a moment before vanished and she strode to them.

She stepped between Alex and Roy, breaking the bond. Both boys paused to shake their heads and refocus on their surroundings. The others stared at them with puzzled looks, especially Java.

"Okay, guys, they're all right," she announced. "Everybody back to work."

As she moved off to her desk, Alex and Roy exchanged a perplexed look. What just happened?

***

The lunch bell hadn't finished ringing before Alex and the others were out of that classroom and gathered around their table. Even Israel ignored the taunts directed at them from passing students hurrying to the cafeteria.

"What'd she say to you?" Alex demanded, causing Roy to pull away in surprise. Alex must've seen the hurt expression and softened his tone. "Sorry, but you looked super pissed."

Roy nodded. "She said if I didn't ditch you she'd make you kill my dad."

"The hell?" Israel blurted, his eyes bugging out.

"She told me the same thing." Alex glanced around at the faces of his friends. They were all leaning in to hear above the surrounding noise of lunchtime. "Said they'd make me kill all of you."

Israel recoiled, Java flinched, but Cuong just stared impassively and Jorge handed him a slip of paper with a red "V" scribbled on it.

"That's bullshit, Alex!" Roy blurted in anger. "You didn't kill nobody, so stop that shit already!"

Everyone stared at Roy with surprise.

"I don't remember, Roy," Alex murmured, squeezing the wheel handles of his chair. "I had blood on me. I might a done it."

Roy felt his blood boil with anger. "No way! You're too good. We all know that, right guys?"

Israel had pulled back and was making a weird face, but the others nodded.

Roy forced himself to calm down enough to talk about what he saw when he grabbed Alex's hand. He and Alex shared their "vision" with the others. They listened, though Jorge kept drawing "Vs" on his bare forearm the whole time.

"You *saw* her kill Ms. Ashley?" Java said, for once looking almost scared.

Alex nodded.

"That bitch!" Israel spat in fury.

Alex told them his plan to visit Father Pat after school in the hopes the priest could make sense of all the stuff they'd found in the grave.

"Freaking cats," Israel spat in anger. "Give me a gun and I'll take out those assholes!"

Java turned with an upraised fist. That was all Israel needed to clam up.

"Okay, I'm gonna get some shit they call food," Israel said in his machine gun style. "Anybody want some?"

Java, Jorge, and Cuong all rose to follow.

"You guys want something?" Java asked.

Alex shook his head, and Roy said, "Naw. Not hungry."

Java shrugged and led the way, with Israel bobbing along behind. The other two walked with their eyes downcast so no one would think they were looking at them.

Alex and Roy sat in awkward silence.

"You could never do those things, Alex," Roy said, his voice almost a whisper.

Alex opened his mouth to respond when suddenly Tami stood before the table, hands to her hips, fury in her eyes.

"What the hell were you doing calling me at three-thirty this morning, Alex?" she demanded, her wavy hair wafting across her forehead in the breeze. "My ringtone went off and my parents had a fit!"

"I'm sorry, Tami, I…." Alex began, but couldn't finish.

Roy watched him, slightly bothered by the fact that Alex hadn't told him he'd called Tami in the middle of the night.

"You what?" Tami demanded, throwing her arms across her chest.

"I, uh, I had a dream," he said. "And I thought you were in trouble."

Her face told the story – she didn't believe him. "Don't bullshit me, Alex."

Alex forced himself to meet her steady gaze. "I'm not. And I meant what I told you, Tami. Stay away from me. You'll get hurt."

She looked confused, the anger dissolving beneath his obvious sincerity.

"Alex, what are you talking about?"

"I don't know. Just stay away."

The hands dropped to her sides, and she stepped closer, her face etched with worry. "Alex, you're really scaring me. What's going on?"

Alex said nothing, and stared at her as though looking right through her.

Roy knew the signs. Alex was spinning.

"It has something to do with the murder on the news this morning, doesn't it, the one like Maribel?" Tami asked, her voice less fearful than a moment before.

As Alex fixed his eyes on her, Roy noted traces of her fear in him, and Tami must have seen it too because she flinched.

"Don't be afraid, Tami," Alex said. "It'll be cool."

"Alex, I *am* afraid. You're scaring the–" Then her face became calm. "I feel better all of a sudden. It's like I'm not even–"

She stopped and stared open-mouthed at Alex's face. Roy realized that she could *see* her own fear reflected back at her. He wanted to say something, but didn't know what.

"Oh, God, it's you!" Tami cried, her hand to her mouth even as she stepped back. "Isn't it? Like all those times before, when I felt bad, and then I didn't…. It's you! What did you do to me?"

Alex looked so guilty Roy wanted to cry. "Nothing, I…." He clearly had no idea what to say, and looked devastated by her horrified expression.

She backed away. "Alex, what have you been doing to me?"

"I don't do nothing," he said, his voice sad and broken. "I'm just me."

She stared at him like so many other kids had looked at him over the years – like he was a circus freak. Then she turned and ran.

"I'm sorry, Alex," Roy said. "She'll be back."

Alex shook his head, and Roy felt his heart lurch at the look of loss on his friend's face.

Before he could say more, the others returned with cardboard trays of burritos and nachos, plopping them down on the table and sliding into the benches after.

"Stupid bitch," Israel was saying as he tore open the plastic around his burrito. "Never gives me seconds." He bit into the sloppy burrito, causing beans and sauce to dribble down his chin.

"Ttthey nnnnever gggive ssseconds, Iiizzy," Cuong said as he unwrapped his food.

Israel flashed him the eye roll. "Iii kkknow ttthhat, fffool," he said, drawing a big grin from Cuong. "I just like calling her a bitch."

Even Jorge laughed as he dug into his nachos.

"Heard that asswipe Saul tried to off his self," Java mumbled as he gnawed off a bite of his chicken burrito.

Alex whipped his head up. "What'd you say, Java?"

Java swallowed his food, but before he could answer, Israel surfaced from his nacho bowl with orange cheese framing his lips, and said, "That asshole who always makes fun of you, Spinner. Tried to hang his self on Friday."

Alex gasped, and Roy studied him. Something about Alex's reaction....

"What happened?" Alex asked, his face ghostly white.

"Everybody's talkin' 'bout it," Java went on. "Fool tried to hang his self from some pipe in the garage, but it broke."

Israel nodded. "Yeah, and now his ass is in the nuthouse." He laughed. "What he gets for callin' us dummies."

Roy couldn't take his eyes off Alex. Why was this news getting him so upset?

Alex finally found his voice, as though for a moment he'd forgotten how to speak. "Do they, uh, like, know why he did that?"

Israel laughed and Java elbowed him. "What?" Israel chortled. "Didn't they say he started to feel like shit in the bathroom here on Friday? That's funny, ain't it, feelin' like shit in a bathroom?" He guffawed.

Alex paled even more. Suddenly, even Israel understood that something was wrong.

Roy's hand went to Alex's shoulder. "What's wrong, man?"

Alex's breathing became hoarse and raspy, his eyes wide with horror. "I did that, Roy," he whispered. "I made him do that!"

"No shit?" Israel blurted, but Java's hand in his face prevented any further outbursts.

Roy glanced at his friends. All of them had the same baffled expression on their faces. He scooted closer to Alex. "Made him do what?"

"Try an' kill his self!" Alex hissed, his fingers wrapped around his wheel handles like he would bolt at any moment.

Haltingly, as though barely able to admit what he'd done, Alex confessed his sin, how he'd taken all the good feelings from those two boys on Friday, leaving them empty.

"And Saul almost died. Cuz of me." His guilt-filled eyes found Roy's sympathetic ones. "Oh, Roy, I *am* evil, like Jane said."

He was breathing hard now, his body hitching from the emotions twisting up his insides.

New anger swelled in Roy, and his eyes burned with passion. He reached out and gripped Alex hard by the shoulders. "You are not evil, Alex! Stop that shit!"

Alex shook his head, as though Roy's words had just bounced right off. "What I did was evil, Roy."

"Alex, listen to me. Evil means you wanna hurt people," Roy pressed on. "You didn't wanna hurt that dude."

Alex locked his wide blue eyes onto Roy's worried face. "Lots of people do evil stuff and don't mean to," he said in a whisper. "Don't make it not evil."

"Alex–" Java began, but Alex's look of hopelessness stopped his mouth cold, and he looked to Roy instead.

But Roy didn't know what to say, or do. He was too dumb to even help his friend through this.

"If Father Pat can't help me, Roy," Alex mumbled, his eyes downcast, his fingers toying with the friendship bracelet on his right wrist, "I'm gonna–" But he stopped himself and refused to look up.

A chill rippled through Roy's entire body that had nothing to do with the cold breeze surrounding him. "You're gonna what?"

Alex didn't respond, and Roy's breath stopped. He was sure he understood what Alex was *not* saying, and it terrified him.

They all tried to draw Alex out for the rest of lunch, but he remained silent. Even Israel cussing up a storm didn't bring him out of his shell.

They did agree to ignore Ms. G. and just do their work for the final two hours, and that's what they did. The substitute tried to engage them, but they refused to cooperate. She kept eyeing Alex, but he never once looked her way. Then it was two-fifty-eight and the dismissal bell chimed its way throughout the campus.

As he wheeled himself out the door behind Roy, Alex was startled to feel a hand on his shoulder. He whirled to find Ms. G. right behind him.

"Remember what I said, Alex."

He spun around and pushed his way through the door into the sunlight without looking back.

***

Roy took the others home and then swung by St. Joseph's to drop off Alex before picking up his dad. Alex promised to go straight to Roy's house after his meeting with the priest.

"You sure?" Roy asked, his voice tense with anxiety. "You'll come right to my place?"

Alex nodded. He tried for a grin, but didn't much succeed. He wheeled away without another word, but then turned back around. "You're the best, Roy," he said, his voice catching slightly. "Sickest friend ever. Just wanted you to know that."

He turned and fled across the church parking lot without once looking back.

Roy wanted to follow, but a quick glance at his phone confirmed the time. He needed to get his dad. Concerned about that look on Alex's face, he climbed into his truck and pulled away from the curb.

***

Alex watched as Father Pat checked out the pictures and read the papers his mother had left. He'd already watched the DVD, glancing over in confusion when Alex stuffed the buds into his ears so he wouldn't hear that music box again, and was now reading everything else. The priest had been surprised by Alex's unexpected visit, and Alex was equally surprised to find him wearing sweat pants and a tee shirt with something written on it that he couldn't read. The priest had laughed and said he was "Off-duty for the moment," before listening to Alex's explanation of why he was there.

Alex told him everything, the whole story of his life, and what had happened since last week. The man listened without interrupting once, which Alex thought about now as he watched Father Pat flip through the stuff he'd brought. Most adults never let him talk without interrupting him.

When he finished, Father Pat's face looked really worried, and that scared him. But he waited with growing anxiety while the man read through every paper in front of him.

Finally, the priest removed his reading glasses and leaned back in his chair, gazing at Alex with wonder. The intensity of that gaze made him fidget and squirm and not want to meet Father Pat's eyes. Somehow, he knew he wasn't going to like what he heard.

"Wow," the priest said, expelling a heavy breath as he did.

Alex brushed the hair from his eyes and said, "What does that mean? Am I… evil, like Jane says?"

Father Pat frowned. "Of course not. If anyone is evil, it's her, especially after what you just told me. And the teacher. We need to report both of them to that police officer you know."

Dread filled Alex at what the man *wasn't* saying. "But what about me? What am I, Father? Can you read me some of that stuff?"

The glasses were slipped back on and Father Pat leaned forward in his chair. "Of course, Alex, I didn't mean to exclude you. Sorry." He looked embarrassed as he scooped up the papers and shuffled through them while Alex squirmed and waited.

"Uh, this one is a line from the Bible. 'One day the evil spirit answered them,' Jesus I know, and Paul I know, but who is the one to come?"' He squinted over his reading glasses at Alex.

"What does that mean?" Alex asked, frustrated at his stupidity. "Are they talking about me?"

Father Pat nodded. "That's what many scholars think."

"Sca-what?"

"Sorry. It means people who study a lot and know a lot. There's this passage here, from Book 3 of The Essene Gospel of Peace. They were a group of people in Jesus' time who believed they could heal others by the power of angels. That's why this picture is on the cave wall."

He held up the photocopy of the cave wall with the blond boy healing people and an angel standing behind him.

"It says, 'one may heal with goodness, one may heal with justice, one may heal with herbs, and one may heal with the wise word, amongst all the remedies this is the healing one, the one that heals with the wise word and the one that will best drive away all sickness.'"

He must've seen the blank look on Alex's face because he added, "From what you told me, you heal by words, people telling you their pain."

Alex nodded. Okay, that made sense. Kind of.

"Then there's the Iroquois legend from your mother's side of the family. It goes like this." Father Pat squinted at the paper. "'A son will be born to you who will be distinguished among his nation as a peacemaker. He will be a white boy as well as an Indian, a boy with round legs and great compassion. His name will reach from the East to the West, the North to the South. His sun will rise on Indian land and set on the white man's land'."

Alex listened intently. Round legs? What the hell did…? And then he lowered his gaze to the wheels beneath him, and understood. They *were* talking about him!

Father Pat set down the papers and scooped up the necklace Alex had found and twiddled it in his fingers as he stood and wandered around the room. Alex watched him, worried about what all of this stuff meant. But he also worried about Roy. He didn't know how long he'd been there, but it was dark outside the windows.

Roy'll be worried, he thought, but just picturing his friend calmed his heart.

"This medallion is supposed to be a portal to another world, if you believe that sort of thing."

He looked thoughtful as he stopped pacing.

"Uh, what's a portal?" Alex asked.

"A kind of gate or doorway, to let creatures, like demons, into our world from theirs," the priest answered matter-of-factly, like he was teaching a class.

Alex shivered. He'd seen movies about demons that took people over and made them do bad things. Even kill.

"I'm sure it was left there for you to find," Father Pat went on, "probably by that substitute teacher."

"Why? Who am I? *What* am I?"

Father Pat looked at him as though seeing something he never expected to see. "A miracle." He crossed the room to squat before Alex. "In college, I did a lot of research on stuff like this, prophecies and ancient sects and so-called demonology. That's why I didn't believe in any of it. It all just seemed like superstition to me." He stopped, because Alex had taken on a stricken, embarrassed expression. "You don't understand the words I'm using, do you?"

Alex shook his head, feeling disgusted *again* for being a dummy who, like Roy had told Dane, needed to be talked to like a baby. "I'm sorry."

Father Pat smiled. "Don't be. I'll try to keep it simple." He paused and took a deep breath. "I told you I didn't believe in demons or angels or other dimensions, for that matter, but I was wrong."

He stood and paced as he talked. "You're what's been called by people who study these things 'The Healer' because of what you can do, how you can take things out of people and make them better." Then he stopped and stared at Alex in shock. "You did it to me before, didn't you?"

Turning red around the ears, Alex nodded.

But Father Pat didn't look angry the way Alex expected. He looked happy. "Wow. It's really true."

Alex waited, feeling confused and scared and almost desperate.

He doesn't know! He doesn't know what I did to that boy!

"Basically, Alex, people dreamed about you, somehow knew about you, thousands of years ago, in different countries and cultures," Father Pat went on, and then paused again. "You know that word, culture?"

Alex nodded. He'd heard a lot about every culture in school, except about white kids like him. He'd always figured he didn't have any culture until his mother's video said he was part Indian.

"Anyway, people have been waiting for you to be born for a long time. Even the Native Americans of your mother's tribe. All of these people believed that you can make humans better, Alex, with your gift. They believe you've been touched by God in such a way as to interrupt the spread of evil throughout the world."

Alex looked confused, and the priest added, "I told you before evil is like a virus that spreads from person to person. The Healer would be able to slow that virus down, and bring people closer to their own goodness."

His expression grew thoughtful. "But others think they can use your gift to control people, to make them worse than they already are. I think those are the ones who killed your parents, from what your mother said on that DVD."

When Alex heard that part he spun his chair away to look out the window. He felt so guilty he was sure Father Pat would see it on his face.

"What's wrong, Alex?"

Without turning to face this man he respected, Alex haltingly told of his crime against those seniors, his voice hitching as he forced the words out. When he finished, there was nothing but silence. He felt a gentle hand on his shoulder.

He nearly jumped he was so nervous, but turned instead and looked into Father Pat's compassionate eyes.

"Did you hurt him on purpose, Alex?" the man asked, his tone even and not at all what Alex expected.

"Hell, no, it just happened, Father Pat. I swear I never wanted to hurt him!"

The man nodded. "Now that you know you can do that, do you plan on doing it again?"

"No way!" Alex insisted, his whole body shaking at the thought. "I don't wanna hurt no one."

Father Pat smiled and squatted to face him. Alex's hair had fallen in front of his eyes and the priest brushed it aside. "That's why you're not evil, Alex. We all have a choice to do right or wrong. You're choosing to do right, and that makes you good. Do you understand?"

Alex had never thought about his power in terms of choices. It was just something he did because it was part of him. "You mean I can control it?"

"Of course, you can. You can control everything that's part of you. It's called making choices."

Alex felt like someone had punched him. He'd never thought of his power as a choice that could be turned on or off. "But what if I can't learn to control it?"

"You will. I'll help. So will your friends. They sound pretty kickass to me." The priest smiled at Alex's comical expression. "Yes, priests are known to cuss once in a while."

Alex fell silent a moment. Then he whispered, "Father, I think maybe I done those killings, too."

Father Pat looked horrified. "No way."

"But I don't remember nothing, Father, and I was there," Alex went on, frustration at his inability to remember tempering the elation he'd momentarily felt. "I was in Mrs. Rhodes' house. I had blood all over me!"

All the emotions he'd been juggling cascaded into a waterfall of tears, and Father Pat leaned in to engulf him in a hug.

"Don't be afraid, Alex. You didn't kill anyone. I know you too well."

"But I might've, right?" Alex sobbed into his shoulder. "I mean, if you was wrong and them things *are* real, they could get inside me, couldn't they? They could make me walk. They could make me kill, just like Ms. G said!"

Alex pulled back to gaze at the priest's uncertain expression.

"Look, Alex, I need to learn more about all this. I'll look through some of my old books, search the Internet. Please try to be strong. If God has chosen you, He won't abandon you. Can I keep all this stuff?" He indicated the papers and pictures scattered on his desk.

Alex nodded, swiping at the tears streaking his face as Father Pat stood.

"Can you stay with your friend Roy for now? I don't want you near that woman until I talk to the police about her. Do you still have that officer's business card?"

Alex fished it out of his pocket. It was wrinkled and beat up, but looked readable to him. He handed it over. “Roy and his dad’ll protect me.”

“Good,” Father Pat said, looking relieved as he took the card and slipped it into the pocket of his sweats. “We’ll talk again tomorrow, okay?”

“Okay,” Alex said, feeling weak and childish. “I’m sorry for crying. I’m too big for that.”

“You’re never too big for feelings, Alex. If you ever were, you wouldn’t be human anymore.”

Alex offered a small smile in return. He was happy he’d confided in this man. Somehow, Father Pat would help him get through all this. But now he needed Roy. And Nathan. They would make him feel good, like they always did.

***

The sun was setting and the streetlights had come on. The night sky sported ominous-looking clouds ready to douse him with more rain. But he also knew the rain only hit when that cat was somewhere nearby. He didn’t understand it, and hadn’t even told Father Pat that the cat, and the doll, had talked to him. *No* adult would believe that, he was sure.

He wheeled himself through the dark and empty parking lot to the sidewalk, and started on his way home. He hadn’t gone far when that feeling of being watched assaulted him like a snowstorm. He stopped just short of the corner he needed to take and looked around. He fiddled with Roy’s friendship bracelet as his gaze roamed the shadowy street.

There should be more cars right here, his frightened mind told him. *There just should be. There’s always cars on this street.*

But not tonight. Tonight, the street might as well have been that graveyard they were in. Was it Ms. G. again? Was she following him? Or was it that damned cat? He shivered, and flipped the hood over his hair and ears. But the cold remained. The sensation remained. It filled his heart and soul with dread.

I could call Roy, he thought. *He’ll come get me.* But then he cursed himself for being selfish. Roy’s dad needed him at home.

Steeling himself against the fear, Alex wheeled forward. Closer and closer to the corner. The house had a tall hedge in front of it and

Alex couldn't see what was around that corner. His breathing on hold, he stopped at the edge, where the sidewalk turned right. Exhaling, he gripped his wheel handles and spun forward, turning the corner like a racecar driver. A man stood blocking his way.

He gasped and tried to turn, but was grabbed hard from behind. A hand clamped itself over his mouth. There was a wet cloth in that hand, and a weird, sickly smell attacked his nostrils. Alex fought against his assailant, but the other man grabbed his hands, yanked them away from the guy behind him and held them tight. Alex felt himself getting sleepy. He vaguely noticed Roy's friendship bracelet slip off his wrist and wanted to scream at his attackers that he needed it back. But his voice didn't work. His lungs didn't work. He was drowning. That's what it felt like – drifting off to sleep under water.

The hand slid off his face, taking the cloth and the weird smell with it. Alex couldn't focus his eyes on the man in front of him. Everything was getting dark. He thought about his bracelet.

"Roy, help me," he managed to whisper before everything went black.

CHAPTER TWENTY-THREE

YOU THE GUY WHO KILLED MY PARENTS?

Roy nibbled at a chicken sandwich in his dad's room, while Nathan sat up in bed eating from a tray resting across his lap. After getting his dad home and upstairs, Roy had retreated to the kitchen and prepared the best meal he could with the supplies on hand: sandwiches, soup, a little salad, and French bread. He'd brought enough for both of them and sat in a chair beside Nathan's bed, but was barely able to stomach anything.

He checked his phone every fifteen minutes, even though he'd left the ringer on and would know if Alex called. Nathan had a bandage wrapped around his head, but looked healthier and more alive than he had in the hospital, not so gray and ashen. He'd been assuring Roy that Alex would be fine with the priest, but Roy worried because it had been two hours since school ended, and still not a word.

Suddenly, Roy sat bolt upright in his chair, his plate of food flying from his lap to land with a *splat* on the carpet by his feet.

"What's wrong, son?"

But Roy couldn't even focus on his dad. Movie-like images played out in his head. There was a man in a coat and tie, but the image kept moving back and forth, and it started to blur. Just before everything went black, he heard it: "Roy, help me."

Alex!

He snapped out of his momentary daze to find Nathan staring at him, looking worried. "What's wrong, Roy?"

"Dad, Alex is in trouble!"

"How do you know?"

Roy tried to focus his thoughts. "I just… saw something. A man. And Alex called to me. Dad, he needs help!"

Nathan set the tray of food to one side and threw off the bed covers, but Roy jumped up. "No, Dad, you need to rest."

Nathan shook his head. "It could be those people his mother talked about on the DVD, son. No way I'm letting you go alone."

As scared as he was for Alex, Roy felt warmed by his father's devotion. He placed a hand on Nathan's shoulder. "Don't worry, Dad. Dane'll go with me."

Nathan's eyes widened in astonishment. "Yeah?"

"Yeah. We're cool now. I'm gonna call him to meet me over at the church."

He was already across the room to the door, slipping out his phone as he walked.

"Roy."

Roy turned, shaking the hair from in front of his eyes.

Nathan looked afraid. "Be careful, son. These are dangerous people. They killed Alex's parents."

Roy tried for a smile. "I'll be okay, Dad. Got me a badass big brother."

He turned and hurried through the door into the hallway.

***

The second Dane heard Alex was in trouble, he wanted in. "Be there in five."

Roy drove more slowly than usual along the route Alex would've taken from the church to his house. The rain had not returned, but there were residual puddles. He used his high beams to better illuminate the sidewalk and street as he cruised along. It wasn't fully dark yet, but the clouds overhead cast everything in deep shadow.

Just as he approached the corner where a left turn would take him to St. Joseph's, something floating in a puddle beside a hedge caught in his beams, and then vanished.

Could be anything, his mind told him. *Just trash.*

But something made him stop and back up. Leaving his truck idling, Roy jumped from the cab and sprinted to the corner. Pulling out his phone, he activated the flashlight app and aimed the beam around in the water.

He gasped.

Reaching down with trembling fingers, Roy picked up the cloth friendship bracelet he'd given Alex shortly after they'd met.

A bracelet Alex swore he'd never take off.

A bracelet that looked like it'd been torn from his wrist in a fight.

He turned and bolted for the truck.

***

Roy had never spoken with a priest before. Even when Alex started going to St. Joseph's because he said it made him feel good, Roy had never accompanied him. He hadn't wanted to get up early on weekends.

Dane stood beside his truck, leaning against it in a way most people would interpret as casual, but Roy noted the coiled nature of his body. Dane was afraid.

"You tried his phone, right?" was the first thing Dane said when Roy pulled into the space beside him and jumped out.

"Yeah. Just the recording," Roy replied. "I think the phone's off."

"Shit," Dane cursed. "If those assholes hurt him…."

Roy was surprised to see Dane so angry, but it filled him with a sense of peace, because it meant Dane would do whatever it took to get Alex back.

"Let's find that priest," Roy said and started off across the parking lot.

Since it was dinnertime, the housekeeper who answered the door was reluctant to call Father Pat for them. But Dane glowered at her in such a way that she relented. She did make them wait outside while she went to find him, however.

It didn't take long for the door to reopen, and a man wearing sweat pants and a t-shirt introduced himself as Father Pat. The moment Roy told him something happened to Alex, the priest led them down a series of hallways to his room.

To Roy it looked like an apartment, but with not much stuff in it: some pictures on the wall, what looked like family photos on the desk beside a laptop, a sofa and a coffee table. Atop the coffee table Roy spotted all the paperwork Alex's mother had left, and that necklace. There were also some books open atop these papers, books that Roy didn't recognize.

He clutched the friendship bracelet in one hand as he sat on the edge of the sofa, while Dane stood to the side and listened.

Roy told them what happened, and showed them the bracelet.

Dane noted the ragged threads, and said it meant Alex had fought with someone. Father Pat agreed with Roy that the group Alex's mother mentioned had probably kidnapped him. He also told them he'd learned a lot about Alex from some of his old books on weird stuff. He'd used a bigger word, but Roy figured it just meant weird and went with that.

Father Pat paused in his pacing and slid a hand into his pocket, extracting a beat-up looking card. "Alex said this detective has been trying to help him."

He held the card out to Roy, who recognized it as the one that cop had given Alex.

"Screw the cops," Dane spat, and Roy looked at him in surprise.

"If Alex has been kidnapped, Dane, the police need to be told," Father Pat said, ignoring Dane's tone.

"'Sides, Dane, the guy was cool with us Saturday at the graveyard," Roy added.

Dane scowled. "You can't trust cops. They do you dirty every time."

Father Pat glanced at Roy, clearly not sure what to do. But Roy knew. He stood and faced his brother. "I say we tell him, Dane. We got no other way to find Alex, right? They could be doing stuff to him right now…." He trailed off, shivering at the thought that something horrible might be happening to Alex.

Dane had sulked, but hadn't fought the idea, and now they all sat around awaiting the arrival of that cop. Father Pat told them the man wanted to meet here instead of the police station, which suited Roy just fine. Dane would likely go off on one of those guys if they entered the station. He wanted to ask why Dane hated cops so much, but didn't want to make his brother madder than he already was.

While they waited, Father Pat said he needed to check something in one of his books, so Dane rifled though the photos Alex's mother had left for him. True to his silent nature, Dane said nothing about any of the images, and just tossed them onto the coffee table when he was finished looking.

A hard knock on the door sounded like an explosion as it broke the awkward silence. Father Pat rose and crossed the room, opening the door to admit Cole.

Dane stood to one side as Roy told the detective what he'd experienced, and showed him Alex's friendship bracelet.

Cole examined the broken threads. "Definitely yanked off."

He began pacing the room, looking to Roy more like a worried parent than an investigating policeman.

Father Pat showed him all the paperwork Alex had given him, including the necklace. Cole lifted it by the chain and examined the design. Roy could tell he'd seen it before, but Cole said nothing. Then Cole flipped through the photos and papers, without any visible expression.

"Demonic creatures?" he finally said, his voice riddled with derision. "Yeah, right. You boys ever see Alex walk?" He turned his gaze from the papers to Roy and Dane.

Roy froze. He might be a dummy, but he could tell what the cop was thinking.

Obviously, Dane could, too, because he said, "He didn't kill them people."

Cole squinted at him. "Did you?"

Dane balled his fists. "Screw you, cop!"

Surprisingly, Cole didn't lash out as Roy expected him to. He set down the papers onto the coffee table, but held out the necklace. "Look kid, the image on this medallion was carved into the forehead of that old lady. You saw it. And now you tell me this medallion belongs to Alex. What would you think?"

"I think you're an asshole, like all cops."

Cole sighed and lowered his hand, but Roy noted he held onto the necklace. "Okay, kid, spill. What did I do to you? Did I give you a jaywalking ticket when you were in middle school? What?"

Dane glowered. "All you cops're assholes. You all knew I was special ed and couldn't remember shit, but you still busted my ass every day after I turned eighteen and forgot my I.D. before going out!"

Again, Cole surprised Roy by keeping his cool. Father Pat looked uncomfortable as the officer kept his eyes on the furious Dane. Roy had never known about those incidents till now.

"Did I personally harass you and bust you for that?"

Dane flinched. "No, but your homies did."

"And they were wrong. But since I didn't, and since Alex needs us, can we call a truce and work together?"

Dane pulled an uncertain face, and Roy knew why. To save his brother's pride, he asked, "What's 'truce' mean?"

"It means make peace so we can get something more important done."

Roy turned to Dane, standing like a statue in the corner. "Sounds like a plan to me, Dane. Alex needs us."

Reluctantly, Roy could tell, Dane nodded, losing that angry dog look. "So, Mr. Cop, how do we find out who gots him?"

Cole had a look on his face that confused Roy, as though he wasn't surprised about Alex being kidnapped, and yet he *was* surprised at the same time.

"I don't know," the man said, glancing at his watch like he needed to be somewhere. "There's nothing specific in any of this paperwork. I'll make some calls, put out an APB on him. About all I can do right now."

He turned toward the door, but Roy called out, "Excuse me, sir."

Cole turned, eyebrows raised.

Roy pointed to the man's hand. "That's Alex's chain."

Dane and Father Pat both looked at the detective, who opened his hand to reveal the medallion clutched within it.

"You're so right, Roy," the man said as he handed the chain to Father Pat. "My bad."

He pulled open the door. He hesitated, and turned again to face the three silent observers. "Let me know if you hear from him." Then he was through the door and down the hall.

***

Alex heard voices, but they were muffled and far away, like they were under water, or he was. Maybe it was a dream?

A man's voice sounded mad. "Dammit, Phil, how much chloroform did you give him?"

A second man sounded like he was apologizing. "Sorry, Mr. Shaw, but I didn't want him using his black magic on me."

The first man made a grunting noise and sounded even madder. "Get him down to the lab. I'll be in my office making calls. Tell the docs to move quickly. We're running out of time."

"Yes, sir."

Alex started moving. What the hell? Was he in his chair? He couldn't tell. And why couldn't he open his eyes? He made out the squeaking of wheels along some kind of hard floor. The sound lulled his senses and then the blackness returned.

***

Davalos paced his office, awaiting confirmation of the grab. The phone jangled, and he snatched it up. An agent, blond, dressed in a dark business suit, stood at attention by the door.

"Davalos." He listened, frowning, not liking what he heard. "How the hell did that happen? We're about to close in and this could be disastrous!" He listened again, cursing under his breath. "All right, I'll get on it. We may have to make a deal with them, thanks to your stupidity. I'll call you when we make our move!"

He slammed down the phone and cursed. He turned to the silent agent, dutifully awaiting orders. "Get ready to take a road trip."

***

Dane paced the room while Father Pat continued to flip through old books on his coffee table. Roy held several of the photos in his hands, staring at the crude depictions of Alex. He marveled at the Indian one, especially, with Alex's long blond hair so different from the dark-skinned people around him. Seeing Alex wearing only a small piece of something covering his privates and nothing else kept his eyes returning to that image, and made him feel dirty.

Don't go there, jerk! He's your best friend!

He dropped the pictures onto the table. "I wonder if Jane knows who took him."

Father Pat looked up from his books in surprise. "Why do you think that, Roy?"

"Alex told me Jane made him spin Juan last week, to fix a black eye, and she had cameras filming him."

Dane clearly didn't understand where Roy was going, but Father Pat did. "You think maybe she gave the tape to someone and those people kidnapped Alex?"

Roy bit his bottom lip, and twirled one of his snakebites as he considered. "Maybe."

Father Pat stood. "Let's go."

***

Shaw had finished his calls and was checking new company promo ads when Phil entered with the female doctor. The name "Stiles" was stitched into the left breast of her lab coat right beneath the company logo. She appeared excited, as though she had just discovered a cure for cancer.

"Have you finished your tests, doctor?"

"Yes, Mr. Shaw. We did every test we could in the limited time we had, including a brain scan and blood analysis."

"And your findings?" Shaw leaned forward and clasped his hands together on the desk.

"Except for the dormant spina bifida," the woman said, "he's a normal fifteen-year-old. There's nothing physically different about him, nothing to explain how he does what he does. He claims to have been able to 'spin' many ailments from people over the years."

"Spin?"

"That's his word for what he does. But, there's no indication that he, himself, has *ever* been sick."

"What do you mean?"

Her face took on an almost awed expression, and her voice sounded like that of someone who'd witnessed a miracle. "There's no indication that he has ever had any normal childhood ailments, not the flu, not even a cold. His white cells look like those of a newborn baby before they ever had to fight a germ. Mr. Shaw, this boy shouldn't even be alive."

Shaw appeared to digest that information. "Bring him in."

Phil strode to the door and opened it. Alex sat just outside in the corridor, Bob behind him. When Alex stared across the length of the room at Shaw, Bob began pushing the chair. Alex shrugged him off, feeling anger course through him, and pushed himself inside. Bob followed and closed the door.

Alex stopped in front of the desk, and gazed long and hard at the man sitting across from him. When he'd awakened in that hospital place downstairs, the two doctors refused to answer any of his questions, and put him through more tests than he'd ever had before. In fact, while they were taking his blood and hooking him up to this machine or that one, Alex realized that he'd never been to a doctor that he could recall. Because he'd never been sick, and had never developed the other symptoms of spina bifida except paralysis.

"Good evening, Alexander," the man said, his voice deep and flat, but not cold like Jane's.

"It's just Alex," he said, studying the man's face. He was terrible at guessing ages, but this guy had to be at least as old as Jane, except he didn't dye his hair. There were streaks of silver running through the black, and they made him look somehow more important.

The man studied him, and Alex wanted to look away. But he didn't. "My name is Shaw."

Alex took in a breath and expelled it. Here goes. "You the guy who killed my parents?"

That got a surprised look from the man, which confused Alex. "Your parents died in a traffic accident."

Alex shook his head. "They were my aunt and uncle. Somebody killed my real parents. And took my brother. Was it you?"

Again, the man looked puzzled, and Alex began to wonder what was going on here. The man turned to the two guys who had grabbed him out on that street.

"Phil, Bob, do you know what he's talking about?" He sounded mad, Alex noted, like he hated *not* knowing something.

The one called Phil stepped forward. Alex knew because they told him their names downstairs. "No, Mr. Shaw. We were able to access his children's services file, but the only parents mentioned were the Maracles."

Shaw sat back in his chair and stared at Alex, making him squirm with discomfort. "How do you come by this knowledge, Alex?"

Alex wasn't sure what to tell this man who had taken him against his will. But it was obvious the guy had no idea about his real parents. Alex knew he was a dummy in every other way, but his spinning ability told him this man was telling the truth.

"A DVD I got last week, sent by my real mother," he answered, his heart thumping at the images flitting through his mind. "She said people were after her and dad. And me. That's why she pretended my aunt and uncle were my parents."

Shaw considered that response a few silent moments, while Alex glanced around him at the fancy office. He'd never been anywhere this nice in his life.

"Was it because of what you can do, Alex?" Shaw went on, interrupting his roving gaze. "What you call spinning?"

Alex nodded. "She sent pictures from, like, way back, pictures of me from caves and stuff. I guess people knew about me 'fore I was born."

Shaw looked from Alex to the doctor. She shrugged. He turned to the other men. "It seems you did not do your job, Phil. I pay you for complete information."

Phil looked pale to Alex, and he wondered if maybe the Shaw guy might pull out a gun and shoot him like they do in the movies. "I'm so sorry, Mr. Shaw, but there was nothing about this in any files on Alex."

He sounded so tough downstairs, Alex thought, *when he kept threatening to tie me to the chair if I didn't do what the doctors said.*

Not sure why, Alex felt an urge to save the man's ass from whatever punishment Shaw might dish out, so he asked, "You, like, work for the government?"

The question had its intended effect. Shaw pulled his angry gaze from Phil and settled it on Alex. "The other way around, actually," he offered in a much calmer voice. "Money and power can buy anything."

Alex studied *him* this time, and the man looked almost amused. "If you're not the guy who killed my parents, why'd you take me?"

"I won't hurt you, Alex, I promise," Shaw said, and his tone told Alex he was being truthful. "I apologize for the secrecy, but I couldn't very well have met with you at the local taco stand."

Alex spun the voice, and the tone in it. "You do a lot of bad things, don't you?"

Shaw titled his head as he examined him, making Alex wonder if he'd said something wrong. "By the standards of a boy your age, I suppose I do. But it's just business. I like being in control, Alex. I do what needs to be done. That's the world, like it or not. Did you know that the woman you live with offered to sell you to me for five million dollars?"

Alex flinched, and expelled a heady breath. Now he understood what that hidden camera was for, what Jane had meant about becoming wealthy.

"Sell me?" was all he could manage.

Shaw nodded. "Body and soul."

Alex shook his head in disgust, hands trembling as they gripped his wheel handles. He shouldn't be surprised, but this seemed bad even by Jane standards.

"That figures. I been pushed around my whole life. Everybody wants me to spin 'em when they's sick or feeling like crap, but then they shove me away for being a freak. Or they try to kill my friends if I won't do what they want."

He must have sounded angry because Shaw leaned away, and from the corner of his eye he spotted Phil taking a nervous step backward.

"I am aware, Alex, of what's been going on this past week. Do you believe the same people who killed your parents killed those other people?"

Alex shrugged, afraid to tell the truth – that *he* might be the killer. He shivered.

"You're not a freak, Alex, from what I know. Just quite extraordinary."

Alex felt his face burn with shame. "I don't know that word."

But Shaw didn't rub his stupidity in like most people. "It means you're very special."

Alex grunted. "No, I'm not. I'm different. Like no other kid. A freak."

"How do you do what you do, Alex? 'Spin' people, as you call it?"

Alex saw the man was genuinely curious, and not the least bit afraid. "Dunno. It's just me. I hate seeing people sick or sad, you know? So, I spin 'em." He forced himself to look Shaw in the eye, his body trembling with anger. This was all Jane's fault. Something could be happening to Roy or one of the others and…. "You gonna pay Jane the money?"

Shaw snorted with disgust, which surprised Alex. "No. I often buy people's services, but I do not buy children. I have a request of you,

Alex. Whether you agree or say no, you're still free to go. I won't harm you, you have my word."

That confused Alex, and sent his anger meter into decline. But he also felt stupid, *again*! "Sorry, what's 'request' mean?"

Again, Shaw didn't make a face or roll his eyes. He simply said, "I'm sorry, Alex. It means I would like you to do something for me."

"What?"

Shaw suddenly looked sadder and smaller as he leaned forward in his chair and clasped his hands together on the desk. "Alex, I have enough money for ten lifetimes. I can buy anything, the best medical equipment, the best doctors. But I cannot buy a cure. I cannot buy what you do."

"You're not sick. I spinned you and you're fine."

That news surprised Shaw. "So, you always know when people are sick?"

Alex nodded. "And sad, too, like sad in the heart." He paused a moment. "You're sad in the heart, Mr. Shaw. I hear it."

Shaw sighed, and suddenly the sadness was on his face. The eyes lost that in-control look they'd had when Alex first came into the office. He pressed some buttons on his desk and the bookcase slid open behind him, revealing several video screens.

One flickered to life and displayed a teen girl, bald, thin, and pale, under some kind of plastic tent with a lot of tubes and wires running into and around her. She wasn't moving, and looked almost dead.

"My daughter, Allison," Shaw said, his voice heavy with emotion. "She's my everything, Alex. Do you know what that feels like?"

Alex thought of Roy, how he felt about his best friend, and nodded.

"She's dying, Alex. You've seen my lab. I've spent millions. But it's not enough. I'd gladly give my life if it would save hers. Hell, I'd sell my soul to the Devil if I knew how to contact him."

Alex flinched at the word "devil," images of demons filling his mind. Demons that could make him walk, and make him kill. He pushed those thoughts aside. "What's wrong with her?"

"Leukemia. Do you know what that is?"

"No, sir." As always, he felt stupid. *Another* word he didn't know.

Shaw turned from the screen and looked solemnly at Alex. "It's a cancer of the blood. She's going to die."

Alex's heart lurched as his gaze returned to the girl on screen. He wanted to help her, like he always wanted to help people. Or was it that he *needed* to help people?

"So, you want me to spin her?"

Shaw stood and walked around the desk. Phil and Bob instantly moved in closer as though to protect him, but Shaw waved them off. He stopped before Alex and looked down at him. "I've seen the video that woman took of you healing another boy. Have you ever cured someone of a disease like cancer?"

Alex knew he should feel weak, as he usually did when adults stood tall and looked down on him, knowing he could never stand and meet them eye-to-eye. But somehow, he didn't sense this man was doing that.

"No," he answered truthfully. He'd spun colds, the flu, broken bones, deep sadness from people's hearts, but he'd never known anyone with cancer, especially a kid his age.

"Your opinion, Doctor Stiles?" Shaw asked the woman, who snapped to attention.

"If he's never attempted a cure of this magnitude, there is a danger."

"Explain."

"If he succeeds in 'spinning', as he calls it, the leukemia out of Allison into himself, he may not be strong enough to purge his own system. He could die."

Shaw considered her words a moment. Then he did something most adults never did – he squatted down so Alex could look him in the eye. "Do you understand what she said, Alex, that this could be dangerous for you?"

Alex nodded. "If I do it, can I go?"

Shaw flinched ever so slightly. "Alex, I told you, you're free to go now if you like. I can only ask this of you. I cannot force you. But if you do it, and succeed, anything you want will be yours. Anything in the world."

Alex considered a moment, his gaze drifting past Shaw's head to the unmoving form of the girl in the hospital bed. "Okay, I'll do it."

Shaw reacted with visible surprise at his quick response. "Just like that? You would risk your life for a stranger?"

Alex thought a moment, struggled to collect his thoughts. Images of his whole life flashed before him, images of people he'd spun and made better. But then he fixed on the two seniors he'd spun in the bathroom at MTS, and pictured Saul hanging from a pipe in his garage. That spin made him evil. He had to make it right somehow. Maybe this was the way.

"It's like, well, you're good at making money, and she's good at being a doctor. I'm not good at nothing 'cept this. It's like, what I am. Plus, I think I owe it to God cuz of something I did that was really bad. If I can spin Allison, maybe God won't be mad at me."

Shaw looked at Alex with wonder, as though in his whole life he'd never seen or heard anything like that. "You're beyond extraordinary, Alex," he said as he stood up.

Alex turned red, feeling, as always, more freak than special.

"Let's go," Shaw said, and gestured toward his office door.

***

Roy and Dane parked their trucks in front of Jane's house and jumped out. Father Pat stepped from Roy's cab and looked up at the dark, silent house. It looked like no one was home. Fear for Alex impelled Roy forward, and the others followed.

He pressed the doorbell and stood on the porch a shifting on his heels. There was no answer. Dane reached for the knob and turned. It didn't budge.

"Shit," he said and looked at Roy with a "what now?" expression.

"Hey, Roy, what's up, man?" Roy heard from behind him, and spun in fear. But it was only Juan and Carlos heading up the walkway toward them. Roy sagged with relief.

"Somebody took Alex," Roy explained, "and we think Jane knows who. This is Father Pat from the church. He's helping."

Roy wasn't sure what reaction he'd get, but the anger twisting Carlos's face surprised him. "That bitch. Let's find out."

Carlos slipped a house key from his pocket and inserted it into the lock.

Juan gazed shyly at Roy. "Hi, Roy."

Roy turned to the younger boy a moment. "Hey, Juan." But his mind was on Alex.

Carlos opened the door and they streamed into the house.

"Jane, where are you?" Carlos demanded, his voice blasting through the silence like a sonic boom.

But no one answered.

"Carlos," Juan murmured, "maybe we should–"

Carlos had already started up the stairs two at a time, leaving the others scrambling to follow. Roy knew Carlos was on Alex's side now, but the intensity of his reaction surprised him.

Carlos peeled off to the left as soon as he hit the second-floor landing, and Roy followed, the others close on his heels. They all stopped when they found Carlos standing at the door to Jane's room. It was open, and Carlos stood frozen, looking in.

Something was very wrong here. Jane never left her room unlocked.

Roy moved to Carlos' side, noting the broken door lock. Someone had busted it open. But his gaze was drawn to something inside the room, lying on the white carpet. Except the carpet wasn't white anymore. It was red. With blood. And Jane lay there in a large pool of it, her eyes wide open and staring at him. Roy knew she wasn't staring at him at all. She was dead, with a knife sticking out of her chest.

"Oh, Lord," Father Pat mumbled, and crossed himself.

Juan made nervous little sounds with his voice, like he might wig out at any moment, and Carlos stood looking at the smaller boy without emotion.

"Shit," he said. "We're dead meat."

Juan nodded.

"We need to call the police," Father Pat said.

"No!" Carlos hissed, and everyone looked at him.

"Why not?"

"Cuz that's my knife sticking outta the bitch," Carlos replied.

Father Pat flinched, but didn't take a step back like Roy expected him to. He observed the burly Carlos with caution, but said nothing more.

"Why?" Juan asked Carlos, his voice trembling. "Why did somebody shank her with your knife?"

Carlos shrugged, and turned to glower in the direction of the body.

Roy had never seen a dead body before, and he felt sick to his stomach. The smell of the blood almost choked him. Carlos's cold reaction surprised him. Then he realized it shouldn't have. Carlos had probably seen other dead people before, so this was nothing new.

Roy's mind raced, Juan's question flitting about like a moth. Why use Carlos's knife? That would make the cops think Carlos killed her. Who would want.... then he had it!

"Alex said you guys were cool now," he said to Carlos and Juan. "That you had his back?"

Carlos squinted at him. "Yeah. Us against the bitch. So?"

"So, somebody's been tryin' to get Alex alone, to keep his friends away from him," Roy went on, his anxiety rising with every word. "If you guys are in jail, that's two more outta the way."

Carlos's whole body tensed up, and for a second Roy thought he might punch him. But Carlos hissed, "Hell with that!" He turned and strode to the body like it was a pile of trash on the floor and reached down to pull out the knife. He closed the blade and slipped the bloody instrument into his pants pocket.

Even Dane regarded him with surprise. "Why'd you do that?"

"Hell if they're gonna find my knife in her," Carlos said as he rejoined them, looking at Dane as though daring the man to challenge him.

Father Pat said, "Uh, I'm not sure that is–"

A glare from Carlos made him leave the thought unfinished.

Roy knew the killing of Jane would cause all kinds of questions, even for him, because everyone knew he and Alex were tight. And they didn't have time for questions.

"Let's go to my house and figure out how to find Alex," he said, feeling a deep sense of urgency. The bond he shared with Alex had amped up when they'd shared that vision at school. Now it thrummed with danger signals. They needed to hurry. "My dad can help."

Dane said, "Everyone in the neighborhood probably seen us walk in the front door." He glanced at Father Pat. "So, we gotta move fast 'fore the pigs come snoopin' around."

"Janitor's right," Carlos said with a snarky tone in his voice.

Dane stiffened.

Roy's anger flared, and he stepped between Dane and Carlos to squint down at the shorter gang member.

"That *janitor* is my brother, and he can kick your ass any day, gangbanger or not. Now if you wanna help us find Alex, I'm down. Otherwise, shut the hell up!"

Carlos took a step back, a look of surprise flitting across his face. "My brother's in prison, so yeah, janitor's an okay job. Sorry, homie."

Roy saw that the apology was real, and calmed down. "Let's go."

***

Alex rode in the elevator with the others in silence. They were going down, probably, he guessed, to somewhere near that hospital where they'd had him before. With the girl that sick, she must need to stay close to the doctors.

He kept seeing her pale face beneath the plastic tent and felt his heart lurch with pain. He followed Shaw and the two doctors down a long hallway. Phil and Bob trailed after him.

To make sure I don't try to bail, he thought as he pushed himself along with determination.

The doctors entered a room near the end of the hall. Shaw stopped at the door and turned to usher Alex inside. He wheeled past without a word.

Allison lay just as she had on the television screen, silent and unmoving. The tubes and cables crisscrossed into and out of her so that she looked part robot. Alex examined the purple bruises all up and down her arms and the ghostly white face beneath a shiny bald head.

He pulled his gaze from her and looked at Shaw. "She's not awake."

"She's been like this since yesterday."

"But she's gotta tell me. That's how it works. She's gotta tell me all the hurt. She has to. Otherwise I can't spin her."

Shaw observed him a moment as though wondering whether or not to believe him. He turned to the doctors. "Wake her."

"Mr. Shaw, she's fragile. A shot of adrenaline and she could–"

"Die?" Shaw's face was set, hard and determined. Only Alex heard the sorrow in that one word.

The male doctor stepped to a large cart beside the bed. He prepared a shot and injected it into the tubing attached to Allison's scrawny, pale arm. A heavy silence fell over the room as everyone watched the girl's unmoving form.

For a moment, Alex thought the shot hadn't worked. But then, almost like a butterfly he once saw poking out of the white stuff it was wrapped in, the girl opened her eyes and looked around, obviously confused. Shaw stepped forward to look through the plastic tent. Alex was surprised to see the man smile.

"Hey, Allison," he said, his voice gentle and soft. "There's someone here to see you. He can help."

Shaw stepped back and looked at Alex. That look of desperate hope mixed with fear touched Alex and made his stomach tighten. He wheeled himself as close to the bed as possible. Allison peered through the plastic tent at him, her eyes wide and curious. Brown eyes, Alex noticed for no obvious reason.

"Hi. I'm Alex."

Allison smiled, but Alex could tell it was hard for her. "Allison," she croaked, her voice weak and raspy.

Alex heard the pain, heard the sickness in just that one word, and knew he didn't have much time. "Tell me about the hurting, Allison, all about it. Every place it hurts, all the bad stuff. Tell me. *Hurry.*"

She looked at her father.

"Do what he says, honey," Shaw said, the desperation still there.

She opened her mouth and began speaking.

***

They gathered in Nathan's bedroom to plan how best to locate Alex. Roy had called Java and told him what happened, and wasn't surprised to find him, along with Israel, Jorge, and Cuong waiting in his driveway when he pulled up.

Now all ten of them sat in chairs or on the floor debating what to do next.

"I say we find Ms. G. and make her tell us," Israel growled. "You know she got something to do with it."

They talked about going to her place and busting in. Dane said he had guns at his pad and could bring them. Nathan looked surprised to hear that, but didn't say anything.

Father Pat sat in one of the chairs rifling through a book he'd brought along from his place. He held it up. The cover had weird pictures on it and a long name Roy couldn't begin to read.

"This is one of the oldest books we know of," the priest said. "I found references in here to the Healer."

"What healer?" Dane asked, his tone derisive, as usual.

But Roy already knew the answer. "He means Alex, cuz Alex heals people. Right, Father?"

Father Pat nodded. "According to this and some other books, that medalli-, that is, that necklace Alex found, is a kind of gateway to another world. Only the Healer wearing it could unlock the gate and release the creatures inside."

Dane snorted in disgust.

"Creatures?" Nathan said, his tone one of incredulity.

"For want of a better word," Father Pat said, "we can call them demons because the ones in the Bible are based on these things."

"It's bullshit," Dane said, his frustration mounting.

Roy felt the same frustration. Anything could be happening to Alex and here they were sitting around talking about demons.

If Father Pat was angry at Dane's outburst, he didn't show it. "I never believed in any of this either, Dane. But I think we have to."

"That stuff only happens in movies," Carlos said in disgust. "Even I know that shit."

"I-I-I b-b-believe i-i-in… d-d-d-demons," Cuong managed to get out, his voice trembling with fear.

Jorge reached out and placed an arm around Cuong's neck. He didn't pull the boy in close, but for Jorge that simple touch was almost a miracle. Cuong looked shocked, and smiled.

"My grandma says demons is real," Juan added quietly. "She gots little statues of the Virgin Mary all over the house to keep 'em out."

"Yeah, my grams got that shit, too," Carlos said. "Don't mean it's for real, lil homie."

Father Pat made no attempt to argue. "Here's the part that caught my eye." He looked down at the book and read, "The metal amulet that

I retrieved is a gateway into our world. Once pushed back through it, the creatures can only be contained if the amulet catches the light of the full moon upon its face, and the Healer and the six are joined as one. Amulet is another word for that necklace."

Roy explained to Nathan and Father Pat how they broke into Ms. G's apartment and found that same spider web thing in her bedroom.

"I still say we go and make her talk," Israel suggested. "Don't even matter if she's screwing some crippled guy in there. We gotta find Alex, and she knows who gots him."

Carlos and Juan looked at Israel like he was crazy, but Java just sighed.

"What?" Israel said. "She's one a them."

"Whoever 'them' is," Nathan added from where he lay propped up in bed.

Roy met his dad's eyes and understood. None of this talk was helping them find Alex.

"You guys don't buy into that demon bullshit, do you?" Dane scoffed, breaking the silence.

"Whatever these creatures are, Dane, humans have written about them since humans could write," Father Pat explained. "I always dismissed it as superstition." He noted Dane's blank expression and added, "You know, people imagining things. The main goal of these creatures is to possess or destroy anything good."

"Like Alex," Roy said.

"Like Alex," Father Pat agreed. "They want his power, and so do the people who killed his parents. It's up to us to stop them."

"How?" Israel asked. "We're a bunch a dummies. We almost got our asses handed to us in that graveyard. Now we gotta go after people and demons and shit? Yeah, right!"

"Everyone has a role to play in life, Israel," Father Pat said, surprising Roy with his calmness in the face of Israel's increasing outbursts. "Alex needs you. He can't send those creatures back without help. Look at this."

He flipped to another page in the book and held it out. Everyone but Nathan scooted closer to see the image spread across two pages.

It was a painting of some kind. In it, a white-haired figure stood within a circle made up of six other people holding hands. Descending onto the figure in the center were horrible, misshapen things that chilled Roy's bones.

"The guy in the middle ain't in no wheelchair," Israel noted.

"Yeah, but look at the hair," Roy added, pointing to the boy standing inside the circle. "And the blue eyes. That's Alex."

"Alex can't walk, Roy, you know that," Java said, his gaze pinned to the image.

A chill enveloped Roy, despite the thick hoodie he wore. "Could those things make Alex walk?" he asked the priest, his voice sounding small and far away.

Father Pat didn't answer. He didn't have to. The truth was on his face.

Roy shivered.

***

Alex stared at Allison as she spoke. He felt the presence of the others in the room, but from far away, like they weren't right beside him. All he felt was the sound of her voice as she described her pain in a strained, but slightly stronger voice. At his urging, she added more and more details of how she hurt and where, and the level of pain.

Alex had never heard anything like this before. No one he'd ever spun had this much hurt in them. Even her blood hurt as it moved through her veins. But he listened, he spun, and felt the same things she did. His whole body ached worse than ever before. He wanted to cry from the pain. He almost did, and wasn't sure he could keep the tears away as more and more of her hurt became his. But he struggled for control, to focus on the sound of her voice, on the pain in that voice. He could do this….

***

Nathan held the book in his hands and studied the image the others had already seen. "That's Alex, all right," he said, shaking his head in amazement. But then he frowned. "If there be these demons, like you said, Father Pat, and they want Alex, then who are the *people* after him?"

Father Pat stood beside the bed, the youngsters gathered around him. "Evil always comes from people, so the people helping these creatures take over Alex must want his power, too."

"Why?" Nathan asked. "He helps people get better when they're sick, but that's a good thing, right? Why would bad people wanna do somethin' good?"

"Some believe his power could be used for evil, too. From what I've read, it's important that Alex give up his power willingly. If he won't, they'll make him hate himself so maybe he'd…."

He trailed off as Roy gasped, and everyone looked at him.

"What, son?" Nathan asked, face creased with concern.

Roy felt his whole body stiffen with fear. He almost couldn't breathe. "Alex told me if he was the one doing the killing, he'd, you know, kill *himself* so he could stop it."

"Oh, shit!" Dane spat.

"The hell?" Israel blurted, as Father Pat paled with fear.

"We gotta find him," Nathan said, and Dane nodded.

"You think Alex killed them people?" Carlos asked the others at large. "I don't. Alex ain't no killer."

"Carlos is right," Nathan said, with a look aimed squarely at Roy. "I know that boy, and my son knows him better than anyone. He couldn't kill nobody."

"Less demons made him," Israel murmured. "I seen lots of them movies and that shit happens."

Roy could tell by the fact he wasn't moving around that Israel was really scared.

Father Pat looked thoughtful. "Did Alex know the people who died? Did they know each other?"

"Maribel was a girl at school who treated him like shit, but she got hurt last week and Alex spinned her. He hated seeing anybody hurting. The old lady was nice to him, and he liked her. I guess her brother died the other day and Alex spinned the sad out of her. He wouldn't never kill her."

"Oh, shit," Father Pat muttered, his body stiffening.

"Are you guys allowed to cuss like us?" Israel asked in his usual random way.

"Shut up, Izzy," Java snapped, as he stared at the priest. "What?"

Father Pat turned and walked to the chair he'd been sitting in. Lowering himself into it, he looked up as everyone followed his movements.

"What?" Roy asked, terrified by the man's facial expression.

"Evil always takes what's good and tries to twist it," Father Pat said, almost like he was talking to himself.

"Huh?" Israel said.

And then Roy understood. "Oh, shit…." He looked at Dane, his dad, at every face now focused on him. "Everybody Alex makes better is gonna get killed. Right, Father?"

Father Pat nodded.

CHAPTER TWENTY-FOUR

YOU THINK HE'S DEAD?

ALEX'S WHOLE BODY FELT POISONED, like his own blood was trying to kill him. Faintness assailed him, and he gripped his wheel handles hard to keep from falling. The voice in his head grew stronger and stronger with each word as he grew weaker and weaker.

Hold on!

Almost there!

His eyes glazed over. He no longer saw Allison, or anyone else. He no longer felt his heart beating. He didn't know if he was even breathing. He focused on that voice in his head, that voice that had started out so feeble and now sounded powerful and strong.

Just a little longer....

***

A dark silence hung around the room. To Roy, it felt like death. Like when his mom died. Only this wasn't his mom who might die. This was Alex. And everyone Alex spun. A thought hit him, and he turned to Juan.

"Alex told me he spinned you, Juan," he exclaimed. "When was that?"

Juan's face darkened, and he glanced at Carlos.

Carlos looked guilty, something Roy had never seen. "Last Wednesday. I punched him in the face cuz Jane told me too." He turned to Juan. "Sorry, lil homie."

Juan smiled.

"What does the time matter, Roy?" Father Pat asked as he sat up in his chair.

Roy considered what had happened last week. He was good with details like that. One of his strengths. That's why he was good at fixing things – he always remembered the exact order he took something apart so he could put it back together.

"Alex spinned Juan *before* school that day," he said as his mind replayed the week, "and he found that necklace when we *got* to school. After that, the only people he helped were Maribel and that lady...."

Father Pat foraged in his pants pocket for the necklace as Roy and the others watched. He slipped it out and held it in the palm of his hand. "Alex opened the gate when he put this on."

Now Java approached, puffing out his chest and looking like a grown-up. "So how do we close it? How do we help Alex?"

Dane grunted in disgust, and everyone looked at him. "You guys don't believe that demon bullshit, do you? It's a crock. There's no God and there's no demons. There's only us, and the us in this room is a bunch a dummies and a little ass kid and a sagging-ass gangbanger. It was *people* that took Alex and it's people we gotta find to get him back."

Roy gaped at his older brother. He'd never heard Dane say so much at one time. The others stared at him in stunned silence. Carlos pulled up his sagging pants.

"Dane is right," Father Pat said when no one else responded. "We need to find the people who kidnapped Alex. That's our first priority."

He paused to think, and everyone else waited.

Father Pat put a hand to his chin as he stood and began pacing. Then he stopped and whirled around. "Roy, remember you told me when you touched Alex at school today you saw what he saw?"

Roy nodded.

Carlos and Juan looked surprised.

"Do you think if you held that bracelet you found and concentrated really hard on Alex, you could see what's in his mind right now?"

Roy shrugged, not understanding. "Maybe. Why?"

The excited priest stepped closer. "Because maybe you'll get a clue where he is."

Now Roy got it. He fished in his tight pants pocket and slipped out the multi-colored bracelet, clutching it in his hands.

He felt the others gather around him, almost like a protective circle. But his focus was the bracelet in his hands. He'd made it himself. A girl in middle school had taught him how to weave them out of colored threads, and he'd found the activity soothing when he felt down or alone. But he'd never made one for anybody except Alex.

He focused on Alex, on every memory he had of his friend's face, of his gentle blue eyes and crooked smile, and his giving nature. He focused on Alex, and gradually the room around him fell away and he was somewhere else. But he felt strange, weak, and his whole body ached with such intense pain he wanted to cry. A girl's voice sounded far away, and a blurred image of the girl came in and out of focus. Was she sitting up in bed? Was this a hospital? It looked like the same bed his dad had been in. But the image was fuzzy, and he couldn't focus.

C'mon!

Roy fought the pain, and concentrated.

***

Alex had never felt this sick before, this weak, this out of control. What had been inside Allison was inside of him now, and he struggled against it. He heard her voice, strong and healthy and alive – so different from when she'd started.

He was nearly finished. He could tell. Her hurt was all in him now, except he'd never felt anything so powerful. Always before, he could endure whatever pain he spun and quickly push it away until it was gone. This time it wasn't going away. This time it was too strong, or he was too weak. His stomach clenched, his heart thumped wildly, like it was fighting to keep the poisonous blood moving through his body, and his head felt light and fuzzy.

I'm going to die, he managed to think through the numbing pain.

But then, without warning, he felt Roy. Not thought of him, no – *felt* him! Roy was there, inside of him, trying to make contact. If only….

"Roy…" he muttered, not sure if he actually said the name or not. He fell forward, and blackness took him.

***

"Alex!" Roy shouted as he felt the sensation of falling overwhelm him, and then nothing. Alex was gone.

He opened his eyes.

"What?" Nathan said, off his bed and propping Roy up so he wouldn't topple.

Roy fought to clear his mind, to regain control. He became aware that Dane was at his other side, holding him with strong arms.

Did I fall?

He shook his head, his eyes focusing on the bracelet in his hands. But no images filled his mind. Alex was gone.

His eyes welled with tears against his will, and he turned to engulf his father in a tight hug.

***

Shaw had stood in awe of what he was witnessing. His emaciated, dying daughter, the reason for his existence, became stronger with each word, each passing second, and the remarkable boy in the wheelchair became weaker.

Shaw had seen so many facets of human nature, most of it destructive, that he almost couldn't believe someone so good still existed. So much happiness infused his being as he heard the strength in Allison's voice increase, saw color return to her face, saw the bruises fade on her arms, that he almost didn't notice the exact same bruises covering Alex's face and forearms. When Alex suddenly toppled from his chair and crumpled onto the floor, he was caught by surprise.

"Alex!"

He bent down to the boy as Allison clambered from the bed to crouch beside him. He looked from Alex's unmoving heap to the healthy young girl beside him in amazement.

"Oh, dad, what happened? I feel fine, but he's–"

Shaw cut her off with a crushing hug, the first impulsive act he could remember in his adult life. He reluctantly pulled away long enough to address the doctor.

"Get him to the lab. Save him."

Stiles looked uncertain. "Mr. Shaw, I don't–"

"Do it."

She recoiled, and nodded.

***

Roy felt Dane's hand on his shoulder as he held onto Nathan in the same desperate way he had when his mother had slipped away in that hospital room and he'd felt like he'd died along with her.

Was Alex dead? That was what it felt like.

"Little brother," said Dane's deep, insistent voice. "What did you see?"

Roy pulled away from Nathan's compassionate, questioning look to focus through blurred vision at the older brother he barely knew. He noted Father Pat and the others staring at him, all with the same question on their faces.

Weak, but no longer in pain, Roy slid down to sit on the edge of the bed and struggled to comprehend what had happened so he could answer.

His breathing ragged, Roy explained what he had seen and felt.

Even Dane couldn't say the words Carlos finally uttered. "You think he's dead?"

Roy turned to Carlos in anger. But he realized the other boy wasn't being heartless on purpose. It was just how he'd grown up – he was used to kids his age dying.

"I don't know," he whispered, barely able to breathe.

***

Alex lay stretched out on an examining table. Stiles and several nurses hovered about him, checking his readouts. Nearby, Allison sat watching the scene, her now-unblemished face scrunched with concern. She was attached to a machine while another doctor and several white-coated lab technicians checked her vital signs.

Shaw stood by Allison's side, as though afraid to leave it, but his gaze remained fixed on the unmoving form of the boy on the table.

"What did Alex do to make me better, Dad?" Allison asked, her look also directed at the unconscious boy.

Shaw glanced at her, and smiled. "I don't know, honey." He looked at the doctor examining readouts on the machine. "But she is better, isn't she, doctor?"

The doctor looked up from the information he'd been studying, clearly astounded.

"Every test comes back normal, Mr. Shaw. It's like the leukemia was never there."

Tears sprang to Allison's eyes as Shaw leaned in to wrap one arm around her.

"But it was there," Shaw murmured. "And now it's in him." His gaze traveled to the soft, gentle features of this boy who'd just given him the whole world. And his heart beat faster than it had in years. With fear.

***

"Roy!"

Dane's voice cut through the sorrow enveloping him, but he couldn't respond.

Alex was dead…

"Roy!" came that sharp, deep voice once again. This time hands gripped his shoulders and shook him.

Roy focused, pulled himself from inside his heart and looked at Dane's stern face.

"Alex isn't dead."

Roy blinked, and those words struck home. "How do you know?"

Dane looked straight into Roy's eyes and said, "I just do. I'd feel it. So would you. So would all these guys."

He stood and looked around at the other kids. "You know what I'm talkin' about, don't you?"

They all nodded.

"He *is* alive, Roy," Israel said, more quietly than he'd ever said anything. "I can feel him inside me. Can't you?"

And then Roy could. He'd been so terrified of losing his best friend that he had closed off his heart and soul. Now that he allowed himself to feel again, Alex was there. Deep and weak, but definitely there. Alive.

He sagged with relief. "Yeah, I can."

"Use the bracelet again," Dane said. "See what you can pick up."

Roy took in a huge gulp of air. He released it, glanced around at the anxious faces, and pulled himself together. Gripping the cloth bracelet in both hands once again, he closed his eyes and pictured Alex.

At first, there was only darkness. But he felt Alex, felt his heartbeat. It was slow and irregular, but it was there. And pain. Roy felt intense pain attacking every inch of his body. Through gritted teeth, he ignored it. He sought Alex's mind. What he found were dreams, flashes, wisps of memory. Alex wasn't awake, but his mind was. There were people in white coats. Doctors, from the look of them. And equipment like he'd seen in his dad's room. And his mom's before she died.

"There are people," he murmured aloud, "in white coats. Doctors, I think. Alex is afraid, but not for…." He trailed off, and even with his eyes closed felt himself turn red around the ears.

"What?" Nathan asked.

Keeping his eyes closed, and forcing down the smile that had risen to his lips, Roy said, "He's afraid, but not for him. For me."

"That's Alex, all right," Java said.

"What else do you see?" Father Pat's voice intruded now. "Do you see anything to tell you where he is?"

Roy concentrated. The images kept changing, flitting in and out. Alex was dreaming, but he was doing something else, too. Roy felt his blood almost boiling, and his body temperature rise.

Focus!

Those white coats kept returning to his mind. There was something on them, an image on the left side, right over the heart. "There's something on the coats, kinda like the 'MTS' teachers at school have on their shirts. But it's not just letters. It's a picture or something."

"Can you draw it?" came Father Pat's excited voice.

Roy opened his eyes and looked at the anxious face of the priest. That thing on the coats remained in his mind, as though Alex wanted him to see it. "I can't draw. That's Cuong." He felt helpless again.

Father Pat turned his fiery eyes on Cuong, who cowered a few feet away, his thin face twisted with fear, his eyes wide and nervous. Father Pat led him to where Roy sat on the bed.

"I need you to hold Roy's hand, Cuong."

Cuong recoiled. "Th-th-that's g-g-gay."

Roy felt himself flush red, and glanced at Dane standing beside him, but his brother said nothing.

His voice gentle and soothing, Father Pat said, "He's your friend, Cuong. It's okay to hold his hand. And it might help Alex."

Cuong looked uncomfortable as he extended one of his hands. Roy shifted the bracelet to his left, reached out with his right for Cuong's trembling hand, and grasped it.

Cuong's eyes flew open in shock and he snatched his hand back like he'd been bitten by a snake.

"I w-w-wanna g-g-go h-h-home," Cuong said, his voice quavering.

Roy watched him with sympathy. He understood the feeling. He was scared, too. Only his need to save Alex kept him together.

"You saw it, didn't you, Cuong?" Father Pat asked, his voice rising in pitch.

"I w-w-wanna g-g-go h-h-home!" Cuong insisted, cowering into himself

Father Pat leaned in and placed a gentle hand on the boy's trembling shoulder. Cuong flinched, but didn't shy away. "Cuong, what you saw, it could help us find Alex. You want to help Alex, don't you?"

Cuong nodded.

"I know this is all pretty scary. But Alex needs you."

"Alex is my friend," Cuong said.

Roy gasped.

Israel blurted, "The hell?"

Cuong hadn't stuttered. It was the first time since Roy had known him that Cuong hadn't stuttered when speaking.

"Is there pen and paper in here?" Father Pat asked Nathan.

Nathan pulled open the night table drawer and handed a pad and pencil to Father Pat. The priest eased Cuong to a sitting position on the bed and placed the objects in his lap. Cuong took the pencil in his right hand as Father Pat flipped open the pad to a blank sheet.

The priest placed Cuong's left hand back into Roy's right. Cuong's eyes bugged out, obviously seeing something that scared him.

"You see what's on those white coats, Cuong?"

The boy nodded.

"Draw it, Cuong. Draw what you see."

Cuong began to draw.

***

Shaw and Allison stood beside the examining table on which Alex was laid out. The doctors had taken off his shirt when he'd been brought in so they could attach pads to his chest and arms that linked to the machines monitoring his vital functions.

Allison had gasped when she'd first seen Alex shirtless, and Shaw understood why. The boy's entire torso was one enormous bruise, as though the blood in his veins had leaked out everywhere in his body and pooled just beneath the skin.

Exactly like Allison had looked before Alex cured her.

Only now the bruises were fading. Fading faster by the moment. As they stood and watched in awe, the bare skin of Alex's torso slowly returned to normal, looking pale and milky white, but healthy and unblemished.

Dr. Stiles stood by one of the large machines, checking the information as it updated itself on screen. "White count decreasing, platelets returning to normal." She turned to Shaw in stunned disbelief. "By God, Mr. Shaw, he's beating it! He's purging his body of leukemia before our very eyes!"

Shaw and Allison stood in silent reverence, his arm around her shoulders, hers around his waist, as little by little, Alex returned to life. Shaw had been certain the boy would die when he'd collapsed, but in less than twenty minutes the second miracle of his life unfolded before him.

Never having given God any thought since he was a child, Shaw had long ago decided *he* would be a god on earth. And he'd succeeded beyond his wildest dreams. His tech business was bigger than Apple, Microsoft, and Virgin Enterprises - computer parts and chips, medical equipment, aerospace engineering, cell phones and just about everything people needed. He'd diversified all his assets through dummy corporations to keep the government busybodies at bay. Not even the IRS knew just how much money and power Shaw wielded, and he intended to keep it that way.

But here before him was a boy beyond price, someone unlike anyone on earth, someone more powerful than himself. He felt an odd sensation waft over him, something so foreign he'd forgotten what it felt like – humility.

Alex stirred, shifting his shoulders, followed by a tilt of the head, as though he were thinking something deep. His lips parted and he whispered, "Roy…."

With a fluttering of lashes, his eyes opened, the blue of them strikingly bold beneath the fluorescent ceiling lights. The eyes blinked a moment, and the head tilted in their direction.

"Welcome back, Alex," Shaw said, his voice less steady than he liked. More emotion coursed through him at this moment than he could remember.

Alex smiled at Allison. "You okay now, Allison?" His voice sounded parched and weak.

Allison broke into a huge grin and pulled away from her father to step up to the table. "Yeah, thanks to you," she gushed, and leaned down to kiss his cheek.

Alex knew he'd turned red, but he also felt good, strong, successful. He'd taken a lot of hurt and sick from her, and he'd beaten it.

"Welcome," he said, offering a shy smile.

Shaw stepped closer to Alex and took one hand in his, clasping it as though they were best buds. "Alex, 'thank you' doesn't even come close."

Alex smiled again, and then yawned.

"You rest, get your strength back," Shaw said and released Alex's hand. "We have a room for you and food – whatever you want. Just ask. I'll be in after you sleep a bit."

Alex nodded, his eyes returning to Allison, who grinned down at him like he was Santa Claus in the flesh.

The doctor called Stiles waved Shaw off to the side and Alex watched as the man followed her. Allison took his hand and squeezed it.

"Your hand feels warm again," she gushed. "It was ice cold when you came in here."

Alex smiled. But then he frowned as he overheard what the doctor was telling Shaw.

"He has the potential to cure any disease known to man, Mr. Shaw," she whispered. "Cancer, AIDS, you name it. Think what that could be worth."

"It's worth nothing to you, Dr. Stiles," Shaw snapped. "I will not repay this boy by selling him to the highest bidder, and neither will you."

"Yes, sir," she replied curtly, and returned to Alex to unhook him from the machines.

Alex looked past Allison at Shaw. The man's expression was

unreadable, but the other people in white coats standing around him had a look Alex had often seen on Jane, a look that meant they liked what the woman doctor said. He shivered.

***

Roy held the image of that white coat in the center of his mind as he felt Alex awaken. His heart pounded with joy. Alex was okay!

He wanted to scream it out to the others, but held back until Cuong could complete his drawing. He saw a bald girl and a man talking to Alex, but could not hear what was being said. A bald girl?

Cuong said, "Th-theerre," and Roy understood he was finished.

Roy released the image from his mind and said, "Alex is okay now."

Jorge smiled. "Alex is okay now," he repeated, sounding eerily like Roy.

It was as though everyone in the room had been holding their breath, because now they crowded around to see what Cuong had drawn.

Dane grabbed the drawing and looked at the image.

"What's it say?" Roy asked, because no one else wanted to admit once again that he couldn't read.

"ShawTech," Father Pat answered. "I've heard of it. Big company – computers, phones, you name it."

"Let's Google it and find out where it is," Dane said, with an intensity that surprised Roy. "Then we go get our boy back, and take down anyone who tries to stop us."

Even with as little time as he'd spent with Dane growing up, Roy knew well enough that it was bad news to piss him off. And right now, Dane was *really* pissed.

Carlos broke into a huge grin. "Works for me."

Java gave him the head nod. "Me, too. Let's go."

CHAPTER TWENTY-FIVE

I'M THE CLOSEST THING TO GOD ON THIS PLANET

Alex lay in a luxurious bed, bigger than any he'd ever slept in, like something he'd expect maybe at the White House. He never imagined himself in such a fancy bed with thick soft bedcovers, sheets that felt like smooth fur, and a blanket warm enough to unfreeze a snowman.

He'd fallen asleep the second his head hit the large cottony pillow, and awoke to find a cart filled with delicious-smelling food beside his bed, along with plates and utensils. Realizing he was starving, he sat up, pulled the cart closer, and dug in.

There was fried chicken and hamburgers and French fries and soda and pudding and cake and cookies and just about everything else a teenage boy could want. He scarfed down the burger and fries, and was wading into the chicken when the door popped open and in strolled Shaw and Allison.

"I guess you're feeling better," Allison said with a light laugh. "You didn't save any fries for me."

Alex stopped in mid-chew, a big chunk of chicken leg ground up in his mouth, and looked mortified.

She only laughed the harder. "I'm just messing with you."

Alex liked how she looked bald, and didn't even wonder what her hair would look like when it grew back. She wore pants and a plain blue shirt and looked so different from when he'd first seen her.

Alex grinned as he swallowed the food and washed it down with a swig of Coke. "Sorry. When I woke up, I was so hungry I couldn't help myself."

"Typical boy," she said with a shake of her head.

"How long did I knock out for?"

She glanced at her smart watch and shrugged. "About an hour. You recover fast."

Alex liked her round pleasant face that was the opposite of her dad's closed and guarded one. Hers was open and inviting, and her soft brown eyes were wide, gazing at him like he held the secrets of life and death.

"You feeling better now?" he asked, spinning her voice for signs she was still sick.

Her grin grew even wider. She stretched out her hands and twirled around like a dancer, the grin turning into a laugh of pure joy. "I've never felt better."

Alex smiled. "Yep. The sick is gone. That's cool."

She turned to her father in exasperation. "The boy saves my life and all he can say is it's cool?"

Alex was surprised to see Shaw smile

Allison put both hands on her hips as though she were mad at him. "Alex, what you did is only, like, the most amazing thing anyone's ever done for anyone, and you act like it's nothing."

Against his will, he felt his face burn with embarrassment. He wasn't used to people fussing over him, not since his parents, well, aunt and uncle, died in that car crash.

"It's just what I do," he offered as he looked down at the uneaten chicken on his plate.

Her mouth dropped open and her eyes bulged for a moment. Then she shook her head and leaned in to kiss him on the cheek. "You are the most incredible boy I ever met, Alex, and tomorrow we hang out. Deal?"

She raised a closed fist like the guys always did. Despite his uncertain future, Alex liked that idea. He raised his own fist and they bumped. "That'd be wicked."

Her face brightened. "You like emo?"

Alex nodded.

"Hawthorne Heights?"

Alex lit up. "My favorite."

Her eyes widened. "Put Me Back Together?"

"Best song ever."

She grinned. "Oh, yeah, you and me are hanging."

She laughed, and Alex joined her. Other than Roy, he'd never felt a kinship with any peer like he did with her. She was natural and easy to be with.

Shaw eyed Allison with concern. "I know you feel good, honey, and

I believe Alex when he says the disease is gone, but I still want you to get some rest. And Alex needs sleep."

She looked like she wanted to argue, but Alex noted the expression on Shaw's face and knew she wasn't going to. She went to the door and turned to Alex. "Tomorrow." She tossed off a warm smile and vanished into the hallway.

Alex watched her leave the room, and only after she was gone did he realize Shaw was staring at him with an unreadable expression. "You're her hero, Alex."

Alex glanced down. "I'm no hero."

Shaw stepped closer, rolled the cart to one side, and sat on the edge of the bed, facing Alex with a look of deep gratitude. "Closest I've ever seen. Now, have you thought about what you'd like? I said you could have anything, and I meant it."

Alex paused a moment, having forgotten the man's offer. Then it struck him what he'd like most of all. "I was kinda thinking… you think maybe them doctors could fix it so I could walk?"

"You can't, you know, yourself?"

Alex shook his head. Oh, the number of times he tried…. "It don't work on me."

Shaw flashed an "I've got the whole world in my hands" kind of look, and said in a firm voice, "If it's possible, consider it done. What else?"

Alex gaped in surprise. "You mean I can get more than that?"

Shaw's mouth dropped open ever so slightly before he closed it again. "Alex, you just gave me my daughter's life. Anything you want is yours."

"I wanna go home." Images of Roy and Nathan filled his mind and heart.

Shaw snorted with disgust. "To that woman? Alex, I can find you a real home. You could even come live with me, if you'd like. I've never had a son."

That surprised Alex since he barely knew this man. In less than a week he had two offers to adopt him. Life was crazy. "It's okay. I'm gonna live with Roy. His dad's adopting me."

Shaw sagged a bit and looked disappointed. "I already told you, Alex, you're free to go now, if you want."

Alex spun him and could tell this powerful man wanted him to stay around longer. In truth, he *did* want to leave now. He was worried about Roy. But he was also exhausted and needed to sleep some more. And he *had* promised Allison he'd hang with her tomorrow. Just the thought warmed him.

"I'll stay tonight and leave tomorrow, if that's okay. I'm really tired."

Shaw nodded. "So, what else do you want?"

Alex fell silent, a dark mood settling over him. For some reason the image of Saul hanging from his neck in the garage sprang to the forefront of his heart and mind, and plunged him into despair.

Shaw leaned in. "Think big, Alex. I'm the closest thing to God on this planet."

Alex exhaled, and finally admitted what he wanted even more than being able to walk. "Can you make me like everyone else?"

Shaw's eyebrows scrunched with puzzlement. "How do you mean?"

Alex held his gaze with his own. "So I couldn't spin people no more?"

"But that's what makes you so special, Alex."

Alex felt tears behind his eyes, but refused to let them out. "Maybe I don't wanna be special, you know? Maybe I just wanna be like other guys -- have a girlfriend, go to dances. Maybe I don't want people runnin' from me cuz they's scared, or tryin' to sell me cuz I'm different, or kidnap me cuz they want my power. Maybe I just wanna be like everyone else." He paused a moment to brush the bangs away from his eyes so he could see into Shaw's. "Can you do that?"

"No, Alex, I can't."

"Then I guess you're not God after all."

Shaw frowned.

***

Roy rode shotgun while Dane drove, navigating the surface streets around El Segundo where the ShawTech complex was located. It was a short drive from Hawthorne, but Dane insisted on swinging by his apartment for the guns. Roy's eyes widened as his brother exited the building with a large duffle bag, which he slid onto the floor of the backseat beneath the nervous feet of Father Pat, Jorge, and Cuong.

"Yes, they're legal," he said tersely to the priest's questioning face, and Father Pat knew enough to remain silent.

Dane's truck was a black F-250 with front and rear seats. The rest of the guys had piled into the bed, trying not to freeze beneath the icy wind as the truck navigated its way along the rain-slicked streets.

Father Pat had suggested Roy hold onto Alex's friendship bracelet to see if he could pick up any more clues about what was happening. Roy could "see" Alex talking to that man in the suit, but it didn't feel like anything bad was happening. Alex felt relaxed, so Roy felt relaxed. The room behind the man looked like a bedroom you'd find in a house, not in the kind of office building he'd seen on the computer screen when Father Pat Googled ShawTech.

The whole thing confused Roy, and Father Pat was puzzled, too. Dane and the others didn't do much thinking – they were more like the action heroes in movies he used to watch with his dad, the guys who just ran in blasting and took out the bad guys. He was different. He was more of a thinker, even though he was a dummy who couldn't read well. It confused him that someone would kidnap Alex – the man in the suit, probably – and then everything would be fine and Alex all relaxed. Made no sense. But they'd know soon enough, *if* they could find a way to get in.

***

Shaw stood by Alex's open door, ready to leave, almost looking sad about it, like he wanted to stay and talk, but didn't really know how. "Good night, Alex."

Alex gazed at him from beneath the warm covers, exhausted, but also shivering. Not from cold. From fear. "Lock me in, Mr. Shaw."

"You're not a prisoner here, Alex. I told you that."

Alex swallowed. His throat felt dry, despite the Coke and water he'd just drank. "I know. But there been them murders. You'll be safer if you lock the door and put a guard outside. Please."

Shaw looked mystified. "Alex, what could you possibly have to do with those murders?"

"I think maybe I done 'em and can't remember." His voice barely rose above a whisper.

Shaw looked aghast, shifting his body weight and tilting his head as though wondering if Alex was trying to be funny. "You? I'd never believe that, not after what I saw today."

"But I was there every time, and I don't know why. I had blood on me, Mr. Shaw, and I don't remember nothing!" His voice rose in pitch. "*Please*. I don't want you to get hurt." He shivered again. "Or Allison."

Shaw squinted at him, his face revealing nothing, but Alex noted a slight flicker of the eyes when he'd mentioned the blood. "I think you're letting your imagination get the better of you, Alex," he finally said after a long pause. "I will lock the door, if it'll make you feel better, but that's all."

Alex had a feeling that might not be enough, but realized it was all he was going to get. Besides, he thought, that nasty-ass cat had always been around the other times, and how could a cat get into this place? He had a feeling Shaw didn't leave the doors unlocked.

Dumbass, he told himself. *The freaking cat talked to me! You think it can't get through locked doors?*

But all he said was a hollow, "Okay."

Shaw tried for a smile and Alex could tell it was something he didn't do very often. "We'll talk in the morning." He turned and stepped into the hall, closing the door behind him. A key turned in the lock and then footsteps fell away until only silence filled the room.

Alex shivered again and pulled the coverlet up to his chin, sliding down and settling into the monstrous pillow that felt like a giant, soft marshmallow. He reached out to flick off the table lamp beside him, but thought better of it.

The dark is my enemy.

He wasn't sure where that thought had come from, but it was true, wasn't it? He decided to leave the light on and settled down to sleep. But his mind filled with images bouncing from one to the next: the cat, Mrs. Rhodes, Jane, the graveyard, that doll, and Roy. He opened his eyes and sat up.

My phone!

He'd been so caught up in everything with Allison that he forgot about it. Would Shaw have taken it away? It's not like he could tell anyone where he was since he had no idea. But at least he could tell Roy he was okay.

He turned to the bedside table and spotted a small drawer, yanking it open. His phone and school ID lay within.

Breathing a grateful sigh, Alex reached out to snatch up the phone.

That's when the music box began to play.

He barely had time to look at his closed door before everything went black.

***

Roy gasped loud enough to draw the attention of Dane and Father Pat.

"What do you see?" the priest asked from behind him as Dane glanced over.

Roy shook his head, attempting to make sense of what was in his mind. "Alex was reaching for his phone. He was gonna call me." He paused to reset his emotions. Alex was thinking about him, and that made Roy feel good beyond measure. "But then everything went dark, like the lights went out, but even darker. I can't see nothing no more!"

He twisted his head around toward the priest behind him. Jorge and Cuong looked at him with wide eyes.

"Are we almost there, Dane?" Father Pat asked.

"Yeah," Dane grunted, glancing at his GPS screen. The voice told him to turn left at the next light. "Few more blocks."

Father Pat met Roy's gaze. "Keep trying, Roy."

Roy turned around, stared at the bracelet clutched in his thin, trembling fingers, closed his eyes, and thought of Alex.

***

Alex blinked. His light was on, the night table drawer open. The door to his room stood ajar. And the music box had stopped playing. His wheelchair sat beside the bed.

As he took in his surroundings, Alex spotted the twin trails of blood leading out into the corridor.

Oh, no, not again!

Terrified, he slid himself off the bed and into his chair. As he grabbed the wheel handles to spin himself around to the door, he yanked his hands back in revulsion. They were slick with blood.

Fresh blood.

No!

Fighting down his disgust, he wheeled to the door and yanked it open. The hall outside was dimly lit, but Alex could make out the bloody tire tracks leading away from his room. Shivering, he forced himself to follow them.

***

Roy spotted a lot of big buildings through the windshield, and knew they were leaving the homes behind and entering the business section of El Segundo.

"See anything yet?" Dane asked him, his normally unemotional voice sounding worried.

"Yeah," Roy whispered. "It's like the lights just came back on. 'Cept it don't look good."

"What is it?" Father Pat asked from behind him.

"There's blood on the floor," Roy answered, "and Alex is following it, down a hall or something. There's lights, but it's not clear. I can feel Alex being scared. Real scared."

Dane pressed on the gas, and the truck sped up.

***

His hands were sticky, and his gorge rose at the coppery smell attacking his nostrils. Alex rolled down the hall, following the twin trails of blood made by *his* wheelchair.

Except I don't remember!

Dread welled up within him as the trails stopped at a closed door, disappearing beneath it. His heart jackhammered as he reached out a trembling hand. There was smeared blood around the brass colored knob.

Fresh blood.

What did I do?

His unsteady fingers grasped the slippery knob. "Please God, not again," he whispered.

He pushed open the door and wheeled himself into the dark room.

***

Roy sat staring through the windshield at the tall buildings ahead, some dark, others lighting up the night like boxy Christmas trees. But he wasn't seeing them. His mind fixed on that bloody doorknob, and he watched as the door swung inward.

"Well?" Father Pat asked.

"It's dark," Roy said, struggling to "see" more clearly. "I can't… Wait! He's turning on the light." Suddenly, he let out a loud scream, causing Dane to slam on the brakes and stare at his brother's open-mouthed look of terror.

"What?"

***

Roy's scream echoed through Alex's numbed brain as it mingled with his own.

The bedcovers were thrown back, as though whoever occupied this bed had leapt out from under. And there was blood everywhere. Fresh, coppery-smelling blood on the sheets, the covers, the pillow, and the floor.

Revulsion overpowered Alex as his wide eyes scanned the walls and saw Hawthorne Heights posters abounding.

"No, no, no…." he stammered, his horrified eyes searching for Allison's body, but finding only blood, and a large kitchen knife on the floor beside the bed.

A knife glistening with red.

He fixed on that knife, on the weapon that had killed her. She was dead, despite her body not being there to mock him. And he'd killed her. Lifting his hands from his wheels, Alex stared at the blood staining them. "Oh, Allison, I'm so sorry, I'm so sorry…."

He began to cry, to sob with all the remorse he'd built up this past week. Ms. Ashley. Maribel. Mrs. Rhodes. Saul. And now this.

I'm a monster. I can't do this anymore. I can't.

His teary eyes focused once more on the bloody knife near the bed.

He wheeled himself toward it, knowing what he had to do. Roy would be mad, but there wasn't a choice anymore.

I told you what I'd do, Roy, he thought as he bent down and gripped the slippery handle, lifting the enormous knife to his lap.

Father Pat talked about making choices, and Alex knew he had to make this one. It was the only way to keep the people he loved safe.

He thought of his best friend, felt Roy's love for him wrapping itself like a warm blanket around his soul. Could he really do this to him? To Nathan who wanted to adopt him? To Java and Izzy and all the others? Then his gaze fell on the blood-soaked bed sheets, and his resolve hardened.

I'm sorry, but I got to.

He gripped the knife handle hard with his right hand, the blood staining his fingers and dripping onto his lap. He focused on those droplets of blood like they were the answers to all his questions.

Face twisted with painful determination, he brought the blade down to his left wrist and began to cut.

***

Roy leaned toward the windshield like it was a television set and screamed, "Alex, noooo!"

***

Alex froze, the blade against the soft skin of his wrist, as Roy's "Noooo" pierced his brain like a bullet and caused him to look behind him, halfway expecting to find Roy in the doorway.

But it wasn't Roy who stood there with an open-mouthed look of stunned disbelief on his face. It was Shaw.

Alex gasped, frozen in place, as the man, still clad in his gray suit, zombie-walked past him to gaze in horror at the blood-soaked bed. He turned his grief-stricken face on Alex.

"I…." Alex stammered, trying to say something, anything. "I…."

Shaw focused on the bloody knife in Alex's grasp, causing Alex to look down at it, too. As though suddenly realizing what this knife had done, he flung it to the floor in disgust. He shook his head in confusion.

"I wasn't... I didn't... I don't know if I... I found...."

Unable to tolerate Shaw's devastated, betrayed look any longer, Alex turned and bolted from the room, out into the hallway, searching for a way out, any way out. He gripped his blood-slick wheel handles like he was doing stunts at the skate park, and pressed forward with increasing speed toward the end of the corridor. He had no idea where he was going, and lost all thoughts of killing himself. He spun right, and nearly toppled as he sped off down another hall.

***

Shaw was sitting on Allison's bed, oblivious to the blood, when Phil and Bob bolted into the room, guns at the ready.

"We heard a shout, Mr.–" Phil began, and then stopped suddenly, sliding to a halt beside his partner, gazing in disbelief at all the blood.

"Oh, shit!" Bob exclaimed, his trained eyes taking in the entire scene at a glance.

Shaw stared at them as though they weren't even there. "Find him."

"Who?" Phil asked.

"Alex."

"Alex?" Bob blurted, his gaze traveling from the splattered blood to the gory knife near Shaw's feet. "How could he–"

"Bring him to me. Alive."

"Yes, sir."

The two men sprinted from the room.

CHAPTER TWENTY-SIX

THEY'RE RIGHT BEHIND YOU!

ALEX SURGED FORWARD WITH DESPERATE intensity. His heart hammered and he could scarcely breathe. This hall looked exactly the same as the last one! He knew what "Exit" signs looked like and scanned the walls for some indication that one was near.

There was nothing!

He began to sweat, the perspiration mixed with blood causing his hands to slip off the wheel handles as he fought to pick up speed. From somewhere behind him came a shout. "There he is!"

Alex didn't even try to look back. The chase was on.

***

Roy gripped the bracelet with such passion his fingers turned white.

Dane glanced over. "Chill, little brother, we're almost there."

"He's in trouble. *Hurry*."

Dane did.

***

Alex whipped his chair into another gravity-defying turn that lifted his right wheel off the floor and nearly toppled him. He righted himself and poured on the speed down yet another endless hallway. Suddenly, Phil and Bob rounded a corner at the other end and sprinted his way. Bob raised a walkie-talkie to his mouth.

"We have him!"

They ran like guys Alex had seen on the track team at school. He turned his chair so sharply it slammed hard into the wall to his left, nearly tossing him to the carpeted floor. Gripping his handles, Alex held his breath as he turned around and pushed back the way he'd come.

He pressed on with increased desperation, his breathing labored, his bloody hands slipping off the wheel handles. He could hear the pounding footsteps of his pursuers even against the carpeted floor. He had to find a way out soon or he was lost. When he hit the end of the hall he spun right this time and barreled forward. Behind him, Phil and Bob rounded the corner in pursuit.

Alex kept his eyes straight ahead, knowing if he dared to look back they'd be on him. This hall was shorter than the last one. He hit the end at breakneck speed, imagining himself in the wheelchair games, and went for broke. He almost collided with the wall as he spun hard to his left, but kept his focus and pushed on.

As Alex whipped around the corner, two more men in suits came into view from the adjoining hallway and raced toward him. Alex would have gasped, except he had no breath left. These two held guns in their hands, aimed straight at him. One had a walkie-talkie in his other hand and raised it to his mouth.

Alex didn't wait to hear what he said. Another hallway veered off to his right between him and his pursuers, and he took it. His arms were throbbing now, and his shoulders had long since gone numb. The men behind him were gaining. He considered stopping and letting them shoot him. It would all be finished then, all the death and misery and horror he'd caused. His eyes widened in fear. Two more men bounded around the corner up ahead and sprinted in his direction.

Alex thought of Roy and his friends. He had to protect them, like he'd protected Roy in Eucalyptus Park. They needed him. Killing himself would be selfish.

He spotted a looming side hall on his left and whipped into it. His chair slammed hard into the wall and he just yanked his hand away in time to keep it from getting crushed. The impact nearly threw him to the floor, and rattled his resolve. But the pursuing footsteps spurred him on. Once more gripping his wheel handles with numb hands, Alex pressed forward.

Still no "Exit" in sight.

***

Dane roared through the slippery streets of El Segundo's industrial section, just off Sepulveda Boulevard. He spotted the building at the same moment Father Pat exclaimed, "There it is!"

Roy held the bracelet in one hand and got ready to spring into action, whatever might be required. Alex was in trouble. Guys were chasing him. Guys with guns. They had to get there in time. They had to!

***

Finally, Alex found a bank of elevators and slammed into the wall in his haste to stop. He pounded on the button repeatedly, staining the clear "Down" arrow a smeary red. He glanced over his shoulder, panting and heaving. His pursuers were closing fast.

Hurry!

The double doors slid open with a *ding*, and Alex rolled inside the little box. He slammed the flat of his fist against the button with the two arrows pointing inward and held it, staring wide-eyed at the group of six men closing in. He pounded the button again, and the doors eased shut with maddening slowness.

Phil reached out a hand to try and grab one of the doors, but Alex lashed out with a fist and struck his forearm as hard as he could. Phil yelped and yanked back his hand. The doors closed, and Alex punched the button with the star on it.

***

Dane swung the truck onto the curved driveway leading into ShawTech headquarters. The building loomed large in front of Roy's wide eyes, a massive glass and steel structure that looked like something off the Syfy channel. Dane whipped around the expansive driveway toward the glass front entrance that had a giant version of the logo Cuong had drawn right above it.

***

Alex panted as panic rose in his throat, and the elevator descended one seemingly endless floor at a time. It finally stopped and the doors slid open so quietly Alex shivered.

Quiet like that graveyard.

He bolted from the elevator and barreled his way across the empty lobby. There was a desk of some kind to his left, and wide double glass doors leading to freedom straight ahead.

Every inch of his arms, shoulders and torso ached with throbbing pain. He'd never exerted himself this hard before, not even when practicing stunts at the skate park. Fearful of breaking the glass of the doors, he skidded to a halt and pushed the blue handicap symbol that was supposed to open them. Nothing happened.

Just then, a big truck outside raced right toward him, and his heart nearly stopped.

Oh, shit!

He spun his chair around to look for another way out and spotted a door with a lit car image above it.

That must be the parking garage, he thought desperately, and started forward.

A door popped open at the far end of the lobby and two new guys burst out, one with a gun and the other a walkie-talkie.

Crap!

Alex propelled himself toward the garage entrance and slammed into the push bar, knowing if it were locked they'd have him for sure. But the door swung out and hit the wall behind it and Alex found himself inside a parking structure. He didn't even slow, just pressed forward and ignored his numbness and panting breaths as he flung himself around a concrete pillar.

There!

Just ahead he spotted the exit, the bar lowered so cars couldn't get out without paying, but not low enough to keep him from ducking under. He pushed and strained, blinded by his sweaty hair spilling into his eyes, but knowing he had no time to swipe it away. A shout came from behind, "Let's get the car!"

Alex knew he was in serious trouble.

***

Dane slammed on the brakes right in front of the glass doors and Roy spotted two men in suits race across the lobby and disappear through another door.

"Look," he pointed at the men. "They're chasing Alex." He focused on the bracelet as Father Pat leaned over the back seat, and Dane waited, hands on the wheel. Roy looked up. "He's where the cars park."

"Parking structure, Dane," Father Pat said. "Around the side."

"I got it," Dane said and floored the accelerator.

***

Alex lowered his head and cleared the wooden bar that separated him from freedom. Then he was out of the structure and onto a sloping road leading down to the street. His momentum picked up as the downward grade steepened, but he pushed his wheel handles all the harder anyway. The area was deserted. He flicked his dripping hair from around his eyes and scanned the street ahead. No sign of the truck he'd seen from the lobby. He didn't dare look back for his pursuers.

If I can just get to the street, I can hide somewhere!

The screeching of tires as a car peeled out of the parking structure caused Alex to gag with fear. He poured on the speed, sailing down the slope.

I'm gonna crash, he thought in a moment of blind panic.

But he wouldn't. He controlled his chair better than most guys could drive a car, and his "fearless" gene had kicked in.

No way they're gonna get me!

Just then, with another screech of tires against pavement, from around the corner of the building careened the massive pickup he'd seen before. It barreled along the street and would intersect him within seconds.

Alex knew he was caught. At his current speed, there was no way he could escape that truck. It would arrive at the intersection with the driveway before he did, and then he was screwed.

"There he is!" came Izzy's unmistakable voice, and Alex peered ahead to see several figures in the back of the truck standing up and waving their arms like those guys did at the airport.

"Alex, it's us!" Izzy screamed again before another shadowy figure grabbed him from behind and clamped a hand over his mouth. That had to be Java. Alex almost laughed. They were here. His friends. They'd come to rescue him.

Roy's voice called out, "Slow down, Dane!" and Roy leaned out the window of the cab. "Hurry, Alex! They're right behind you!"

Every muscle strained and weak, his entire body drenched in sweat, Alex put even more power into his hands and arms, and pressed ever closer to salvation.

***

Roy stared in horror at the sight of his best friend speeding down the ramp toward them, a black car not far behind.

Oh, God, they're gonna run him down!

He leaned further out the window of the truck as they began to pass the ramp. Alex was almost there. Almost close enough to grab.

The handle! Dane had one on his truck, too!

"Alex!" he shouted. "Grab the back handle!"

Alex clearly heard him because the chair turned and aimed itself at the rear of the truck. It would be close, Roy knew, glancing at Dane. He saw at once his brother understood what Alex was going to do and slowed his speed even more.

The truck passed by the ramp. Alex let go of his wheels and flung out a hand for that handle at the rear. He missed, regrippped his chair wheels with rock-solid stability and turned the chair to his right, speeding after the retreating truck. The headlights from behind illuminated Izzy leaping around in the bed yelling for him to hurry. Alex again threw out his left hand for that elusive extension of smooth metal. His fingers caught this time, slipped around, and held.

The truck picked up speed and pulled away, Alex hanging on to the rear. The wheels of his chair wobbled and rattled as the truck accelerated.

"Hang on, Alex, I'm coming!" Roy stuck his whole body out the window of the moving truck as it raced down Continental Avenue away from ShawTech. The black sedan followed less than a block behind.

Dane shouted, "Roy!" but Roy didn't stop. He climbed out the window, still facing inward, and gripped hard to the underside of the window casing, hauling his feet out so he was crouched like a cat ready to leap from the moving truck. The cold wind whipped the beanie off his head and sent his hair waving into his eyes, momentarily blinding him.

From the corner of his eye, he spotted Alex clinging to the back of the truck and the black car closing in. Ignoring his panic, he let go his left hand and rapped hard on the back-seat window. It dropped down at once and Father Pat's terrified face filled the space.

"Roy, what–"

"Sit back, Father!" he shouted, not caring if he sounded rude.

Father Pat complied at once. Roy gripped the metal bar separating the front and rear windows, and swung his left foot out onto the rear window frame. Having been a decent skater, Roy's footing was good, and his balance better than most. He stood against the wind and stepped fully onto the open window frame. His heart pounded as he gripped the truck roof with both hands, and then stretched out his left leg toward the bed.

The truck careened down Continental and veered onto Grand Avenue. Roy's leg was almost into the bed, where Java stood reaching for him. The sharp turn caused Roy to lose his footing and slip off the truck. One hand snaked out for the lip of the bed and the other seized the open window ledge. He felt Father Pat's hand grab him from inside as his feet dangled dangerously close to the pavement. Then Java had his left arm and muscled him up toward the bed. Roy let go of Father Pat's hand and flung his right arm toward Java. The bigger boy grabbed hold and stumbled backward, falling onto his back with Roy sprawled on top of him.

Panting and heaving from fear, Roy had barely a second to nod his thanks to Java when Alex called out, "Guys, I'm slipping!"

Java scrambled to his feet and yanked Roy up hard. The two stumbled to the rear of the bed and looked down at Alex. The wheels on his chair wobbled like crazy, looking like they might snap off from the high speed. Roy knew the chair was built to withstand a lot, but this much? He looked out into the street-lit darkness and saw the black car bearing down on them like an angry dinosaur.

Israel, Jorge, and Cuong cowered near one corner of the bed, clearly unsure what to do. But Carlos and Juan stood ready for whatever was needed.

"We gotta grab Alex and the chair and pull 'em both in," Roy shouted against the wind.

Juan's eyes bulged, but Carlos and Java didn't hesitate. They leaned over the tailgate and stretched out their hands. Roy took the corner closest to Alex and reached out for his friend.

"Gimme your hand!"

Alex glanced fearfully at Roy, and then over his shoulder at the pursuing sedan. It was closing the gap. He returned his gaze to Roy.

"Come on, Alex, we got you!" Carlos yelled out, and Java shouted, "Take Roy's hand and I'll grab for the chair!"

Java hauled himself over the back of the tailgate and stood on the bumper. "Hold my arm, Carlos," Java called out.

Carlos gripped him hard and hunkered down with his weight for support.

Squatting, Java reached out to Alex.

Craning his neck, Alex leaned around to see what was up ahead. Confused, Roy followed his gaze and spotted Nash Street approaching. He knew that street. There was a big soccer field on it and lots of businesses and big driveways.

"Hurry, Alex!" Roy cried out, afraid of what Alex might do.

"Not enough time!" Alex shouted back. "Keep going, I'll meet ya at home!"

Dane swung the truck into a left turn onto Nash. As he did, Alex released his slippery grip on the handle. His chair sailed off to the right and disappeared into the darkness of a large, tree-lined driveway.

Roy's heart nearly stopped. "Alexxxx!"

The sedan whipped around the corner. Roy grabbed for Java, hauled him into the bed and the two of them tumbled backward. Scrambling to his knees, Roy crawled to the tailgate with the others and saw the car in pursuit. He breathed a slight sigh of relief that at least they hadn't seen Alex slip into the shadowy driveway.

The truck flew toward Imperial Highway at breakneck speed. The boys in the bed huddled near the tailgate and watched the pursuing sedan.

Roy crawled to the side of the bed and looked toward the front. Imperial loomed, and a green light faced them. For the moment. Once it switched to red, cars would be racing back and forth in both directions.

Roy held his breath, praying the light would stay green. His heart pummeled his chest, and he had to restrain his untamed hair with one hand. Closer. Closer. He glanced back. Damn! The other car was gaining! Must be a Mercedes, he absently thought, one of those big-engine types.

The light switched to yellow.

Oh shit!

Roy felt the truck beneath him accelerate. He closed his eyes. The truck zoomed forward. Nothing happened. He snapped his eyes open in time to see the intersection behind them and the traffic starting to cross it. The sedan tried to run the red, but a Metro bus crossing into the intersection slammed into it with an ear-splitting crash of metal against metal.

The sedan spun into the eastbound traffic and two more cars smashed into it.

Dane swung the truck onto a side road heading in the direction of Hawthorne, and the wreckage was lost to Roy's view. He released his breath. Leaning over the edge of the bed, he stuck his head toward the cab. "Dane, back to the house!"

His brother's head nodded, and Roy collapsed in a heap against the side of the bed. The others stared at him. Even Carlos looked a little spooked by the episode, but at least Izzy was too scared to start one of his rants. Roy fought to control his breathing.

Alex, please make it home!

***

Bob entered Allison's room with his cell phone in hand. Shaw still sat on Allison's bed, oblivious to the blood staining his pants, his gaze glued to the empty, blood-soaked pillow.

"He, uh, got away, sir," Bob confessed. "But we have the plate number."

As though he were a marble statue coming to uncertain life, Shaw turned his head and fixed his devastated eyes on Bob.

"Find him. Follow whoever has him. Do not engage until I give the order."

"But, sir, you don't really think he could've–"

The searing look on Shaw's face stopped Bob in mid-sentence.

"Find him."

"Yes, sir." Without hesitation, Bob slunk from the room.

Shaw reached out for a framed photo on Allison's night table, a photo of himself and his daughter taken several years earlier. They were yucking it up at the beach and grinning like fools. He clutched the photo to his chest like it was his whole life.

CHAPTER TWENTY-SEVEN

IF I'M LUCKY, HE'LL KILL ME

Everyone gathered once again in Nathan's bedroom, but this time Roy paced while the others sat around on the floor fiddling with their phones. Father Pat sat beside Nathan's bed, and Dane stood looking out the upstairs window into the driveway below.

"He shouldda been here by now." Roy finally said what everyone was obviously thinking. Dane turned from the window, and Roy fixed a hard look on him. "We shouldda gone back to look for him."

Dane's face flashed with anger. "I already told you, little brother, the place would be crawling with cops. They'd have made us for sure."

Roy simmered, but said nothing more.

Father Pat cleared his throat. "Roy, is there anywhere else Alex might have gone? He wouldn't have gone back to his own house, would he?"

Roy stopped pacing a moment and shook his head. "No. This is his house. He was coming here. Oh, God, maybe they got him after all!"

Java piped up with, "Still nothing on his phone. Must be off."

Father Pat flinched, as though just remembering something. "Roy, is there anyone else Alex has spun lately?"

Roy stopped cold and his eyes went wide with fear.

Oh, shit!

He hadn't even thought of that. If the people being killed were the ones Alex helped.... His mind raced to remember. So much had happened the past week. "He tried to spin *me*."

"Why, what's wrong with you?" Israel asked, squinting with suspicion.

Roy flushed red and glanced down at the carpet. "Nothing. There were them two seniors." His eyes widened.

"What?" Father Pat asked, leaping to his feet.

"Tami. He spinned Tami today."

"Oh, shit," Israel muttered.

"Let's go," Dane said, looking relieved to finally be doing something.

Nathan threw off his covers and clambered out of bed, pausing to maintain his balance. "Not so fast. I'm goin' too."

Roy rushed past Father Pat and tried to force his dad back into bed. "No way, Dad. You're hurt."

"You're my son. Dane is my son." He glanced past Roy at Dane's unreadable expression. "And Alex is my son. You're in danger and I'm going."

"But, Dad–"

Nathan gripped both of Roy's shoulders and forced their eyes to meet. "We're a family, Roy, and a family sticks together." He looked across at Dane, standing before the window. "That work for you, Dane?"

Roy turned to his volatile brother, and thought he noticed just the flicker of a smile grace those normally pursed lips.

"Yeah, pop, that'll work," Dane replied.

***

Dane's truck screeched to a loud stop in front of Tami's house. There were no lights on and the place looked deserted. The street around it seemed unnaturally dark, despite the full moon lighting up the sky overhead. Roy tumbled out of the cab and rushed to the unmoving form in the wheelchair planted on the damp lawn like a misshapen garden gnome. The others piled out after him.

Roy crouched before Alex, his heart beating with equal parts joy and trepidation. Were they too late? Roy scanned Alex's lap and shirt – no blood! But his friend's eyes were vacant, staring at the darkened house without actually seeing it.

"Alex, man, where the hell you been?" Roy asked, as the others crowded around.

Alex stared, silent and unseeing, and made no move to answer.

Father Pat squatted down before him. "Alex, are you all right?"

Roy watched Alex's eyes lose the vacant stare. He blinked several times, and then looked at Father Pat with confusion. "Huh?"

Roy and Father Pat exchanged a look of dread.

"Where am I?" Alex asked, sounding groggy.

Roy gave him a solemn look. "Tami's house."

Alex's face screwed up with horror. "No!" He grabbed his wheels and spun around Roy toward the front door. "Tami!"

Three small steps leading to the wooden porch halted his progress, and he whipped his head around to the others. "Help me!"

Dane and Java got there before Roy, hefting Alex and his chair up the short climb to the porch. Roy grabbed the doorknob, certain it would be locked. But the knob turned, and the door swung wide to reveal a dark, empty, and way-too-quiet entry hall.

Alex didn't hesitate. He rolled over the threshold and pushed his way forward. Roy followed, phone out, flashlight app engaged. Dane flanked him and the others crowded in behind. Despite their past, Roy felt relief at having Dane's strength and unflinching will beside him. His dad's, too. It occurred to him as he shone his light around the empty living room and hallway that the three of them had never done anything together as a family. This was a first.

Off to the right, down a short hall, a sliver of light spilled from an open door, looking like a pale lightning bolt ripping across the carpeted floor. Roy nudged Alex, and they hurried down the hall toward it.

Alex got to the door first, but Roy was right there with him. It was a small kitchen that looked a lot like the one at his house. His gaze traveled to the open refrigerator – the source of the light streak.

Alex pushed his way inside, the others following until the tiny kitchen was suddenly alive with ten moving shadows.

Everyone stood frozen, staring at the contents of that refrigerator as though they explained everything that had been happening. But Roy knew mayonnaise and milk wouldn't tell them what they needed to know.

Father Pat crept forward. He spotted a piece of paper on the round kitchen table and picked it up.

"What's that?" Roy whispered.

The priest scanned it. "A note, to Alex."

Alex turned to him. "What's it say?"

Father Pat held the note sideways, so the refrigerator light could illuminate the blue ink and feminine script. "'Dear Alex: I'm sorry for running away. I was confused and upset. I don't care if you're different or not, you're still the nicest guy I know and–' That's all there is."

While Father Pat read the letter, Roy found himself inching closer to the open refrigerator door. He bent closer, and then recoiled. A smear of blood graced the edge. He turned to find Dane and Alex staring at the same smear. Roy knew he should close that refrigerator door, but couldn't bring himself to do it. Somehow, he felt certain he knew what they'd find behind it.

Dane pushed forward and swung the door shut, causing Roy to stumble back in surprise, and Israel to cry out, "Oh, shit!"

On the wall, next to the refrigerator, was an address, scrawled in blood, and a note to go with it. A large splash of blood streaked the floor at Dane's feet.

Alex paled with dread. "That's Tami's blood."

Nathan stepped forward and wrapped his arm around Roy's shaking shoulders. "What's it say, Father Pat?"

The priest returned the note to the table and stepped forward. The other kids crowded around him. Roy heard Israel whimpering, and in the back of his mind thought, *forgot his meds again*. Doing his best to keep his phone steady, Roy aimed the beam at the bloody, dripping message. It was wet and sticky looking, and he felt his gorge rise at the smell.

"It says," the priest began, his voice sounding strained, "the girl for the cripple. Come to this address or she dies."

Stillness filled the room as everyone digested the reality of those words. Roy looked at Alex with terror, but it was Dane who broke the silence.

"Sounds like they want a showdown." He slid a handgun from his pocket and held it up to the group. With no light except Roy's flashlight app, the gun glinted in the shadows. "Demons or humans, we're gonna take these assholes down and put an end to this shit. Tonight. We might be a bunch a dummies, but we take care of our own. And *nobody's* gettin' Alex."

Israel's eyes bulged with surprise, but both Carlos and Java nodded.

Alex looked at Dane with gratitude. "Let's go."

***

They piled into Dane's truck, with Alex in front, sandwiched between

Dane and Roy. Jorge, Cuong, and Father Pat clambered into the back seat, while the others climbed over the tailgate to crowd together in the bed. Father Pat had the location programmed into his phone, and looked at the screen a moment as Dane started the engine. The bright headlights hit the street with startling illumination, almost causing Roy to jump. He was scared, and he wasn't afraid to admit it.

"Head north on the 405," Father Pat said.

Dane grunted and pulled away from the curb, leaving Tami's empty house behind.

Dane drove with caution. Nathan had warned him against speeding. Last thing they needed was a cop stopping them, especially with all the guns in the truck.

Roy was so fixated on the brooding Alex that he paid little attention to his side-view mirror. He barely noticed the dark sedan following them, and gave it no consideration.

Alex sat in silence, staring out the front window.

"Alex, say something," Roy whispered, knowing his voice sounded frantic, but that's how he felt. He'd gotten Alex back, but something had changed. The image flashed through his mind of Alex bringing that bloody knife to his wrist, and his gaze lowered to his friend's hands, clasped in his lap as though in prayer. His heart lurched. Along the left wrist was a thin line of dried blood.

"Alex?"

His best friend said nothing. Roy glanced over the seat at Father Pat, who got his message at once and leaned closer to the back of Alex's head.

"Alex, who kidnapped you?"

Alex didn't move his head, but Roy noticed him flinch. "A man who wanted me to help his daughter. I killed her."

Roy gasped, and even Dane looked sideways at Alex.

"Alex, I don't believe you killed anyone," Father Pat said, his voice calmer than Roy felt. "Why do you think you did?"

Roy wanted to grab Alex's hand, wanted to hold him like he had when they'd been alone. But he couldn't. Not here.

"Who else could have?" Alex answered in a creepy monotone voice. "Blood on my wheelchair, all over her room. Just like the other times."

"You didn't kill no one," Dane asserted with a conviction that surprised Roy. "Even if that guy thinks you did."

A terrifying thought occurred to Roy. "Is that why they were after you, for payback?"

Alex just stared. His unresponsiveness was creeping Roy out, big time. "If I'm lucky, he'll kill me."

"Alex, you can't give up," Father Pat said from the back seat.

Like an echo, Jorge's voice filled the cab, "Alex, you can't give up."

When Alex didn't respond, Roy leaned in and placed a hand on his arm. "Alex."

Alex didn't react to Roy's touch. He didn't move a muscle. "I don't wanna talk no more."

Feeling sick, Roy sagged back into the seat and gazed out the window.

***

Davalos sat at his desk absently tossing a handball up and down, bouncing it off the far wall. The phone rang. He grabbed the receiver in his right hand, plucking the handball out of midair with his left. "Talk to me."

Leaning back in his chair, he listened. Then he said, "Okay, we have the twin now, so we might have to barter. I'm sending in a full company of men, but I'm sure they are, too."

He listened for a moment. Frowning, he leaned forward in his chair and stared at the clippings across from him.

"Under no circumstances allow either of them to fall into enemy hands. If you have no other choice, and I mean *no* other choice, kill them both."

CHAPTER TWENTY-EIGHT

ALEX IS STILL IN THERE!

Roy had no idea how far they drove, but he absently noted that they had ascended higher and that meant they were heading out of Los Angeles over the mountains. He didn't care. His heart and soul were with Alex. He wanted to say the right things, wanted his friend to stop hating himself. But he had nothing, so he sat and brooded like the emo boy he was.

No one spoke, not even Father Pat. The priest's phone rested against the dashboard, attached to one of those sticky pads so it wouldn't fall when the truck made a turn. The robotic female voice kept intoning things like "Go four point five miles on the current road" and "In one quarter mile, turn...."

Roy tuned it all out after a while and did something he hadn't done since his mom took sick – he prayed. He asked God to keep Alex safe, to make sure nothing bad happened to him. The prayers hadn't worked for his mom—she died anyway—which was why Roy didn't bother praying after that. But with all Father Pat's talk of demons and other stuff he didn't understand, Roy decided to give God another chance. Alex needed all the help he could get.

He emerged from his heavy silence when he felt Dane begin to slow, and that weird Google voice stated, without inflection, "Your destination is five hundred feet straight ahead." Roy peered through the dusty windshield at a large, burned out structure looming in their path. The fact that it had been a church was obvious – a huge cross sat atop a steeple that had been gutted by fire. It reminded Roy of Father's Pat's church, with big windows surrounded by fancy carvings, but no glass anymore. The outside was made of bricks, which, Roy guessed, was why the whole place hadn't burned to the ground. There were towers rising high into the misty darkness, and large buildings attached to either side of the main structure.

No lights welcomed them into the weed-infested parking lot. Only the full moon gave the relic a hint of illumination, but the cloud cover filtering the moonlight made the place look especially creepy. Roy felt something, too, similar to what he'd felt that night in Eucalyptus Park. He didn't understand what he felt, just knew that there was something in this building that was wrong, something that wasn't… human. Demons? He shivered and glanced at Alex beside him as Dane eased the truck to a stop in front of the steps leading up toward chained-up double doors. Then he popped open his door and stepped out onto the cracked pavement.

The boys in back clambered over the tailgate and stood shivering in the chill night air. Java lifted out Alex's chair and rolled it to the front, while Carlos looked around. Roy noted Carlos's gaze flitting everywhere, and realized that this place was perfect for an ambush if someone wanted to take shots at them.

Juan looked like a frightened rabbit, his thin frame trembling from a combination of cold and abject terror. Jorge, Israel, and Cuong huddled together. Jorge silently stared at the church and Israel looked from one end of the empty lot to the other. Cuong gripped his Gameboy like a weapon he intended to use if anyone came at him.

As Roy helped Alex into his chair, Java stepped away and touched Israel's shoulder. Israel opened his mouth to scream, but Java clamped a hand over it. "Quiet, Izzy!" he hissed.

He pulled his hand back, and the visibly shaken Israel lowered his clenched fists. "Shit, Java," he hissed, his breathing ragged, "don't do that shit!"

Java shrugged. "Sorry, Crack Head."

Dane reached into the rear seat and hefted out his weapons bag, laying it on the ground beside the truck.

Alex wheeled forward, stopping in front of the truck, gazing intently at the monstrous wreck of a church in silence. Roy followed him. Alex's wheels rolling against the gravel of the lot was the only sound Roy had heard since they arrived. This church was pretty far out, with no houses anywhere in sight. But the town wasn't far away, and yet he heard nothing. It was almost as if the place had a dome covering it, like in a show he'd seen on TV, keeping out everything but them.

Roy watched Alex staring at the dark, scary-looking building, and was so intent on his friend he didn't hear Juan creep up from behind and touch him on the shoulder.

Roy jumped. "Shit, Juan, you scared me!"

Juan shivered. "I'm scared, Roy." His voice sounded tiny and weak. "Real scared."

Alex turned. "Tell me, Juan. I'll take it."

As Dane pulled his weapons out of the duffel and laid them side-by-side on the cracked pavement, Alex spun the fear from Juan like it had never been there.

Roy was terrified. He could ask Alex to spin him, too, but thought he might be better off scared. After all, he was more afraid for Alex than himself.

With a grateful little smile, reminding Roy of a mouse in some animated movie he'd watched, Juan whispered, "Thanks, Alex."

Roy had been so focused on the two of them he hadn't noticed Nathan approach and stand beside him.

Gotta be more alert, he told himself.

"You okay, Dad? Need Alex to spin you 'fore we go in?"

Nathan looked at Alex, and Alex tilted his head upward. But Nathan placed one hand on Roy's shoulder and one on Alex's. "I think Alex needs to stay strong. If what the priest says is true, he's gonna need every bit of whatever he's got to fight these things."

"It's okay, Mr. Phillips, I can spin you," Alex said at once. "Let me."

Nathan shook his head, offering a slight smile. "No. I'll be fine. And when are you gonna stop calling me Mr. Phillips?"

"What should I call you?"

"Nathan, Dad, Pop," Nathan replied with ease. "Just don't call me late for dinner when you cook."

Roy couldn't help but smile, which really helped relieve his pent-up tension.

Alex offered a grin. "Thanks… Dad."

Then Dane was at their side along with Father Pat and the others. Everyone stood a moment looking at the forbidding structure that had once been a place of worship.

"They're here," Alex said. "Can you feel 'em?"

Roy didn't need Alex to say who "them" was, because he already knew. Demons. Creatures. Evil. He glanced above Alex's head at Dane, saw strength in his brother's eyes, and a total lack of fear.

"You guys ready?" Dane asked, scanning their faces. Roy thought he was practically daring anyone to say they weren't, but even Jorge nodded and repeated, "You guys ready?" He held up a can of spray paint. Roy didn't even remember Jorge bringing it.

Dane squinted at Jorge a moment, as though he thought the autistic boy was mocking him, and then grunted. He stepped around the group to where he'd laid out his weapons, and Roy turned to follow.

He froze when he saw the lineup of guns. The uneasy feeling came over him that they might not all be legal.

Nathan must've thought the same thing because he stepped forward to examine them. "Uh, that one looks military, son."

He pointed at one that looked to Roy like an Uzi from the movies.

Dane reached for the indicated firearm. "Friend of mine in the Marines gave me this. Not supposed to, but he did, so screw it. You want?"

He handed the gun toward his father, but Nathan shook his head. "Wouldn't know what to do with it. I'll take the rifle."

He reached down and snatched up the rifle, hefting the weight and the feel of it against his shoulder, making sure not to even brush his finger against the trigger.

Dane grabbed a handgun and passed it to Roy, who held it nervously. "Uh, I don't know, Dane. I never shot one before."

"I have," Carlos said, stepping forward and holding out his hand. "Gimme."

Roy looked to Dane for approval, and Dane nodded. Roy handed the gun over.

Carlos checked it, slipped out the chamber to make sure it was filled, and slid it back into the handle. "I'm ready."

Dane nodded and offered another handgun to Father Pat. The priest shook his head. "I wouldn't even know how to use that. Besides, this battle is more spiritual than physical."

Dane grunted, but said nothing.

Israel stepped forward. "I'll take it."

Dane looked at Israel as though he was crazy, and Roy felt sure he'd say no. But in a surprising move, he handed the gun over. Israel took it into both hands, his eyes wide and excited.

"Prob'ly shoot yer foot off," Dane said with disdain in his voice. "It's automatic, kid, so just point an' shoot."

Israel nodded, and Roy noted how less scared he looked now that he had a weapon.

Dane lifted the remaining handgun and passed it to Java. He held the Uzi at his side. Everyone froze a moment, and then turned to gaze once more at the silent, expectant building.

They're waiting, Roy knew. *The whole building is waiting.*

"They'll try to trick you," Father Pat announced, like he was a coach with last minute instructions before the big game, "to draw you away from Alex. You can't let that happen. You can't leave him alone."

Every head nodded solemnly, even Jorge's.

"It's time." Alex pushed himself forward toward the steps leading up to the blackened entrance.

The wood of the doors was carved into fancy patterns, almost like giant flower petals. When Roy had first looked, he'd seen the lock and figured the doors were sealed. But now that he was closer, as they stood at the base of the steps, Roy saw the padlock had been purposely broken.

They want us inside. He shivered.

Alex turned around and Roy hurried behind him, grabbing the chair. Tilting it back, Roy muscled Alex to the top one step at a time. The *thunk, thunk, thunk* of Alex's wheels sounded like bomb blasts against the eerie silence. Dane hurried up after, and the rest followed.

***

Cole sat in his car and observed the group entering the abandoned church. He lowered the binoculars and glanced at the time on his phone. Thumbing in a quick text, he slipped the phone into his pocket. Reaching into his glove box, he pulled out his service weapon, checking to make sure it was loaded.

Stepping from his car, he scanned the deserted street. He was certain the kids hadn't noticed him following, but wanted to be sure they were well inside before he went in after them. His car was hidden from view of the church by a copse of trees fifty yards outside the parking lot. Seeing nothing around him, he turned and sprinted toward the building.

***

Phil eased the sedan to a quiet stop a hundred feet behind Cole's. He watched the detective sprint around the side of the old church and head toward the rear. Cole was lost in the gloom within moments. Phil and Bob exited their car and stared at the dark, silent hulk of a church.

Bob turned to Phil, and gasped. The muzzle of Phil's gun was right in his face. Before Bob could blink, the weapon discharged, blowing a hole through his forehead.

Phil watched his former partner drop to the ground in a heap, grateful for the silencer Shaw had provided them both. He took off at a run toward the church.

***

Once Dane had knocked off the broken lock with the butt of his Uzi and pulled open the double doors, the smell of burnt wood and masonry assailed Roy's nostrils, and he noticed the others recoil. He hadn't been inside a church since his mother's funeral, but he could tell as they stepped into the gloom that this was some sort of lobby, like the main school entrance at Mark Twain.

Glancing side to side as he followed Alex into the dark, blackened interior, he noted stairs on either side ascending to another level. There were little dishes for holy water on either side of the door, only these were blackened and the glass of the bowls had melted into solid, ugly blobs. Roy remembered putting the holy water on his face and hands at the funeral service, hoping it would make him feel better. It hadn't.

The remains of fancy wooden doors hung askew before them, revealing the vastness of the main church straight ahead. Roy didn't need Alex to confirm the presence of something evil in there – the feeling was stronger than the burnt-wood smell. It assaulted every one of his senses at the same time. He shivered, more from that feeling than from the intense coldness of the place. It felt a lot colder inside than it had out, and Roy knew why.

Alex didn't even stop to look around. He rolled forward and shoved the dangling interior doors to one side like he was the Hulk. The doors tumbled off what was left of their hinges and crashed to the smoke-blackened tiles with an echoing *bang* that startled Roy, and caused Israel behind him to erupt with a stifled, "Shit!"

But Alex paid no attention. He rolled forward into the church, and the others crowded in behind him.

This place is huge, Roy thought as he nervously scanned the cavernous ceiling and upper balconies extending the entire length of the building. Holes in the roof sent streaks of moonlight down to the floor like flashlight beams, illuminating burnt overturned pews, what looked like blackened bibles or prayer books scattered amidst the rubble, and fallen beams or charred masonry that had dropped from above.

Fancy dangling light fixtures hung askew from the pitted ceiling. Some of them had pulled loose from their moorings and crashed to the floor, smashing into pews that would have held people had a service been in progress.

Roy absently wondered what had happened here, but his focus was on Alex, and whoever their enemy was, and when that enemy might strike. Burned and blackened statues seemed to leer at him from shadowy areas along the sides. Roy felt eyes on him, and kept returning his fearful gaze to these faceless statues that had been burned beyond recognition.

He glanced at Dane, who cradled his Uzi, his face tight with expectation. Java and Carlos crowded in behind him, their eyes roaming, their senses alert. Juan shivered and Roy offered him a nervous smile. The others encircled the priest as they inched their way forward, and Roy wondered if they thought a man of God could protect them better than guns.

This is a spiritual battle, Father Pat had said, and somehow Roy knew that was true. Even though some of their enemies were human, this fight was for Alex's soul as much as his life.

The altar lay far in front of them, almost like it was at the other end of a football field, but the darkness ahead was more pervasive, and Roy could make out no details. Everywhere was the smell of death and decay.

Alex inched forward, rolling his chair around fallen debris and scorched wooden support beams that had crashed down from the roof.

The burned rafters strewn about the floor made his passage toward that distant altar increasingly difficult. But he pressed on like metal drawn to a magnet.

***

Bringing up the rear, Israel glanced at Jorge beside him, but the autistic boy didn't look at all afraid. He held out his spray can like it was a machine gun, and looked at Israel with that blank, but calm expression he always wore.

Looking around at his group, taking in everything at once the way his ADHD allowed him to do, Israel sensed a mix of fear and excitement in Java and Carlos. They were stoked for this, he could tell, while he felt like crapping his pants. If he lived through this, he'd never watch another horror movie again!

Then his hyper-attuned gaze spotted a red dot floating amongst them. The hell? The dot skimmed the top of Java's head, passed over Father Pat heading for Alex. Something Israel remembered from a movie kicked in. As the dot stopped on Juan's forehead, Israel screamed, "Look out!"

Both Alex and Juan spun around, and a gunshot rang out. Israel barely saw the fear in Juan's wide eyes before his head exploded in a shower of blood and brain matter that rained gore onto Alex's blond hair, and splattered Roy and Dane across the chest like they were some horrible modern art project.

***

Carlos and Dane reacted at once, raising their weapons and firing up at the balcony, while everyone else scattered, hurrying down the cluttered center aisle toward the front entrance.

Alex gaped as Juan's small body twitched and spun before dropping in a heap at his feet, the top half of his head gone.

"Oh, shit!" Roy exclaimed, leaping aside as the body collapsed. Dane and Carlos began sweeping the upper floor with gunfire. Israel's hand flew up, the gun rapidly firing toward the ceiling, his arm sweeping randomly about. He wasn't even trying to aim.

Roy looked up at the ceiling and saw the danger at once. The bullets had weakened the beams above them, and the charred wood was crumbling.

Alex must have seen it, too, because he shouted, "Get back!" and shoved Roy with all of his strength.

Like when Ms. Ashley had done experiments on motion with Alex and his chair, shoving Roy toward the front entrance propelled Alex backwards toward the altar.

Startled, Roy stumbled into Dane, and Dane stopped firing to glance upward.

The entire roof was caving in on them.

"Back!" Dane shouted. "Get back!"

He grabbed Roy and shoved him into the others. Everyone backpedaled as the first of the wooden beams and ceiling supports slammed into the floor where they'd been standing.

The debris rained down on them and Nathan yelled, "It's all coming down! Back to the parking lot!"

Roy was aware of Dane dragging him, of Izzy shouting "Oh, shit, oh shit" again and again as the silence of the church was violated by the rending and splitting of wood, the crash of beams and loose glass, and dangling light fixtures striking the floor in front and around them like an insane hail storm.

Father Pat urged Jorge and Izzy to hurry while Carlos shouted, "Move, move!" But Roy's gaze remained fixed on Alex, separated from the group by a rising mound of debris as the entire ceiling collapsed inward and build a wall between them, a wall cutting him off from the friend he loved.

"Alex!" he shouted in despair as he fought and struggled against Dane's iron grip. "Let me go, Dane!"

Dane ignored him, gripped him hard around his torso like a linebacker taking down an opponent and powered him toward the door as a huge light from above slammed into the floor where they'd been standing.

"Alex!" Roy shouted again. He could barely make out his friend in the gloom beyond the pile of rubble. Even though more moonlight was entering because the roof had collapsed, the dirt and grit rising from the wall of debris blinded him. He made out Alex's hand rising into the air, a final wave goodbye before the rest of the roof toppled in on itself and cut him off from view.

Roy screamed in despair and fought Dane like a wild man. But Dane was strong as hell and Roy couldn't budge him. He found himself back in the lobby area with the others before Dane finally released him.

Everyone looked shaken, even the unflappable Java, but all Roy could picture was that final wave goodbye from his friend. He whirled on Dane in fury and shoved his brother hard. "Alex is still in there!"

Nathan placed a hand on Roy's shoulder, but Roy shook it off. "Dad!"

"Dane did the right thing, Roy," Nathan said in that quiet voice of his. He sounded rattled, but somehow managed to stay calm, and didn't even react with anger to Roy's throwing off of his hand. "You'd be dead if you tried to get to him."

"The hell with *me*," Roy spat with fury. "Alex is more important!"

Everyone stared at him, breathless and shaken and uncertain.

"Alex is more important," Jorge echoed, and Roy looked at him with anger. But Jorge smiled in that disarming way he had, and Roy's anger dimmed.

"All along they wanted to get Alex alone," Roy went on breathlessly. "To keep us away from him. And now they got him! Don't you see?"

"Roy's right," Father Pat agreed. "We have to get back in there."

Dane and his dad exchanged a questioning look, and then surveyed their surroundings.

"Stairs are no good," Nathan began, as though examining a construction problem that needed solving. "Side buildings?"

Dane nodded. "Yeah. Must be a way back into the main church through one a them. Pop, you take half and go through the building on the right. I'll take the other half and go left."

Nathan nodded.

Dane swept his gaze over all of them. "Carlos, the priest, stutter kid, and the one who repeats everything go with my dad. Roy, Java, and hyper kid go with me. Whoever gets in first, go right for Alex. Who's got phones?"

Everyone pulled theirs out. Dane told them his number, and they thumbed it in. Dane had to spell his name for them, but he needed them to do the same for him. "I got Pop's number so if I get in, I'll call. Pop, you do the same back. You others too."

Roy looked imploringly at his big brother, a man he barely knew, but a man he needed more than anyone right now. "Dane, we *hafta* save him."

Dane looked at him with determination. "We will, little brother. No one hurts my family."

Roy was surprised by the intensity of his brother's words, but heartened by them too. He turned to his dad. "Be careful, Dad. I love you."

Nathan looked soberly at his son. "Love you, too. Stick close to Dane. He'll keep you safe."

They scattered.

***

Alex stared at the rubble before him, blinking against the dust swirling in the air, his eyes watering from irritation, his lap covered with white powder from above. He felt Juan's blood in his hair, sticky and fresh, and shivered with disgust, wanting to jump under a shower and wash it all out. The unnerving silence following the cave-in seemed even worse than it was when they'd entered.

He observed the mountain of rubble before him. The way out was hopelessly blocked. He supposed if he wasn't in the chair he might be able to clamber up the hill of debris and get to his friends, but even that looked risky with so much loose and unsettled chunks of wood and broken glass and weakened beams. But he *was* in the chair. His friends were on the other side. And he was alone.

Exactly the way the enemy wanted. He'd heard Roy shouting his name, but nothing after that. They would come for him.

But will they get here in time? Do I want them to?

He realized he didn't. Too many had already died, or been hurt, because of him. He saw again in his mind's eye Juan's head exploding outward, the split-second of horrified realization on the boy's face before death snatched him from this world like someone spearing a hotdog from a pot of boiling water. He couldn't see Juan's body at all now. It was completely covered, giving Alex the weird feeling of having seen his death, funeral, and burial all at the same time.

Juan was a good kid. He shouldn't be dead. Allison shouldn't be dead. Mrs. Rhodes and Ms. Ashley shouldn't be dead. Even Maribel, who'd treated him like shit, shouldn't be dead. Everything was his fault.

Because he was a freak.

But Roy and Nathan were alive, and so were his friends. The only way he could keep them safe was to give his enemies what they wanted. If they wanted his spinning power, they could have it. His friends and family were more important.

As though knowing exactly what was in his mind, a voice purred enticingly from behind him. "Welcome, Alex."

A chill ran through him, freezing him in place. He recognized that voice. Even as he began a slow turn of his chair, he knew what he would find. Atop the altar in the gloom ahead sat an object he recognized: the music box. And right beside it, grinning with evil finality was the big, fluffy, inhuman cat.

"We've been waiting, Alex," the cat purred in that scratchy, guttural voice punk singers employed. "A very long time."

Alex's breath froze in his chest, and his heart thumped with dread. Even as he began pushing himself forward to meet his fate, his thoughts were on Roy and the others.

At least they're safe.

CHAPTER TWENTY-NINE

THEN DIE FOR YOUR FRIEND

Roy followed Dane, but kept an eye on Izzy with that gun. He wasn't sure Dane should've given it to him, but then Izzy had great coordination and a good eye, despite his ADHD. Or maybe because of it. He'd just proven that inside the church. He recalled Ms. Ashley saying kids like Izzy had brains that were super aware of everything around them. Still, he worried his friend would panic and accidentally shoot him in the back.

They crept along the outside of a large building attached to the main church. The full moon cast the blackened structure in a weird light, almost making the burned and scorched wood look beautiful, rather than dead. His eyes roamed everywhere at once as Dane held his Uzi at the ready and skirted the rows of blown out windows. Glass crunched beneath his boots as he slunk along, and the crackling sound unnerved Roy. He heard in his mind that hideous doll in the graveyard talking to Alex. The crunching glass reminded him of that evil, scratchy voice.

And, despite his best efforts not to, he couldn't erase the image of Juan's twitching body, half his head gone, as it crumpled to a heap at his feet. He'd always liked Juan, and images of his encounters with the boy flitted through his mind as he glanced side to side. It suddenly occurred to him that Juan always looked at him the same way *he* used to look at Patrick. Could Juan have been crushing on him? He'd never know for sure. But he did know he would never forget that final look of stunned horror on Juan's face as he collapsed.

Dane stopped at a single door, blackened, but secured with a large padlock. He raised the Uzi to shoot off the lock, but Roy put a hand on his arm. "Too loud. Lemme."

He slipped the small tool kit from the front pocket of his jeans and stepped around Dane, who watched with curiosity. Roy examined the lock a moment before sliding out the appropriate tool, and proceeded to stick it inside the keyhole, wriggling it this way and that. In seconds, there came a satisfying click, and the lock snapped open. He slipped it off the door and handed it to Dane, feeling, despite the danger, proud to show his big brother something he could do. And the look of surprised respect on Dane's face would stay with him forever.

"Slick, little brother." He stepped forward and raised the Uzi, nodding to Roy and the others. Israel raised his handgun and pointed it at the door. Java scooted around Roy and gripped the door handle. He looked at Dane. Dane nodded. Java yanked open the door and jumped back to avoid any hidden booby traps.

There was nothing. Only darkness, and a blast of cold air spilling out from within.

Dane stepped around everyone and entered first. Roy followed, with the others trailing behind.

***

Nathan led his group toward the right side of the massive complex, around Dane's truck and past a side entrance to the main church. He paused a moment to examine the location of this door relative to where the cave-in occurred, and knew it was no good. Entering there would just bring them onto the same side of the blockage as before. They needed to move on.

He held the rifle Dane had given him. He'd learned to shoot from his old man when he was a teen, and he supposed it must've been in the blood since Dane had taken a liking to guns, too. Looking at the others, he wasn't surprised to see Carlos alert and all business. Gang members like him knew how to survive. He just hoped if push came to shove, Carlos wouldn't save himself and leave the rest of them to die.

Cuong looked wide-eyed and terrified, and Jorge simply curious. Jorge always looked curious about everything, Nathan had noted more than once. Even when Jorge cut himself once while helping Roy fix his truck, he'd just stared at his bleeding hand in wonder, like it was the coolest thing he'd ever seen. Cuong had his Gameboy turned on and held out in front of him like a space-age flashlight.

Nathan stopped and studied the building adjacent to the church. He glanced at Father Pat.

"This looks like a separate chapel," the priest whispered, "but it *should* lead back into the main church."

Nathan nodded and continued on along the building, noting the gaping holes where those fancy colored windows had once been. He could make out bits of colored glass reflected in the moonlight, wedged into the wooden copings.

He led the group toward the rear of the structure. There was another door. It was padlocked, but unlike the front entrance to the main church, not busted open. They obviously weren't invited to enter through here. He noted the location of the door relative to the main part of the church and saw at once it was far enough back to be on Alex's side of the cave-in.

Slipping the rifle strap over his shoulder, Nathan reached into his workpants and pulled out his own set of pick tools. Having worked as a locksmith before going into construction, opening a door like this was a piece of cake. As he inserted a pick into the lock and felt around for the mechanism, he wondered if Roy had brought his own set to use on the other side.

Nathan couldn't help a slight smile at the memory of finding eight-year-old Roy with his pick tools in hand, trying to break into that cabinet to retrieve his Xbox. It had been locked up for a week because Roy had been disrespectful to his teacher, and Nathan had wanted to teach him a lesson. Instead, Roy had taught him one – the apple didn't fall far from the tree, in more ways than one.

The mechanism clicked, and the padlock popped open. He slipped it off and set it down. Not knowing who might be lying in wait, he determined to be as quiet as possible. Sliding the rifle off his shoulder, Nathan gripped it firmly, glanced at Carlos and saw the boy had his handgun raised and ready, and then reached out to turn the doorknob.

***

Roy kept to Dane's side as they slunk down a hallway. It looked to him like maybe before the fire these rooms had been offices. He spotted the remains of burned out toys in a couple, and what was left of some kind of playpen. Those rooms looked like places where small children hung out while their parents were in church.

Other rooms had charred sections of door hanging from melted hinges. Inside some of these were pieces of chairs, and even a metal desk that had partially melted into the floor and looked like a weird piece of art Roy had seen on a school field trip one time.

It looked to him like the building split off into two sections, either one of which might lead into the main church. He touched Dane on the shoulder as they approached some crisscrossing hallways. Dane turned, eyebrows raised.

"We need to split up, Dane," he whispered, indicating the two different directions.

Dane flinched. "No. We stick together."

"Dane!" Roy hissed, his entire body tensed for action. "Alex could be in trouble. We gotta split up."

Dane looked uncertain, something Roy wasn't used to seeing, and turned to Java. Java stood awaiting orders, like a soldier in the army.

"Can you take hyper kid and check out that direction?" Dane asked, pointing to their left.

Java looked at him without fear, tossing off that cocky grin he sometimes had. "You got it. C'mon, Izzy." Without even waiting for an answer, he strode down the hall to their left.

"Izzy, if you find Alex, beep my phone or scream like hell," Roy said. "I'll come running."

He raised a fist. Israel bumped it and hurried down the hall after Java.

Roy turned to Dane, who stood tautly.

"You okay, little brother?" Dane asked.

Roy swallowed his rising panic. "Yeah. Let's go."

***

Carlos led the way, with Nathan and Father Pat right behind him. Sounds came from up ahead, rustling sounds. Carlos stopped and cocked his head to one side, listening. The sounds stopped. Carlos stepped forward and the two men followed.

***

Behind them, as Jorge glanced around at the charred remains of this smaller church, he spotted an area that looked like it used to have a lot of candles stacked up, the kind his mother always burnt at home. There was broken, melted glass and puddles of hardened wax splattered across the floor. But that wasn't what drew him away from Cuong and toward this side room. It was the red Vs someone had spray painted all over the blackened walls. He smiled and moved in that direction.

***

Cuong saw Jorge going the wrong way and froze. He wanted to tell the other boy to stop, but feared he would stutter and make the gangster kid mad. He started following Roy's dad, hoping to get his attention, and then stopped. The Gameboy in his hand vibrated. He turned it around. It displayed a game - a game he didn't own.

On screen was a game version of the church. Four figures moved around damaged and burned seats and statues that looked exactly like the ones they'd just been walking through. And the figures on screen looked like them!

Cuong's breath almost stopped, his eyes wide and afraid. It was like when Link had attacked him through the TV last week. He watched as the Gameboy-Jorge entered the area with all the Vs, but the one that looked like him wasn't standing where he was. It was moving off to the left, through a door into another hallway. Looking up, Cuong spotted that door just ahead, and moved toward it.

***

Jorge's eyes widened with fascination at the intricate pattern of Vs all around him, the bright red of the paint – some still fresh – contrasting with the black and burnt chunks of wall and stonework on which they'd been sprayed. Even the ceiling above him had Vs of all shapes and sizes, upside down and right side up. This was how he wanted his room to look, only his mom kept stopping him every time he'd bring the ladder in from the garage to spray his ceiling.

Feeling calm and secure in this dark, but comforting space, Jorge approached one wall and raised the paint can. With sheer delight, he added his own Vs, filling in all the empty spaces he could find. A click sounded behind him, but he kept on painting.

"Hey, kid."

Jorge turned. A man stood in front of him, a strange man with white hair like Alex's, a man Jorge had never seen before. He was dressed nice, like some of the men always dressed on Sundays at his church. But he held a gun in his hand, a gun pointed straight at Jorge's face. The man smiled.

***

Carlos, Nathan, and Father Pat all stopped to listen. There was definitely movement somewhere in the building, slithery animal movements. Nathan recalled what Roy had told him about the attack at the cemetery. "Might be cats."

Carlos squinted at him in the gloom. "So? Cats can't hurt us." He held up his gun like it was the answer to everything.

Nathan looked grave. "A *lot* of cats."

Carlos's eyes widened, and then he was distracted by something behind Nathan. "Shit, where'd them other two go?"

Nathan turned, but Carlos was already jogging back the way they'd come, past the blackened altar, deftly leaping over beams and shattered pews. Father Pat trailed behind, and Nathan stumbled after, his head injury forcing him to move with care.

From an alcove ahead, an unfamiliar male voice said, "You willing to die for that cripple?" and Jorge's unmistakable imitation followed, "You willing to die for that cripple?"

By then Carlos had rounded the corner out of Nathan's sight. A shot rang out. And then another.

***

Israel caught up to Java as he was about to enter a hallway that looked like it led to a school. He recalled seeing a play yard off to the side as they'd entered, so it made sense. The church his parents took him to had a school next to it. But he didn't think the school would have a way back into the church. Even without his phone in hand, he knew it had been awhile since they'd left Alex alone.

"Muscle Man," Israel whispered, stopping at Java's shoulder and bouncing up and down like a rubber ball.

Java turned.

"This way goes into the school," Israel said. "Look, there's burned out desks in that room." He pointed to the nearest room, its door burned off, charred and pitted and melted remnants of children's desks visible amidst the rubble.

Java shrugged. "So? Might be another way into the church through the back."

Israel didn't think so. "I seen another hall. We just passed it. Looked like it goes to the church."

Java hesitated. "Dane said to check this way."

Israel knew Java well. He liked being told what to do. That's why the football coach liked him – until Java beat the crap out of another kid one night. "You go this way. I'm gonna check that other hall. If I find nuthin', I'll come back."

"You're not scared?"

"I'm scared outta my mind, Java," Israel hissed, his voice trembling. "But Alex needs us. 'Sides, I got this." He hefted the gun like it was his best friend.

"'Kay. Come find me if it be a dead end." Java moved on down the hall, but then turned back. "Member what Dane said – don't shoot yer foot off."

Despite his fear, Israel grinned.

***

Alex stared long and hard at the cat. It seemed the animal was mad-dogging him, but it was hard to tell since those reddish eyes never changed. Gunshots echoed from somewhere nearby, and he stiffened. But his focus remained on the cat.

"Where's Tami?" he demanded.

The animal licked its right forepaw like any normal cat.

"Tell me, bitch!" Alex hissed, feeling his temper begin to rise.

From deep shadows behind the altar stepped a figure wearing black pants and a black sweatshirt, a figure Alex knew all too well.

"Cats can't talk, Alex," Ms. G. said in a smooth voice. "I didn't think you were *that* stupid."

She held a leash in her hand, like people used for walking their dogs. But whatever was attached to it, Alex couldn't make out. This part of the church had its roof intact, and not much light filtered through the holes above him.

Alex had been called stupid more times than he'd been called "crip." Usually, it didn't bother him. He *was* stupid, after all, in some ways. But he understood a lot more than people gave him credit for, and he was *tired* of being called stupid.

"I'm not stupid. And I want Tami!"

Ms. G. smiled, and Alex shivered. Her smile looked so much like the cat's it sent chills straight into his heart. She brushed strands of blonde hair off her forehead and gave a hard tug on the leash.

Alex froze as Tami stumbled out of the darkness. Her hands were tied behind her back and she had a scarf around her mouth, gagging her so she couldn't speak. The end of the leash was attached to a dog collar around her neck. Alex took in the blood on her face and tee shirt, and his temper surged.

"Let her go!"

Tami's eyes bulged with fear.

Ms. G. pulled the leash hand over hand, dragging Tami in like she *was* a dog instead of a real person. She gripped the leash so close to the collar that Tami choked from lack of air.

"That all depends on you, Alex."

***

When Father Pat rounded the bend into the shadowy alcove, he found Carlos standing in front of Jorge, who held out his spray can defensively. A body lay on the ground, a blond man wearing a brown suit. Father Pat approached, with Nathan moving cautiously just behind him.

Carlos grinned. "Looks like Quiet Man didn't need no help."

Father Pat shone his phone light on the body. A hole in the man's upper back oozed fresh, slippery-looking blood that pooled onto the charred floor beneath him. It sickened the priest that a boy Carlos's age could kill someone and not think twice about it, but then kids like Carlos had never been nurtured in life to begin with. To them, it was kill or be killed on the streets.

Carlos bent and rolled the body over, and Father Pat gasped. A big red "V" covered the man's pallid face, each rising arm of the letter turning the open, staring eyeballs a ghastly shade of red and staining the tips of his blond hair.

Father Pat looked at Jorge, but the boy just stared at the dead man, as though he'd never seen anything so fascinating in his life.

"Quick thinking, Quiet Man," Carlos said with admiration.

Jorge looked at Carlos and smiled. "Quick thinking, Quiet Man."

Carlos shook his head and turned to Father Pat and Nathan. "Just when I got here, he sprayed the guy and the guy's gun went off. Hadda shoot or he might a killed him."

Father Pat nodded. The seminary sure never prepared him for anything like this.

"It's okay, Carlos," Nathan said, clapping the boy on one shoulder. "You saved Jorge."

Father Pat had a sudden thought that terrified him. "Yeah, but where's Cuong?"

Carlos stiffened, and Jorge said, "Where's Cuong?"

***

Java crept along in the shadows, his gaze darting from side to side. The blackness enveloped him. The roof in this part of the building had not burned completely, so only a little moonlight filtered through. He didn't want to use his phone for fear of being seen. He crept through the fallen rubble, glancing into each classroom as he passed. Israel had been right – this was a school, but one for little kids. He spotted cartoon animals peeling off the walls and saw bits and pieces of posters with pictures of young children on them

Stepping over a discarded fire extinguisher, he suddenly stopped to listen.

Footsteps. He definitely heard footsteps! But from where? Looking back over his shoulder, Java took in the empty hallway.

Nothing.

He turned to face forward, and gasped.

A beautiful young woman stood before him wearing a negligee, and only underwear beneath. Java's eyes bulged and dropped instantly to her breasts, pushing against the lightweight material as though they had a life of their own. Only a thin little belt looped casually around her waist kept those breasts from spilling out. Mesmerized, he felt warmth replace the cold all through his body and lowered the gun to his side as his heart pounded.

"Do you like what you see?" the woman asked, her voice like the soft droning of a new car engine.

Java nodded, his mouth hanging open, his eyes riveted to those breasts.

"I'm yours if you want me." She reached out to grab at the front of his jeans, smiling with glee. Java gasped. "And I can tell you want me."

Java was stunned. He'd never had a girlfriend. Sure, he was badass on the football field, but pretty much sucked at getting girls to like him. He always looked too mean, they told him, too scary.

"Who…" he began, his voice almost a croak as her hand rubbed against him. "Who are you?"

"Does that matter, Java?"

His legs felt weak. "How… do…you know me?"

She sidled even closer, those amazing breasts rubbing against his chest, exciting him even more. "Who cares? Leave with me now and we'll put this to good use."

She squeezed his crotch harder, causing him to practically jump out of his pants. He leaned in closer as her lips moved toward his. Then he heard Father Pat's words echo though his enflamed brain: "They'll try to trick you."

He pulled back and stepped away from her, breathing hard. But that short distance cleared his mind.

"I'm not leaving Alex."

She stepped forward. "Forget him. He can't give you what I'm offering."

Java's eyes narrowed with suspicion. "How you know 'bout him?"

She rubbed herself against him. This time it had no effect. He was onto her game.

"Java–"

"You're one a them, ain't you?" he spat, cutting her off. "Like Ms. G."

Her eyes flashed with violent anger. "I'm offering you pleasure. And you choose a cripple."

Java bristled, puffing out his large chest in defiance. "That cripple is my friend."

"Then die for your friend."

Sharp pain pierced his abdomen and he grunted, the air in his lungs frozen with shock. He looked down and saw a knife sticking out of his abs, just below the belly button, her finely manicured hand gripping the hilt.

"Oh, shit," was all he could mumble before crumpling to the rubble at her feet. The gun dropped from his hand and he looked at her in astonishment.

She held the knife in her hand, its blade slick with shiny blood that glistened in the shadowy moonlight. Stunned, almost in shock, Java stretched out one arm to feel for the fallen gun as she raised the knife and bent toward him. He couldn't find it. All his groping hand could grab was the remnants of a burnt book that crumpled to ashes as he snatched for it.

Her leering face swam above him, the shimmering blade raised for the killing blow. As the blade made its arcing way toward his chest, Java took the coward's way out and closed his eyes.

A shot echoed through the building. The woman grunted in pain, and Java popped open his eyes in time to see her drop into an unmoving heap beside him. Those breasts were practically in his face, but rather than feel turned on, he felt revolted and squirmed away from her body in horror.

***

Dane and Roy both heard the shot at the same time, and whirled to face that direction.

"That's where Java went," Roy exclaimed.

"C'mon." Dane sprinted back the way they'd come. Roy started to follow, but an ethereal voice floated out of the darkness behind him.

"Roooyyyyy."

The voice drifted along in the cold breeze wafting through the building.

Roy froze. He recognized that voice. He hadn't heard it in four years, but he knew it better than he knew his own. He turned, and gasped.

"Mom?"

***

The graveyard hadn't bothered Java all that much, except when they'd actually opened the grave and had to look at the dead body inside. But seeing the lifeless woman mere inches from him, her glassy eyes open, but unseeing, and the blood rolling out of a hole in her upper chest pushed his fear button big time, even more than finding Jane dead.

He struggled to prop himself onto one elbow, but the pain in his lower body was excruciating each time he shifted position. He glanced down at his blood-soaked hoodie and jeans, and knew he was badly hurt. Oddly enough, that didn't worry him.

Alex will spin it, he thought, *like he always does.*

That thought cleared his mind. Alex!

A hand reached down for him and Java raised a meaty fist to swing.

"Hold on, kid, it's me!" a male voice said, and Java squinted upwards into the shadows at the figure looming over him. "Detective Cole," the man went on, his hands stopped in mid-air.

Java blinked a moment. Cole? Then he remembered. The cop who'd been following Alex around.

Java lowered his fist, but remained wary.

Cole looked at Java, and then at the body of the woman beside him. He knelt and checked for a pulse. "Dead." He noted the knife beside her and peered at Java through the gloom.

"What's going on here, kid? Where's Alex?"

Java wasn't sure he could trust this man, and said nothing.

"Look, kid, I'm on your side," the man said, his voice sounding almost angry.

Java debated a moment, and then nodded toward the dead woman.

"Chick tried to off me." He pulled his blood-soaked hand away from his wound so the detective could examine it.

Cole lifted the wet hem of the hoodie and scrutinized the wound. Slipping out a penlight, he shone the tiny beam onto Java's exposed flesh. The hole wasn't large, but it was ragged and bloody. Just the sight of it sent renewed spasms of pain arching through Java.

"This looks bad," Cole said. "You need a doctor."

Java shook his head. "I need Alex. He's trapped in the church. We be tryin' to find a way back in."

Cole looked upset at that news, and Java began to think the man told the truth about being on their side.

"Let me help you up, kid," the detective said, reaching for Java. "We'll find a way in."

Cole grabbed him under each armpit and began hefting him to his feet. Java grimaced as more slivers of pain ripped through him.

And then another gunshot rang out, shattering the silence.

Cole was flung backwards and stumbled over the body of the woman, toppling into a heap just beyond her.

Java's mouth fell open in shock as he dropped back to the hard floor amidst spasms of stabbing pain.

Heavy footsteps leaping over the broken desks and rubble forced Java to crane his neck and seek out the large figure running through the gloom toward him. Even in the dark he made out the weapon before the face. "Dane!"

Dane stopped and looked down at Java breathlessly, the Uzi up and pointed toward where Cole fell. "You okay, kid? Who was that?"

Java had to catch his breath. The pain was terrible, and he felt light-headed, like that time he'd gone helmet to helmet with a big kid on the line and been knocked out for a few seconds. "Shit, Dane, that was the cop!"

"Oh, hell!" Dane muttered, deflating before Java's eyes.

"Help me up," Java said, wheezing.

Dane reached down and grabbed Java by the right arm. Java gripped Dane's forearm and allowed himself to he pulled to his feet. Leaning on Dane for support, Java felt his head swim and stood a moment to let the little white dots stop dancing before his eyes. "Think he's dead?"

Dane grunted, but said nothing. Instead, he held Java's arm at the bicep and guided him around the dead woman, barely giving her a glance. They stopped and looked uncertainly at the police officer sprawled on his back.

Cole groaned, and Java nearly jumped back in terror. But Dane held him tight and watched as the man opened his eyes and looked around. Seeing Dane and Java standing above him, Cole groaned, "You really do hate cops, don't you, kid?"

Dane dropped his weapon and lowered himself to one knee. He still supported Java, but reached out for Cole too. "Oh, shit, man, I didn't know it was you. Thought you was hurtin' him!"

Java's eyes widened at Dane's sincerity, and even Cole looked surprised. "It's okay, kid," he grunted as Dane pulled him to a sitting position. "I'm vested, front and back." He used one closed fist to tap against his chest. "Just stunned, is all."

Dane whistled with relief. "What happened, Java?" he asked, and Java filled him in.

"Member how the preacher said they'd try to trick us?" Java asked. "Roy was right. They wanna keep us from Alex."

Suddenly, Dane remembered something, and turned to look behind him. "Oh, shit."

***

She stepped out of the darkness, and glided toward Roy like a ghost. She looked beautiful, with auburn hair and a photo-perfect smile, wearing a long, colorful dress.

Roy gaped, his mind flashing back to the sight of her in that coffin, wearing this very same dress, her eyes closed, her lips forced into a horrific imitation of her real smile.

"Mom?" His breath nearly ceased, and his heart pounded harder than it had all night. *This wasn't possible.* He *saw* her in that coffin. He *saw* her lowered into the ground. She was dead!

"Yes, beloved, it's me."

That voice! Exactly as he remembered it. He often dreamed he could hear her calling to him, using the pet name that had always made him feel so special: *Beloved.*

She stopped in front of him, close enough for them to hug, and he stared in wide-eyed astonishment. He was taller than her now, even though, until she took sick and shriveled up like a grape in the sun, she'd been five feet ten, tall for a woman, she'd always told him.

She smiled, her light brown eyes alive with joy, the same joy she'd always shown. He couldn't remember a time she ever looked crossly at him, or with disappointment. She opened her arms, and Roy found himself within them, his own wrapped around her. Memories of her hugs when he'd fallen off his skateboard or had bad dreams filled his heart and soul with tenderness and safety.

Tears sprang to his eyes. "Mom, how can you…? You died… didn't you? I was… there, in the room, when you…."

She pulled away and gazed into his teary eyes. "Yes, beloved. But they're giving me a second chance, Roy, a chance to make up the years we haven't been together."

Roy's head spun with confusion. "Who's giving you a chance?"

His mother's lovely face clouded over with uncertainty. "I don't know. I was… somewhere. Heaven, maybe? It was peaceful, I know that much. But I missed you, Roy, oh, how I missed you. Someone, an angel, maybe – I can't even tell you what it looked like – told me I could come back. That I could have you back."

Roy's eyes widened with surprise, but a tingle of fear raced up his spine. "Mom, I missed you so much. There been so many things I wanted to tell you, about me, about, well, everything."

"I know, beloved. And now you can. Come with me, we haven't much time."

She took his hand and tried to lead him down the corridor. He hesitated, Father Pat's words ringing in his head like the fire alarm at school: *They'll try to trick you.* He stopped and her hand left his abruptly. "Where we going, Mom?"

She turned to him, glancing around and above them as though they might be attacked any moment. "We have to leave this place. We have to leave right now or they'll send me back!"

She reached for his hand again, but he pulled it away. It was trembling. His whole body trembled, not from the cold air, but from the cold realization of what was going on here.

He released a tense breath, and looked deep into her eyes. She sure looked like his mom, and felt like her. Could this be real? "Mom, we gotta get Alex, first. He's my best friend, he's–"

"I know what he is to you, Roy!" she snapped, more sharply than he ever remembered her talking to him before.

He recoiled, and her look softened. But her nervousness didn't, and her gaze kept flitting about with fear. "Roy, I've always known about you and boys, honey. I saw it when you were little. But Alex can't be what you want him to be."

She reached out her hand a third time, and again he stepped back. His eyes filled with tears, and he could barely breathe. "I know that, Mom, but he's still the best friend I'll ever have. We have to go back for him. Dad's gonna adopt him. Mom, we gotta go back!"

He was crying, because he was now sure just what cruel trick was being played on him.

"Roy, it *is* me, truly. But…." She trailed off, and Roy saw the pain in her eyes. "You can't have Alex. You can have me back, but you can't have him, too. You must choose, beloved."

Roy felt his insides collapse as tears worked their way down his cheeks. His chest tightened like he was having a heart attack, and he nearly crumpled with grief.

"No, Mom, no! Don't make me pick. It's not fair. *Please….*"

He cried as she stepped closer and once more engulfed him in a warm embrace. "Roy, I want so much to be with you, and this is the only way. You have to choose. I'm sorry. I know you love Alex. But I love you, too."

Roy continued crying as he pulled away from her. "I can't, Mom, I can't leave him. If you're really her you know that, 'cause you're the one who taught me."

Through blurred vision that doubled the image of his mother before him, Roy saw a tear force its way from her eye and roll down her cheek.

"Loyalty is everything. But if you don't leave with me now, Roy, they'll kill you. Your influence over Alex is too great. Please, Roy. I don't want you to die!"

Her imploring look and fear-filled eyes touched Roy's heart, and set off more tears of his own. He shook his head and backed away from the woman who gave him life, the woman he loved more than he would ever love any woman again.

"I can't leave him, Mom. I just can't. Not even for you. I'm sorry. I'm *so* sorry."

She offered a smile. It was sad, but her face displayed a look of pride, as though she'd hoped he would choose Alex over her. "Alex is lucky to have you, Roy."

His mother faded into the darkness, becoming ethereal and gossamer. Her final words were faintly audible. "You make me proud, beloved...."

She vanished.

"Mom! I love you!" Roy cried out in despair, but she was already gone. He dropped to his knees and wept.

He didn't know how much time passed before he felt a hand on his shoulder. Whirling, he lifted a balled fist to fight. But it was only Dane, and he wore a look of relief, mixed with compassion, on his face. Behind him was that cop, which surprised Roy for a second, and the cop was supporting a bleeding Java. But the loss of his mother – again – consumed him with grief. He jumped up and threw his arms around Dane, crying into his big brother's strong shoulder. Dane wrapped his arms around Roy, and just held him.

***

Alex's heart lurched with empathy for Tami. He wished she could talk so he could spin the fear and pain from her. But she couldn't. He had to focus on Ms. G.

"What do you want from me?"

That question amused her. "We want *you*, Alex, not something *from* you."

"Why? I help people. I don't think you wanna help anyone."

She laughed – a hollow laugh that cut through the silence like a sickness. "You don't know half of what you can do, Alex. But you will. When you join us."

That scared Alex.

You don't know half of what you can do.

He thought of Saul, who he'd spun into almost killing himself.

He thought of the murders. But he fought down those fears. "I won't join you."

She laughed again. "You already have, Alex." As though reading his mind, she added, "Or have you forgotten the boy you almost killed?"

He flinched, but said nothing.

"We're your friends, Alex, not those dummies you hang around with," Ms. G. went on, giving Tami's leash a little tug and eliciting a whimper from her. The teacher smiled again. "You haven't even thanked me for killing Jane."

Alex gasped.

Phil stepped out of the shadows and approached Ms. G.

Alex's mouth dropped open. "The hell?"

Phil smiled.

***

Israel held his gun steady, his brain taking in all of his surroundings at once. So much information might overwhelm him, especially since he hadn't taken his meds for two days, but without those meds he "saw" more of his surroundings than the other kids. This hallway ended at another that branched off in the direction of the church. Israel was positive he was at the rear of the main building by now.

He moved along the rubble-strewn hall, not even looking down as he stepped over a wooden beam, or chunks of masonry that had collapsed inward from above. His brain simply knew where these things were before his eyes did, and he skirted them with ease. His heart pounded, but he didn't feel the panic swelling in his heart like it had at the graveyard, or at Ms. G.'s apartment building. He felt in control, something so unusual it almost made him laugh.

He squinted in the dim light, noting speakers and cables lying on the floor as he passed. The walls appeared to have panels in them with lots of switches and places for plugging in equipment, reminding him of his guitar amp at home.

Must be where all the lights and mics used to run from, he thought.

He heard something from the dark shadows straight ahead.

"Wh-wh-who's th-th-there?"

Israel expelled a nervous breath. Just Cuong. Grinning with relief, he whispered, "Cuong, it's me, Izzy."

No answer. That was odd.

"Cuong? You okay?"

Still nothing.

Tendrils of fear crept around Israel's heart as he stepped forward. The air became colder, if such a thing was possible. It reminded him of reaching into the frozen section of the supermarket when he'd go shopping with his mom. With each step, the air grew icier. Israel shivered, his light hoodie barely providing the slightest protection.

Nothing was visible. Even the walls seemed to have vanished in the extreme blackness surrounding him. He stopped and listened. It was someone breathing, but sounding raspier than it should, like an old man who'd smoked too much and then passed out on a park bench.

"Cuong? Where are you?" His voice almost made no sound. It was weird, like he was in some kind of soundproof room. In fact, other than that breathing, he couldn't even hear the wind outside anymore. His mind kicked into defensive mode. He felt like he was going to be attacked, like he was in a video game and the zombies would leap out at any moment.

"Come closer, Izzy," came Cuong's voice from the blackness ahead.

Israel's heart pumped into overdrive. No stutter. Something was *very* wrong.

"Cuong?" he whispered, and waited for a reply. None came.

Gun raised and pointed straight ahead of him, his gaze darted everywhere at once. He inched forward, his sneakers crunching on bits of wood or stone, but making no sounds his ears could hear. *That's crazy!* He looked down and stepped on a piece of glass with his sneaker. He felt the crunch, but heard nothing. He should turn and bolt. Every fiber of his being screamed at him to run and not look back.

But what if Cuong's hurt? I can't just leave him.

He advanced until he heard movement ahead. Actually, he *sensed* it more than heard it.

Something split the darkness. A figure. Small. Thin. Familiar.

Israel broke into a grin of relief. "Cuong, man, you scared the shit outta me!" He laughed, but the blackness took the sound like it had never existed.

He lurched forward to meet his friend, and stopped up short as Cuong's thin face slid into a sliver of moonlight entering through the ceiling.

Israel screamed.

***

A human scream echoed through the cavernous church.

Alex glanced from side to side, trying to figure out what direction it came from. "That sounded like Izzy."

Ms. G. shrugged. "It doesn't have to be this way, Alex. They don't all have to die like your friend Juan." She turned to Phil with a smirk. "Nice shooting, by the way, his head exploding. Artistic."

Phil grinned, and Alex's blood boiled. She turned that smirk on him. "You could join us willingly, Alex. If you don't…."

She let the thought trail off. But the knife she produced from her pants pocket and pressed to Tami's throat left no doubt as to her meaning.

Alex's mind spun. Did this mean Shaw was in on it? That didn't make sense. Why would he put Allison's life in danger?

Besides, he already had me, so he could've just turned me over to Ms. G.

"Mr. Shaw doesn't know about this, does he?" That was a guess, but he was pretty sure he was right.

Phil chuckled. "No way. I'd be dead if he knew I double-crossed him."

Alex swung his gaze back to Ms. G.'s smug face. "You *really* killed Jane?"

"She was a murderer anyway. We knew that before I bought the music box from her. Once we found where you lived, she was just another means to our end."

All this information was almost too much for Alex to handle. Jane dead? Really dead?

Ms. G. seemed to read his mind. "Yes, *really* dead. But that's what *you* wanted to do, wasn't it, many times? Kill the bitch?"

Alex shivered. He had thought about it a few times, but he'd never have done it. "I wouldn't have hurt her."

"Because you suffer from the same terminal affliction plaguing mankind," she answered in a disgusted tone of voice, "the one we need your help to eliminate – conscience."

Despite his vow not to, Alex again felt the immense weight of his stupidity. "I don't understand what you just said."

Phil chuckled, and Ms. G. smiled with great superiority. Her smile pissed off Alex even more because she'd picked words he wouldn't understand to make him feel weak.

Well, it won't work this time, he thought, but didn't say that. Sure, he'd play the dummy for her, but he wasn't going to *feel* the part. Not anymore.

"God made a fatal error when he created humans, Alex," Ms. G. said, teacher mode in full force. "He gave us free will. When you give people a choice between what's good for others and what's good for themselves, almost all choose themselves. I'm sure even a dummy like you understands that."

Alex didn't rise to the bait. "Not everybody's like that."

She laughed. "Not yet. But they will be, once we sic you and your twin on them. Humans will lose all the so-called good qualities because *you'll* spin those out of them, and then *he'll* put in what we want. What's left will plunge the world into darkness, and that will be, as they say, that."

The word "twin" slammed through Alex's brain like a bullet. "You have my brother?" His voice was barely a whisper.

"Of course, we do," she answered casually, while Tami whimpered beneath the tight restraint. Then Ms. G. nodded for Phil to take the leash, and he snatched it from her, yanking Tami toward him and driving the girl to her knees with a strangled yelp.

"Leave her alone, you asshole!" Alex cried out in anger, gripping his wheel handles with white knuckled intensity.

Phil chuckled as he stood behind Tami with the leash in one hand and the knife Ms. G. offered him in the other. "That depends on you, kid."

Alex fought down his panic. He couldn't lose control. That's what they wanted him to do. "You killed my parents, didn't you? You took my brother when he's a baby."

Ms. G. nodded. "We thought he was you, and we did everything we could to bring his powers to light."

She reached out and plucked the music box off the altar. The cat ignored her, and sat licking its paws.

"Since your mother took such pains to send this to you, we thought it might awaken his dormant power, but it only seemed to affect you." When she moved to lift the lid and activate the music, Alex pressed his hands against his ears to keep from hearing it. The tinkling sounds still penetrated his brain, only this time he didn't zone out. There was no darkness. Nothing changed.

She laughed again, and Alex decided he hated that laugh. Too much like all the kids who'd made fun of him over the years. "Don't worry, Alex, I just removed the post-hypnotic suggestion that would make you black out. You can lower your hands."

Alex did, though he had no idea what she had just said to him. And he wasn't going to ask. The important thing was the music didn't affect him like it did before.

Then it occurred to him. "You mean I didn't really kill them people?"

Phil laughed and shook his head with disgust. Again, the mocking tone pissed off Alex.

"Of course not, Alex," Ms. G. said with a nod at the music box as she replaced it on the altar. "We had enough trouble clouding your mind so you'd think you had."

His mouth hung open in shock. He hadn't killed anyone after all!

"We wanted you to think you killed Roy in the park, but somehow you broke through my control. That's the only reason he's still alive."

Alex's head swirled with confusion, and a certain amount of understanding.

I stopped them from killing Roy. That means they really are afraid of me.

Her words in the classroom flashed through his memory: "We may not be able to kill him, but you can."

If that's true, I must be able to stop them. But how?

Her next words hit him like truck, and caused all these thoughts to vanish. "Alex, would you like to walk?"

Alex blinked. "Huh?"

"We can use your brother's power to make that happen," she said as though announcing a quiz for tomorrow's class. "But he needs you to complete him, Alex. You're the key to everything."

"I could… walk…?" He barely spoke those words, allowing what she'd said to consume his brain with hopes and fears and a thousand questions all at once. "Where's my brother? How do I even know you have him?"

Ms. G. slipped her phone from one jeans pocket. "The miracle of modern technology, Alex. I can show him to you, but you'll never meet him if you don't surrender to me."

Alex locked eyes with a terrified Tami while Ms. G. pushed virtual buttons on her phone. He tried to offer Tami a reassuring look, but couldn't muster one. There were too many emotions churning through him just then. He felt like what he imagined the inside of a tornado must be like – everything was spinning round and round and he wasn't sure he could hold it all together.

"Oh, shit!"

He pulled his gaze from Tami to look at Ms. G., who had gone very pale. The dim light only made her sudden whiteness more apparent. Phil rushed over, playing out the leash and giving Tami some space between them.

"What?"

He leaned in to the phone and gasped loud enough for Alex to hear clearly. "You think they got him?"

Ms. G. glared at him with fury. "Who else would blow up the place?"

Phil stepped back.

"You gonna show me my brother or what?"

She looked at Alex from the altar, her eyes blazing with fury. "It would seem our enemies have taken him. That won't be good for you, Alex, I promise you that."

"If they're your enemies, they must be my friends," he retorted, trying to get under her skin.

She looked shaken by whatever she'd seen on the phone screen. "No, they're not."

Alex snorted. "Least they don't want me to ruin the whole world like you do. Like I could do that anyway, even *with* my brother. We're only two kids and there's millions of people out there."

Phil sniggered, but Ms. G. silenced him with a piercing look. "Alex, the Internet can connect you to the whole world, literally. You can spin billions at a time, and the ones you missed would be killed by the others anyway. Like I said, technology is a wonderful thing."

Alex had decided he wasn't going to let her scare him anymore. Spin the whole world over the Internet? He didn't think he could do it because everyone would have to be talking at once, but maybe Andy could? Or the two of them together? Since he didn't know Andy, he couldn't be sure. But *she* seemed sure, and that worried him.

"Let me see the phone," he said in a challenging tone. "You said I could see him."

With a nasty smile, she stepped down the four small stairs to stand before his chair, and held out the phone. He squinted in the dark at the screen. It looked like a big room surrounded by glass, or what used to be a room, because a bomb or something had gone off there. Smoke filled the screen and hid most of the busted-up furniture and broken glass.

"What is this place?"

"That, dear Alex, is where your mirror image spent his entire life," Ms. G. announced like she was laying out a new lesson plan in class. "It was a controlled environment, and completely soundproof to prevent him from doing his own unique spin on us."

That surprised Alex. "He can spin people like I can?"

"Oh, yes, but he can do more than that. Unfortunately, he's weak without you. He needs big brother to make him complete."

This was becoming too much for him to process. "How can I be his big brother? We're twins."

She shook her head. "Dummy, *one* of you has to come out first."

Alex's cheeks burned, despite his resolve not to be the dummy anymore.

"What're we gonna do, Ms. Garrett?" Phil asked from behind her.

Alex noted as she turned to face him that Phil was several feet from Tami.

"They won't kill the twin, just as they know *we* won't kill Alex," she answered, her voice thoughtful as she considered her options. "But we *will* kill Alex's friends one by one until he agrees to come with us. Then we'll take back what is rightfully ours. It *did* take them thirteen years to find him." She chuckled, and swung around to face Alex. "Well, Alex, will you join us? Or do we kill your friends? Starting with the wanna-be girlfriend here?"

Alex didn't answer as Phil raised the knife in his hand and started toward Tami.

***

Just when Roy finished explaining to the others about his mother, Israel's shriek of terror echoed throughout the building. Dane and Cole turned to sprint off in the direction of the fading scream, while Roy draped Java's arm around his shoulders and hurried after as fast as Java could stumble.

By the time he got to a hallway that was filled with pieces of audio and video equipment, Dane and Cole already stood looking around in the darkness, guns raised and ready. Cole waved his penlight here and there, illuminating nooks and crannies. Every cable looked like a snake, and every burnt speaker a severed head. Roy's imagination worked overtime. But there was no sign of Izzy anywhere.

"Here." That was Dane as he stepped forward and squatted down.

Roy eased Java to a sitting position on a fallen beam. Java's caramel-colored face looked pale, even in the dark, and he groaned with pain as he sat.

"Thanks, Roy."

"Hang on, Muscle Man. Alex'll fix you."

Java tossed off that super confident grin. "Course he will, fool." But his voice sounded weak.

Roy looked up as Dane and Cole approached, Dane holding something in his hand. Roy squinted. It was an iPhone.

"That's Izzy's phone," Roy said in a whisper, looking fearfully at the two men. "No sign of him?"

Cole looked at Dane, and Dane at Cole. Suddenly, in that moment, those two were on the same side. Dane turned to Roy. "Just blood on the floor."

"Oh, shit…," Java muttered, deflating even more.

Roy's mind reeled. Could Izzy be dead? But his insides were tingling in an odd way, and it distracted him. "Alex is close." He didn't know how he knew, but he did.

He squatted beside Java, and the bigger boy threw one beefy arm around his neck, allowing Roy to rise to his full height and pull him along like a dance partner.

"How do you know, kid?" Cole asked.

"I just do. This way."

Without waiting for an answer, Roy started down the cluttered corridor, easing the heavier Java along as though *he* were the power lifter.

Roy heard the others following, and averted his eyes from the splashes of fresh, shiny blood splattered across several beams, with the biggest blot creating an obscene-looking face on a ruined speaker cover.

***

Carlos and Nathan both reacted to Israel's scream of horror, and the even more unearthly silence that followed. Carlos cocked his head, and then fixed his gaze at a narrow door across the chapel.

"Came from in there. Let's go."

Without waiting for the others, he jumped over fallen light fixtures and skirted debris, nimbly weaving his way through the charred, broken pews. Jorge followed at once, his spray can out and ready, leaving the two adults to play catch up.

Father Pat noted a half-burned painting of the Virgin Mary crumpled on the floor by his feet as he followed Nathan through the rubble. Saying a silent "Our Father," he quickened his pace.

***

Roy spotted the burnt, blackened door before Dane or Cole, and waved them forward. He continued to support the muscular Java, the back of his mind tingling with the realization that he wasn't the least bit tired from the exertion. He vaguely recalled something in the body that began with an "a" that Ms. Ashley had said came out in times of panic, and made people stronger. He stopped and pointed at the door. Alex was on the other side. He was sure of that.

Just as Dane and Cole approached, pounding footfalls filled the corridor, and both men raised their weapons toward the darkness beyond.

Carlos appeared, seeming to pop out of the gloom, and skidded to a stop at the guns pointed his way.

"Yo, guys, it's me!"

Dane cursed, and lowered his weapon.

"Shit, kid, almost got your head blown off," Cole said, lowering his gun. "One of yours?"

Dane nodded as Jorge, Nathan, and Father Pat all appeared from the blackness like ghosts.

"Who's this?" Carlos asked suspiciously, his own gun up and ready.

"Detective Cole of the Hawthorne PD, kid," Cole responded with irritation, his weapon still raised. "So, unless you want your ass in jail, I suggest you lower the gun."

Carlos bristled with anger, the way a cat's fur stands on end when confronted by an enemy, but he lowered the gun.

"We heard Izzy scream," Nathan said.

"Us, too," Dane answered.

Roy had barely watched the confrontation unfold. His concentration remained on the door, and the presence of Alex on the other side.

"You sure Alex is in there?" Java whispered.

Roy nodded. "I'm sure."

Cole stepped forward, his handgun poised for action. "Okay, I'll lead. The rest of you fall in behind me and keep quiet. We don't want to spook them."

Dane leaned in. "Who?"

"The ones who have Alex," Cole responded, without emotion. Then to Roy he added, "He's not alone in there, is he?"

Roy shook his head. Ms. G. was there. Like he'd expected.

Gun in his right hand, Cole reached out with his left for the blackened, soot-covered doorknob. Gripping it, he pulled. The rotting wood creaked and groaned, despite the officer's attempt to ease the door open. Voices wafted in on the cool breeze. That breeze smelled of burned wood and something else. Something vile. But Alex's voice was all Roy focused on.

Cole stepped through the gaping black maw, Roy pulled Java after, and the rest followed.

CHAPTER THIRTY

BRING OUT THE TWIN

PHIL SWITCHED THE LEASH TO his right hand and wrapped it around the knife hilt. He grabbed a clump of Tami's hair with his left and yanked her head back. She cried out in pain, but the gag muffled everything, making her sound like she was underneath a pile of pillows. The knife flew to her throat with expert precision, and Phil pressed it home, drawing drops of crimson blood that glistened in the pale moonlight.

Tami's eyes bulged with terror.

"Stop!" Alex shouted, not even conscious that he'd planned on speaking. He couldn't let her die for him. Too many were already dead.

"Well?" Ms. G. asked, grinning like she'd just won the freakin' lottery or something! He hated giving in to her, but what choice did he have?

"I–," he began.

A voice cut through the eerie quiet like a bullet. "Everybody freeze!"

Alex spun his chair to the left, shocked at the sight of Officer Cole pointing his gun at Ms. G. and Phil, just like cops did in the movies. But his heart thumped with joy at the sight of Roy unharmed. The others, too. His internal sensing of people's health status told him Java was hurt, and his squinting eyes made out no sign of Izzy or Cuong.

Oh, no....

Alex turned to see Phil frozen in place, the knife held firmly at Tami's quivering throat. Tears streaked her cheeks at the real possibility that she was about to die. Ms. G. didn't seem afraid, or even worried. She folded her arms across her chest like she owned the world.

"How did you find him?" she asked.

"One of yours finally squealed," Cole replied with a small chuckle.

Alex's mind reeled. *Huh?*

Dane said, "The hell?"

The others shifted with shock, as the truth dawned on them.

But Cole and Ms. G. seemed not to care. They continued their stare down, as though no one else was present.

"It won't matter," she said matter-of-factly, "because we have Alex, and you need them both."

Cole chuckled, but his gun never wavered.

Phil glanced from Cole to Ms. G. The knife, however, remained pressed to the soft flesh of Tami's throat.

"Correction, my dear Jeanette," Cole replied. "We have them both."

Rustling movements came from all around Alex. Men in military uniforms carrying large guns emerged from the shadows behind him and the others. Some pointed their weapons at Phil and Ms. G. But the others had the guns aimed at his friends and family, aimed right at the back of each one's head.

"Drop your weapons and don't move!" one of them snapped as Dane and Carlos started to turn. Both froze in mid-motion. Clattering sounds punctuated the gloom as they tossed their guns to the floor.

"What's going on, Detective?" Father Pat demanded, though Alex saw he made no sudden movements.

Dane looked at his father, and Nathan gave a slight shake of the head. It was obvious Dane knew what was going on – the cop had double-crossed them.

"Pig!" Dane spat in fury.

"Least I never gave you a ticket." Cole kept his weapon trained on Ms. G. as he eased his way to Alex, stopping near him, but not close enough for Alex to make a grab for the gun.

"I thought you were my friend," Alex said, hoping to distract him.

"I am your friend, Alex," Cole said, eyes still fixed on the unmoving Ms. G. "That's why I'm keeping you away from her."

Alex said nothing. He looked at Ms. G. The next move, it seemed, was hers. Unfolding her arms, she held them out toward the altar and made a clucking sound with her tongue. The cat stopped licking itself and jumped off the altar to land in her arms. As big as the animal was, Ms. G. didn't even flinch when the enormous cat plowed into her. She caught it as effortlessly as if it were a kitten. Stroking the purring animal, she clutched it to her bosom and smiled at Cole.

Cole kept his eyes on her and yelled, "Bring out the twin!"

Alex flinched.

The twin?

Movement from behind caught his attention, and he spun around to protect himself from attack. His breath stopped, and his heart seemed to freeze.

A boy stood before him. He wore gloves on his hands and something around his lower face that Alex had only seen on dogs to keep them from barking. A boy who looked exactly like him. White blond hair, longer than his, like in the Indian drawing he'd seen, streamed halfway down Andy's back. Piercing blue eyes were fixed on him with astonishment. And Andy was handsome. Really good-looking. Sudden realization hit Alex that he must be that good-looking, too. Tami hadn't just been saying it. Roy, either. But what rocked Alex to the core was seeing "himself" standing tall and straight on legs that looked strong and healthy.

Andy wore jeans and a plain gray t-shirt. His arms, Alex noted, weren't as muscular as his because he hadn't been pushing a wheelchair his whole life. What *had* he been doing? He looked thin and not very buff. Was he locked in that room all the time? Had he never even gone outside? The absolute whiteness of his exposed face and skin told Alex maybe he hadn't.

"Andy?"

The other boy nodded. He tried to step closer, but the soldier behind grabbed him by one bicep and held fast.

Alex's temper flared. "Why is that thing on his mouth?" he demanded, spinning his chair around to Cole.

The cop raised his eyebrows, surprised at Alex's tone. "His voice is dangerous, Alex, especially this close to you. That's why his hands are gloved. We don't know what might happen if you guys touch. But the Pentagon wants to find out. Together, you two could be the most powerful weapon on earth."

Ms. G. laughed. "You see, Alex? He's not your friend. At least you know what we want."

Alex glanced back at his brother. Andy's eyes were big and blue, but Alex sensed no fear in them. *I'm ready*, those eyes said. *Ready when you are.*

Now all I need is a plan, Alex realized.

"So, Jeanette," Cole said, "at the risk of being politically incorrect, we have a Mexican standoff here, don't we?"

"Do we?"

"Well, Alex does, anyway," Cole responded. "Who do you choose, Alex – your brother or your girlfriend?"

"She's not my–" Alex began, but bit the rest back.

"Don't listen to them, Alex," Father Pat said. "They're both liars. God gave you these powers and he won't abandon you!"

Alex looked across the church at his friends, and the priest who'd been so good to him. Father Pat had always told him God didn't let people down when they really needed help. But where had God been his whole life?

"You know the Creator doesn't get into details, priest," Ms. G. said in that know-it-all tone of voice Alex hated. "So, who do you choose, Alex? If you pick the girlfriend, trust me we *will* get your brother back. You can have your cake and eat it, too, as the saying goes."

Alex had heard that saying, but had no idea what it meant, so he didn't respond.

"Two can play that game, Jeannette." Cole said. "You want your girlfriend back, Alex, and your brother?"

Almost as a reflex, Alex said, "She's not my… yeah."

Cole nodded, but kept his eyes fixed on Phil. Tami whimpered, still on her knees, but didn't dare move with the blade grazing her skin each time she did.

"Let her go," Cole ordered.

Phil pressed in more tightly against Tami's back. "She'll be dead before I am."

Cole smiled. "Oh, I'm not gonna kill you." He swung the gun toward Ms. G. In that instant, Phil whipped his head around to face her. She opened her mouth to shout, but Cole's bullet tore through Phil's temple before her words came out, and he flew backward in a shower of blood and brain matter.

Tami lurched forward as the man's hands flew away. The blade nicked her throat before clattering to the wooden floor somewhere behind her. She scrabbled along the blackened floor, her hands slipping against the soot.

Alex watched Phil's head explode with momentary incomprehension at what he was seeing, but as Tami broke free and crawled desperately down the steps in his direction, he gripped his wheel handles and pushed himself forward to meet her. She collapsed at his feet, and he reached out to gently take her arm. Careful of her hands tied behind her, Alex pulled her close enough to untie to rope.

Ms. G. laughed. "Very clever, William, but it doesn't matter. In the end, we will win."

Hands free, Tami yanked off the gag and gripped Alex's hand like a vise.

"Is that your whole army, Jeanette?" Cole asked with disdain. "A cat? My men swept the grounds and found only you and your flunky over there. Oh, and the girl tied up in the rectory. Who's she, by the way?"

Alex flinched at the word "girl." What did that mean?

Roy sat Java down on what was left of a pew and crawled on hands and knees to Tami's side. Guns clicked, and Nathan hissed, "Roy!" But Roy paid no attention.

He crouched beside Alex and pulled Tami down beside him, cradling her protectively between him and the wheelchair. She cried and whimpered. Alex held one of her hands, and Roy wrapped his arm around her.

Cole noted the movement, but said nothing.

Ms. G. laughed again. "The girl in back is an insurance policy, dear William, against an unexpected complication. Don't trouble yourself over her. As for my army, well, I have power at my disposal you couldn't hope to control. I thought Davalos understood that."

"More demonic bullshit, Jeanette? You've been threatening us with that fairy tale for generations. So far, all talk, no creatures."

Jeanette smiled. "Alex knows they're real, don't you?" she said, turning her fierce look on him and making him squirm. "My little boy here–" She stroked the cat, "–spoke with him on several occasions, as did the doll we buried in place of the twin. Isn't that so, Alex?"

Alex froze. *That's* how the cat and the doll could talk? Demons took them over? He considered her words only a moment.

"It's true," he whispered. "We all heard it."

Suddenly, Cole didn't look so confident. His face had paled in the darkness, but the gun hand remained steady. "Even if all that shit your group's been pushing were true, there are gates holding them back, gates you could never open."

"*We* couldn't," she replied, like she hadn't a care in the world. "But the Healer could." Before anyone could comment, she said, "Priest." She didn't even look at Father Pat. Her eyes remained riveted to Alex. "Hold up the amulet for *Detective* Cole."

Alex watched as the confused and fearful Father Pat fumbled in his pocket and pulled out the necklace. He held it up, the weird web design glinting in the thin shafts of filtered moonlight.

Cole kept his eyes locked on Ms. G.

"Once Alex put on the amulet and locked the clasp," she went on gleefully, "well, that was that. Gate open."

"You're lying." Cole's voice sounded confident, but Alex felt the uncertain tremor beneath it.

As though that was the cue, an inhuman laughter echoed all around them. The hideous sound bounced off the rotting beams and filled the place like the roaring of a hurricane.

Alex managed to catch Roy's look of terror before something moving behind the altar drew his attention.

From out of the darkness stepped a figure, pushing a dazed Israel in front of it. The figure's face was hidden in shadow, but Israel looked terrified, and numb at the same time. His shirt hung in tatters around his shoulders – it had been ripped right down the front. Alex gasped as the figure pushed his friend further into a shaft of moonlight – that web-thing had been carved into Izzy's chest like a nasty-ass tattoo! The pattern oozed blood down his torso and into his pants. A lot of blood. Izzy looked dazed, like he was drugged.

Java blurted, "Izzy!" He struggled to his feet and started forward.

The soldiers ignored him completely, their weapons aimed at the figure holding Israel.

Nathan reached out a hand to steady Java. The angry boy flung away the man's hand, but Nathan said, "Hold on, Java. Izzy needs you alive."

Java tottered on the brink of collapse, hand to his head.

"Java, hang on, man!" Alex called out. "I'll spin you. Chill."

Roy met Alex's gaze, and Alex saw in those poignant eyes the same fear he felt, but didn't want to speak aloud – not all of them would get out of this place alive.

The small figure pushed Israel forward, one bony arm around the boy's neck, a stiletto poised at Israel's throat. Israel gripped the gun Dane had given him, only now it dangled by his side, oddly enough, Alex found himself noticing, aimed at his foot. The figure wore a hoodie - a familiar-looking hoodie.

"You have all resisted our temptations," the figure said in a guttural, raspy voice. An inhuman voice. "You surprise us."

Alex clung to Tami's hand. She moaned in fear. "Alex…"

Alex offered her the most reassuring look he had. "I won't let anything happen to you, Tami," he said, trying to sound brave and macho and all that stuff he'd seen in action movies. But he didn't feel brave and macho – he felt like a scared little kid who wanted more than anything to crawl under his bed and hide.

He faced the figure and squinted to see the face through the shadows, even though he didn't want to see it. Because he already knew the truth. He recognized that Pokémon hoodie.

"Who are you?" His voice sounded small and childlike in the vastness of this once-holy place.

The figure laughed again. "Do not be coy, Healer. You already know."

He raised his free hand and held out Cuong's Gameboy. There were gasps from across the room, but Alex's gaze remained fixed on the shadowed face as the figure stepped into a shaft of light and revealed itself.

"Holy shit!" Dane exclaimed.

"Mother of God," Father Pat murmured.

It was Cuong's face, and yet not his face. Cuong's soft features were present, but he looked like one of those phone apps that can change a picture into something ugly or fat. Only this must have been the "evil" app, Alex thought, because Cuong's gentle eyes were harsh and glaring and murderous. His skin looked torn and covered with scabs and dead skin, like he was a corpse arisen from the grave.

Alex's heart lurched. *Oh, Cuong…*

The figure spoke, only this time in Cuong's normal voice. "A-A-Alex… h-h-help m-m-me…"

Those words, in Cuong's so-gentle stutter, ripped through Alex worse than any bullet. "Oh, God!"

The possessed Cuong threw back his head to laugh at Alex's open-mouthed expression. He raised the Gameboy again, only this time the toy burst into flames. The creature hurled the flaming Gameboy like a major-league pitcher straight at Alex's head. Alex pushed Tami aside and tumbled from his chair, sprawling onto the burned-out floor as the Gameboy struck a pew behind him and exploded into a bright fireball. Chips of blackened wood flew into the air and poured down on Alex, Roy, and Tami like poisoned rain. They hid their faces, and Roy scrambled forward to help Alex.

The soldiers raised their guns, but Cole's voice shot out, "Hold your fire!" The men did, but stood tautly, weapons raised, awaiting orders.

The Cuong-thing laughed again as Roy pulled Alex into a seated position. Alex felt weak, like he always did without his chair. And sick to his stomach. Roy gripped his hand and squeezed as they stared at the evil creature that had once been a sweet, gentle boy who hated seeing bugs get squashed.

"You're so pathetic," the creature said, that harsh, inhuman voice ripping through the quiet, and freezing Alex's blood.

"Why?" Alex croaked, tears streaking his face. "Why'd it have to be Cuong?"

Ms. G. stood by the creature's side, gazing at Alex with superiority. "The weak-minded are so easy to control, useless as human beings, but perfect for us."

Alex had heard that kind of shit his whole life. Special Ed kids were useless, or should have been aborted, or shouldn't be in school because they were too stupid to ever amount to anything in life.

"Cuong's my friend, and that's more important than being smart."

The Cuong-thing smiled, stretching the boy's thin lips so wide rips appeared in the skin of his face.

"Your friend has been very helpful in committing those murders. Maribel, Mrs. Rhodes, poor Allison."

Alex flinched as though he'd been slapped.

Ms. G. chuckled. "His simple brain knew he was doing something bad, but he couldn't stop himself. So sad."

Alex felt queasiness well up within him, a heaviness that pulled him down and made him feel like he'd sink through the floor.

All my fault....

***

Ms. G. turned to Cole, who still had his gun raised. "Meet my army, William," she cooed like a dove. "An army you can't defeat."

"Alex can," Father Pat said, taking a bold step forward. "He is God's chosen one. He opened the gate, and he can close it."

Ms. G. studied the priest like he was a bug. "Why would Alex do that when we can give him everything he ever wanted? You can't. My old enemy William can't. Only we can. Isn't that right, Alex?"

She turned to face him, and Roy saw Alex flinch. He didn't know what she meant, but Alex did. And that scared him more than anything else. Alex looked tempted.

To distract Ms. G. and the "thing," Roy addressed the creature. "What are you, the Devil?"

The creature laughed, and Ms. G. grinned even more broadly. "The Devil is a man-made construct, Roy, created to explain the evil that comes straight from the souls of human beings."

Roy didn't understand anything she said, so he ignored her. "I asked *it*, not you."

The Cuong-thing chuckled, and Roy's breath froze. It was so unnatural a sound that his skin crawled. "This dummy has spunk. I like that. Of course, he loves the cripple."

Roy blushed, grateful for the darkness to cover it.

Java shouted, "We all love Alex, asshole, and I'll kick your ass if you hurt him. Now let Izzy go!"

The creature laughed. "You are all amusing. We shall enjoy killing you." He turned to Roy. "To answer your question, *dummy*, the human soul created us. There was so much evil in the world, all created and fostered by human beings, that eventually it came together and became sentient." It sniggered. "For you dummies out there, that means it became intelligent, a living being all its own. Later, you called us 'The Devil'. So, what are we really? We are you."

Roy looked at Tami. Her eyes were wide with terror, and

understanding. He hadn't understood, and looked at Alex to see if he had. But Alex didn't even seem to be paying attention. He had sunk into a dark place, despairing over Cuong and Java and Izzy and everything. Roy understood at once. Alex blamed himself, and that made him weak.

"Alex, this isn't your fault," he whispered into his friend's ear.

Alex lifted his head and Roy's heart pounded. Those blue eyes looked devoid of hope.

Dane scooped up his Uzi and took aim at Ms. G. "Back off, shitbag," he called out to the Cuong-thing. "Let the kid go, or I kill your bitch over there!" His finger caressed the trigger.

The possessed Cuong laughed again. "Feel free. She is of no further consequence."

Roy had no clue what that expression meant, but he did see Ms. G. flinch and drop the cat to the floor. The animal sniffed at Cuong's dirty, blood-soaked sneakers, hissed with fear, and bolted off into the darkness.

Father Pat stepped up beside Dane, affecting boldness, even though he visibly trembled. "If these kids are all a bunch of 'dummies,' why are you so afraid of them?"

The Cuong-thing gripped Israel harder, the arm around his neck pulling tighter, the stiletto drawing blood. Israel's eyes widened with fear.

"Afraid?" The thing affected a harsh, mocking tone. "Of a cripple? Of brainless losers?"

Father Pat laughed, trying to sound brave instead of scared. "These 'losers' have been touched by God. That frightens you, doesn't it? Because it doesn't matter where you came from. The power of God can destroy you."

"You speak of what you do not know, priest, as befits your ilk." But the voice had lost that smug harshness of before, something Roy picked up on.

Father Pat took a step closer to Cole. "Any ideas, Detective?" he whispered.

Cole looked shaken by what he'd seen. "This God stuff is your bag, Padre. I'm about to have my men blow them away."

Father Pat paled. "You'll kill Izzy and Cuong."

Cole shrugged, his gaze back on Ms. G. and the Cuong-thing. "All we want are Alex and Andy. The rest are expendable."

Ms. G. had recovered from her momentary lapse of composure and looked at the cowering Alex. "See, Alex? He's not your friend. We're offering you a choice. He'll just kill your friends and take you. We'll let your friends live if you and the twin come with us willingly."

***

Alex pulled himself out of his funk and looked at her, but kept his head angled at Cole, as well. "You both say you wanna use me to change the world. Ms. G. wants to end it and Mr. Cole wants to make me into a weapon. But I don't get no say, right? 'Cause I'm a dummy? Well, I might not read for shit, but I know shit when I see it. And you're both full of it. So, I say to both sides… screw you!"

Ms. G. frowned. "That's a fatal mistake, Alex. It doesn't have to end this way. We can even take Roy and the others with us."

"Their power must be destroyed," the Cuong-thing snapped. "They have too much influence over the Healer. You know this, woman!"

She kept her eyes on Alex.

"So, I *was* right," Father Pat said. "You aren't that strong yet. That's why you're afraid of Alex and these others. Their power comes from God, and that means you'll lose."

"Not if they're dead, priest!"

Israel's limp arm rose, the gun in his hand aiming at Java. Israel fought to stop it. Gritting his teeth, he forced his arm back down as the stiletto poked his throat. Trickling blood ran down his neck onto his shredded torso.

"No way, asshole!" he hissed, and stomped down with his foot, slamming it into Cuong's leg and pushing himself forward.

The Cuong-thing didn't react to the kick, but snaked one arm around and snatched the gun from Israel's hand before the boy stumbled clear. Israel threw himself to the floor and Dane shouted, "Down!" Israel began scrabbling from the altar toward the others.

The Cuong-thing raised the gun. Without the trigger being pulled, the gun fired, the bullet glowing like fire as it hit Cole in the chest and passed right through his vest, and his body. The exiting bullet struck Dane in the shoulder as he was shoving Java and Jorge down to the floor.

Dane spun backwards and crumpled into a heap, groaning and writhing with pain.

Cole had no chance to even look surprised before he dropped to his knees. Father Pat caught him, turning his back to the possessed Cuong. Another shot rang out, and the priest was struck in the lower back and flung to one side where he lay unmoving. The medallion flew from his hand to lie in the ashes a few feet away.

Cole called out in a hoarse voice, "Fire!"

"No!" Alex screamed.

The soldiers opened fire. The bullets struck Cuong and pierced his small body. Blood burst forth in little fountains everywhere up and down his frame, but the creatures possessing him were not the least bit fazed.

Ms. G. tried to dive under the altar, but bullets raked across her back and she collapsed into an unmoving heap.

The noise was deafening, and the already stuffy air filled up with smoke from the automatic weapons fire. Israel crawled to Java and grabbed his friend's outstretched hand.

"Welcome back, Crack Head," Java whispered, but Israel saw the blood-soaked shirt and gasped.

"Shit, Muscle Man, you're hurt!"

Java tried for a grin as Israel scooted closer. "Just a scratch, fool."

The things within Cuong made his hideous face smile with triumph and aim the gun at Roy. "Now for the most important one."

Alex screamed, "Roy!"

But Roy had nowhere to run. The gun fired. Tami tackled him and tried to push him aside. She cried out in pain as the flaming bullet struck her in the upper back and she went flying off him, rolling to a stop beside Alex's chair.

"Tami!" Alex cried out, his despair becoming overwhelming.

This is my fault!

Stunned, Roy scrabbled to Tami's unmoving form as Alex dragged himself to her side.

"Tami..." Alex whispered, tears streaming down his cheeks. "Don't die!"

The gunfire of the soldiers continued, and now the possessed Cuong targeted them.

The men scattered as the first flaming bullet passed through one of them, despite the body armor. They dived behind rotting pews or fallen beams for cover.

Alex rolled Tami onto her back. Her glassy eyes focused on both boys.

"You saved my life," Roy said in a breathless whisper.

"Protect… Alex," she mumbled as life bled from her body. "Sorry, Alex, for running away…."

Alex took Tami's hand, crying and shaking. "Please, Tami, tell me the pain. I can spin you."

Tami squeezed Alex's hand with her last bit of strength. "Stay special." That was all she could get out before her head lolled to one side.

Alex shook with anguish.

Roy put an arm around his shoulders and pulled him closer. "Alex," he said, "you can stop this. Don't let them emo you out, man. Use your power to kill those things!"

Alex pulled his head from Roy's shoulder and looked aghast at his friend. "But Cuong…."

"Cuong's already dead."

Alex's eyes went wide as he released Roy and turned to look at the grinning "thing." Alex saw the truth of Roy's words. Cuong was gone. It was just a dead body standing there now.

Alex released his hold on Roy and sat up, glaring with fury at the thing on the altar. "I told you when you was the cat I'd spin your ass till there was nothing left, and now I will!"

He focused every ounce of his power on the creature, pulling the venom and evil and hate and malice out of it. He felt sledgehammer blows in his head as waves and waves of blackness filled his being, but he was aware that Cuong's body sagged, and the hand gripping the gun lowered. He wasn't sure how he was doing this since the things inside Cuong weren't speaking. But then, they had no voice that one could hear. They'd been using Cuong's mouth to speak. As Alex plunged himself into their consciousness he could hear their thoughts like words. And he spun those thoughts with everything he had.

***

Andy crouched behind a large beam where the soldier had dragged him. The man gripped his arm, and Andy knew they could electrify his facemask if he tried to shift any of them. He'd listened carefully, and understood that Jeanette hadn't been lying about one thing. He *did* need Alex. And Alex needed him.

Despite being unable to use his voice, Andy focused on Alex, concentrated on the brother he'd thought about night and day from the moment he'd been told Alex existed. They were twins, and so much more. They were connected by a power no one else had. He focused and cleared his mind of everything but Alex. He felt his brother's mind, felt the "spin," as he'd heard Alex call it, and pushed his own spin into that of his twin, mouthing words beneath the mask.

***

Roy rose to his feet, looking from the possessed Cuong to Alex and back. Alex was winning. He felt it. He noted the beads of sweat on Alex's forehead and knew his friend was spinning like never before. It was a battle of wills between them, and Roy knew Alex would win it. Father Pat had been right about that. He felt, rather than saw, Andy's eyes fixed on Alex, and turned to look at the boy who was Alex's mirror image.

Andy possessed every bit of Alex's beauty, but there was something behind the eyes that struck Roy even as he watched one twin help the other against the darkness threatening them. Andy's eyes looked both wary and hard, as though even in his moment of concentration, he was fearful of being out in the open.

Roy looked across at the others. Nathan squatted beside Dane, supporting him, with Java, Izzy, and Jorge hunkered down beside them. Carlos crouched behind a pew with the soldiers, aiming his weapon at the figure on the altar. Father Pat lay unmoving, and Cole groaned weakly.

Roy felt Alex vibrating with energy. His face looked furious and hate-filled; completely unlike the gentle expression that had captivated Roy and made him forget that choirboy Patrick ever existed.

He looked at the "thing." It was on its knees now. On Cuong's knees.

Before Roy knew what was happening, the arm with the gun raised itself with great effort, and the weapon pointed straight at him. Roy had but a moment to think of Alex alone without him when the gun fired.

The flaming bullet flew out and struck him in the stomach, flinging him back in a spray of blood and waves of excruciating pain.

Roy barely heard his father's voice cry out, "Nooooo!" before he landed in a heap, rolled over twice, and ended up on his back. His vision blurred. He could just make out the charred rafters high above as darkness filled his mind, and he discerned only a bit of starlit sky beyond. He hoped he *would* see his mother when he got to heaven. And maybe even hear Patrick sing like an angel. That was his last conscious thought before everything went black.

CHAPTER THIRTY-ONE

AT LAST THE HEALER IS OURS!

THE SECOND ROY WAS STRUCK, Alex stopped spinning and turned in horror to see the best friend he ever had collapse to the ground and roll onto his back, where he lay unmoving.

"Roy!" he screamed. There was nothing in his heart or soul at that moment but the friend and brother who had gotten him through every single day since he'd moved in with Jane, the boy who loved him in ways Alex couldn't return, the boy who understood him better than anyone ever had, the boy who in so many ways completed him.

Roy didn't move. He lay there in the dirt and ash, darkness covering him like the grave. Alex wept, and raised his eyes toward the night sky high above. The moon wasn't visible through the burnt-out rafters, but the stars were. He could almost see God in those stars, the God who Father Pat said gave him his power, the God who was supposed to take care of him, the God who'd just let the best boy in the world be killed.

"I give up," he told the heavens above. "I don't care no more. You hear me, God? I… don't… care!" He bowed his head as if in prayer, his shoulders slumping, his body seeming to cave in on itself. "I give up."

"No, Alex!" Dane shouted. Despite his wound, he crawled to his brother's unmoving form. "Keep fighting!" He bent to examine Roy, and then looked up with excitement. "He's alive!"

Alex lifted his head, his eyes wide with hope.

But it was too late.

Like a translucent cloud of belching exhaust, the creatures within Cuong's body swarmed out, allowing the boy's lifeless form to crumple to the floor in a bloody heap. Dane gasped in horror as the formless, pulsing darkness descended like a missile straight into Alex.

Alex's head snapped back, and his entire body stiffened. His features began to distort, became twisted and harsh, the skin cracking and scabbing with decay. A snarling sound emanated from deep within his throat.

The soldiers rose to their feet and took aim.

"Hold… your… fire!" croaked Cole, who pushed himself to his knees. "Don't shoot Alex!" His men lowered their weapons as he struggled to his feet. "We need him alive."

Nathan helped Java, and Jorge assisted Israel as they followed Carlos on hands and knees to Dane's side, and then they all watched in open-mouthed horror as the possessed Alex pulled his legs under him, and rose to his feet as easily as if he'd been doing it his entire life.

Jorge gasped, and Israel muttered, "The hell…."

"Oh, Alex…," Nathan whispered, his voice filled with dread.

The Alex-thing pulsed with power. It raised Alex's arms high into the air and crowed in that guttural voice, "At last the Healer is ours!"

It turned to lock eyes with Andy. "Come to your brother," the thing rasped, and extended a hand toward Andy.

The soldier who held him in a vise-like grip flew backwards by some invisible force, and Andy was free to stand. So, he did. But he made no move to approach.

"We said come!"

Andy resisted. He unclasped the mask covering his mouth, tossing the dreaded thing aside. Now he could talk. Now he could shift. But how could he shift this thing without hurting Alex?

"Don't listen to it, Andy!" Cole called out from behind the Alex-thing.

That distracted the creatures for a moment, and they turned Alex's head to ogle the cop with contempt.

"You'll never get out of here," Cole said, trying to sound confident. "My men are everywhere. We'll kill them both if we have to."

Andy flinched, but said nothing. Now that the thing was facing away, he started inching forward.

"Not another move, brother," the thing hissed. "Wait until we call for you."

Andy froze, and looked at Alex's friends. The big guy, the one who'd taken a bullet to the shoulder, made eye contact and raised a hand of caution. So, Andy held back, and watched. He spotted the other kid, the one Alex thought had died, stirring, trying to force himself awake, so he concentrated on shifting some of that boy's weakness into the possessed Alex. His lips moved, and he whispered his commands.

"Your men are of no consequence," the Alex-thing said, its voice sandpapery and unnatural. "We will show you what the Healer can do."

Cole flinched.

Alex's twisted features glowed with a kind of black shimmer, and then, like someone flipped a light switch to "off," every soldier in the church dropped to the floor, their weapons clattering from their hands to land in the rubble.

Cole gasped. "My men…."

"Are all dead," the Alex-thing said with a raspy chuckle. "Outside, as well. We used but a fraction of the Healer's power to *spin* the life force from them all. How easy it was. And how much more we can do when we combine the Healer with his twin."

Father Pat groaned.

"He's alive!" Nathan blurted with excitement. He scrambled to the fallen priest and helped him to a sitting position. "Whadda we do, Father? How can we help him?"

"You can't," the Alex-thing said. "The priest was right. We were weak. But soon we will be unstoppable."

Father Pat grunted, "Guys, the circle, like… in the book!"

Despite his pain and loss of blood, Java powered himself to his feet. He staggered, but remained standing. "You heard him!"

He reached out for Israel and muscled his friend to a standing position.

"There were six," Dane muttered. "I remember."

Father Pat glanced at Roy's unmoving form with uncertainty. As though he'd heard Dane speak, Roy moaned and shifted, forcing his eyes open.

Dane cradled his head. "Roy!"

Intense pain filled his stomach area, and Roy felt the blood steaming out of him, taking his life with it. But his eyes took in the possessed Alex and understood at once what had happened. Alex needed him, and he would help if it killed him.

"Help me up," he groaned.

Nathan looked at Father Pat. "He's so weak. It might kill him."

"If he doesn't do this, we're all dead."

Nathan hurried to his sons. Between him and Dane, they hefted Roy to his feet.

Roy felt the blood drain from his face, and little white dots danced before his eyes. He was going to faint.

No!

He fought down the dizziness and reached out a hand to Java. Java took it without hesitation and thrust out his other hand at Israel. Israel grabbed it and started moving into a circle.

"Jorge, grab Izzy's hand," Java hissed, fighting his own lightheadedness.

Jorge didn't hesitate either. He dropped the paint can and reached for Israel.

The Alex-thing watched as the circle took shape, and Roy knew the creatures understood what they were doing. He spotted Andy in the background, his lips moving, staring at his possessed brother with an intensity he'd only seen in Alex, and knew why they hadn't been attacked yet.

To further distract the creatures, he said, "Alex, it's me, Roy. I'm alive. Fight!" His voice cracked at the end, and the intensity of speaking nearly sent him to the floor in a swoon.

The thing looked at him with a face that was at once Alex's and not Alex's, and Roy had to fight to maintain eye contact. Alex's normal blue had gone blood red, and the hate coming from those eyes was almost painful.

But then, for a split second, the eyes turned blue again, and Alex muttered, "Roy?"

Roy's heart pounded, and he almost couldn't answer. "Yeah, man, it's me. Hang on, Alex. We're gonna save you!" He paused, keenly aware that everyone was watching him, and decided Alex was more important than his shame. "I love you, Alex. Remember? I'll always love you."

Alex's face softened, and Roy saw a single glistening tear at the corner of one eye. The creatures possessing him had frozen for that brief second. But then Alex's eyes burned red again.

Father Pat nodded to Carlos. "Go, Carlos."

Carlos looked stunned. "Me? I treated Alex like shit."

"Now's your chance to make it right."

Dropping the gun, Carlos leapt forward and reached for Jorge's other hand. Again, Jorge didn't hesitate. He gripped it and said, "Now's your chance to make it right."

Carlos nodded and cast his nervous gaze at the possessed Alex, now almost surrounded. There was room for one more in the circle.

"You said six," Dane said to Father Pat over his shoulder as he continued propping up Roy. "We only got five."

Father Pat winced from the pain in his back. "It's you, Dane."

"Huh?"

"You complete the circle."

"That's bullshit, man," Dane said, but there was an edge to his voice that hadn't been evident before.

"God chooses who he chooses, Dane," the priest intoned like he was giving a sermon. "Alex needs you."

"I don't believe in God," Dane muttered, his gaze fixed on the wounded priest.

Father Pat met that gaze straight on. "I guess He believes in you."

"You're dummies," the possessed Alex spat like venom.

Roy looked past it at Andy. Alex's twin was on his knees, fighting to control the demons and losing ground.

"You'll always be dummies." The guttural voice reeked of mockery.

Roy's blood boiled at that hated word. He turned his head to Dane. "You believe that shit, Dane? I don't. I'm no dummy and I say we take down these assholes!"

Dane hesitated a moment longer, and then turned to his dad. "Hold him, Pop. Don't let him fall."

"I got him."

Nathan stepped behind Roy, gripped him around the chest, and held him up.

Dane moved to Roy's side and took his free hand. The brothers made eye contact for a split second – a look of understanding. Dane stepped sideways and closed the gap between himself and Carlos. He stretched out his hand, and Carlos took it.

The circle was complete.

The Alex-thing froze, like time itself had stopped, its body going rigid. Alex's twisted face contorted with rage, and his head snapped at them like a rabid dog, but his body was paralyzed, unable to move.

"I feel weird," Israel muttered.

"That's 'cause you *are* weird, fool," Java tossed off in his confident tone, his body looking strong and healthy.

"It's like electricity inside me," Roy added, feeling a surge of energy pour through him. His bullet wound, nearly fatal moments before, now faded into the back of his consciousness. He was still dying – that much he could feel. If they couldn't free Alex from these things, Roy knew he was a goner.

But we will free him. We will!

Every face glowed with strength and resolve. Looks of fear and uncertainty dissolved into expressions of determination. They stood upright, their postures fierce, like warriors prepared to launch themselves into battle. Locked in their unity and single-mindedness, the six focused their intense gazes on the invisible 'things' that controlled Alex, and willed those things to leave him.

As power coursed through the boys, Alex's normal face flashed in and out – the demonic visage would fade, replaced by Alex's gentle, strained features. Red eyes turned blue, and back again.

"Come on, Alex, fight," Roy said, feeling beads of sweat on his forehead. "Come back to me!"

Slowly, steadily, the creatures emerged from Alex, one at a time, to coalesce in a kind of luminescent cloud over his head.

"Oh, shit," Israel muttered, eyeing the floating mass nervously.

"Concentrate," Father Pat hissed. "You've almost got him!"

As more and more of Alex returned, Roy's heart soared. The face of his friend had almost returned to normal. Alex looked dazed, but kept his eyes on Roy, and Roy knew that he needed to maintain eye contact.

That's right, Alex. Almost there.

The mass of writhing, formless creatures swirled and spun and twisted above Alex's head, but could not flee the circle. The power of the six contained them. Finally, Alex's face became clear and free, and his mouth cracked a tiny smile.

"Roy," he muttered before collapsing in a heap onto the floor.

Roy started to release Dane's hand, but Father Pat's voice cracked like electricity, "Don't break the circle!"

Roy halted, gripping his brother's hand all the harder, and the circle remained unbroken. The creatures swam above the fallen Alex as one coalesced, pulsating energy force.

Alex stirred, and Roy's heart lurched. *Thank God!*

***

Alex opened his eyes, confused and disoriented. He put one hand to his head. Man, did he have a headache! What had happened? Then he suddenly remembered. Those things had invaded him.

Oh, no…

What did I do?

He looked up from his prone position. The anxious faces of his friends gazed down at him, and the huge, translucent mass of demons hovered just above him.

They want me back. Well, screw that!

Forcing himself to will down the weakness and lightheadedness, Alex pushed himself upright, pulled his legs under him, and looked with gratitude around the circle at his friends. "Thanks, guys."

Roy inclined his head toward the panting, kneeling Andy outside the circle. "He helped."

Alex turned to look between Carlos and Jorge at his twin. "Thanks, bro."

Andy nodded, but said nothing, fighting to regain his breath.

Alex looked again at the creatures swirling above him, their individual countenances snaking out of the whole, snapping at the boys with what seemed like loud, smacking, gaping jaws, trying to scare them into breaking the circle. The boys sweated from the exertion of holding them at bay.

"I'm… gettin'… tired," Israel croaked, the damage from his wounds, coupled with the energy he was expending, taking its toll.

Java's legs wobbled, and he looked ready to crumple. "Me, too. What now?"

Alex surveyed his friends in horror. He took in the blood, the wounds, and the exhaustion. And he didn't know the answer. But then, as though God himself put it into his mind, he *did* know. "The necklace. I need it."

Israel looked panic-stricken again. "I don't got it."

"Shit, who does?" Dane blurted, sagging, the bullet wound oozing a steady stream of blood down the front of his jacket.

"The preacher gots it!" Carlos shouted, his voice tight and strained.

***

Father Pat spun his head around, searching for the medallion. Carlos was right. He'd had it when the bullet struck him and vaguely recalled letting go of it as he fell. But where had it fallen?

There!

He spotted it a few feet away, lying among ashes and burned pieces of a crucifix. The pain in his lower back was excruciating, and he'd lost enough blood to make sudden movements dangerous. He remembered that from his college science class. Too sudden a move and he'd pass out, maybe never to awaken. He crawled on hands and knees, one hand and one knee at a time. Closer. Closer.

"Hurry, Father!" That was Alex's voice, though Father Pat didn't dare look over. His goal was almost within reach. His head swam and he paused.

No! Not now. Please, God, not now!

He lay on his stomach, his vision blurring, and fought to keep his head straight. He reached out his right arm. His fingers scrabbled in the ash and dirt. But his reach fell short by two inches.

He forced himself to stay calm. The pounding of his heart only pumped more blood out through the painful hole in his back. He slithered forward, feeling oddly like that snake in the Garden of Eden that had started all the trouble. Another myth, but a powerful image all the same. His fingers groped, and found the chain. *Yes!* He began sliding it toward him.

A black dress shoe planted itself on his hand, and he cried out in painful agony. Raising his eyes, he made out gray pants and craned his head upward with great difficulty. His back throbbed, and his hand went numb. A man towered over him pointing a handgun at his face. An austere man, the priest noted through his pain and weakness, an angry man wearing a suit, a man preventing him from saving humanity. All priestly poise vanished. "Get the hell off my hand!"

***

Crouched inside the circle, legs pulled under him, Alex watched Shaw turn his gaze from Father Pat and look at him.

"Alex."

Alex squirmed, but didn't break eye contact. Tears blurred his eyes, the image of Allison's bloody bed sweeping in like a hawk and threatening to pull him down into hopelessness. "I'm sorry." It sounded weak, and lame. But it was all he had. And he meant it.

Shaw continued staring, his hard eyes pouring more guilt into Alex, threatening to overpower him before he could finish what he needed to do.

"Allison's dead because of you."

Alex tried to swallow, but his throat was too dry and there was no spit left. "I know. If you wanna kill me, that's okay." Roy gasped, but Alex ignored him. "But please give me that necklace first so nobody else gotta die like she did."

Shaw's mouth dropped open in amazement. "Even now, when you know you're about to die, you put others first."

Alex almost shook with hopelessness. The creatures kept snaking little tendrils down into his hair, electrifying it, as they fought to overcome the power of his flagging friends. "I just don't want nobody else to die for me. Please let me have it, Mr. Shaw. *Please.*"

Shaw stared at him with an unreadable expression.

Father Pat said, "He's the world's only hope."

Shaw never even glanced down. "I don't believe in hope anymore."

Alex sagged, and saw Israel almost ready to drop. Only Java yanking his hand kept the flagging boy on his feet.

"*Please*, Mr. Shaw…."

Roy trembled with weakness. "Can't hold 'em much longer, Mr. Shaw!"

Shaw eyed the murky mist reaching down to grab at Alex. He lifted his foot, and Father Pat pulled his hand free.

Clearly fighting pain and dizziness, the priest pulled himself to his knees, medallion in hand. "Alex, catch!" He tossed it high into the air.

The medallion arced over the heads of the boys in the circle and

Alex plucked it from the air as it descended. It pulsed beneath his fingers. Ignoring the fleshy feel that sent shivers throughout his body, Alex held the medallion high above his head. It began to glow a blood-shade of red.

The misty mass of formless creatures began funneling downward. They passed through Alex and into the medallion. Like the strands of a spider's web, the spun metal trapped them.

Alex had to fight the urge to drop the medallion. Its touch felt like death, and those things passing through him felt like he was buried alive and couldn't breathe. The webbing pulsed with their presence, and the medallion grew heavier by the second.

Something wasn't right. Alex knew that at once. The creatures pushed against the webbing, fighting to get out. The gate wasn't closed yet.

"Something's wrong!" he shouted. "We ain't done everything yet!"

"Somethin' about the sun, right?" Roy blurted. "No, the moon. Hell, I can't remember!"

Suddenly, Jorge's soft voice intoned, "The metal amulet that I retrieved is a gateway into our world. Once pushed back through it, the creatures can only be contained if the amulet catches the light of the full moon upon its face, and the Healer and the six are joined as one."

Dane scanned the roof above. The boys shuddered with their encroaching weakness, and Alex knew they were ready to collapse. His grip on the medallion became shaky. It felt like he was holding up a thousand pounds, and his arms quivered with the exertion. The web pressed outward even further, like a nasty-ass blister ready to burst.

"Do something! They're getting out!"

Frustrated, Dane spat, "There's no holes up there!"

Shaw looked up at the rotting rafters and support beams, took aim at a selected spot, and began firing round after round.

The burned-out ceiling showered down bits of charred wood, and a hole emerged. A shaft of moonlight, almost like a spotlight at the MTV Awards, shot down through the hole and struck the medallion full on its face. The creatures emitted a blood-curdling shriek as the gate snapped shut and trapped them within.

The medallion stopped pulsing, but the glow remained. Alex knew the gate was still active. It could be reopened.

Like hell....

"Andy," he croaked. "I need you." He didn't know how he knew, but he did. Twisting his trunk around, he lowered his left arm to support himself as he turned. But the right hand remained aloft, holding the damnable necklace as far from him as he could. His twin crouched in the ash and debris, soot from the falling timbers raining down and darkening his long white hair. Andy looked back, but didn't move forward.

"Andy," Alex hissed again, his voice breathless and weak. "They said we're stronger together. I need you." Drained and almost ready to pass out from the exertion, Alex held the gate aloft, but his arm trembled. Now it felt like ten thousand pounds.

Andy didn't move. "You don't need me. You have them." He indicated the circle of sagging young people.

Alex understood what Andy meant. Before he found Roy, he'd felt alone, too. "I do need you, Andy," he said, groaning under the strain. "You most of all."

Andy's eyes widened, and Alex saw the deep blue of his own reflected back at him. His twin scrabbled forward on hands and knees, squeezing between Carlos and Jorge to Alex's side. "What do I do?"

Alex offered up his free hand. Andy hesitated, as though he'd never held anyone's hand before. He slipped off the gloves and tentatively took Alex's hand.

Alex felt power surge through him, like a fully charged battery. The medallion in his upraised hand no longer felt heavy. He felt so powerful he didn't think anything would be heavy ever again. "Reach up with your other hand and hold this thing with me."

Andy hesitated. "Any idea what might happen?"

"No clue."

Andy reached up and closed his fingers around the other half of the medallion.

A surge of energy poured through Alex like a raging river, and Andy's wide eyes told him his brother felt the same.

The medallion exploded in a blinding flash of light that made everyone duck for cover.

When Alex opened his eyes, there was nothing but his fingers entwined with those of his twin.

The necklace was gone.

The boys let go of their circle, and slumped to their knees, panting and heaving. Nathan held onto Roy and gently lowered him to his knees, keeping his arms wrapped around Roy's upper torso.

Java toppled onto his back and lay unmoving, and Israel scuttled to his side. "Hang on, Muscle Man!"

Java lifted his head. "Fool, you're gettin' your blood all over me!"

Israel jerked back, and Java chuckled.

"Asshole," Israel muttered, and grinned.

Alex exchanged a look with Andy as they lowered their upraised arms and let go of each other's hand. The strength and power retreated as quickly as it had arrived, and Alex felt a wave of tiredness wash over him, like he was about to fall asleep. He'd never used so much spin at one time, not even with Allison. Just the thought of her drew his attention to Shaw, standing outside the circle pointing his gun.

"Thank you," Alex said, his voice heavy with sadness.

Shaw kept the gun leveled on him.

Dane crouched, looking like he might rush the man.

"She was all I had," Shaw said in a hoarse whisper that suggested deep emotion being held in check.

"I know." Alex waited with breathless expectation.

Shaw lowered the handgun, and then offered his free hand to Father Pat. He assisted the priest to his feet and helped him sit on a burned-out pew. He slipped the gun out of sight beneath his jacket.

Alex looked around at his friends who'd risked everything for him. "Thanks, guys."

They nodded.

Roy grunted, his head bowed.

Alex turned to him. The best friend he'd ever have raised his head, and smiled. Beads of sweat covered his pale, pasty face.

"I love you… Alex." He swooned and slipped from Nathan's embrace, sprawling onto his back on the floor, where he lay unmoving.

Nathan dropped to his knees beside him. "Roy!"

Alex gasped, fear rippling through him. "No!" He pulled himself forward as a shell-shocked Nathan cradled Roy's head in his lap.

Dane scuttled over and pressed his ear to his brother's chest, listening for a heartbeat.

He looked up, and Alex's breath stopped. Tears glistened in Dane's steely eyes, and he shook his head in disbelief. Nathan made a kind of gagging sound, and Dane began to cry.

"Noooo!" Alex shouted. He grabbed for Roy's hand and pulled it to him. "Roy! You can't die, you can't!" He sobbed.

His whole body shook and his stomach clenched like a fist. His mind filled with every moment he'd ever spent with Roy, every smile, every gesture, every crazy emo moment since they'd met. Roy couldn't be dead. He couldn't! And yet Alex could feel his friend leaving, Roy's soul departing. It felt like his own was going with it.

A hand slipped into his, and the power surged through him again. He looked up to find Andy gazing at him in wonder.

"You love him, don't you?"

Alex nodded.

Andy looked amazed. "I never thought it was real."

Alex's chest heaved as his emotions churned through him. "What?"

Andy glanced down at the unmoving Roy. "Love."

Alex didn't have time to respond because Andy spoke in a voice filled with strength and power.

"Roy, you're not dead," he said in a calm, steady tone. "You don't have a bullet in you. You have not lost any blood. You are whole and healthy. You have given all of your hurt and weakness and pain and death to me." He paused, and Alex looked aghast at him. But nothing happened. "I know you can hear me, Roy," Andy went on in a voice deeper and more commanding than his normal one. "I won't let you die. My brother needs you."

Suddenly, Andy stiffened.

Alex lurched as he felt the searing pain of being shot, of having that flaming bullet rip through his gut, but it didn't feel the same as when he spun people by himself. This pain had come through Andy, somehow, all at once, and he had no control over it.

Blood seeped from the lower part of Andy's shirt.

And Roy stirred.

Alex looked at Andy in astonishment. "They have to talk 'fore *I* can spin 'em."

Andy offered a weak smile. But his face had gone a ghastly shade of gray, and he looked ready to pass out. "*I* can talk stuff out of people. One problem, though."

Alex raised his eyebrows.

"I can't get rid of it like they said you can," Andy went on, his voice now small and childlike, and growing weaker. "Unless I shift this into somebody else, I'll die."

Dane muttered, "The hell?"

"But," Alex began, spluttering with indecision. "That means we… hafta… kill somebody."

Andy nodded as more blood soaked his blue shirt, staining it with death. Sagging, he whispered, "Or I can just die." He shrugged. "Might be better that way."

Alex squeezed Andy's cold hand all the harder. "No, Andy, you can't die! I just found you!"

Cole's hoarse voice came across the room to them, "My people are… on their… way. Hers, too."

Alex looked up. Cole staggered toward them, one hand on the gaping hole through his upper chest.

"You need to… go now, or you'll never… be free again." Pale and weak, he stopped and looked down at Andy. "Use me, kid."

Alex felt Andy's life slipping away. "Why are you helping us?"

"I'm… dead… anyway." Cole fixed his gaze on Andy and rasped, "Do it."

Alex felt a rush of something pass through his body, almost like his soul leaving, and a burst of red blossomed on Cole's stomach, spilling through his shirt and dripping onto the ground. The man collapsed into a heap and lay unmoving.

Alex looked at Andy, and his brother offered a weak smile. But there was no more pain in either of them. They were healthy.

"Alex?"

Roy!

Grinning with joy, Alex watched as Nathan and Dane helped Roy to a sitting position. Nathan engulfed him in a tight hug.

"I thought I lost you," Alex said, his choked voice filled with elation.

Roy pulled away, looking confused and embarrassed with everyone staring at him. He glanced down at the front of his shirt. The fabric was sticky with blood, but when he pulled up his shirt there was no wound.

"Did I die?"

Nathan nodded, his cheeks damp with tears. "Looked like."

Wide-eyed, Roy regarded Nathan and Dane with confusion.

Dane broke into a huge grin. "Scared the shit outta me, Roy. Don't do that again, little brother."

Roy turned to Alex and offered a shy smile. "You saved me again, didn't you?"

Heart pounding with joy, Alex shook his head and pointed to Andy's blood-soaked shirt, using a hand motion to indicate that Andy should lift it. His brother did, and revealed soft white flesh beneath. But no wound. "It was Andy."

Roy's eyes widened in shock as he took in the situation, and understood what had happened. "Thanks, man," he said, flipping the hair away from his eyes so Andy could see them.

Roy gazed at Andy with wonder, and Alex understood why. It amazed him, too. He looked at his twin with the same color hair draping his shoulders and absolutely identical facial features and felt like a movie special effect had come to life.

Andy didn't respond to Roy's gratitude. He just stared, and those deep blue eyes caused Roy to squirm and look away.

Carlos and Jorge sat on the burned-out floor, catching their breath and observing the resurrected Roy with the same awe-struck expression.

Nathan helped Roy stand. Then he supported Dane with an arm around his waist, and Roy extended a hand to Andy. Andy ignored him and rose to his feet unaided. Roy frowned and pulled back his hand.

Alex glanced up to find Shaw standing beside him with the wheelchair. Andy bent to assist Alex, but Roy said, "Uh, he gets pissed if anyone helps him."

Andy tossed him an angry look that clearly confused Roy.

Alex noted the exchange with curiosity. He caught Roy's eye and shrugged. Andy stood aside as Alex hauled himself up and settled into the chair, pulling his feet onto the footrest. He felt Andy studying his every movement and it unnerved him. He offered his twin a smile. "See? No prob."

Andy nodded.

Alex studied each of his friends. Both Java and Izzy needed to be spun, and fast. And Father Pat. Dane was hurt, too, but not as badly. The others just looked tired.

"Java, Izzy, tell me, quick."

Israel said, "You can start with Muscle Man. I'm too hot to go first." He cackled.

Java tried for a grin, but a stab of pain turned it into a grimace.

Nathan, Dane, Father Pat and Shaw watched with awe as Alex spun the injuries from the boys, drawing those injuries into himself, and expelling them. Even Andy's stoic face displayed a trace of admiration.

After, Java pointed to Israel's now-unblemished chest and said, "That would've made a wicked-ass scar, Crack Head, like them emo boys say."

"Then we'd have to listen to that emo shit music? Hell, no!" Israel offered up the loopy grin and they bumped fists.

Father Pat kept feeling around his lower back for the hole after Alex spun him. He grinned like a little boy with a cool new toy.

After Alex finished with Father Pat, Andy said, "Wish I could do that, brother."

Alex glanced at Cole's lifeless body and shivered. "I think what you and me can do together is scary enough."

Andy shrugged.

Alex didn't like the coldness in his brother's eyes, the emptiness of the other boy's heart, suddenly realizing he didn't know this person at all, this person who looked exactly like him, who had a power more dangerous than his own.

Well, he thought, *I'll get to know him. But will I like what I see?*

He turned to Dane. "Your turn."

Shaw stepped forward. "You all have to leave now. Spin him in the car. You heard what he said." He pointed at Cole's lifeless body. "More are coming, from both sides. They'll probably be here within minutes. Use my limo. Martin will take you to a secluded place where no one can find you. The priest and I will handle things here. Then we'll join you."

"We can't go home?" Israel said, his loud voice suddenly quiet, like a church mouse.

Alex looked at him and saw a little boy, not the big, handsome teen who tried to impress every girl on campus, but whose ADHD always got in the way. Java put a hand on Israel's shoulder. "I wanna be goin' home, too, Izzy. But we can't right now."

Israel's eyes widened with fear, and the realization that his life had changed, and would never be the same again.

Java grinned. "I'm still gonna ADHD yer face if you be drivin' me crazy. Don't matter where we go."

That brought a sliver of a smile to Izzy's face, and Alex saw his friend as he never had before. Izzy really *was* good-looking, like he always kept saying. But the bragging about his looks was just to cover up his fear that everyone only saw his ADHD. They never *tried* to see more. Alex knew that was true because all people ever saw about *him* was the wheelchair. If girls could see Izzy's loyalty, they'd go for him in a second. Same for Java, and all of his friends. Like Roy's mom told Roy when he was little, loyalty was everything.

"Dad?"

Alex recognized that voice! Whirling his chair around, he observed Shaw go pale and turn to look behind him. Allison stood amidst the rubble, her bald head covered in soot, her wrists red and blotchy, blood splattered on her nightgown. Her tearful eyes took in the sight of her father, and she smiled with pure joy.

Alex couldn't see Shaw's face, but a gurgling sound came from the man's throat as Allison sprinted forward, leaping over the crumbled remains of a pew to throw herself into her father's arms.

Alex felt his chest tighten, and his breath hitched. He recalled Cole asking about the girl in back, and found himself grinning. He turned to Roy, and saw his best friend grinning along with him.

When father and daughter released each other, Allison said breathlessly, "They had me tied up in back, Dad. But I got away, like you always taught me if I ever got kidnapped."

That surprised Alex, but given what Shaw had told him about his business, it made sense. The man must have enemies.

Shaw wrapped one arm around Allison's shoulders and pulled her in. "I thought I'd lost you."

She hugged him even tighter. "Never." Then she spotted Andy and her eyes widened with surprise. "Wow, there's two of you!"

Alex nodded. "My brother, Andy."

Despite her ordeal, she offered the chin raise. "Wicked cool."

Alex allowed a slight smile to grace his lips as they locked eyes a moment before Allison turned to her dad and gripped his hand like she never wanted to let it go.

Shaw reached into a jacket pocket and pulled out his phone. He pressed a button, and placed the phone to his ear. "Martin, you're going to have a carload of passengers. Take them to the safe house. I'll be in touch." He ended the call and stood staring at them. "Well?"

Alex looked around the remains of the burned-out church, and the reality of everything that happened these past six days, the sheer weight of it all, flooded in on him and almost choked him with guilt. Tami's lifeless body lay in the soot a few feet away. She'd died to save him. He thought of little Juan, who'd tried so hard to be good, and gentle Cuong, who wanted so badly to be understood when he spoke. He thought of everyone who'd fallen, and sadness filled him like lead. He'd live with this guilt for the rest of his life.

He turned to Father Pat, the man who always told him God had a plan for everyone. "Is it right so many people had to die, Father? So many got to give up so much for me? That how God works?"

"Yeah, sometimes."

Alex paused. He hadn't expected that answer. But somehow, it seemed a more real answer than pretending that just because there *was* a God, that meant everything had to be perfect.

"Will I see you again?"

"You bet," Father Pat replied with confidence.

Alex rolled himself over and hugged the priest. Father Pat returned the hug with genuine affection. As Alex pulled away, his eyes settled on Shaw, arm wrapped tightly around the wide-eyed Allison like he was afraid she would vanish if he let go.

"Why are you doing all this?"

A look of revelation crossed Shaw's stoic features. "Because *I'm* not God after all."

Alex nodded, and they broke eye contact.

"C'mon, guys," Dane said, one hand pressed against the wound in his shoulder. "The suit's right, we gotta jam before they get here. You coming, Pop?"

"Never leaving my family again." Nathan looked around at Roy, Alex, Andy, and all the kids. "My whole family." He turned to Dane. "That work for you, son?" He held up a closed fist.

Dane bumped it with his own. "Yeah, Pop, that'll work."

He winked at Roy, and Roy grinned.

They all started walking toward the audio-video hallway when Java stopped and looked around. "Where's Jorge?"

Alex turned to scan the cavernous church, and his eyes fell on the altar. Ms. G's unmoving form lay slumped beside it, and Jorge stood in front holding the big cat in his arms. His right hand gripped the spray paint can, and his left stroked the thick, furry neck of the feline.

Jorge smiled at them and stepped away from the altar. Right behind where he'd been standing was a large, freshly painted red "V."

"For victory," Jorge said, his grin pure and innocent, the cat purring in his arms.

Everyone stared a moment in silence. A shaft of early morning light illuminated Jorge's face, and his peaceful expression filled Alex with hope.

Java held out his fist flatways toward his friends. "For victory."

Roy placed his fist atop Java's. Israel followed suit, and gave Carlos the chin raise. Carlos understood, and added his fist to the tower. Dane eyed the pile of fists a moment and then placed his own atop Carlos's. Jorge let the cat drop to the floor and hurried forward to join them, adding his fist to the top. Alex turned to Andy, who watched them without expression. Alex raised his eyebrows, and Andy stepped forward to add his fist to the tower.

Alex reached up and placed his open palm on top to complete their ritual. "For victory."

***

Dawn had arrived. The clouds were gone. The sun rose orange in the east and the air felt crisp and cool. Shaw, Allison, and Father Pat stood in the parking lot and watched as a man in a chauffeur uniform opened the doors to a black Hummer limo and ushered in the ragtag group of exhausted survivors.

Father Pat felt wistful, knowing that these were children, kids who should be worrying about prom dates, not sinister cabals that wanted to take them by force and use them against their will. This world was diseased, and would become more so before it got better.

But Alex gave him hope. No, Alex *was* hope.

***

Inside the car, Alex sat in his chair in the middle of the bench seats surrounding him. It was the biggest, fanciest car he'd ever been in. There was even a television. However, as the engine roared to life and the massive vehicle pulled away from the church, all he saw were the people around him. The danger wasn't over. He and Andy would always be hunted. But as long as he had these people by his side, he'd be all right.

"We make a kickass team," Java said, looking tired, but satisfied.

"Got that right," Carlos echoed, his chest puffed out with pride, and they bumped fists.

Alex glanced at them, and then turned to meet Roy's eyes. He smiled. His best friend returned it.

"Not a team," Alex said with a contented sigh. "A family."

He extended a hand. Roy took it and turned to Dane beside him, offering his other hand. His big brother gripped it hard. Grinning, Dane turned to Nathan on his other side, and extended his free hand. Nathan took it with love. Carlos didn't hesitate either – he took Nathan's free hand and reached for Java. Java reached for Israel, and then Israel put out a hand to Jorge, who grabbed it. With a soft, gentle smile, Jorge turned to Andy and stretched out his hand. Andy just stared at it. Alex extended his own hand, and Andy turned to face him. The twins locked blue eyes on each other's, a deep moment of connection passing between them.

"Family," Andy whispered, reaching for both Jorge and Alex at the same time. The hands linked, and the circle was complete, a circle of love and solidarity.

Alex smiled, feeling something he never had before - safe.

They were a family.

And they would prevail.

Here is a preview of Book 2 of The Healer Chronicles:

SHIFTER

AGE 12

He held Death in his hand. It was a small death, but it should work. They didn't know he had it. They didn't know the scope of his power. They kept his enclosure sealed so nothing could enter or leave, but that was because they worried about his voice getting out. They never thought about death getting in.

It had.

Now he just had to wait for Teacher.

AGE 7

His name was Andy. He knew that much, but he still didn't know any of *their* names, even after all the time he'd been there. They came and went. Some just stood and observed him. They took notes on clipboards and stared at him like he was an animal in a zoo. He'd learned about zoos from the books Teacher had given him.

Teacher had shorter hair than his and he always wondered how it got like that. It was a different color, too. Brown. His was dirty white. Teacher had brown eyes. His were blue and his hair trailed past his shoulders. It always got longer, not shorter. Since he hated Teacher, he didn't bother asking about the difference in their hair.

Teacher taught him words and gave him books with pictures. That's how he knew what a zoo looked like. Other books were all words. One was called a Dictionary. Many of the words were covered in black. Those were the ones he most wanted to learn, but he couldn't figure out how to see under the black.

Uncle taught him lessons in his dreams, though Andy didn't know if Uncle existed or was just a figment of his imagination. Uncle had long gray hair and his skin looked like wrinkled clothes. He said he was very old, but Andy had no concept of old. He knew what "age" meant, even though he didn't know his own. Teacher never told him.

Since Andy had no friends, he sometimes thought Uncle might be someone his lonely mind had conjured. Teacher taught him that there was no such thing as friendship or love. Andy wasn't so sure. Uncle made him believe Teacher was lying.

Then there was Doctor.

Doctor hurt him.

He despised Doctor.

Those were the only people he ever talked to.

AGE 12

He kept his fist closed. He felt it wriggling against his skin and sensed it didn't have much time left. How did he know that? He wasn't sure. He just knew. He also knew Teacher would arrive in time. They tried to confuse him by not letting him see or hear anything except what they wanted him to know. He had been taught the concept of time but did not know how it worked. He'd seen Teacher wearing something around one wrist that indicated the time, but Teacher never explained the device.

It didn't matter. Andy sensed time anyway and always knew when Teacher or Doctor would come for him.

As though his thoughts were answered, the door to the chamber surrounding his glass cage opened and Teacher stepped inside.

AGE 7

He'd tried breaking the clear walls of his cage many times. Teacher always laughed and said the glass was bulletproof. Andy didn't know what that meant, but he did know hitting the walls with the furniture they'd given him didn't work. At first, the walls weren't soundproof because they didn't know what he could do. He didn't, either, not until he'd begun talking more. He'd only known a few words when he arrived there, like "mama" and "dada," but Teacher insisted those words were no longer of value. Teacher taught him many words and phrases, and he learned rapidly.

Teacher said, "You have a quick mind," which sounded like it was a good thing, though Teacher never said so.

He knew the word "people" because Teacher said that's what they were called. "Human" was another word for people. He'd only ever talked with Teacher until Doctor came for him that first time. He didn't know how old he was then, but he knew how to say many things and his white hair was longer than Doctor's short black hair.

Andy was taken to a place called "Lab." He saw many things he didn't recognize. Doctor only told him that the "equipment" was for tests, to learn what he could do.

"What do you think I can do?" Andy asked, for he honestly didn't know.

Doctor studied him a long moment, as though wondering if he was hiding something. "Your birth has been anticipated for millennia, Andy, but your power has still not materialized. We hope to speed up its arrival."

Andy was confused. He didn't know the word "millennia," but he did know what "power" meant. "What power?"

"That's what we need to discover. You're the key. Only through you can our plan come to fruition."

Andy knew about the "plan" from Teacher, though Teacher had never actually explained what it meant. He only knew it had something to do with destroying humans. Or was it humans destroying themselves? Teacher was always unclear on that point and refused to answer when Andy asked follow-up questions.

Doctor strapped him to a table so he couldn't move and then put little sticky pads on his head and his body. He wasn't even allowed to wear his clothes. He felt strange that first time, lying on that table with no clothes on, but, since his room was surrounded by glass and they watched him change his clothes all the time, he supposed it didn't matter much.

The equipment lit up and made sounds, and then terrible pain shot through his body. His skin felt like his tongue that time he'd tried gulping hot cocoa. He screamed again and again, begging Doctor to stop.

Doctor ignored him.

Andy had never experienced such agony. He wanted to tear off his skin it was so bad. He pleaded with Doctor to turn off the hurt as his body twisted and writhed against the restraints.

"Heal yourself, Andy!" That was all Doctor said.

Teacher stood nearby watching. Teacher kept coughing but tried hard not to. Andy had never been sick, but he understood what it meant. There was something inside of Teacher, a germ making Teacher's body weak, making Teacher cough. Even though Andy understood what "heal" meant, he didn't know how to heal his suffering or that of other people.

Finally, the agony became almost unbearable. Andy didn't know why he did this, but he looked at Teacher and muttered something.

Teacher stopped coughing and stared at him with wide eyes.

Andy began coughing. He glared at Doctor and spoke again.

Doctor coughed. And coughed. And coughed. Doctor staggered back, doubled over with fits of coughing.

The pain stopped when Doctor's hand left the equipment.

That's when they soundproofed his room. That's when they knew his voice was dangerous. And that's when he began to understand the power he wielded.

AGE 12

Teacher entered through the black door. Andy didn't know what else was on the other side of that door except Lab. He didn't feel the pain anymore when they hurt him, though he didn't tell this to Doctor or Teacher. He wanted them to think they controlled him, so he always acted like he was in agony, but he'd long ago trained his mind to ignore the hurt Doctor inflicted on him. Now they put the mask on him every time he was taken to Lab. The mask blocked his voice. It was removed once he was strapped down to the table.

In the Lab, Doctor and Teacher covered their ears with objects he didn't recognize. Then Doctor brought in the clipboard people and tried to force him into shifting germs from a sick person into someone who was well. He always refused to cooperate. Doctor used the machines to send pain throughout his body when he'd remain silent, and Andy cried tears that looked real. His mind, however, sought ways to use his voice against Doctor or Teacher, but that opportunity hadn't yet arisen.

Until now.

Teacher stopped outside the glass wall. Andy stood beside his bed, fist clenched. Teacher reached out to flip a switch on the wall beside his glass cage. Now they could talk to each other.

"Hello, Andy. How are you today?"

Andy didn't answer. Every day was the same and Teacher already knew the answer. He asked the question Uncle had suggested.

"What is the opposite of hate?"

Teacher looked surprised. "There is no opposite of hate. I taught you that."

"Everything has an opposite," Andy said. "You taught me that, too."

Teacher shifted in place. Andy knew Teacher didn't like being challenged. "I taught you that *most* things have opposites. There is no opposite of hate."

"Then what is love?"

Teacher flinched and Andy forced himself not to smile.

"I thought I made it clear that love doesn't exist."

Andy had no intention of telling Teacher about Uncle and the dreams, so he just shrugged.

Teacher frowned. "Is this about the puppies again?"

Andy flinched this time. He'd tried to block out the puppies, but they still haunted his dreams.

"Did I love those puppies?" he asked, forcing himself to stay focused. The skittering movements within his fist lessened.

Teacher stared at him, as though wondering what he was doing. "No. You hated those puppies. Don't you remember?"

AGE 5

He was very small when Teacher put the first puppy into his cage. Andy had never seen anything like it. Teacher told him it was called "Puppy" and that it was an animal, which made it different from people. Andy tried to talk to Puppy. The animal just made little sounds and didn't answer back. Puppy rubbed up against him, licked his face and hands, and always wanted to lie next to him when he slept. Andy vaguely recalled feeling a similar tug in his heart before he'd come to this place, but his experience with Puppy was altogether different from that.

The animal had soft fur that Andy loved to stroke, and its eyes were big, and it had a tail that moved all the time and it made Andy feel…

special. He only had vague memories of two people before coming here, but not many of the feelings associated with those people. Teacher and Doctor had never held him close the way he held Puppy, even when he was lonely and crying from despair.

Andy felt his heart pound with excitement and a sensation he couldn't describe. He only knew that Puppy made him feel… good. Every night he snuggled with Puppy in his bed. He felt safe. Each time, Puppy cuddled against him and seemed happy to be with him, Andy understood "love." He felt the reality of it.

Teacher kept saying there was only hate. Even when Andy tried to explain how Puppy made him feel, Teacher said those feelings weren't real. They were a false belief that made people weak, and he must not become weak.

Over time, Andy couldn't even fall asleep without Puppy beside him, and that was when Teacher did the unthinkable. One day when Andy was playing with Puppy—throwing a ball that Puppy retrieved and brought back to him—Teacher appeared outside his cage holding an object he didn't recognize.

"Hello, Andy."

Andy stopped throwing the ball. "Hello, Teacher. You're early for my lessons."

Teacher looked surprised that he was so keenly aware of time and said nothing for a long moment. Puppy danced around Andy's feet, making that happy sound it always made when playing. Puppy wanted Andy to throw the ball.

"How do you feel about Puppy?"

Andy considered a moment. "I love Puppy," he answered, knowing this wasn't the response Teacher wanted. "Puppy is my friend."

Teacher frowned. "I told you, Andy, love is a weakness. So is friendship. Both must be purged for you to be strong. You do not love Puppy. You hate Puppy."

Andy shook his head and tossed Puppy the ball. The small animal scurried after the ball as it bounced off Andy's bed and rolled under his desk. Puppy scooped the ball into its mouth and ran back, tail wagging.

Andy took the ball and gazed out at Teacher. "I do not hate Puppy. Puppy loves me."

"Put on your mask, Andy."

Andy recoiled. The mask was only used when he went to see Doctor. "Are you taking me to Doctor? It's not time for that."

Teacher looked impressed. "You seem to have gotten very good at telling time. Interesting. No, you aren't going to Doctor. I'm going to enter your cage. Put on the mask. Now."

Andy knew there would be more pain if he didn't obey, so he tossed the ball across the room and strode to his simple wooden desk. Puppy chased the ball as it bounced off one wall and rolled into his tiny bathroom. Andy picked up the dreaded mask. He hated it. It covered the lower half of his face and prevented him from talking.

More importantly, Teacher and Doctor could both send waves of agony through the mask into his head if he disobeyed or tried to speak. He knew if he didn't obey now, Teacher would fill his glass cage with something that put him to sleep. Then he'd awaken with the mask on anyway and be given a harsher punishment for his disobedience.

He slid the strap over his head and the heavy mask over his mouth. A little box called a remote dangled from a chain around Teacher's neck. Teacher pressed a button on the remote that locked the mask into place. Now Andy couldn't remove the mask no matter how hard he might try. Teacher pressed a button on the panel outside his cage and an invisible door slid open. Andy didn't move. When he used to try and escape, the mask shot terrible pain into his head and he collapsed onto the floor, writhing in agony. He'd learned that lesson well.

Teacher entered the cage and pressed a second button on the remote. The door slid shut and sealed itself.

Puppy jumped and raced around Andy's feet as Teacher stared at them with an unreadable expression.

"Step away from the desk, Andy."

Fear gripped Andy's heart. He used to feel afraid all the time. His whole body tightened, and his mind went numb. He'd adapted to the torment of the mask, so it no longer scared him. But now he sensed Teacher was going to do something new, something unknown.

He stepped back. Puppy raced around his feet.

Teacher squatted down and extended the hand that did not hold the object. "Here, puppy."

Puppy looked up at Andy a moment and, sensing that the ball wasn't going to be thrown, happily scampered to Teacher, ball in its mouth, tail wagging. Teacher's hand opened as though to take the ball. When Puppy skittered closer, Teacher grabbed it by the fur of its upper neck and pulled it in close. The ball dropped from its mouth and rolled languidly across the floor.

Andy froze, unable to speak or make a sound.

ABOUT MICHAEL J. BOWLER

Michael J. Bowler is an award-winning author of nine novels.

He grew up in San Rafael, California, and majored in English and Theatre at Santa Clara University. He went on to earn a master's in film production from Loyola Marymount University, a teaching credential in English from LMU, and another master's in Special Education from Cal State University Dominguez Hills.

He partnered with two friends as producer, writer, and/or director on several ultra-low-budget horror films, including "Fatal Images," "Hell Spa," "Club Dead," and "Things II."

He taught high school in Hawthorne, California for twenty-five years, both in general education and special education.

He has also been a volunteer Big Brother to eight different boys with the Catholic Big Brothers Big Sisters program and a thirty-year volunteer within the juvenile justice system in Los Angeles.

He has written three new books for teens and one for middle grade. All are, as yet, unpublished.

His goal as an author is for adolescents to experience empowerment and hope; to see themselves in his diverse characters; to read about kids who face real-life challenges; and to see how kids like them can remain decent people in an indecent world.

CONNECT WITH MICHAEL

Website:
http://michaeljbowler.com/

FB:
https://www.facebook.com/michaeljbowlerauthor/

Twitter:
https://twitter.com/MichaelJBowler

Instagram:
https://www.instagram.com/michaeljbowler/

tumblr:
http://michaeljbowler.tumblr.com/

Pinterest:
https://www.pinterest.com/michaelbowler/

Goodreads:
https://www.goodreads.com/author/show/6938109.Michael_J_Bowler

Online Retailers:
https://books2read.com/u/4Apa8d

YouTube:
https://www.youtube.com/channel/
UC2NXCPry4DDgJZOVDUxVtMw

www.ingramcontent.com/pod-product-compliance
Lightning Source LLC
Chambersburg PA
CBHW030350310726
48979CB00001B/252